Druidic Twilight

David J. Day

Druidic Twilight

By David J. Daly

Published By Green Boat Press
P.O. Box 135
Manlius, NY 13104

editor@greenboatpress.com
www.greenboatpress.com

This book is dedicated to the memory of

Bernard Joseph Reavey
And
Frances Clifford Brennan

And also to wonderful Daniel, who inspired me to finish it.

Many thanks are due to these people for their assistance to me while I wrote and published this book:

Sue Daly, Laurie Caraher, Mike Diflorio, Anne Bourcy

Thanks are also due to these people for their gracious support and assistance and for being my biggest fans and the best promoters of my books:

Kathy Daly, Louise Jerome

As always, thank you also go to all my friends who have contributed greatly to my writing career, too numerous to mention.

Prologue

The man now known as Sean Drood came to Syracuse from downstate in one of those rusty old buses with bars and grills in the windows. That is the way many eventual residents arrive in Syracuse from New York City- the jail bus or the state-sponsored trip on the hospital bus. Drood was under the weight of many mg's of Thorazine and wore donated clothing, rags really. He was gaunt, yellow, and had dark circles under his eyes. He had a scraggly beard and a downcast and resigned expression, like paintings of Jesus on the cross. When he stepped onto the pavement from the bus, in spite of the numbing medication he started a ceaseless muttering and his eyes darted to and fro.

The story given to the people in admitting was that Drood was a John Doe, a homeless man found naked and incoherent drifting in a rowboat under the gaze of Lady Liberty in New York Harbor. Preliminary attempts by the hospital to get out of him who he was and where he came from were answered only with paranoid rantings and fantasies. Drood was diagnosed as a schizophrenic suffering from acute depression, dehydration, and hypothermia. In fact he had almost died. After a few weeks in the hospital in New York, the state had shipped him to St. Francis, a long-term mental rehabilitation facility on the north side of Syracuse. He was to be kept there for observation and treatment and put into the system. His caseworkers, if they cared, would have the job of finding out who he was and from whence he came.

After the admitting paperwork was completed Drood muttered and stared as the bus hauled out. He stood like a pigeon-crusted statue in the antiseptic lobby of the hospital. An orderly appeared with a wheelchair and Drood was plunked into it and strapped in. He was aimed at the elevators and wheeled through the lobby. Nobody took much notice of them at all. As they waited for the elevator, the orderly's curiosity compelled him to ask, "So where you from, man?"

Drood lifted his head and ceased mumbling. Graying matted hair hung in his eyes. He smiled and held the orderly's gaze with his bleary eyes before he smiled and replied, "I'm a Druid from ancient Ireland. I was tricked by Manannan, the God of the Otherworld, into coming here. I've done some really bad things like betraying my best friend Kilty, and I was set up and betrayed by a man named McGrath and now I've lost all, my wife and my daughter, and I can't even die. I am immortal and no one will ever know. I will take my secrets to the grave. They can put as many wires on me as they like, they can force me to sign whatever they want, and they can lock me up as long as they like, but the Gods know and I know, this is the Otherworld but you think it is North America....." and he continued in that vein as the elevator doors opened and the orderly wheeled him in. Drood continued to explain about time travel and the whims of the gods and the orderly began to look sorry he had broken his policy of not talking to the crazies. There were already a doctor and a visitor in the elevator and they edged away from Drood and looked at the orderly with sympathy. The orderly shrugged and smiled. He twirled his finger around his temple.

The elevator doors opened and the orderly bumped Drood down a long corridor with open doors on the right and left. As the wheelchair rolled down the hall, Drood glared malevolence into each room and began to rock back and forth in his chair. There were no windows and each room had photographs and decorations, looked much lived in, and had the appearance that the occupants had all been there a long time. The orderly steered for the last room on the right, but as the strapped-in Drood passed the room before it, a photograph on the dresser caught his eye. It was a woman playing with a girl child, a mother and daughter. Drood's eyes opened wide and his mouth hung down as he stared at the picture. His features contracted into rage and the orderly pushed Drood away and his head snapped back as they swung around the corner into the last room. When the orderly undid the straps Drood went berserk. He screamed and flailed his arms and legs, screamed at invisible people named Manannan and McGrath and struck the orderly in the head and all hell broke loose. Completely against his most fervent desire, Drood had been saved from death.

Several Years Later
Chapter 1

Drood was watching carefully when his friends hauled the old rug out of the corner and spread it over the floor, not bothering to sweep up the cigarette butts, pennies, and old matchbook covers. He was eager to sit down again and drink his beer and this interruption bothered him. A gust of wind from the open end of the room brought in the smell of oil and rust, if rust has a smell, and Drood shivered and pulled his coat closer. He glanced at Shiny patting down the last corner of the rug.

"Hurry up, Shiny, my back is killing me."

"Keep cool my man, keep cool." Shiny waved his hand carelessly at Drood and began moving the chairs back in from the end of the room. Sardonic Tom and Gus weren't moving too quickly either and Drood tossed his head and swore. Watching from a window, if there were one, one would think Drood was the owner of the place and that he had hired the men to set up the slovenly lair for him. It was not so.

"Awright, Drood, here you go. Sit your impatient ass down." Gus kneed the green vinyl recliner into the corner where it had been. Drood sighed and fell into the chair as the others pulled up the other chairs. Now he was ready for the magic to begin. It was his first beer of the night and he was tired and cold.

The wind was really strong outside, the unseasonably warm December was changing back to winter and as the cold front moved in, the trees were flailing wildly outside. The collapsing, burned-out old factory where they were congregated offered a little protection against the weather and they had a kerosene heater, which Gus was tuning up, but the wind pounded the aluminum roof and the booming and shrieking echoed through the empty building. They paid no attention to the ominous sounds. They had come to drink beer and to play cards.

3

Sardonic Tom, as Drood had dubbed him, had a small business repairing TVs, lawn mowers, appliances, anything really, in one corner of the factory, for which he paid a tiny cash rent every month. The owner of the property let them have the extra room off Tom's business as a sort of clubhouse, provided they would generally keep an eye on the place and swear nothing illegal would take place there. The owner didn't care much what they did. The factory was a shambles and he'd take whatever money he could get while trying to sell the location to somebody. Walls had fallen down, somebody had used one corner of the factory as a dump, and rats lived quite well in the piles of junk. Tom's business was sectioned off from the rest of the inside of the factory by walls he himself had put up. The workshop had once been a garage and had a small door next to a garage door in the front. The clubhouse was entered from the back of the garage. There were really only three walls to the clubhouse, the back of it being open to the vast emptiness of the old factory and its dripping decrepitude.

"Hey Shiny, is it me, or do you look happy tonight for some reason?" said Drood.

"Happy?!" Shiny looked over at Drood with a grin, "Why should I be happy? I got no hair, a giant gut, the IRS after me, and a flatulent dog."

Drood smirked. "Must be you're smiling cuz you get to hang around with us."

"Oh, did I mention, I have no social life?" said Shiny.

Gus chimed in. "He's jes happy 'cause he think he finally figgered out a way to keep his poker face. Tell 'em about it Shiny. 'S a man with a system. Gonna win back all his twelve dollars."

"That's right," Shiny grinned. "You boys aint never gonna know what hit ya. Like takin' candy from babies."

"Hmmph." Drood snorted and frowned, though he was actually quite curious to see what Shiny had up his sleeve, so to speak.

Gus said, "You won't be able to hang on to it Shiny, you gonna do jes like you always do. Win a hand, lose a hand, till you git to your fourth or fifth beer and then you'll be bettin' like a madman, end up sittin' in the corner moanin' and fartin' while the res' of us play some serious poker with your money."

They all snorted and laughed, but Shiny said, "Screw you, man. You aint so smart. You'll see."

4

BOOM!!! A heavy punch of wind against the roof and some dust fell over the men. Drood looked up and smiled. Aluminum roofs. "Some innovation," he thought. Cheap, thin, but kept the rain out. Enough metal for a thousand swords hanging over their heads. He stared at the rivets and the cobwebs above him as the first hand was being dealt and he began to relax and feel the confidence the first surge of alcohol into the brain always brought. He looked around at the men and wondered, as he did two hundred times a day, why he was on this planet, how he had gotten to this time and place, and when it would all end. Perhaps the makeshift walls of the clubhouse would collapse on him and that would be it; brief, intense, cleansing pain and then the great relief. He didn't know if the passage through the other side to the next life would leave him better off or worse, but he did think it was time. He was more than ready to shed his current incarnation. He hoped the next one would also be human and wouldn't be 1500 years from now like the last one. Too difficult to adjust.

"Drood, you in or out? Let's go man."

Drood slowly brought his cards up to his chest to look at them. He pondered. Nothing yet. No patterns in the cards, no feelings in his head, no signs he could recognize. Two of diamonds, six of spades, eight spade, jack club, jack diamond, ten heart, ace club. He calculated percentages. He frowned and his lips moved silently and then he emerged from his thoughts to toss fifty cents onto the pot. The action moved away from him again, went around the table, and he stared off into the gloom beyond the range of the lamp. As Gus raked in the pot from the first hand, Drood was about to turn his attention back to the game when a motion in the recesses of the dark factory caught his eye.

A pale presence seemed to appear and then disappear off to the right. Drood blinked and looked at the men around him. None of them had noticed. He peered into the gloom again and waited, squinting. Nothing. He shrugged to himself and looked back at the game. While the front part of his brain engaged itself in numbers and the possibilities in the cards, the back part of his brain wakened and was sniffing around the edges of their lantern-light circle. The back of his brain was anxious, ragged and wild, smelling smoke in the woods, and standing up on the tips of its paws. Something was up.

It might have been nothing or it might have been a person. It could have been a spirit or it could have been a hallucination. As the poker game continued, Drood frequently peered into the darkness but the image didn't return. He replayed the vision in his mind, and as he thought about it, the face of a boy began to emerge from the shadows in his cerebral cortex. Maybe eleven or twelve years old. The boy had pale skin and a shock of pale hair hanging in his eyes. His high Indian-looking cheeks were flushed and he had small dark eyes. Was the boy an illusion? Had the pale flash in the gloom really been a boy?

Drood wondered if the Gods and their spirit-servants were conspiring to deceive him again, or if perhaps he was beginning to slide back into mental illness. He remembered twice waking up in a boat in a new world. When Drood thought of his past, sometimes he believed he had traveled in time, sometimes he thought he had died, and sometimes he thought he had been insane. One thing he knew for sure was it was all very confusing and he wanted very much to just be Drood, the ordinary man. He thought of his time in St. Francis hospital and shivered. He didn't like to remember being a Druid in 5th century Ireland, or a media executive in Manhattan. He couldn't bear the thoughts about a lost family and a betrayed friend. He suddenly saw the face of McGrath, the man who had enjoyed and orchestrated Drood's betrayal and collapse. In his flashback Drood could see the evil intent he had somehow missed in McGrath's face before. McGrath had paid him to betray Kilty. Had broken the deal and turned him in to the police. Had stolen his family from him. Drood clenched his jaw. McGrath. The jug ears and the leer.

He wanted it all to go away and leave him with his fragile grip. He wanted to be a regular human in the early 21st century in Syracuse, New York. He could no longer understand anything that had happened to him before his time in St. Francis and he wanted to just serve out his time on earth in peace. The flash in the dark had started his mind thrashing.

"So now I am going to have visions," he thought, and that made him really nervous. "Will I go insane again? Is Manannan still laughing at me? The great trickster God of the Otherworld, stealing souls from their natural places and sending them into the twilight over the ocean and playing with them, and...." but that was enough. He was breathing hard.

"Drood!"

Drood's head snapped back to the game.

"What's wrong with you, man??!!" Shiny was glaring at him.

Drood looked at Tom and Gus. They too were looking at him from under furrowed brows.

"This is the fourth time we've had to remind you it's your bet. Either play cards or don't, man!" Shiny had that glazing in his eyes that meant he was lubed enough to start losing his money. Drood reluctantly filed the boy-vision away in his short-term memory and sat up straight in his chair. In his fractured life there was plenty of time to pursue idle illusions. Now it was time to play poker.

BOOM! The wind emphasized the change in Drood's focus by slamming the roof hard. The intensity of the game ratcheted up and the temperature dropped three more degrees. The men began to shiver and Shiny got bounced out and they were all really glad to be alive, even Shiny, as he lay sprawled over the recliner, quite drunk by now and happy just to be there, freezing and drunk and listening to the guys banter and bet. He watched the shadows from the kerosene lantern flutter around them as the wind played hell outside. Shiny knew tomorrow he'd be hung over and broke. He'd be the desperate bald bum in the morning light, but right now he was the poker playing man among men, with no ambition, no shame, no fear. He thought to himself, "A man's Saturday night is best when it is served up cold, sharp, and electric in your head."

When the game finally broke up, Gus gave Drood a ride back to his apartment ten blocks away in the heart of Eastwood. Drood got out of Gus' car and watched as the Oldsmobile rumbled away under the giant maple trees out to James Street. Drood watched until the car was out of sight. It was icy cold now and Drood walked over the cracked and heaved-up sidewalk to his porch. He climbed to the top step of the porch and looked out over the neighbor's house below him to the main drag. It was 1 a.m. but there was a consistent stream of cars going by. "Probably had a game or concert at the Dome earlier, or something," Drood surmised. He leaned on the railing and breathed deep and looked at the glowing street lights laced over by the black branches between the porch and the street. Was this then, the real winter, he wondered? Because he was ready, he craved it, the crystal frost on everything, the numbing whiteness, the removal of thought and feeling in a savage absence of warmth. His soul responded to northern winter as if it were a healing devastation. He longed to be punished by winter. He unbuttoned his coat, hoping the cold would help ease his heart, but it just wasn't cold enough yet. Only cold enough to be uncomfortable, not enough to be brilliant. Drood craved a frozen world.

He sighed and thought of the boy-vision again. The boy's face was becoming clearer all the time now and Drood began to feel as though maybe he knew the boy. With a weary shake of his head he began once again to negotiate the complicated pathways of the many emotional and mental lives he had lived to try to place the face. And as Drood had been taught to believe, the future could always invade your life in visions and dreams, so it was possible the boy was someone he had not yet come to know. He decided he didn't have the strength for visions and turned to go inside, for a cigarette, and then bed. The metal outer door was stuck again and Drood had to lift it before he pulled. He jiggled the key and shouldered the door before he stepped into the gloom and the stale smell of his place, his lair. He looked around at his place and felt satisfied. The beat up furniture and the crumbling architecture of the old Victorian house matched his emotions these days: weary, gray, and comfortable. His personal bedraggled life and home also matched the way he looked at the city of Syracuse itself. Although he had come to Syracuse mentally disturbed and tormented, he had managed to find comfort and a home.

Syracuse was an unpretentious city, born in a swamp stolen from the Onondagas (or bought, depending on whom you talked to, a man named Webster married into the Onondagas and then "helped" them sell their land), and raised to glory on the salt trade. Salt, once a precious commodity was drawn from mines in Syracuse. The city could not have had more basic roots, in spite of the lofty Greco-Roman place names that had been overlaid on the Native American holy names. Its salt had provided a swelling new nation in the early 1800's and the Erie Canal had made the city into a real metropolis. Manufacturing had found a comfortable home in Syracuse and enjoyed an uninterrupted reign of prosperity for over 100 years (Great Depression excepted), before the recessions of the 1970's and 80's had turned it into one more upstate rustbelt town. It sits on the most polluted lake in the country and because of the mid-size of the city, the mid-education of the populace, the age of the people and

8

various other factors, Syracuse became a great marketing test city in the 1980's. The "average American citizen" could be supposed to live in Syracuse then.

By the time Drood arrived in Syracuse in the late 1990's the economic boom that had been caused by computers and the Internet was just beginning to take hold in Syracuse. Drood had no interest whatsoever in growth and prosperity, but he found plenty to be affectionate about in the older, rotting parts of the city. Syracuse still clung to its blue-collar and farm traditions and it was a dress-down, casual city. Driving from one end of the city to the other during the morning or afternoon rush hours still took only fifteen minutes. Fashions were ten or fifteen years behind New York and L.A., and the people still said hello and believed in their communities and their families. True, there were enclaves of moneyed yuppiedom in the suburbs, but in large part they were sandwiched in between the gritty, low-rent city and the vast swathes of farm and woods and lakes to really cause too much trouble. In other words, as Drood reflected, lighting a cigarette in his darkened apartment that was delightfully backlit by street lights, Syracuse was a place where there was no disgrace in working with your hands, where driving a rusted and crusted car was okay, and where you could wear any old rags wherever you went.

Drood enjoyed his cigarette, watching the smoke curl in the blue light oozing in through the windowpanes. His mind wandered and he thought of his lost wife and daughter somewhere in the maw of the great city to the south. Or some great city somewhere, for who knew if they still lived in Manhattan? Deirdre would be twelve by now and Claire would be doing the school and soccer-mom thing. Drood's eyes began to feel sore and heavy as his lungs tightened near the end of the cigarette. He thought about putting music on, but in the end he stubbed out the cigarette and dragged himself into the bedroom and peeled off his clothes while falling into bed. The clothes slid down to the floor as Drood fell asleep, ending the nighttime bachelor ballet ritual. As he drifted away, Drood remembered to ask the Gods in whom he no longer believed for dreams. And then Drood began to snore loudly.

He was haunted that night by the face of a man he had betrayed, the redheaded man whose name he could never again say. The face was behind bars and it was sad and lost and Drood knew it so well.

9

The blue eyes begged him for mercy. Drood wept again, as he often did in his sleep.

Chapter 2

Monday morning saw Drood back at work, all his feelings and thoughts stowed carefully away. Time again for another round of bobbing for money while the Overlords laughed nervously and hovered around each other's offices. They whispered into their cell phones, stared at their screens, and talked only to each other, while the cubicled workers struggled to make some sense out of the commercial miasma into which they had unexpectedly fallen. Most of the cubiclists didn't remember a time when they hadn't been treading water in the corporate absence of integrity and soul. Money had different rules than cubiclists had and overlords had yet another set of rules. Drood tried using oracles, visions, spells, dreams, but nothing could help him to understand what was going on. It was a baffling collision of values and ideas that seemed to have been frozen in mid-crash; everyone could look at the scene and wonder what the hell was going on, but nothing changed. Drood had managed to get in as an "information" worker. He had started as a clerk and had managed through persistent use of common sense and commas to be established as the "Processor" for the Corporate Communications department of Meltocom. Meltocom made something or another, but most of its employees had nothing to do with that. They all supported other functions, or something. Drood worked in the Cor Comm department and basically it was his job to see to it that everyone else in the company got what they needed in the way of information, publications, reports, or whatever else they asked for. There were three other workers like him in the department and then there were twenty-five other members of the department whose job it was to confuse, obstruct, blame, and take credit for the work Drood undertook to do. Drood undertook it simply because he didn't know what else to do while he was there.

Mr. Muke came forward bright and early on Monday morning when Drood hadn't quite had time to shake off reality yet and sidled into Drood's cube with a particularly smarmy look on his pasty face.

11

To prevent himself from winding up a roundhouse right, Drood turned his back to the Muke and busied himself with tidying up his desk. He wished he could wear Manannan's cloak of mist to hide himself. Being ignored, of course, infuriated the Muke, who really wanted respect from his subordinates, but could only recognize respect in the form of sniveling fear. Drood knew his kind and made him wait. If he wanted something, the Muke could say so. A daily game of chicken. Finally, the Muke could stand it no longer.

"Seaaaawn," he said, drawing out the name into a singsong, which made Drood's skin crawl. "Did you know that we're going to have to get the Druckerman report out today?"

"Yeah. No shit. I've been working here two years, haven't I? What do you think I do all day?" Drood was really not in the mood.

"Oh. Well excuuuuuse, me. I guess you won't be needing anyone's help then, will you?" And the Muke smirked again and bounced away, having withdrawn any support Drood might have needed to get the report out.

"What next," thought Drood? And no sooner than he had that thought, here came the water cooler warthogs to babble and slap each other's hands in the air and make fun of each other and talk about team sports as if they were involved in them. Eventually they noticed Drood's total and genuine lack of interest and wandered away. "There's got to be a better way," thought Drood. And before the noise of the warthogs had subsided in his head, the phone rang and he had to listen to one of the sales people try to blame him for not doing what they hadn't asked him to do and at the same time flatter him to get him to do something they knew he wasn't supposed to do. When he finally got off the phone and could feel a massive headache building, his fourth level boss (he could never remember which ones were which) came down the aisle of cubicles and cheerily greeted the "team" and asked them to come down to the "Command Room" (conference room) for a strategy and planning session. Drood looked around and saw that his colleagues (the three others who actually worked with him) had seen it coming and had made themselves scarce. Drood knew they would not be held accountable for anything, nor would they be assigned "action items" and really wished he could have seen this meeting coming and had not picked up the phone. Now Drood knew he would be assigned to produce another of the five standard bright new paradigms "in

12

process" and would be expected to answer to a panel of nitwits as to his actions regarding a group of indecipherable half-articulated abstract whims.

Drood came out of the building at 6:30, hungry, with a raging headache, and not even half the will power he might need to destroy himself. He sucked lustily on his cigarette and sat for a minute in his car with his head on the steering wheel, cigarette dangling from his lips. It would be a few moments before he would have the strength to turn the key in the ignition. There had been a man named McGrath in his past, a man who had betrayed him and caused him to lose everything. Drood winced as McGrath's face swam in front of him. "Why does he have to show up to leer at me every time I'm in deep misery?" This line of thinking led him to his ex-wife Claire, and his daughter Deirdre. "Maybe despair can be gotten over if swallowed whole, all at once." He started driving before the emotions swamped him. At least he had learned to shut things down when he had to, a luxury he didn't have when he was younger, when he believed in meaning, when he could still affect his own life. He held on to the wheel and drummed his fingers, quietly scanning the cars and the road and the sky and the passing trees on 481 and then 690 as he aimed back to the city.

He looked at the inane billboards blatting their angry, desperate need for his money and finally pulled off on Teall going north, up the steep hill into Eastwood. Back onto James, into his quiet side street, driveway, and back to life. A little peace and quiet, a little reality. Without warning, Drood remembered the vision of the boy again and thought maybe it was time for a little meditation, a little inspiration.

Inside the apartment, Drood flipped on the light, dropped his keys on the coffee table and slung his jacket over the dining room chair. He flopped into the overstuffed couch and lit another cigarette, pulling the ashtray on the coffee table closer to him with his foot. He breathed a heavy sigh and reached down to pull off his shoes. They were harder to reach than they used to be. Another heavy sigh. Puffing quietly, he let his gaze come to rest on the coffee table. He had long since given up any kind of religious or spiritual meditation, now he just let his mind wander until things would come up. He didn't know any longer where they came from, he had no more understanding of Gods, the unconscious, spirits or

13

anything. He only knew that when you unfocused and let your eyesight go, first of all, it was relaxing, and second of all, things came up and you learned things or noticed things. Drood admired the coffee table first, the inlaid mosaic tile of an Aztec sun on half of the top of it and the green glass on the other half. It was a table for smoking on, for eating on, for drinking wine on. It was always good to look at. Next he looked to the light in the window and observed to himself that human beings are drawn to light, as they are drawn to water and wind because of the energy in them. It is human beings responding to their own source, the energy that, essentially, they are. It was dark outside, but there was a weird purple northern cold glow in the air and he marveled at it. "The color of soul" some part of his brain said. Drood composed an impromptu haiku:

Purple light comes in
   through winter evening window,
I hear my heart throb.

He looked at the top of his neighbor's pine tree framed nicely in the upper left pane of the west- facing window and wondered if he could ever be free and then surprised himself by not caring about being free anymore. He was all of his pain and then some and he didn't care if he got away from it. He knew he was close enough to the end of the road now and he could find enough little everyday pleasures, enough cups of warm tea, and strolls in snowstorms to nourish him until the end came. A mild anticipation of pleasure kept creeping back into him at the strangest times and he was irritated and astonished and grateful for it all at the same time. He mused that the life in us has no interest in who we think we are or what we think we are doing. It waxes and wanes according to its own principles, the principles of energy, and doesn't know anything about us. We bob in the cosmic tide and it doesn't matter whether we flail or not, because the time it takes us to drown is based on the sea, not on our efforts. Drood chuckled at the metaphor he was making and the ugly workday began to leave him for good now. There was a little beauty to be had and now he had a fighting chance at wrestling the demons to a draw before he slept. He looked around the apartment in the twilight.

14

In the dimly lit apartment Drood worked with a pencil to make out the features of the boy. All portraits centered around the eyes of course, and that was where Drood started, focusing all his recall on the vision and letting his hand go to do the translating. As the eyes became more distinct and vivid, to his surprise, Drood saw himself in them. He saw an intelligent, weary, and wary traveler. As he finished the rough sketch and sat back to examine what he had done, he pondered the relationship of himself to the vision. With a frown, he penciled in at the bottom of the portrait, the caption, "The Traveler." He thought about where a boy like that would go in this world and what would become of him. If Syracuse in the early 21st century was the starting point for a soul, where would it end up? Drood stared at it a long time before going to bed. Curiosity.

The next day was Tuesday, and on this particular Tuesday Drood was to have finished a report, but he wasn't sure whom it was for, or what they wanted it for, and he had no idea who had the information that was supposed to go in the report. As far as he could tell the report didn't even have anything to do with Meltocom. He scrambled around the building begging for a clue, and then it got close to four o'clock and the phone calls from people demanding the report began to increase. He decided to wing it, and so he took four old unrelated reports and took turns copying paragraphs and charts from each one until he had at least fifteen slides that could be printed out and stapled together and called a report.

He left the office after receiving many smiles and pats on the back for his achievement. He'd pick up another carton of cigarettes on the way home. Perhaps he should break his rule this week and do some drinking tonight. "Discipline Drood," he told himself, "you didn't come all this way back to the world to give up now did you?" Drood thought about struggles in the mental hospital and once again felt an overwhelming outsiderness, like some great gulf of lost space opened up inside him, from his groin all the way to the back of his skull.

Tonight was visitor's night at the hospital. He headed down the big hill on James Street into the city and swung north on State Street. The hospital loomed above him on the next hill. As usual, he had to park on a side street and haul himself up the hill to the hospital. There was a bitter wind blowing, of course. It seemed as if there always was whenever Drood went to the hospital, and he arrived at the front entrance with burning ears. Several nurses huddled, smoking and shivering, with shoulders hunched in a clump outside the door. Opposite the nurses on the other side of the door, the patients huddled, also smoking. They all eyed Drood grimly as he hustled through the sliding doors.

Drood was the first visitor on the ward every week, sometimes the only visitor. He always felt he was in danger of being captured and admitted when he visited, because they had never had a former patient come back to sit and talk with the patients before. He must have been crazy.

"Drood is here!!!" Margaret shouted from the hallway. No one moved. There was only the hum of the lights, shuffling slippers, and an electronic fizz from the loudspeakers. Drood smiled and said, "Hello Margaret, how's the old crazy lady, tonight?"

"Ahm not as crazy as you are Drood," she smiled and wagged a finger. "She knows," Drood thought, and then corrected himself quickly, nervously, automatically, "Nope nothing wrong with me." He was always on the verge of being found out, although he could no longer remember what he had to hide.

She couldn't seem to erase the smile from her face. She took his arm and steered him away from the nurses' area. They strolled down the hall like an old married couple, Drood a little stiffly, Margaret clinging to his arm and patting his hand once in a while. Drood looked at her hand on his forearm and marveled again at the smoothness of her skin, at the glassy nails, and the porcelain beauty of Margaret's hands. When she was smoking he could stare at her hands for many years. They came to the corner where the hallway turned at the big window. Drood looked out at the hills of the West End, beyond downtown, and wondered if any of the Irish descendants who lived on Tipperary hill were related to him. Drood and Margaret turned their backs on the cool gray city and sat together on the windowsill.

"They want to run more tests on all the bi-polars, depressives, and suicidals," Margaret explained. "They got another drug now. They think they've figured out the exact part of the brain where all the trouble is. It's not just the serotonin now, they say."

Drood shrugged. They'd never completely cure mental illness, and he knew it, until the nature of reality and the reason for human beings could be determined for sure. He had tried to explain his understanding to Margaret one time, but ended up confusing himself. Drood's thoughts since the great disaster were always clear in his head, but for some reason he couldn't get them out right.

"How are YOU doing honey?"

"Me? I'm fine. I'm on 25 mg of Zoloft, 25 mg of Paxil, 25 mg of Thorazine, and I have no idea at all what I feel like. But it's better than it was, right? You know what I mean."

"Yeah. I do. Is Mickey feeling okay today, do you think?" Drood asked her.

"He looked okay at lunch time. You never know with him though. He's probably in his room."

"I'm gonna go talk to him, now. I'll catch up with you later, O.K.?"

"O.K. Drood..." she looked at the floor and pouted her lips out and scrunched up her eyes.

"What's wrong?" he wanted to know.

"Why do you still come? Isn't it...well...uncomfortable? When I get out of here I'm not coming back for five minutes."

"No, it's not uncomfortable at all. I have a lot of training in the workings of the mind and I find this place interesting. And I understand both the patients and the doctors. They don't have enough people like that around here. They need me." He said the last sentence with a sheepish grin and tried to make it come off like he was joking.

"You really are crazy, Drood. Well. Goodbye."

"And," he paused and looked at her and smiled, "I learn a lot when I'm here. See you later Margaret."

Mickey was schizophrenic and when he was off his medicine he was usually delusional. Depending on the levels of Lithium and whatnot, he was either too sluggish to talk, or he was able to sing, talk, and entertain like a troubadour. Drood found Mickey sitting on his bed in a rigid posture with a book held tightly with both hands in front of him. He appeared to be muttering to himself. Drood waited in the doorway. Mickey was priceless to Drood because he knew things he wasn't supposed to be able to know and Drood was always in search of answers and clues about what in the world was going on. The only problem was finding the line. It was hard to know which of Mickey's perceptions were based in delusion, in fantasy, or in genuine insight.

"Drood! I was just y'know, reading, y'know, cause, y'know, I need to y'know learn more about y'know the atmosphere, y'know, because of all the chlorofluorocarbons. If there's too many, we'll all die," and Mickey smiled brightly at him. It made him look ghastly.

"Yes, I had heard that," said Drood, taking a chair across from Mickey. He noticed that Mickey's room was, as always, immaculate. "How are you Mickey? I forgot to bring you those books we talked about. I'll try to drop 'em by on my way home from work one of these afternoons."

"It's okay Drood. I have plenty to read." Mickey had combed his hair carefully and looked as though he was holding on to himself as tightly as he could. His clothes were Salvation Army - a brown sweater, polyester checked pants, and a bright yellow shirt, all mismatched and out of style, and barely fitting. His face was institutional pale and his long nose pointed, bringing one's eyes into his own large soft brown eyes.

"Can you play cards tonight Mickey, or would you rather be left alone?"

"No, I can play, I'm okay. But I'm not as crazy as you are, right Drood?" and Mickey laughed a staccato cackle. Then he sat back down on the bed and hugged himself as he laughed. Drood grinned. It didn't seem like this little private joke would ever die down or go away. And how could it? The patients had so little new stimulus in their lives that whatever jokes and stories they did have tended to last for a long time. And, Drood remembered, their damaged minds collected memories in odd places, in arrangements that sometimes startled the more conventional and less pathological brains.

"Okay, so let's go to the lounge, buddy." Drood headed out and Mickey grabbed a deck of cards from his dresser and followed Drood into the hallway. Mickey walked, leaning forward and slightly hunched, the epitome of anxiety. They sat in the prison-made chairs with the green cushions and faced each other.

"War or fish?" Drood asked. Since Drood had so many choices to make in his life, he always let his friends in the hospital make most of the decisions about his visit.

"Fish. War is too boring, never gets anywhere, never ends. Besides, teach a man to fish…want me to teach you how to fish Drood?" And Mickey cackled his laughter again.

18

Drood began to deal and a couple of male patients came in and sat in chairs near Drood and Mickey and watched them play. Drood hadn't seen them before. They looked heavily sedated and must be new. They looked confused and slightly angry, glaring at everyone they could see as if someone had to be to blame for their sickness and confinement.

Mickey and Drood paid no attention to the spectators. They flipped cards over at lightning speed with the numbers and the pictures flashing and the edges of the cards flapping. They got into a good rhythm and each of them relaxed although their concentration was sharp. Drood had the occasion to marvel again at how many different ways there were in life to lose oneself and to be gone into the moment. And he thought about how necessary it was and if there could be more people losing themselves there would be more "mental health." Meditation, physical activity, work, whatever, anything to lose the grip on yourself and just be.

"Mickey," Drood said, and Mickey glanced up and, as he did, he flipped a card the wrong side down onto the pile.

"Yeah." Mickey retrieved the card and flipped it over.

"I had a vision the other day, I wonder if you could help me figure out what it means." Mickey was Drood's unofficial counselor, oracle, therapist, and confidant. Drood wondered what it said that the only person he could trust in this world was mentally ill, institutionalized, and drugged.

"What do you mean a vision? Were you awake?" Mickey wanted to know. His face changed and a sly intelligence slipped into his narrowing eyes.

"Yes, I was awake, but it was late at night, it was dark, and I'd had a few beers," said Drood. "And, I was in a card game in an eerie old warehouse, so all that probably had some effect on it."

"So what was the vision?" Mickey flipped a card the wrong way again and swore softly to himself. His lips moved as he fixed the card and muttered to himself. His lips kept moving

"These guys have visions." One of the spectating patients said to no one in particular. The two patients smiled at each other.

Drood and Mickey paused and looked at the first patient. There was a moment of silence and Drood and Mickey looked at each other and then finally resumed the card game.

Drood related the vision. "I was looking off into the dark and I noticed a kind of a pale flash. And I thought that was it. But the more I thought about it, I began to see a boy's face, maybe a thirteen-year-old boy."

Patient One twirled his finger around his temple and smiled at Patient Two, who nodded his head. Yup, having visions is crazy; they seemed to be agreeing silently. Their eyes were blurry and they had hospital clothes on and they shivered occasionally. But they were watching and listening to Drood and Mickey very carefully. Seemed important.

"What do you think Mickey?"

Mickey sat back in his chair and held a handful of cards out in front of him. His lips stopped muttering and he stared at the cards. He breathed deeply.

"I have a couple of questions, first. What do you mean by a pale flash? How did it become clearer? Have you ever had an apprentice, and which direction do you think the boy's journey would take if you had to make a guess?"

Drood stared at Mickey, trying to take in the implications of the questions Mickey had just asked. Apprenticeable knowledge? But Drood had never told Mickey about his memories of being a Druid. And it seemed Mickey assumed the boy in the vision was real and that the boy was going to make a symbolic journey. Hence, Drood had named the boy "The Traveler."

"Okay," Drood said and swallowed. His throat had become dry from the hospital air. "Okay, the pale flash. Well.... I guess I was looking over the heads of my friends and into the darkness on the right. There's no back wall to the place we were sitting. I guess it appeared like a different shade of darkness first in a spot I wasn't looking at and then as I noticed it and moved my eyes to it, I caught the last glimpse of someone walking away. The paleness I saw was the skin of the face and the hair of someone turning away and moving off. But I think I saw eyes and face."

Mickey nodded, the game of cards forgotten now. Patient One was leaning over trying to catch a glimpse of Mickey's drooping cards. He couldn't quite see and so sat back and shrugged at Patient Two. "Go on," Mickey said.

"I think it became clearer because by focusing on it I began to get bits of information. And no, I've never had an apprentice."

Drood paused and thought for a moment. He had himself been an apprentice in Ireland for sixteen years, he seemed to remember, and then his modern brain took over and doubted the accuracy of it. As always, reflections on his past ended up with the visions of the doomed redhead, and the big-eared, leering McGrath arising and then the fear in his stomach rose and he had to shut it all down again, force himself back to the present.

Patient One and Two were on the edge of their seats; suddenly eager to hear the next thing Drood was going to say. Drood and Mickey turned and looked at them.

"What?" snarled Patient One.

Drood turned back to Mickey to speak and Patient One said to Patient Two "Nosy." And Patient Two nodded. Drood grimaced with annoyance and the tension swelled again.

"I don't know about the journey," Drood said. "What do you think?"

"I think those are the things you need to think about." And Mickey smiled and nodded. His eyes were deep and confident now. No muttering, no slurring, Mickey was all soul now. And Drood accepted what Mickey said and resolved to think about Mickey's questions. Drood had gotten the hearing and the direction he had come to the hospital for. Mickey resumed the card game, smiling craftily whenever he caught Drood's eye.

As Drood wandered down the icy sidewalk toward his car, lost in thought, the night became silent in the heart of the city. The snow fell in silence and cars moved in silence and Drood was alone in the scene, hunched forward, chin tucked to his chest, breathing in the flakes and coughing once after every tenth step. He looked up at the streetlights and their holy orange glow, so high, so steady, and so considerate. "An apprentice, a boy, a journey," he thought to himself, and he sighed. Did he have enough left in him to try again to place some meaning somewhere, to teach somebody something, to care? Who was he, the failed Drood, the shattered Drood, the mentally disturbed Drood, to have any interest in the affairs of other humans? Was he not now on borrowed time? Hadn't he proven beyond all doubt that he did not belong in this world, that he wasn't worthy of trust and respect? Just ask his daughter and his wife. Wherever they were. And the redhead.

Chapter 3

Wednesday came down on Drood without mercy and he tried to brace for the next trudging day of purgatory in the weird Otherworld of the Meltocom building. He slid his badge through the scanner and opened the door and looked down the long hallway toward the row in which his cubicle nested with all the others. Drood said hello to several nameless, faceless drones and then made his way to the final corner into the cubicle farm. He went down his own hedgerow and finally to his space. It wasn't much - gray, gray, and gray, with paper, but it was better than having an office. The people in the offices tended to get pressure put on them more often by the other people in the better offices, whereas the cubicle dwellers were accorded a sort of dignity of their own. This was due to the office people's belief in fear, in rules, and in hierarchy and the cubicle people's belief in fate and comfortability. The office people were therefore susceptible to pressure from above (indeed they craved and twitched for it), the cubicle people were therefore immutable in their thinking and their ways (can't move 'em off a dime with a bulldozer).

The office people were also afraid of the cubicle people because the cubicle people had less to lose and so were more likely to be truthful and forthright. In his days in New York, Drood had at one time been an executive, motivated by specific ideas and plans, but here in Syracuse as a cubicle dweller, he could observe better as a disinterested participant. He mused that spiritual growth was only possible for the cubicle dwellers; the office dwellers were doomed.

Mr. Muke came into Drood's cubicle again to point out that there was a spelling error in the memo Muke had made Drood transcribe. The memo explained, incorrectly, a project that Drood was responsible for. He had asked Mr. Muke not to write it, because it would make people think Drood could provide them with information he didn't have and couldn't get. Mr. Muke had asked Drood to write it because Mr. Muke didn't know how to use the word processing software. Drood had edited carefully, but somehow Mr. Muke had figured out how to use the software enough to turn Drood's clear memo into a detailed explanation of rules that no one had ever heard of and didn't use and that weren't related to the project that Drood was responsible for. Mr. Muke was angry about the typo.

When Drood finally got Mr. Muke to accept that it could indeed be changed to the correct spelling, Drood noticed that it had been spelled correctly when he had sent it to Mr. Muke. He settled back in his chair with a sigh. No sooner had his boss left than the phone rang and he got three e-mails at once, all demanding the information he didn't have and wanting to know why they were always kept in the dark and why couldn't Drood have let them have the information earlier and why were they only able to find out about this kind of thing because of his boss, Mr. Muke.

By lunchtime Drood had received fifteen more requests for the fictional information and since he knew Mr. Muke's feelings on the matter, he decided it would be pointless to try to argue. It would be better to invent the information and pass it along. As he was typing, he overheard two people in the next aisle discussing how difficult he, Drood, was to work with, always hoarding information and keeping it to himself. Drood gathered the latest quarterly reports submitted by the department heads and culled paragraphs from them for a montage report. When he had finished, the report almost made some sense, so he knew he had some more work to do to fix it. It would never get through with reason in it. He pulled out his list of corporate jargon and threw buzzwords liberally into the document. He added nominalizations, sports phrases, malapropisms, and incorrectly used mixed metaphors. He scanned it again quickly and deemed it worthy of submission. Incomprehensible. A gem. He would begin distributing it immediately. Of course, it had nothing to do with the topic he was supposed to be providing, but that would go completely unnoticed. Drood was confident he would be commended for being on top of things.

The rest of the afternoon became a panic when the Local Area Network crashed at the precise moment the king of sales arrived at Drood's cubicle to demand the final draft of something he had never requested from Drood but a very important customer was demanding from the king of sales within the next ten minutes.

Drood knew the king had gotten the request from the customer six months ago because of the dated letter attached to the request on top, but the king probably hadn't actually looked at the request. He sure was mad that Drood didn't have it ready. Drood simply parroted the king's demands back to him. This seemed like agreement, but didn't promise any action. The king couldn't figure out this cooperative but unsatisfying agreement and eventually went to complain to Mr. Muke. Drood knew that for the rest of the day he would be repeating statements without committing to or admitting to anything. He wouldn't be disagreeing with anyone so they couldn't punish him (in their way of thinking), but he would also be avoiding trouble.

After five o'clock Drood ran to his car and got in and lit up. He put his arm over the passenger side headrest and looked at the black branches in the park across the street. How much longer could he keep this up? The inanity, the absurdity of the whole world threatened to cave in his mind almost every day and every day he had to fight it off. His mind cast about for a way out and he thought, as he often did at the end of the work day, if he could only find his daughter and see her and talk to her, he would have a reason to keep going. He would suffer anything if he had someone or some reason for doing so. "Deirdre," he muttered dispiritedly to the dashboard. He wondered again if he really did have a daughter after all and what had happened to her. He saw the other workers filing to their cars and he had to leave. He just had to find his daughter.

Back in his lair Drood got out his folders and his notepads and put them on the coffee table. He got a fresh pack of cigarettes, opened it, and laid it next to the pads with his lighter. He wouldn't start with the grog just yet; he had to do some talking and thinking still. He was about halfway through his investigation of the list of private schools in Manhattan his daughter might be attending, but he could rarely find the time to make phone calls during the day. So he had to content himself with trying the types of businesses Claire might frequent with her credit card. Drood knew her numbers and could honestly pass himself off as her husband, and so he could get a general idea of her whereabouts since they moved. Of course, he was assuming they were still in Manhattan, and his search of dry cleaners, the big department stores, and catalog sales hadn't turned up much yet. Drood preferred to search by phone. The Internet bothered him and he knew Claire wouldn't use it, though Deirdre might by now. He had tried a few perfunctory searches, but they kept coming up with the old address. And he didn't have the money to hire a private detective.

Drood took a break from the search and went back to work on the drawing of "The Traveler." He smiled and remembered he had called his daughter a traveler when she was born. He believed she had returned from the spirit-world for her next life and he had also called her the traveler. That was before all the disasters began or, if he looked at it another way, it was in the middle of the disaster that was his life. Drood's mind had been to so many different planets by now that he no longer knew where one life began and another ended. He read somewhere that every molecule in your body changed every few years and so when and where he had been born were irrelevant as far as figuring out what his life was. Clearly, that birth was in a different time and the little baby that he must have been was not, then, really him. As he continued to sketch the face, Drood's thoughts wandered to his family, to his youth, to old friends, to captivity and confinement, to home, and he wondered, for the sixteen thousandth time, what was the point of it all. It was only a mild kind of wondering though. Really he was just waiting. He expected some kind of revelation at the end. And now he was waiting for the boy. He glanced at the pile of papers by the phone and sighed. The boy. His wife. His daughter. What could he possibly do to be of any use to any of them? Despair sent him to his bedroom. His conscious mind thought about his bed and sleep, but the back part of his brain, the part that never sleeps, was begging the great darkness for a more permanent relief. He dropped onto the bed and closed his eyes. Another long night ahead.

* * *

Drood usually spent his Thursday morning trying to enter his time for the week into the mainframe program, and then spent some time writing about what he had been writing about for the weekly report. After those were done, he would have four or five quick meetings in an attempt to arrange a meeting for the following week. Then he would finish writing his report on the corrections he was making to the "corrective actions" program plan that he was writing for the people he was substituting for on the quality steering committee that came about as a result of a lack of focused participation in the original quality program. He hoped there were no errors in it. And finally, before lunch arrived, he would do his round of "helping" all the much higher paid people use the keyboard to enter their time for the week. Keyboard design hadn't changed much really in the first twenty years of the information age, but every Thursday the keyboard was a brand new phenomenon to the decision-makers and risk-takers who had the expensive plastic new houses lined up facing each other in the sterile and coveted Beamer neighborhood. Drood sighed as he pulled on the door of the building and made his entrance. The weariness flooded over him again as the first genius saluted him and he smelled the already stale coffee. Some people seemed to be able to avoid stress in these environments and Drood marveled at them. When he thought about how they did it, he reflected that all you really had to do was to think of yourself as important and then it seemed you were allowed to ignore phone calls, e-mails, memos, and tasks of any kind. You could wander around the building talking on your cell phone to other important people and occasionally you could stop someone who was busy to pontificate to them and harangue them on the evils of the policies the company had set up before you arrived and were powerless to change. There were no special skills, experience, education, or training required to achieve this special status of "self-imposed carrier of protective bubble of oblivion". You just had to decide one day that you were IT. And no matter what happened from that point forward, you could not be dislodged from the privilege, although occasionally you might be obliged to transfer to another oasis of luxurious harmlessness if your current spot required you to get out of the way of some work or some actual pressure. Drood grimaced as he reached his cubicle. This was the price he paid and this was how he earned his bread. Those Christians and their penance were really on to something, he thought. Drood wondered how long this current phase of hell would last. Well, he had no time for thoughts of the Traveler now. It was time to make the numbers and letters fly around the electronic universe, somehow to the advantage of the company, he supposed. The senselessness, the uselessness of life inside the company buffeted him about and he understood more fully every day he worked there, the meaning of "post-modern". Sans meaning. Ceaseless activity without any attachment between cause and effect. Drood lived in a perfectly calm, even boring world, where there was no reason, no explanation, no adherence to any principles of any kind, and yet there was no chaos, no violence, and no seeming confusion. All the struggle that had been expended to create this extremely evolved existence, somewhere in the Third World maybe, or in the cracks and chinks in the "First" world (children shooting up schools, pedophilia, domestic violence, rage and insanity), still existed and supported this soulless undriven unpressured life in corporatia, but it was far away most of the time. "Best to think of it as service," Drood remembered, even though he knew for certain it was not service of any kind. "But think of it as patiently serving. That attitude will get you through anything. Assign your own master and pretend to be serving it while you scrape and bow. Trick your mind. That is the way to live in America in the twenty-first century. Trick your mind, and hope your body goes away or else manages to negotiate some existence on its own."

Drood went home from work with a massive headache and staggered around the apartment reading the mail. He thought idly of quitting his job and heading out onto the road somewhere. Unfortunately, he grimaced, there was no purpose and no reason to drive him to believe there was anything else to do. The phone rang and startled Drood out of his musings.

"Hello," Drood said.

"Yeah, is Tag there?" a young voice wanted to know.

"I think you have the wrong number." Drood politely replied.

"Oo-oh." Click. The young person sounded impatient.

Drood glanced at his pile of folders, compiled in the hunt for his daughter. He glanced at the unfinished drawing of the traveler on the table. He thought about the name "Tag" so similar to the old Irish word for traveler "Tagh." So many things starting to come together, he thought. Now events would run together and coincidences would build. If he had seen it once he had seen it a thousand times. Whether you could trace the cause and effect yourself or not, the events and objects of life ran in patterns and once you identified a pattern that meant that you were in the middle of it already.

Drood thought about traveling. He himself had traveled thousands of miles, thousands of years, light years, galaxies, universes and now he was about to encounter another traveler or perhaps his daughter who was a traveler. "What does it mean? What is it about traveling that is important? Okay, so the bumper sticker can tell you the journey is the destination," he thought. "What is it, what about journeys? You see things, different things, but you don't participate in all of them. You notice other paths, other scenes, other people that are different. You go out of yourself and your world. What does it do to you? It stretches you, it teaches you, and it weakens you and drains you. You are getting knowledge and experience and you are trading it for time and energy - which is the basic process of growing in life, but a journey has a set beginning and an end. At least ideally. Some journeys don't end, but don't you then have to remove the definition of journey?" Drood wasn't sure, but he continued tracking this line of thought. "The fact of motion prevents adherence, meaning adherence to a place with its rules. No rules apply when you are traveling. Only the rules of traveling. Which are what? 1.Keep moving. No adhering. 2.Sustain life. Food. 3.Keep a destination in mind. Even when delayed or detoured. That's it. Pretty simple although pretty difficult to do." This was a simplified system, the perfect system, it occurred to Drood. "Now if you can translate all of life both personal and universal into a journey with these rules you then really have something." Drood knew about not adhering, having several times now been uprooted and tossed from his place into a new place. No adhering. That's good, he thought. He liked that. It was Buddhist and Christian at the same time. Keep living, obvious, but a subtle and constant discipline in its requirement of maintenance. Keep a destination in mind, now there is the hard part. Because if you translate the laws of travel into the laws of life, keeping a destination in mind means you have to have an overarching goal or meaning. You not only have to choose your destination, you have to maintain it through all detours. Drood knew for sure that it took most people half of their lives to identify a worthy destination, and then all of their energy for the rest of their lives to keep that destination in mind through detours and sabotage. Drood would develop this travel philosophy further, he determined. It was worth looking into, and if the Traveler ever showed up, Drood wanted to be ready.

Drood glanced at the drawing of the Traveler and noticed that there was a detail missing, something that didn't match with his memory, or maybe with his imagination. Something not quite right with the mouth. It was slightly down-turned and gave the boy a serious, almost grim expression. Drood was dissatisfied. He sat down to finish the drawing, and immediately his headache began to dissipate. The rigors of maintaining sanity and discipline in the face of the cultural, psychological disaster that was Meltocom took their toll and Drood's circuitry was strained and smoking. He lit a cigarette and as it burned into his lungs and the nicotine soothed his brain, he turned one corner of the boy's mouth up, giving him an unbalanced, mischievous smile and somehow adding a glint to the eyes. Something clicked inside him, and Drood knew the picture was done. He sat back on the couch, put his feet on the Aztec sun tiles and smoked contentedly, head tilted back, staring at the infinite swirls in the white ceiling and watching the wisps of smoke evaporate as his headache disappeared and he finally began to relax. He began to feel infinity.

Chapter 4

Friday was Drood's devious day. He filled it with traps, tricks and harmless but infuriating deviltry. He did it to make the weekend more palatable and to ensure that he left the office week behind him without a headache. He had long ago learned the things that were the most prized and caused the most anxiety in the office environment: time (measured and counted with excruciating jealousy), space (parceled out and ferociously fought over), and materials (office supplies and cutting edge equipment were given out as favors, withheld as punishment.) The overlords watched your time, controlled your space, and counted and prized all your materials. Some of the more enthusiastic managers, such as Mr. Muke, actually became physically ill when they couldn't control closely enough their subordinates' time, space, and material. On Fridays, Drood made it his mission to work against these principles. He had been an executive himself once, before the catastrophes that had brought him to Syracuse, and he knew all the intricacies and intimacies of the corporate environment. He was a master player when he chose to be.

In the resource of time, he had several Friday strategies to frustrate those who frustrated him all the rest of the week: coming in late, not leaving for lunch at noon, either being the first one at a meeting or coming in last after the meeting had started and, when no one was around, he would adjust all the clocks to be no more than five minutes off. He'd spend many moments on Fridays just standing and staring, as if he were deep in thought or trying to remember something. These strategies irritated people, but didn't bring them to the actual level of conscious anger, and so people didn't consciously recognize the difference, but Drood enjoyed their discomfort nonetheless.

For space, he would move people's furniture slightly, stand too close when talking, shorten chairs, always take the seat next to someone and move it even closer to them. He parked in the forbidden visitor's space or the handicapped spaces, right next to the CEO. People had to accommodate him, but again, for one day a week people were used to making mental adjustments, and so it never came to confrontation.

To raise anxiety over materials, payback he told himself, he'd walk around all day with extra blank pieces of paper and inconspicuously leave them everywhere like a wake or a scent. He'd raid all the supply cabinets for one particular item, say staples, and stock pile them in the empty drawer of an empty desk in an empty cubicle. He'd move books from one manager's office to another. He'd turn up the volume on sound cards and phones. He'd disconnect cables to computers whenever he'd have a moment unobserved. He'd turn pictures to the wall or lay them face down on the desk in people's cubicles. He'd post inane documents and memos in prominent places on walls and cubicles where they were forbidden to be. He'd move all paper supplies for a printer to a stack on the floor in front of the printer. Garbage cans would be removed from under the desk and placed under the chair so that they'd be knocked over without being noticed. Anything that belonged to a group in common, such as reference material or supplies, would be sneaked into a manager's office and left in an inconspicuous corner. Drood had searched everywhere and found a methane spray can that fit in the palm of his hand. He sprayed it behind people when they walked.

Drood's rebellion also included eating dinosaur-sized lunches on Fridays. He'd go to any one of the Central New York style diners where they'd serve fried potatoes and heaping mounds of an egg-meat-vegetable hash called a fretta or fish fries, and he'd gulp down beer on his lunch hour. In the afternoon he'd sit, stunned by his morning efforts at sabotage and general mayhem, by the huge globules of brain-melting lovely salty fat smush that were bulging through his circulation and depositing their load of oily soothing silt in the synapses causing him to smile and drool a little. Friday afternoons passed slowly, but fortunately no one expected any work from anyone else on Friday afternoons. Drood looked at his cubicle wall for a while until its gray began to seep into his mind and then he looked elsewhere.

Finally, it occurred to him that surfing the net looked a lot like working if someone couldn't get a careful look at your screen.

Particularly if you wanted to do the kind of surfing he wanted to do: looking for his daughter and getting in touch with her. At 3:00 Drood launched his effort. He'd been in Meltocom long enough to be comfortable doing something so blatantly not supposed to be done, and he had begun to understand the Internet a little bit, and he had nothing else to do and so now he was ready to dive in and use the electronic stream to carry him where he wanted to go. Drood also knew that the various search engines, and formatted lists, and sites and locations etc. could look a lot like "business" documents. It really only meant that there was alignment, ruled lines, and structure to the information on the screen. If he turned off the color he could make any web site look like work. Use of color by cubiclists made the managers suspicious. Though the managers of course took every chance they could to get color into their presentations, (appropriately or not), if lots of color showed up on an inferior's screen it could only mean one thing. Creativity and freedom. Bad. So anyway, if Drood turned the color off, he knew that the managers didn't actually know how to use the Internet or any other applications, so they would have no idea whether they were looking at work or not. As long as it was only words and numbers and no pictures and colors.

Drood still didn't have a name. Had his daughter changed her name because of him? Or because Claire had remarried? By quitting time he was no further along than he had been. The different types of searches, directories, web sites, files, organizations, networks and individual users were so vast, multiconnected, infinite and cryptically coded that he had no idea if the lists or leads he found were connected to anything useful, whether or not they were valid, or what next steps he had to take to activate them. Every time he thought he was getting somewhere he was asked for his credit card and he couldn't do that while on the company computer. He knew they could track all the sites he was on, but if the big Meltocom headquarters didn't know who or what he was looking for, or what his job entailed, they had no reason to flag his searches for investigation. As long as he didn't start buying a bunch of stuff. And each time Drood would get to the point of credit information he was never far enough along the certainty curve to know whether what he would be buying would actually help him in his search for his daughter. He had assimilated quite a bit of information in his lifetime, more than anyone should be expected to, really, but the web and all its codes, nicknames, abbreviations, and acronyms seemed to him far too disorganized and poorly articulated to be of much real use finding things. If you already knew where you were going, maybe.

In any case, the weekend arrived on Friday afternoon and Drood sprinted to the car fumbling for his cigarettes and keys at the same time. As he sat in the car and sighed with great relief, he finally got the cigarette lit and looked around him. The people trudged to their cars without looking at each other. The executives all looked embarrassed, the cubiclists all angry and defensive. They moved so slowly in such contrast to Drood's desperate race to escape. Perhaps this was a culture from which they knew they could never escape. Drood knew of other cultures, of other times, and that was a big difference between him and the others. He had special knowledge and at times like this he wished he could spray it out all over everyone else. Altruism existed yet in his damaged and degenerated heart. He wanted them not to trudge; he wanted them to hold their heads up. Okay, they were stuck in this place, in this disaster of a soulless existence, but he wanted them to at least believe there were other ways of being.

Drood hit 690 and revved up. He got up to 80 mph and weaved in and out of the traffic. The automobile. Drood felt its power and ease. He hadn't been driving long enough to know that his vehicle was old and that the engine had far less pick-up than most other vehicles. He only knew that he was in command of the world when he was behind the wheel. The original "detached reality" experience, long before video games, the automobile abstracted the landscape, made people and trees, houses, whole villages and towns nothing but blurred images. With the heat on and the radio on and the shade pulled down and his seat reclined Drood soared through the world. With just flicks of the wrist he surged into one lane and out of another. He watched the cinder block and brick warehouses go by and he read the billboards advertising chiropractors, car dealers, and insurance companies. The sun was right in his eyes as he came round the curve and zipped over to the right lane to get off on Teall Ave. Drood passed Longo's bar and grill and went up the steep hill past the Ukrainian bowling alley. He considered visiting Mickey again, but it was Friday night and he was tired of thinking about the unknown. His inner eye was developing a permanent squint from trying to divine the omens in the murky future. Drood knew how to read signs, and had been around long enough and in enough different settings to be able to pick out patterns. It was the one skill he still had and that he could use in any situation, and it was clear to him that a major pattern was now developing around this vision he had and all the little ripples that made up his life were beginning to point in the same direction. He was not quite ready though to see the big tsunami coming, whatever it was, and it was Friday night and he needed relief. His searching for his daughter and for the mysterious Traveler boy would have to wait. His week was over and it was time to punctuate it. He had only to decide which bar to go to and plan for the return trip by cab.

* * *

"No problem, I'll lock up," said Drood. Tom slowly turned away and went out the door. As Tom disappeared through the frame, Drood turned again to face the dark cave. He put his hands out again and plunged in. At first he couldn't see anything, but his sight quickly adjusted. He moved toward where he had heard the footsteps thudding away. It was around the corner and into the section that had been the main floor of the factory. The smooth cement floor was still intact, but there were places where debris and wreckage had been piled high. At some point there had been a fire and somebody had put half-burnt lounge furniture in a heap right in the middle of the floor. Drood looked to the corners of the main room and couldn't see them. He went into a side room off the main floor and saw that at the other end of the room there was an entrance to another room. Drood slowly moved through the place looking at the fantastic, shadowy debris and the ruined rooms and the makeshift architecture where walls had apparently been erected and removed many times, until he finally lost track of where he had started and chuckled to himself. He was in a genuine, man-made labyrinth by himself late on a dark Saturday night. He wondered if he would encounter a Minotaur as he had read about in the Greek mythologies. In ancient Ireland it was believed that caves could be the entrance to the Otherworld. Drood pondered that for a minute and wondered if somewhere in the factory-cave there was an entrance that could take him to ancient Ireland. What would it look like? The stories said it would be a small entrance that you had to squeeze through and that you would fall when you were finally in. Drood stamped on the cement floor. He was pretty sure there was no basement to the place, nothing below.

Drood began to feel really cold and the thrill of exploring began to wear off, so he decided he would try to find his way back to Tom's workshop, or find another exit and walk around to lock up the shop. It shouldn't be hard to find at least a way out. The place was in such decrepit shape and connected in a haphazard way to a series of sheds and garages that he figured there had to be at least one place where he could squeeze out. Sure enough, he heard the noise of a car going by not far from where he stood and when he turned to face the sound, he noticed a double door with a rusted chain and padlock on it that had enough give in it to slip through. Drood bent and struggled to contort himself through the opening, not as young as he used to be, and finally popped out into the frosty night. The smell of grass was strong and there was a rusty chain link fence with high ugly trees right in front of him. He could see no road. He figured he had to be on the other side of the "complex" from the workshop and so he began to walk around to the front where he had to lock Tom's workshop. Noticing the abandoned cars, the high weeds, the rusty barrels and industrial parts lying about everywhere, he continued the ruminations he had entertained while inside the building about what kind of people had been through here. What were the circumstances of their leaving things behind? So much evidence of life and choice, surrender, and passing on. One could expect to stumble on a decaying corpse here. Drood finally came around to the door of the workshop and put the seal on the evening by locking up. He went home with no further sign of the boy.

* * *

This is my first entry in this journal and I don't really know what to say. My uncle told me that it's good for you to write in a journal, but he didn't say why. I don't really see how writing in a journal can be good for you, but I'm kind of bored so I might as well do it. The Knicks rule! They're going to have every body they need this year to win the whole championship. No way the Lakers are going to win even though they got Kobe and Shack. Mom's downstairs moving everything around again, she's all nervous because Charles or Charlie or whatever his name is coming over again. She always gets like this when she has a new boyfriend and I can't stand it so I come up to my room and play Nintendo. But only now I'm writing in the journal. Who is reading this anyway? None of my friends has a journal, at least I never heard of one until my uncle gave it to me. He told me all kinds of famous people keep journals, he says it like you would say keeping a pet, and that maybe if I'm famous some day the journal will be really valuable. I'd like to be famous, but I think it would be embarrassing if someone read something stupid like this. I want to be on the Knicks some day, but I never heard of Patrick Ewing writing a journal. My hand's kind of tired now. This is more writing than I ever did in school, but I hear the music now from downstairs so that must mean the guy is here. I might as well call him Charles, because he told me to call him Charlie and acted all friendly, so I'm going to call him Charles. Because I don't know him at all and I get the feeling he's just being fake friendly to me, like most of them are. Hopefully he'll just leave me alone. I wish my mom didn't have to have boyfriends; they can be a real pain.

Anyway, it's almost my birthday, and I hope I get the Knicks starter jacket. Mom said when I got to be ten I could get one and here comes number twelve. But she'll probably forget like usual, and when I go to remind her, it'll be like I'm bringing it up for the first time and she won't want to get one. It's not her fault, she just doesn't remember too well, and anyway I know she doesn't have the money. She just wants to get it for me when she tells me she does, but she only tells me she will when it's really far away. I wish she would just say no the first time. I don't really want a Knicks starter jacket anyway. Somebody would probably steal it and I'll have to worry about it all the time. Well, now I'm really going to stop writing because my hand is killing me, and I've used up three whole pages in the journal. It's kind of funny, I didn't think I wanted a journal and I didn't think I would like writing in it, but I did three whole pages. That's more than I did all last year in school. Well that's all now. Bye to whoever you are. Oh yeah I forgot to say. I got beat up after school today and I can't open my left eye and both of my lips are split.

* * *

At the same time, across town, drunk, Drood's hand scrawls in his journal:

I came to in restraints and feeling all numb and tingly in the arms and legs. I had tubes in my arms and there was a TV in the corner of the room but there were no people right near by. I couldn't believe it. The spite and the vicious stubbornness of the Gods, and the tortuous resilience of the human body had foiled me and here I still was in this world with still no reason to live and now a resentment that bordered on rage. I pushed with silent fury on the restraints until the needles and the tubes began to leak on my arms and a light began to *flash and a beeping noise filled the room. My head was pounding and nothing outside moved and I couldn't believe I was in store for yet more torment. The beeping continued and nothing happened. I wondered what hospital I was in and had I ended up in New York City again or was I somewhere else on the east coast? Never would have predicted Syracuse, federal relocation of mental patients on Medicaid, and listed as John Doe. Faceless, nameless man, retrieved from a row boat in the Atlantic ocean, naked and ranting, sedated, sedated some more, and finally sedated some more until, comatose, all the paperwork could be done, and then, trussed and motionless, I could be bussed from Staten Island all the way up the Thruway to St. Francis in Syracuse. When I looked in the mirror the day of that first reawakening, I looked like the mad Suigne, who perched in the branches of the trees and played bird until the cause of his grief could be assuaged. Well, maybe it hasn't been assuaged but it's definitely been delayed and postponed.*

I went into that boat to die and I don't remember much else beyond a few hours of anguished solitude and drifting. No idea where the clothes went, no idea how I was discovered and the rescue, the subduing, and the subsequent repatriation. Now who was I to be and for how long before I could escape. was my only thought. The doctors interfered. They would keep me in this world long enough to weaken me to where I couldn't escape and the disease of life in this world would take hold again. I passed judgment on those doctors as well as all other citizens. They would be repaid some day. Hopefully before I was finally called home. Wherever that might be.

Gradually, I came to remember my ex-wife and daughter, indistinctly, and will and purpose snuck back in. There was a dark misery in me, something I tried to purge and could not, some compelling reason to step into the rowboat and shove off, but I wouldn't face it in that hospital. I know now how I destroyed everyone around me. And that is all I can bring myself to say.

Chapter 5

Tag Clifford was running as hard as he could and he was panicked. He knew they were going to catch him no matter what he did. They had caught him before. He hadn't expected them to be in his neighborhood on an early Saturday evening. He'd never seen them here before. Maybe they came just to find him and get him. He whipped his head from side to side and grabbed the corner of the fence as he got to the end of the churchyard on Midler. He swung around into the side street and he heard their sneakers slapping down on the sidewalk not far behind him. Nobody on the side street either, lots of parked cars, and Tag was sure he was going to catch a beating again. He started to cry and wished he were dead and he felt their hatred right behind him. He didn't even know why they hated him. As far as he knew he'd never given them any reason to, they just did. And they were after him all the time, threatening to cut his balls off, to shave his head, to flush him down the toilet, to make him bend over for them. As Tag stopped running and flinched, hunching his shoulders, the tears pouring down, he thanked God that it was at least on a public street and in broad daylight, so that they wouldn't be able to do much to him that was really terribly awful. He would keep all his body parts and his clothes although he was in for some pain and some blood.

As he felt the first punch in the back of his head, the door in a brown car parked on the side of the street swung open and a man sprang out and caught the lead pursuer, the first puncher, by the throat. The momentum of the other two carried them right into the man, who paused and then kicked one in the stomach and grabbed the other by the hair. Now the three pursuers were stopped, one held by the throat, one held by the hair, and one gasping for air on the sidewalk.

"Leave now and you leave in one piece!" the man, Drood, shouted. The gasping boy struggled up and tried to jog away. As the man released his grasp the other two started to walk away, glaring at him over their shoulders. Drood hadn't surprised them or frightened them. He had merely stopped them and they were letting him know it with their stares. This might increase the trouble for the young boy, Drood thought. Instead of a persecution, it might now become a war, which the young man looked ill prepared to wage.

Drood turned to Tag and looked him up and down. Thin and pale, with scruffy hair, noticeably younger than the picture Drood had drawn, but unmistakably the same boy. The tears were drying on his face and he looked up at Drood with large eyes and a down turned mouth. He stood still and simply stared at Drood, as if waiting to see what would happen next. Drood didn't move or say anything. The boy was real and had run right into him. The "Traveler."

"Thanks." Tag offered in a lifeless monotone.

Drood saw that being saved from a beating didn't necessarily give the kid any hope. Must be in serious trouble this kid. What should he do now? "No problem. You okay?"

"Yeah, I'm O.K." Looking at his sneakers now.

"You live around here, or you need a ride to get home?" Drood asked.

Suspicion seemed to creep into the boy's eyes and he edged away. "I don't live far. I'll be O.K. They won't find me, the way I go." Tag said and looked at his feet.

"O.K. You're sure?"

"Yeah. Thanks," and the kid was off, running down the side street and cutting through a gate to run through the church property. Drood watched as the boy slipped through a hole in a fence and disappeared, evaporated just like a dream. This boy seemed to have the gift of mysteriously appearing and disappearing, Drood mused, a skill for which the Druids had been famous. Well he had made contact with the boy, now what? Wait for the Gods to make their next move. Drood instinctively looked to the sky and muttered, "Manannan…." and then clenched his jaw and shook his head.

* * *

Drood was distracted during the poker game that night and had constantly to be called back to attention by Shiny's swearing or by

Gus' good-natured teasing. Even Tom had to ask him once "What's up?" Drood kept watching the darkness, the opening into the factory, looking for the boy. He felt sure the boy would come now. He must have really seen him last week when he thought he was having a vision. He probably foraged around the old ruin in the dark; the way kids like to do. Drood wanted to talk to the boy and find out why the others had been chasing him, why they wanted to hurt him. He wanted to help the boy and at this point he was pretty sure the boy was in serious trouble and that whatever powers there were had sent him to take care of the boy or to help him. Where Drood came from the mentorship and sponsorship of children who were not blood relatives was a common thing and it was not required that you had any connection to the child other than something to teach or offer. It was a time and a place far away and long ago that this was possible. Drood was not so familiar with children in this time, but he read about and watched with dismay the spread of the disease of pedophilia and the increasing fascination with it in mainstream culture. It appeared to him that all nouns now could be sexualized, and in this culture anything that was possible would occur. The basic drives of humanity were being perverted. Well, to mentor this boy he would have to be careful of perception and careful of communication and misunderstanding. Drood pondered his next move as the cards slapped down, the beer flowed, and the temperature dropped.

Drood shivered as the sound of dripping water stopped and he imagined the source of the water had frozen somewhere on the aluminum roof. In the dark and the gloom they couldn't see the water, but heard it everywhere around them. It rained all the time in Syracuse when it wasn't snowing. But no wind tonight and now no dripping water. The silence seemed to outline their voices and edge them with a humming treble. Drood heard a rat scuffle somewhere in the main factory. He forgot his preoccupation with finding the boy and concentrated on the card game.

"Gimme two." Click. Click.

"Shit."

"Three." Clickclickclick.

"One." Click.

"Dealer takes one." Click.

Dead silence. Eyes squinched, glances at each other, staring at cards. Breathing. A cough. Resume with speed.

"Bet five."

"See."

"Out"

"Yeah. And five more."

"See."

"Call."

"What it is, my man!!!" and Shiny laid down two aces and two jacks.

Gus chuckled and dropped three fives and a pair of two's. Drood just dropped his cards on the deck. As Gus raked in the money, they resumed talking while was Drood's turn to shuffle the cards.

"Anyhow," says Shiny, continuing a story thread he had started earlier, "I think I'm gonna go back to the Cue Ball and kick the shit out of that old dude." He looked around the table eagerly and Tom avoided his eyes, while Gus looked doubtfully at him. Shiny concluded that Drood was the only possible ally and looked for support.

"What do you think Drood, you were there, man?" And all eyes were on Drood as he continued to shuffle without looking at Shiny.

He paused and waited for full dramatic effect. Though supposedly crazy, Drood knew they all respected his opinion because he had been around quite a bit and clearly had a great deal of experience to draw on. Gus, Shiny, and Tom had lived in Syracuse most of their lives and had been who they were consistently and thoroughly all their lives, but they somehow sensed that Drood was another kind of being and they deferred to him in opinions and in conversation although they also at the same time teased him, dismissed him, and joked with him about his time in St. Francis and his craziness.

Finally, Drood spoke, "I think you won't be kicking anyone's ass Shiny," and as Shiny began to swell and turn purple and get ready to spit, Drood continued, "because you're too nice of a guy and too grown up to go back after a loser like that. I've seen you restrain yourself too many times when you had a right to go after somebody. You know the score. You're too sweet."

And at that Shiny didn't know what to say. He lost the impetus and the moment for feigned rage and he gazed at the other two with furrowed brows. Gus just nodded his head and mumbled "s'right" as Drood threw the cards around the table. Tom was trying to refrain from smiling and turned his face slightly away from Shiny. Drood had restored the dignity and respect Shiny was posturing to get, but it wasn't the way it was supposed to go, and so Shiny felt better and relieved and, at the same time, a little embarrassed for putting on the show when he didn't have to. Shiny stared at Drood as the rest of the men read their cards.

"You're something else, Drood" was all he could manage. "I still think the guy should be taught a lesson." Shiny had been who he was all his life and couldn't quite give up the act.

Drood replied, "Life will take care of that, Shiny, don't you worry about it. It probably already has."

"What the hell does that mean?" Shiny was getting his anger together again.

"Nothing, never mind." said Drood. "Your bet Tom."

And they resumed, betting, seeing, raising, taking cards, swilling beer and shivering. This time they had a tape player and Otis Redding wailed his loneliness and pain into the cold, empty moonlight streaking the factory floor at symmetrical interludes, through the busted window frames and skylights of the old dump. Drood stopped caring and he played automatically, winning and losing, mostly losing, while his mind wandered the hills of his native Ireland, remembering his people and their land, thinking of the barefoot summers he knew as a boy and the lonely lands and the smells of the animals and the fires and the turf. He could almost feel the soft rain of home in the two weeks of Syracuse spring when it rained every day in May. Almost, but not quite. The rain was stronger and more determined here, no hint of the Gulf Stream. Maybe that's why he stayed here in Syracuse, the almost Irish nature of the weather before the winter.

Drood didn't know how long he had been musing this way when he looked up from his cards and saw that all the other players had stopped moving and talking and were looking at the back of the garage where the boy stood by the corner watching the game. The boy looked surprised as though asking: how had he given himself away and who had noticed him? There was a brief standoff in the gulf between the boy and the poker game, before Gus said in a kindly voice, "You want something?"

The boy shook his head.

"You want to watch the game?" Gus had six children of his own and many grandchildren. He was comfortable around kids. The boy nodded and curled almost completely out of sight around the wall. Just his intent eyes peeked into the room.

"Well, come over here then and pull up that old crate." Gus said. "We won't bite you."

He stepped into the light and Drood noticed the boy had the same clothes on he'd had on in the afternoon when Drood had rescued him from his tormentors.

"What's your name boy?" said Gus.

"Tag."

"Tag?" And the boy nodded.

"Okay Tag, we playin' five card draw, you know how to play poker?"

The boy nodded again.

"All right then. Here we go. Jus' speak up if you have any questions."

Drood considered that it was kind of Gus to take over the situation this way and to invite the boy to watch and learn. He looked at Tom and at Shiny and concluded that neither of the two of them had any experience or understanding of children and would probably have just driven him off. Gus was not only allowing him to watch but was going to offer to teach him to play. Shiny and Tom fell in with this scheme because they didn't care one way or the other. Drood could tell by their stiffer body postures and their deeper than usual frowns as they studied their cards for the next hand that they felt a little self-conscious, but they would go along with Gus and Drood if Drood stepped up to help the boy.

Drood watched the boy watching the game and he could see the kid, in his concentration, had lost all sense of fear. Tag looked wary, he fidgeted and glanced to the exits often, but the boy was absorbed in the game and in trying to understand the plays and the odds. Every once in a while Gus commented to the boy about a particular move or percentage. Drood could see Shiny was getting a little impatient with Gus. He huffed and blew air out and sat back and looked at the ceiling.

"You live around here?" Drood asked the boy.

"Mmhm. On Midler." Midler was the main North/South artery that bisected Eastwood, an incorporated village in the city of Syracuse. It was mostly rental houses between Erie Boulevard and 298, with a few factories toward the North Side. The burned out factory of the poker game was just a block off Midler.

"Your parents know you're out here?"

"I just have a mom. She doesn't care where I am as long as I'm home when she wakes up in the morning."

"Hmm." Drood considered that and the others looked concerned but resumed the game. "Not dangerous around here on a Saturday night?" Drood continued.

The boy eyed Drood and didn't speak. He began to shrink away from the game and Drood decided to pursue another tack. "What school you in?"

Shiny burst in, "C'mon, Drood, quit interviewing the kid, we're playing cards here!"

"Awright, Shiny, just being friendly, keep your shirt on." The game continued and the boy visibly relaxed and once again gave close attention to the game. Drood noticed anticipatory smiles and sympathetic frowns on the boy's face and he realized that the boy had more or less figured out the nuances of the game and the personalities of the players, and quickly. Drood could see intelligence in the boy's gaze and wondered about his background. As it grew late, Gus leaned over to show the boy his cards and asked him, "Now, what would you do here?"

The boy leaned forward and whispered in Gus' ear and Gus pulled back his head and stared at the boy in apparent surprise.

"You kidding me?" The boy just shook his head no and gazed very seriously at Gus. Gus looked at his cards again and shrugged. He bet high. Shiny called and raised, Gus called and raised again. Drood and Tom had dropped out. Gus took two cards. Shiny took one. The betting continued, a death struggle now, Shiny looking ferocious and sweating and Gus smiling and occasionally glancing around the table. He looked uncertain.

The cards were laid down, four sevens for Shiny. Exclamations: "Whoa!" "Lookit that" and "Man!"

Gus flipped his over, straight flush.

"All right boy, good call. He said go for the straight flush!" and Gus looked around the table at the other players with a smile. "The boy called it, he did. My pro-tuh-jay!" Gus crowed. The boy had an impish smile on his face and he looked calmly at Gus and then at Drood. Shiny was purple, but he knew he had no cause to be. He had been fairly beaten, and so he restrained himself once again. Drood was confirmed in his opinion of the boy's intelligence. There might be much he could teach the boy.

"Screw this," Shiny said and he stood up and stretched his arms over his head. "I'm going home while I still got some money to go with."

Gus chuckled, and Drood remembered that Gus took particular pleasure out of beating Shiny because of the energy it required being around Shiny and because of Shiny's constant eruptions. It was payback for Gus to beat him in cards.

The game broke up and Gus handed the boy a ten-dollar bill for helping him take such a large pot. The boy didn't argue or thank Gus; he just put the money into his pocket. Drood thought the boy's eyes looked cold when he was taking the money, like the eyes of a hawk as he swallows a frog. "Just doing what he's supposed to do, not feeling anything in particular about it, just acting in concert with the laws of nature, unconscious and un-self-conscious," Drood thought. Drood used his considerable psychological training and skills to notice every detail about the boy. He watched the boy's nervous feet, his quick and searching eyes, noticed his almost total silence, and saw recognition and deep cogitation in his eyes.

As they were leaving, Gus said to the boy, "You come back here any Saturday night you want and watch. We here o'most every Sat'day, except holidays." The boy nodded and turned away from the front door as Tom locked it. Drood watched as the boy sprinted to what must have been a fence smothered by bushes and vines. Tag disappeared into the middle of the wall and there was nothing left of him but the moonlight on the path he had run. Vanished. "What next?" wondered Drood.

On the ride up Midler to James and on James through the little village of Eastwood, Drood thought about his next move. He assumed the boy would return to watch the poker game and, compelled only by a general sense of destiny and curiosity, and with serious misgivings about the plans of the Gods, Drood thought he

46

should make a move to unofficially sponsor the boy somehow. He had to be ready to take action by the next card game. He'd look for clues in the world and formulate a plan of approach. Perhaps the reason for this boy entering his life would be made clear.

Drood didn't follow conventional thinking when it came to decisions and choices. He saw a greater range of options than normal people saw. As he drove by the tax preparer's, the used bookstore, and the furniture store, into the residential area where he lived, Drood considered how other people must live their lives. They hadn't been to other worlds and other times. They hadn't (mostly) been mad and lost and so they had to look around themselves and base all their opinions on their families, their jobs, and their friends. Opinions based not on Gods, not on the history of their people, not on the earth around them, not on the nature of human beings, not on dreams or omens or signs. They had no recognition of patterns, of intersections, and no appreciation of coincidences and magic. The known ruled them and therefore they could be completely destroyed by the intrusion of the unknown. In the case of the boy, Drood was relying on coincidence, vision, and potential (as well as his own unconscious longing regarding parenthood, of which he was not unaware), rather than on the known. He KNEW he was connected to the boy. Coincidences always, always, always preceded awareness of cause and effect connections. Drood was old enough not to question these things. He went in the right direction before the right direction revealed itself. Timing was everything and Drood had been trained to look into the future.

"O.K.," he said to himself, "so I'm going to need to figure out a way to work with the boy and a reason to give him. It will probably all present itself to me, so I'd probably better prepare anyway so that when the situation does properly present itself to me, I will recognize it right away and be prepared." And he decided that he would need one more meeting with Mickey to get himself ready. And he'd have to be a little more aggressive at Meltocom this week so that he wasn't quite so tired and passive when his next opportunity to work with the boy came. He had to get on top of things.

* * *

I watched a bunch of old guys play poker last night in that old factory that's falling down on the next block. I was just fooling around in there looking for stuff to take home and I saw their light was on again so I went over there. They said I could watch and I figured it out real quick how to play and then I helped one old black guy win money. He gave me ten bucks for it, so that was pretty cool. They play in there every Saturday and the guy said I could come to watch whenever I want to. I think I'd be pretty good at poker, because I know all the cards and the rules for what hand beats what, and I should just practice at it. Maybe eventually I could be one of those guys who goes around the country and plays poker for a living, like those pool players in that movie. Mom always says how smart I am and I beat her in every game we play, which isn't saying much because she doesn't pay attention, she's usually just playing to be nice to me. But maybe I'm smart anyway you never know. School doesn't count; it's just a bunch of bull anyway. Just a place where you go to get beat up and have stuff ripped off from you, and then if you say anything to any of the teachers or anybody they look at you funny and pick on you whenever they can after that. But anyway, one of the guys in the poker game was I think this guy that stopped them from beating me up yesterday. I don't know why they were on Midler because they don't live near here, but they were chasing me and this guy stopped them and even kicked one of them in the stomach. He looked real serious at the poker game, but he might be a nice guy, except he offered to give me a ride home too, so he could be a creep. I don't know. But anyway, he helped and he didn't say much at the poker game, so maybe he's all right. Well, Mom's yelling at me again, so I better stop writing now. I'm going to go back to the poker game and learn to be a great poker player so I can get rich. Then I can buy a bodyguard who will do whatever I want.

Chapter 6

Drood and Mickey were deep in conference, but it had taken Drood a full hour and a half to get Mickey to concentrate and talk about the real world. Either the medication wasn't working or Mickey had stopped taking it again. But finally, as Drood stayed off topics like electronics, technology, government, or the mafia, he was able to keep Mickey reasonably coherent enough to get some advice from him on how to deal with the boy. Mickey was a genius but he was completely incapable of functioning or taking care of himself due to his schizophrenia. He would spin amazing tales of connections and conspiracies and he came close to being a science fiction writer in the level of detail and coherence of his tales. He seemed believable. When Mickey would get to talking and get really into a subject, a listener would often be grateful and enthralled by the insights, and by the unexpected opening up before him. There inevitably came a moment, Drood remembered, when the listener realized that Mickey was mentally ill and that Mickey really believed these stories. The poor man was genuinely frightened, excited and tormented by his own delusional tales. In this condition Drood would have Mickey talk on particular subjects and then he could glean general information and advice indirectly, rather than having Mickey be analytical about it. As Mickey spoke to Drood about the removal of blood and bone marrow from the patients in the hospital for the purpose of decreasing the mass of the cadavers they hoped to create, Drood considered which subjects he should direct Mickey toward. Perhaps "teaching," or "parenting," or "spiritual mentorship." He wasn't certain what direction the relationship with the boy was going to go, but he needed a clue for how to proceed. Perhaps he should have Mickey talk about creating world-views, or about inventing one's self. That could be really promising. In

Drood's several lives he had found no one who knew as much about it as he himself did, except Mickey, whose madness seemed to give him access to many other lives and times. Drood wondered suddenly how he, Drood, had managed to keep his sanity through all his progressive lives. But enough pondering, time to get Mickey started and let him spin, and sit back and take it all in and work on a clue.

"Well Drood you got yourself a problem because you can't have a custody ward, because you're already a number, an identified problem for the state what with your insanity, institutionalization and all, of course they had that planned from the beginning."

Drood thought about protesting that he didn't want a custody ward, he just wanted to know how to deal with the kid, but he knew better than to interrupt Mickey at this stage. Mickey spewed words and ideas and Drood always pictured them running into each other – racing to get out into the air.

"So, what you gotta do is sort of un, un, un, un, un, unofficially get involved and it's clearly to save the boy's life from your description the little minions of Satan are after him and chasing him and beating him and whatnot and it's doubtful he has any kind of protector, because having the marks on him and catching them in the act of getting ready to mark him again, well, that's surely a sign that he's on his own. Otherwise, the Secret Services and Child Monitoring Control Systems would step in, because once you've fallen through the cracks and no one can protect you, well then they want to make sure the final destruction of your life goes according to their plan with foster homes and whatnot. Well, we don't know for sure that they're evil in the services; they just try to manage an evil that has already occurred. You see my drift here, Drood, don't you, we're onto good and evil now and that's the structure of things we have to work with, so for the side of good, you've got to claim the boy and protect him from evil."

Mickey paused here to stare significantly at Drood. Drood merely shrugged and Mickey took a deep breath and continued in a rush,

"Right. So, anyway, as it turns out, there must be some reason they've chosen you, and for now, we'll have to assume it was those 'Gods' you keep talking about, although I have my suspicion that it was a doctor in the hospital here. He works on the next floor in neurosurgery, that's just a cover, he does the actual repairs and implants into the gray matter, works the electrical controls and all that, even does reprogramming jobs on the side, but it's only to keep him occupied while he's doing his real job of reassigning various souls to other various souls for his ultimate purpose, which presumably, we have yet to discover. So, now we have to figure out why the doctor, I'll call him Doctor Zulu to protect his real identity, you see they have these programs that filter all the noise in the hospital and then digitize it, and then it's automatically scanned for keywords. And since Doctor Zulu is behind the project, they scan most frequently for the use of his name and then they put full time surveillance onto whoever speaks about him. Since I'm not using his actual name the monitors won't pick it up."

Drood began to suspect that Mickey was moving off the subject into a more personal delusion and so he shifted in his chair and coughed a little. Mickey, without altering his tone or his pace, picked up the signals and returned to the subject at hand without any acknowledgment that he was conscious of having strayed.

"So we have to figure out why you have been chosen. I suspect it has something to do with one of your previous lives. Probably some latent skill that you have and probably some particular attachment to the boy. Of course, we can't see into the future like Zulu's technicians, so we don't know where it will lead. If we have to guess though, we would have to assume that you are just a signpost for the boy to find his direction and a pawn for Zulu and the gods to accomplish their purposes. The trouble is you've got all these skills, Drood, and you won't tell all your experiences, so we can't really narrow it down much."

Mickey paused and suddenly leaned into Drood's face and his large brown eyes absorbed all of Drood's vision and he said with urgency, "Don't have any children yourself, do you Drood?"

Drood was startled and sat back in his chair. Mickey continued leaning forward and staring intently at Drood. Drood pondered how to respond. If he told Mickey about his previous life, he'd have to tell him about the life before that, and eventually Mickey would have to know the whole thing. Of all the people in this world, Drood couldn't think of anyone he'd rather tell than Mickey. But at the same time, he had been concealing everything for so long that it had become second nature to him and though he couldn't think of any logical reason not to tell Mickey - he was an institutionalized schizophrenic after all and no one would believe Mickey about anything - he still felt strongly about his secrecy. Just because it was a long and strong secrecy he wanted to keep it and to break it would hurt him. It would be violence. The question was, would it be the kind of violence that allowed healing afterward, setting the bone, lancing the boil, or the kind of violence that would lead to slow bleeding and then the attack of the sharks and wolves who loved the smell of blood?

"Well, yeah, actually I have a daughter somewhere. I've been trying to find her."

"Ah, ha," said Mickey, "the reason for this boy may be to help you find your fatherhood, maybe even to find your child, literally. If I were you I'd help the boy fulfill his purpose, meanwhile let him lead you to your daughter or to your feelings of responsibility and parenthood. It makes sense, psychologically, mythologically, and from the point of view of a good story."

Drood considered this and it had the click in his mind of a lens coming into focus and it seemed to him to be just about right. Of course, he considered, it was ludicrous, random, and reading into things, but wasn't that really what life was all about? Whether it was determined by Gods, by chance, by fate, or by free will, all human connections and purposes involved a certain amount of absurdity. Literally, there was no meaning, but clearly he had to have some kind of meaning. So Drood pasted a meaning together from the scraps of reality he could, and he used Mickey's verbal glue, as a temporary solution until events created a new pastiche for Drood to contemplate.

"I think I got enough to go on Mickey. Thanks," said Drood. He wondered how to take his leave now that he had got Mickey stirred up. He knew Mickey could go on for hours in this condition.

"No problem, Drood, you see I've found that Dr. Zulu may appear sometimes kind and sometimes wicked, but one thing should always be known and that is that he is watching and taking part. You haven't had to have what they call an MRI lately have you?"

"No," said Drood.

"Well, avoid it if you can. If you get one of those they map out all the pathways and they put it into their databases and they program it and with the wireless signals the way they are now, they can change your thinking with just a couple of quick programs they write, and then there you go, off into having an affair, or launching a campaign for a social cause of their choosing, and sometimes they do it just to amuse themselves, like those old cheap magicians who could hypnotize you and make you cluck like a chicken. Zulu is the chief of the program, I'm convinced of that, but don't worry Drood, I'm monitoring him at the same time, now that I've discovered the situation, and I'll keep you informed, so he can do what he likes with all the other souls wandering through the hallways here, but you and I we'll be okay, we can counteract any reprogramming he does."

"Right." Drood was now realizing he would have to just get up and go and interrupt Mickey, and he did. "Gotta go now Mick. I'll catch you next week, ok?"

"Drood, find the kid, Drood, find your own kid. Dr. Zulu…" and Drood was up and moving as all patients turned their lonely eyes to him.

Now Drood had spoken with his oracle and he added his own little interpretation and came up with the following: lead the boy out of his troubles and back off on the search for his own daughter. Good news for him, because he really didn't know how much longer he could face the depressing search for his daughter. The government system wasn't actively against him, but there were complications and inertia seemed to hold sway and all of Drood's magic couldn't seem to make it happen. The boy had some kind of magic power and for lack of anything better, Drood was going to go with it. "O.K.," he thought, "I've got to speak to the boy and offer to help him out of his troubles. Be direct, go right to the source of the trouble." And, in truth, he was happy to give up the fruitless search for his daughter, at least for a while.

* * *

A young girl stared out the window of a 15th floor apartment in an expensive building on the upper West side of Manhattan. Her forehead pressed the window pane and her eyes followed the ants below. She was thin and small and she had to stand on her tiptoes to see down to the street. Her hands were on the windowsill and she leaned on them. After a few minutes, she sighed. She turned from the window and quickly looked around the room. It was a dark and voluminous living room. The lights were off and the pale light from the windows penetrated halfway into the room. It was completely silent in the apartment. She looked around again as if hoping or waiting for something. No noise at all.

The girl's black hair and vivid blue eyes gleamed in the weak window light, but there was no one there to see it. She hugged herself and walked through the empty gloom to the hallway and then down the long hallway to the front door. Her slippers made a shuffling noise on the carpet. The little girl reached up to check the locks on the door, her fingers running expertly over the deadbolt, the chain, and the button locks. She turned and walked slowly back through the ghostly rooms to her own bedroom. She sat at her desk and turned on a desk light and opened a book. She picked up her pen and began to write.

I am alone again. Or still. There is only one person in the whole world who understands what I am like and why I am always so sad and that is Rebecca. She's so pretty and so nice to me, I am very grateful to her for being my best friend. I will always love her no matter what, even if she decides she doesn't want to be my friend anymore. She knows what it's like for me, and she does little things that help, like she'll give me a card, or like if I'm around some perfect family at some school thing or something, and the family is all happy and everything, she will hug me without saying anything. She is the prettiest girl I ever met too. I really hope my mother doesn't decide to send me to the St. Andrew Academy next year. Then I would never be able to see Rebecca, although we could e-mail and talk on the phone all the time. Rebecca would hate it too, even though her Mom and Dad are great and she doesn't have all the problems that I have. As long as we can hang out together everything will be okay, she can ignore me around those other friends of hers and I won't care.

My Mom wants me to go see Gramma and Grampa again in Iowa, but I just can't face all that boredom for the summer. She thinks farm life is good for me. Maybe they'll come here to visit instead. I wish my penmanship were better. I wonder if Mom will ever let me find out about my father, even if he was killed right after I was born there should be more to say. And that he was a media executive. She never tells me any more than that and she also said he didn't have any living relatives. Oh yeah, and he was Irish. I wish she wouldn't get so upset whenever I ask her about it. And I wish she didn't marry Lewis, he is a pain. He's not my father. I hope Mom never reads this. Well I'm going to stop now because I am supposed to do homework. Next week we are going to California for a vacation, so Mom can rapid bond before she ships me off to Iowa.
Dee Dee Dewar, December 10, 2000.

Chapter 7

The boy became a regular at the Saturday night card games and he came to trust Gus and Drood because they were kind and consistent. They didn't want anything from him and they taught him how to play. The kid irritated the hell out of Shiny and so of course the boy resented him back. Shiny felt the game had been compromised by the presence of an innocent and he couldn't restrain himself from swearing. What kind of a Saturday night poker was it anyway when you couldn't talk about women and cuss all you wanted? He even had to drink less because of the boy. Drood could have told Shiny that the boy didn't need to be handled with kid gloves, any twelve year old has already heard all the swear words they were ever going to hear, and as for women, well, might as well be honest, the boy was going to get his own ideas no matter what. But Drood also felt compelled to watch what he said, and so the boy garnered far more attention and power in the card game than might be expected. As the weeks went by Drood observed that the boy was cautious, but sharp. He was mostly silent, but always watching from behind the shrewd, dark eyes. His occasional comments indicated a curious, but self-conscious and defensive boy. His immediate grasp of poker was fascinating to watch. He quickly understood not only the patterns in a deck, but the percentages, and more importantly, he got to know the emotional, mental part of the game. The kid quickly became as good as or better than the rest of them and it wasn't long before Shiny began to insist to the others, when the kid wasn't around, that the kid use his own money. There was an argument over that, but in the end, the kid settled it by bringing ten dollars one Saturday night, and the winter went on. They would have felt bad taking money from a kid, but the kid usually held his own and never complained when he lost. The winter got colder and the Saturday nights got more vivid. The kid seemed happy with the men.

Drood kept waiting for his chance to speak to the boy or to intervene somehow. Finally he felt he could wait no longer. The time for Mickey's recommended course of action had come. "Does your Mom worry about you are when you're here?" Drood asked one night as they settled in to play cards.

"She thinks you guys are all my age. She doesn't care, as long as I'm there when she wakes up on Sunday. She's probably pretty drunk right now anyway. Charles came over again."

"Who's Charles?"

"This guy she wants to marry. He's a loser."

Drood nodded. Maybe it was time to ask about the kids who had chased him. They had never spoken about it and Drood didn't even know if the kid remembered that it was him who had saved him. "You remember when those kids were chasing you over on the next block and I stopped them?"

Tag looked warily at Drood and then looked around at the other men. He wanted to keep playing poker. The back of his brain was telling him that attempts by grown-ups to get involved in your life usually weren't good things. He had been happy just to stick to the poker and to listen. But he had been asked a direct question and if he wanted to keep playing, he'd better play whatever this game was that Drood was after.

"Mmhmm," was all Tag said.

"What was that all about? Why were they chasing you?"

"No reason. They hate me and they try to kick my ass every time they see me."

"But, I mean, why do they hate you? What started it?" Drood persisted.

Tag had nothing to be ashamed of here, but he didn't know it. He stammered, but he told the truth, as he understood it, "I don't know. I was walking down the hall in school one day and those three guys were standing by some lockers and they were watching me as I came up the hall. They looked like they had just done something, you know, like all tense and nervous, but I didn't see anything. Anyway, they just said 'What are you looking at?' And I said 'Nothing.' And they grabbed me and started punching the hell out of me. Ever since then they try to get me whenever they see me. And they say all kinds of stuff, like threatening me, you know. They even came to my neighborhood looking for me. I think they live over by Burnet, down the hill toward 690."

"Do you ever say anything, or talk to them at all?" Drood asked.

"Nope. I just run whenever I see them. They're older, so I can avoid 'em most of the time at school."

"What does your mother say?"

"She doesn't know. She thinks I just had one fight. I told her I won it, anyway."

"What about telling the teachers and stuff?"

"I'd get in trouble and they'd only get their hands slapped, and then they'd kill me for sure. They probably have guns, anyway."

"Does Charles know about it?" Drood continued. He was after information about the boy's situation, but he was also making a point to Tag.

Tag just sneered. "Charles! He doesn't know shit about shit."

"So, are you just going to keep running from them for the rest of your life?"

"What else can I do?" And tears began to show in the corners of Tag's eyes. Drood had him cornered now and Tag began to get scared. He scraped his money and stuffed it in his pocket and said, "I gotta go." It was much earlier than he usually left the card game. Drood said, "I'll walk you out." Shiny threw down his cards in disgust.

It was snowing outside when Tag and Drood emerged from Tom's workshop. The vines on the fence had lines of white traced all around them, making a supernatural fleur-de-lis. Drood stared, entranced for a moment by the white curls and the delicate patterns in front of him. He felt faint. They stood at the hole in the fence through which Tag usually zipped to navigate through the broken down neighborhood and wend his way home.

"I think I can help you with your problem with those kids," Drood said.

Tag said nothing, just watched Drood's face and listened. It occurred to Drood that Tag's eyes looked so intense, so sharp and focused, that he must have a very old soul. There was something noble and stoic about the boy's silent suffering; he seemed to understand intuitively how to bear it. Drood sensed a great strength there.

"I know you could use a break, and I think I can help you,

but it will take a little cooperation and some courage from you to make it all happen. I don't want anything from you, I just like to help." Drood hesitated for a second, on the brink of revealing his own status as lost parent, mentally disturbed, Druid from another time, etc., but that would only put pressure on the boy and after all, if he was to help the boy, he should keep his own needs out of it as much as possible, focus on the boy and the problem at hand. His own needs could be dealt with incidentally and by osmosis. Drood suddenly realized he had become a parent after all and had grasped the very first concept in parenting. Sacrifice. He chuckled at the irony of it.

"What do you think?" he said to Tag.

Tag shifted his sneakers around in the snow and watched the slush at his feet. "I don't know," he said, "maybe." And then, "I gotta go" and he zipped through the fence and was gone.

"Hmmm" Drood thought. "Well, planted the seed, made the offer, see what the universe has planned here."

Shiny was going on about a confrontation he had at the Cue Ball, another run-in with a big mouth. He interrupted his monologue to take some shots at Drood, "Hey, Drood, what are you gonna be the kid's father or something? I don't think you're gonna be too good at it, you can't even take care of a straight flush, let alone a twelve-year-old boy."

"Shut up Shiny, let's play some cards."

* * *

Drood says he's going to help me with Loomis and those guys. I don't know if I should let him, because he could make it a lot worse. I think those kids might kill me, literally kill me if I do anything other than avoid them. But, he's not like my Mom, and he's not involved with the school. If he could stop them without connecting me to it, that would be best. I wonder what he would do? Probably threaten them or something. Anyway, Ewing got hurt again so the Knicks gotta get another center and things aren't looking too good for them. The guys at the card game think the Knicks will never win the championship with Ewing because the offense centers around him too much and they never should have got him back again. I think he's the best center ever. I wish I had more friends. I've only been in this school for four months, but I should have at least one friend by now. And a girlfriend. I'd like to be in love like in the movies, but nobody is really going to even like me, let alone love me. That's just stuff for the movies. Shiny talks about women all the time, but I don't think he knows as many of them as he says he does, because he talks about them all like they live just for him and like they're stupid or something. My Mom isn't stupid, she just doesn't get it sometimes, she's all confused a lot. But I think any woman who got around Shiny wouldn't stay very long, he's just too much to handle. That sounds just like something my Mom would say. Maybe I'll give Drood a chance to help as long as he keeps me out of it. Those kids aren't going anywhere and neither am I. If we make it all the way through junior high school and high school they'll probably always be in this town, even if I end up going to New York or California like I plan to. Once I get to those places I can start over and have a really cool life. I could get a really cool job, like a bicycle messenger in New York, or a taxicab driver in L.A. Then, when I have enough money saved up, I can get a place with a pool and hang around with some friends there, who would be really cool. Maybe Drood can even help me figure out a way to get to those places, Shiny said Drood used to live in New York. Wonder why he ever came to Syracuse, there's nothing exciting or interesting going on here. Anyway, maybe I'll see what he can do.

* * *

Drood was back at work Monday morning and he came in an hour early so he could have time to think. Sunday was a hangover day so he hadn't made any progress on the plan for the kid. The office, before people came in to bother him, was a good place to sit and work quietly. Drood's experience told him that all good work was done alone.

He considered that he didn't know as much about teenage boys in this society as he needed to if he was really going to get involved in saving Tag. So, the first thing would have to be inconspicuous observation of teen-aged boys. Then he would have to teach the boy some strategy. Drood remembered all the things he had learned about manipulating people, about dealing with enemies, and about managing perceptions. Oh yes, Drood was the right person to teach him the skills. The boy would become powerful, but who would teach the boy about loyalty and justice? Drood shuddered, knowing he was incapable of addressing those subjects with anybody. So Drood would observe.

Drood also knew the plan to save Tag would do the boy no good unless Tag took control of the plan and made some decisions and changes himself. The boy would have to take risks. He would have to be convinced to do it. He was too young to have the big picture and too young to know how simply bullies can sometimes be vanquished. He would have to begin training the boy in some basic concepts of life. Clearly there was little or no support in the boy's home life, and yet Tag had picked up quite a store of observations and experience. Drood would have to help Tag contextualize all he had been through

"What should I train the boy in? Observation. People. Honesty. Those are the only tools we really have," Drood mused. "The Right Action makes itself clear to us without us having to force it." He remembered his teachings well. "O.K." Drood thought, "Now I'm getting into the details too much and pushing ahead too fast. Let everything come to me." And he made some notes on his thoughts and pushed the pad back and stared at the cubicle wall, thinking nothing at all.

The outer door crashed and Mr. Muke came bustling in. With pursed lips and anxious glances around the office he silently announced his arrival with as much self-importance as he could muster. Drood wondered where Muke came from and where he went every night. What was the Muke, after all? No one knew anything about Mr. Muke's private life, except that he could be available at all hours at any time, day or night, weekend or week day, to work for the company. Drood watched him as he sniffed around the empty office, inspecting all the cubicles as he went by. Muke glanced at Drood and Drood grimaced before he could catch himself.

"Working early, today, eh, Mr. Drood?" the Muke sang. Drood grimaced again. "Uh huh" was all he said. Mr. Muke would be sure to come back and pounce once he had deposited all his carrying stuff in his office. Never leave the workers unattended was Mr. Muke's motto. The workers suspected him of being a religious zealot because he was so eager to instruct people how to think and how to be. Drood turned his computer on and waited, because he knew Mr. Muke would be there any second. The muscles in his neck hunched up.

Even though he was expecting it, he started when Mr. Muke appeared beside him. "Ready for the big meeting today?" Mr. Muke crowed. He was clearly excited. Drood didn't remember anything about a big meeting.

"What meeting?"

"The Cowdermill meeting!!! He's going to tell us about the next re-organization. We'll find out how things are going to change around the old marketing department. I'm really looking forward to it, because we need to get those people to figure out the strategic plan earlier so we can..." and then all Drood heard was "Blah blah blah." The chimera of reorganization seemed to energize the people doing the re-organizing, but basically, everybody always ended up doing the same thing, or not doing it, and the same people usually got stuck doing all the work. Being somewhat downhill from the re-organizers, Drood was pretty sure it was just a matter of changing the voice on the other end of the phone line that was asking Drood to come up with a way to make the voice a lot of money without any risk or even evidence later on. Mr. Muke had finished speaking and Drood just shrugged. His lack of enthusiasm seemed to offend Mr. Muke.

"Well **I** think it's important. A lot of people have worked really hard to make this all happen and we're sure it's a great new direction for the company." Drood couldn't possibly fake enthusiasm, but he could at least reign in his scorn. He tried "Ok, good. We could use a new direction." That was honest at least. "Let's see what happens." The Muke was slightly placated, distracted enough to wander off in search of more prey that was now steadily streaming in the doors in the form of cubiclists.

Drood said only, "The Cowdermill meeting..." and began to search for some electronic or paper evidence that might establish for him the time and the place of the meeting. He began to assemble the day in front of him when he was interrupted by the first phone call. It was Johnson, Mr. Muke's superior.

"Drood, do you have a few minutes? I want to talk to you about something in my office."

"OK" said Drood with a sigh. Johnson probably wanted Drood to write a memo for him. Johnson had never learned to read and write, but fortunately he was a Vice President and so had never really needed either of those skills. Drood trudged through the cubicle farm and found himself outside Johnson's office. As the door swung closed behind him, he noticed that the other Mr. Johnson, the first Johnson's boss, was there as well. They were both smiling broadly. Drood thought, "This can't be good." And then the first Johnson spoke.

"Drood, we have a plan in this reorganization that's coming up to make things different." Drood now believed he was about to be let go. But reality struck with an even more vicious force in Johnson's next utterance,

"We want you to run the Support and Service group for us."
Promoted. Drood's knees trembled and he had a moment of collapse before he remembered who he was and smiled back at them.

"Any chance you'd reconsider?" And they chuckled, and the second Johnson said, "Not a chance."   As Drood staggered away, he thought that Mr. Muke probably hadn't been told, for whatever reason, or else he would not have been so overbearing that morning. Instead he would have been downright hostile. He saw Mr. Muke headed for Johnson's office and figured he had better prepare for dealing with an infuriated Muke. An underling being made an equal was a devastating event. Drood felt that indeed, things were beginning to happen all at once and he took a deep breath and started to pray, but then remembered how he felt about Gods. They didn't exist any more, the evil bastards, and so he just exhaled loudly. And Support and Services? They were not exactly the easiest people to work with and now he would have to be their boss? "Ach", he thought. This is a big problem.

Drood walked to the coffee pots, strolling through Support and Services to refresh his perceptions of the group. They were exactly five men and five women and those who bothered to look at him glared as he passed. Drood shuddered. Those who were on the phone or talking to each other each had the same expression on their faces: wounded, victimized, righteous indignation. They all felt they had been screwed by life and they were determined to make Mommy and Daddy pay for it. And who was Mommy and Daddy? Anybody they could make take on that role. And now it was Drood's turn. Mother and Father both of a brood of poisonous snakes who were well entrenched in their pit. Drood's headache began early. And now it was time for the Cowdermill meeting. As he got back to his desk he saw Mr. Muke watching and waiting for him with a barely controlled smirk on his face. Muke's lips were quivering. As he spotted Drood on the path back to his cubicle, he began to walk toward him and Drood, avoiding eye contact, made a quick left hand turn into the hallway and zipped into the men's room. He sat in the stall and held his head in his hands. Why had he ever come to this world and hadn't he already paid enough? He lost his family, his friends, his homeland, his best friend, and finally his wife and daughter. Why couldn't he just get to know Deirdre a little bit? Why was she kept from him? Even the Gods weren't supposed to do that sort of thing. What kind of magic power could Drood summon to overcome existence? He had to shut his thoughts down, he had to, he could feel the craziness coming back into him. He could feel himself start to spin and wobble and he felt the world starting to slip away. He breathed deeply for several minutes and practiced saying to himself "Some day I will die and it will all be over, some day I will die and it will all be over..." until he had calmed down and could face the day. He washed his face with cold water and headed back out to the Cowdermill meeting.

Chapter 8

Tag was late for class because he had helped his mother get his old mattress out to the street for the city to pick up. He didn't have a new mattress yet, but Charles had said he had one for him and would bring it over whenever they wanted. Tag sort of doubted whether Charles really had one, but he wasn't thinking when he had complained about the mattress again at breakfast. It was lumpy and squashed and made him roll off to one side. His mother had heard it for the last time and so it had taken them a half hour to wrestle it down the two flights of stairs, snarling at each other when they got stuck at every corner. When they finally got it out to the curb, Tag had missed the bus and she had to drive him and they were both pissed off. He was grumbling to himself about his mother when he came around the corner to the row of classes where the English classes were held. Standing right in front of him was Loomis, the largest and meanest, the ringleader of his tormentors.

"Well, look who's here!" And Loomis grabbed Tag's shirt at the shoulder and punched him hard in the stomach. Tag doubled over and gasped and looked up at the hallway. Nobody there. Loomis looked around the corner and there was nobody coming that way either.

"What do you want from me... I never did anything to you?" Tag groaned.

"Shut up faggot. We're gonna get you and hurt you, understand, bitch?" Loomis stooped to his backpack and pulled a hunting knife from a sheath. Tag was on the verge of screaming and he couldn't breathe.

"You ever say anything and we'll gut you with this, or maybe just cut your asshole out, whatta ya think of that?" Loomis smiled and put his face right next to Tag's.

"Now get on your knees and kiss my foot right now, or I'll do it to you right here!" Tag was already on his knees and he just dropped and did as he was told. He tasted dust and then he tasted bile and thought he was going to throw up. Loomis walked away and laughed over his shoulder.

"We own you, bitch. We're gonna make you do whatever we want."

And he was gone around the corner. Tag stayed on his hands and knees for a moment, breathing. He heard footsteps from around the corner and he thought it might be Loomis coming back, so he got to his feet and prepared to run, but it was only Mr. Edwards, the security guard.

"What do you think you're doing out here? What class you supposed to be in?"

"English." Tag pointed to the classroom down the hall.

"Well, get there. You got no business bein' out here in the middle of class. Who do you think YOU are?"

"No one," said Tag.

He walked slowly to his class. His brain was wobbly and he reeled a little bit and Mr. Edwards suspected him of being high. At least he no longer felt like vomiting. The door was locked of course, and so he had to knock, which would disrupt the class and irritate Mrs. Wallenda. She opened the door frowning.

"Well, if it isn't the late Mr. Clifford. So glad you could join us. Late, as usual, and probably without having done any of the reading or the homework, right?" She smiled her fake, angry smile and Tag shuffled in and flopped into his chair, his breathing and his heart rate still weren't quite right. The rest of the class was half asleep, so he was hoping Mrs. Wallenda would let it go at that. He was wrong.

"Can you tell us why Ambrose Bierce used the bridge and the watch in his story, Mr. Clifford?"

Tag tried to speak and croaked. The class giggled. He tried again, "No, I didn't finish it." He actually had lost the book weeks ago and rather than get yelled at for it by the teacher and have his mother yell at him for having to pay for it, he just resigned himself to failing English, because what was the point of it after all.

"Didn't finish it. Do you ever finish anything? Do you intend to finish this class? Or are you finished already?"

"I wish," he said. He couldn't help it. And of course, then came the rage, and the yelling, and the lecture. The rest of the class was grateful. They had some drama and some entertainment and the teacher had been thrown off the track from tormenting them. Tag just closed his mind while Mrs Wallenda ranted in his face. He considered that she was lucky that it was only someone small and worthless like himself. If she tried yelling at some of the other students they'd scream back at her, or have their brother or sister or uncle come in and yell at her and threaten her. Some of them would probably even hit her. But, Tag thought, it's only me and she knows she can get away with it, and so I have to just sit here and take it. It was only 8:30 in the morning and Tag didn't think there was any reason to go on living through the rest of the day. He fantasized about killing himself and imagined all the different ways he could do it. It would have to be at the school so they'd all see and feel bad. And his mother would have to come to the school all sobbing and everything. And the whole thing would be over and he wouldn't have to be scared anymore and he wouldn't have anything to worry about. He'd be free.

* * *

Dee Dee wandered through the party and watched her mother playing hostess. Dee Dee kept an eye on her and avoided Lewis as much as possible. She hated to be presented to people, to perform and to have them compare her to their own children. She preferred to be left alone, but her mother insisted on her making an impression on all these rich people. Dee Dee hated all her mother's parties. It was all about who was better than whom and in the end they all ended up drunk and pawing each other and embarrassing themselves anyway. Once in a while one of the men would even try pawing her when they thought no one was looking. She hadn't even hit puberty yet. She thought the whole thing was disgusting. When she complained she got a lecture from her mother, or worse, from Lewis, about making connections and the importance of friends later on in life. As Dee Dee looked around the room at the overweight, overdressed, over-surgeried, over-monied crowd, she didn't see how anyone like these people would ever be her friends. They never brought kids over. Finally, she knew she had been out in the mix long enough and she made her way to her room.

* * *

California was incredible!!!! I love it there and when I get a little older I am going to live in Los Angeles and spend all my spare time at the beach. They have the best-looking boys there and all the movie stars and everything. I am going to live in Beverly Hills and come back to New York once a year to visit my mother and to go shopping. I will have a whole wing of my house for Rebecca and her family to live in and I will fall in love with a talented young actor who is also a writer and sensitive. How could you ever be unhappy there with all that sunshine? We went to San Diego too, and that was beautiful too! Everybody had told me there were too many people there, but it's no worse than New York. I can't wait until I live there. What is the point of going through the motions until I am eighteen, I wish I could be out there now. Maybe I can get Mom to send me to school out there. She'd never go for that, but if I went to St. Andrews she'd see me just as infrequently. Lewis doesn't care, just as long as I'm gone. I'll go on the web and find a private school out there and I'll find somebody's parents to sponsor me. If I set the whole thing up myself, she won't be able to argue. I know I'm only fourteen, but maybe it's time for me to take control of my life. Clearly Mom and Lewis cannot be responsible. They don't know what they're doing. Gee I hope Mom doesn't read this.

* * *

Drood took Tuesday off, and sat in the city park near his house watching young men play basketball and baseball. He didn't want to appear to be some kind of pervert so he brought a newspaper and a cigar with him and engaged himself in scanning the headlines and casually watching everything going on around him. "Okay, the obvious thing about these boys is aggression," he thought, "spilling out all over everything. Pushing, challenging, looking for an outlet. It's like a tide that can't be controlled." He watched the mildest of the young men play basketball and considered that even he wanted to beat the others, to conquer. Drood knew that there was a biological imperative in all this, surging hormones, and he knew from bitter experience that overt aggression in this Otherworld would be paid for dearly. The young men would have to be tamed as they made it into adulthood, or at least learn to sublimate their aggression into carefully controlled activities. Drood knew that while the media celebrated adolescence and aggression, in actuality they were severely punished in real life. Drood watched the game continue.

"Observation One: Aggression. Observation Two: extreme self-doubt and self-centered fear."

If someone has to conquer, someone else has to be conquered and the boys seemed to fear that most of all. They believed their lives and their newly established self-images were on the line with every play, with every utterance, with every gesture.

Swagger and challenging gave way quickly to anger and self-loathing. They were so easy to read. Drood reflected that it must be difficult for the young men to survive the teen years with a small measure of self-worth.

"Observation number three: sexual desperation."

Any girl that came near the boys caused an instant and total change in their behavior. They lost their attention and their focus and became confused and half-crazed. They bumped each other and made noises and got up on the tips of their toes. "Some things never change," Drood reflected.

"And observation number four: curiosity." This seemed to Drood to be a little harder to spot, but it showed in the eyes. They noticed everything and when they were unfamiliar with something they moved slower and stared at it for a long time. Drood saw this behavior repeated several times in his afternoon of observing. One of the boys even gave him the long, slow stare, no doubt wondering what the old man with the newspaper would be doing in the park in the middle of the day.

These observations would all have to be taken into account when Drood made his plans. It didn't seem right that the major characteristics of teenage boys, although biologically determined, should be the exact characteristics society desperately fears and goes to great lengths to stamp out.

"Aggression, self-doubt, sexual desperation, and curiosity are just not what 21st century America is able to cope with. Because they are seen as wrong, morally wrong, not biologically driven." Drood reflected briefly that somebody needed to show some mercy to these kids. Where he came from, these things, aggression, sexual need, modesty and uncertainty were considered virtues and boys were taught about them and how to use them and when to use them. Aggression was for battle and sport and making a name and a place for yourself in the world. Sexuality for pleasure and for children. Modesty indicated character and perspective and doubt drove one to seek the counsel of wiser elders. The satisfying of these adolescent needs was a major part of his culture and achieving adulthood without making use of these basic instincts was considered impossible. The definition of manhood had definitely changed. "Or," Drood reflected, "Maybe it's just that we had a definition of manhood and now there is no definition."

Drood watched the basketball game as the best player repeatedly crowed his triumphs over the other players and taunted them. He watched the game stop as two pretty girls walked by and the boys drifted silently after them in their wake. He saw the uncertainty in their frowns and their twitchy eyes. And he saw how they watched everything around them, soaking it all in, learning fast. They couldn't help being who they were.

Drood turned his thoughts to the three boys who were trying to destroy Tag. Clearly something had gone wrong with them and they were taking it out on Tag. What was it? Aggression run amok, without purpose. Self-doubt raised to the level of psychosis. Sexual desperation misdirected. Total absence of curiosity, of feeling for other sentient beings. Would there be a way to save Tag and also to help those boys? Drood doubted it, but it didn't matter to him, what was right was right and those boys had to be stopped. He'd give them a chance to do it the easy way and then they'd have to do it the hard way. It would be tricky. He'd want Tag to take all the actions to save himself. He'd want to avoid the schools, parents, and the law. He'd want to do no lasting harm to the other boys, and even help them if he could. And he'd want Tag to grow through the whole thing, to achieve some kind of positive and permanent identity, or, more accurately, solidify the positive aspects of the identity he already had and burn away the rest. A diamond in the rough. It would have to be a sneaky, smart, and effective campaign. This was just the kind of thing at which Drood excelled. He remembered his own training in the arts of war, deception, and mind control and realized with a start that Tag was at exactly the age that he had started training with Mylvwyn. "Great Lugh!" he said and sat up straight on the bench in the park.

"Mickey was right. I've got an apprentice!" Drood realized he would have to broaden the scope of his plan to include Tag's development and the teaching of all Drood's skills. Drood knew psychology, mythology, religion, language, history, poetry, and so much more. The plan would have to be a much larger plan. A master plan.

A little hint of meaning, a goal, crept into his soul and the ashes stirred and the embers in his heart glowed. It had been so long since he had cared about anything and he felt a little confused, but the tingling of interest felt good. He enjoyed the surge of adrenaline in the sunshine for a few moments. He thought, "It's been some time since a significant quantity of dopamine has saturated those particular receptors in those particular neurons in my brain and I would like to enjoy it. An apprentice! And me, a teacher," he mused. "Crazy."

The next part of his plan for Tag's salvation was to directly observe the enemy, the three boys. He knew what Loomis looked like, but he couldn't remember the other boys. He thought he might be able to recognize them if he saw the three of them together. He knew they were all in Lee Middle School over on the corner of James and Teall, but there was no good place to park. Had to be especially careful on this one because of the pedophile problem, didn't want to be seen lurking around the school ground following some young boys. He also didn't want Tag to see him. He wanted this to be completely covert. Drood decided to park on the street in the expensive Sedgwick neighborhood behind the school and do a little walking. He'd have to be careful to spot them right away and he'd not be able to make too many more trips to the school before somebody would get suspicious.

The next afternoon Drood walked to the corner of Teall and James and stood as if waiting for the downtown bus. He watched as the first wave of kids came out of the school at the end of the school day. Most of them walked singly, heads down, looking like they wanted nothing more than to get home and lie down. "School must be stressful for kids," he concluded. The kids that walked in groups were noisy and playful. No sign of Tag. Drood decided to walk toward the city on James in front of the school, just once, as most of the students were coming out, and then to continue in a big loop back into Sedgwick and his car. He hoped for luck because it would be too conspicuous to go around twice.

As Drood approached the school he thought he spotted Loomis. He had a baseball hat on backwards, a large gold chain on his neck, baggy shorts and a swagger. Loomis was quickly joined by his two buddies and to Drood's satisfaction they walked to the sidewalk ahead of Drood and turned west on James St. Drood slowed his pace to give them some room so they wouldn't know he was following them. He looked away whenever they turned back toward him. They shoved another kid out of the way, off the sidewalk.

Drood noticed that they picked on each other almost as much as they picked on other kids. They tired to outdo each other and to humiliate each other, pushing each other into traffic or into bushes, grabbing things from each other and throwing them, and bizarre for Drood to see, fake humping each other. They called each other "Bitch" and "Ho" and "Girl" and said vicious things about each other's families. He wondered if they had yet gotten into the crime and drugs that they were clearly headed for. He saw them insult an old man waiting at another bus stop, calling him "Pops" and laughing at him. They taunted him for a while and then left. Drood had seen enough and he turned off James to head back around to his car. He felt he had learned some things about the enemy and he'd be able to help Tag.

When he got home Drood looked at the stack of folders and papers on the coffee table and with a heavy sigh, he gathered them up and moved them into the closet in his bedroom. The search for his daughter was going to have to take a back seat for a while. He just didn't have the mental energy to handle a new job, the problem with Tag, and his own strained and stressed mental situation. Being the boss of Support and Services alone would be enough to drive someone insane. In fact, as Drood thought about it, it had done just that to the last three people who had the job. Fading sunlight poured in through the windows in the late afternoon and Drood considered what to do with his day now. He had observed all those kids; he had not gone to work, he wondered if Tom might need him so he called him.

"Sure, Drood, come on over, I can always use a hand."

"Okay, I'll be there in ten minutes."

The splintered and cracked side door was open and he picked his way through the middle of the factory and around to the poker room and through it to the back door of Tom's workshop. He came in under a shower of dust and noticed that it was very cold in the workshop.

"Why don't you turn the heat up?" Drood called out by way of a greeting.

"Out of kerosene. Gonna get some more tonight," Tom answered. It didn't appear to be a big deal at all to Tom.

"What are you working on?" Drood asked as he came around the bench where Tom was hunched over.

"Look at this old clock, it's beautiful isn't it?" Tom was shining the brass of an antique clock.

"I didn't know you could fix clocks," Drood said.

"Anybody can fix anything," Tom answered. He didn't have to expound on it. Drood was familiar with Tom's philosophy. He believed that patience and persistence were the only requirements for technical expertise. A few basic principles of machinery and physics were all you needed. And then you applied common sense.

"Well, what do you want me to do?" Drood surveyed the many entrails of all the various equipment on benches around the shop.

"Sit down right over there, and take apart and clean out the motor on that blender and see if you can put it back together again." Tom pointed to a bench just a few feet away from himself.

"What do you want to hear?" Tom indicated his CD player and stacks of CDs over by the "office" which was really just a corner bench where he put his books and cash box.

"How about Ellington?"

"Right." Tom and Drood shared an enthusiasm for music of all kinds. They had, without speaking, agreed that music was The Way.

Tom went back to work and Drood set to work. They spent the next two hours dreaming and making small motions with their hands. They barely spoke at all, except when Drood needed another screwdriver or when he had to ask Tom the motion or meaning of a particular part. They hunched over and listened to jazz and worked carefully and quietly and the time ticked away and they could hear the occasional honk of the truck horn outside and once they heard snow slough off the roof inside the factory. The notes slid out of the speaker and wobbled in the dusty air and the piano tinkled and their minds were resting in the sounds while their hands were resting in the business of all the little parts. They engaged more parts of their brains in those two hours than most people do in an entire year. As Drood worked he had fantasies of rescuing his daughter from a burning building, of Claire coming back to him and accepting him for who he really was after everything that had happened. If only he had been honest, owned up to everything right from the start, how different the story would have been. But then he realized he would never have had Claire to begin with and his mind started spiraling with the infinite possibilities of what might have happened. He thought about old Ireland once again and wanted to make a trip there. He wondered where he would stay and maybe next summer he really would go there after always talking about it and never doing it.

Drood didn't think at all some times for many minutes as the songs drifted through him and he tried to puzzle out the equipment in front of him. He smoked the most satisfying cigarette of his life in the middle of the two hours. Some of the time he just sat and watched Tom work. Tom was fast and expert and it was a pleasure for Drood to try to follow what he was doing.

Tom, for his part, grunted once in a while and seemed to be emotionally involved with the machinery. He took his job personally, it was what had made him an expert, and he undertook each repair job with the passion of a zealot. It didn't matter if it was just cleaning contacts, or rebuilding something from scratch. He was meticulous and scrupulous and he cleaned to sterility every piece of equipment no matter what condition it was in when it came to him. The music penetrated his thoughts once in a while but he wasn't aware of melodies or harmonies; he just caught the occasional phrase or riff and his mind snapped them up like pieces of candy. He liked having Drood nearby and would like to have spoken more with him but he felt that he really didn't have anything to say. He just was and did. Tom was an old hippy from way back when and Drood never knew if he had burned out his brain or if he had always been so sedate and so quiet. Tom was very interested in music, in machines, in various other little ideas and projects, but he was totally self-contained.

As he sat working, Drood remembered one time last summer when he had driven all through the city with him while Tom searched for a part for an old washing machine. They went to at least ten little repair stores, a couple of warehouses, and even to the great megalithic mall and Drood had a chance to observe Tom in action in his natural habitat, behind the wheel on the streets of Syracuse. They went mostly in silence. Tom had a long tape of Miles Davis and they smoked and drove, Tom's forearm resting coolly on the steering wheel, the other over the back of the seat behind Drood's head. Tom drove a gigantic late '80s model Caddie, with red plush faux velvet interior. The smoke in the car had room to twirl and expand into interesting patterns and the air conditioner had been on and he kept it so clean you couldn't even hear the engine. Drood remembered it as a day he could have driven around forever; it seemed like they were floating in space. They smoked and listened and drove and occasionally stopped to get out and inquire inside. Tom didn't want a car phone to call the shops; he wanted to go investigate the places anyway. He told Drood he liked to stay on top of who had what. Nice perk to being self-employed, if you wanted to do things a different way, you certainly could.

As they drove, Drood watched the city go by the window and the muted trumpet was the perfect accompaniment, a depressed, demented jazz-blues riffling sound that would forever be mixed in Drood's mind as the sound of the soul of Syracuse. They had started at the workshop over between Court and Midler and had gotten on 298 and driven back Court Street over the other edge of the north side. All the neighborhoods had the same type of houses. Drood's research told him most of the current structures had been built in the early twentieth century and were in need of repair. There were many many two-family houses. Going through Lyncourt, the houses were nicely manicured, there was a bank and a bar and every third corner had a neighborhood market, the precursor to convenience stores, a converted first floor of a house, with a Pepsi or a LaBatts sign hanging outside on the corner. There were pale kids hanging out on the corners and lots of old trees. As they came further down Court Street, Miles was blowing it hot and they saw a very overweight young teenage girl carrying a baby and screaming at another little boy. The old Maria Regina College that had become a daycare and a library was on the corner of Grant and they saw weeds and dogs on chains at every other house. Some broken windows and an old bicycle or two lying around. They turned right and went down the hill toward the ballpark and the old factories. The road had potholes all the way down the hill and Tom swerved smoothly to avoid them. Drood looked at Tom who seemed to be in a trance, one finger over the steering wheel moved to the music and that was the only sign of anything other than the required motions for driving. Overgrown grass everywhere. They stopped on the corner of Hiawatha one block up from the ballpark and Tom pulled in to an appliance store. The sign was beat up and falling down and there was garbage on the sidewalk in front of the building. Drood stayed in the car. He looked around and saw another overweight teenaged girl with a baby. A Viet Namese family wandered by, chatting. A dirty stray dog ran past. The engine was still purring and Drood sat in the coolness taking it all in. It was probably eighty-five degrees outside, one of the hottest days of the year.

Tom came out and they continued over Hiawatha to the west side, past the remnants of Oil City and the sewage plant and its concomitant stench. They turned back onto Genesee and Drood marveled at the spires of the Cathedral there in what had been a Polish neighborhood. The streets were empty of people, just lots of cars. They continued on Genesee up into Tipperary Hill past the muffler shops, delis, and diners and turned left on Avery. Four blocks of two-story, two-family homes, again with weeds everywhere and no curbs or sidewalks. Drood saw six different people walking dogs as they pulled into the little repair shop three blocks from Burnet Park. Tom went inside and Drood thought about the Irish roots of the neighborhood. In his time in the city he'd never seen anything that would mark the place as being connected to Ireland, except the shamrocks on the pubs, and to Drood that wasn't really an Irish thing, it was more of a Christian thing, as St. Patrick had first used the shamrock to describe the Trinity. He granted that some of the people he saw in the neighborhood did look a little familiar. He wished he could show them what the real Ireland was like, before the Christians, but he sighed and supposed that was gone forever and certainly he, Drood, would never have access to it again anyway. Drood wondered how many businesses there were in the first floor of homes in this city. It seemed that Tom knew where every one of them was.

They left Tip Hill by going down Avery, through the marsh on Velasko and turned left onto Onondaga. They went through Skunk City, filled with empty houses and garbage in the streets (you could really see the depletion of the city population here) and continued all the way over to South Avenue. The neighborhoods they went through now were poor, and they saw more damaged looking people here. Some vacant eyes, some drugged or crazy people and many suspicious glares at the car. More teenaged girls with babies. Beer bottles in the gutters. They headed down South Avenue into the South Side, reputed to be a dangerous neighborhood, but here also were two-story, two-family houses straddling the ancient Onondaga Creek, source of life for the

76

Iroquois Onondagas, who miraculously still lived on the reservation further down the valley. The South Side was predominantly African-American and Drood and Tom were two conspicuous white guys driving around in a big Caddie in the middle of the day. Everyone was outside in the heat and Drood listened to the piano twittering behind Miles' pensive, dripping sounds from the horn. Drood pondered briefly the plight of the African-Americans, compared it to the history of the Irish, and then abandoned it as fruitless. What was the point of rating suffering, the point was to do something, right? And then Drood wondered idly what could be done. They came out eventually onto the Seneca Turnpike by the ball fields and headed over to Salina Street. They turned right and headed down to the furthest edge of the city in Nedrow.

There were several strip malls on Salina heading down to Nedrow and Drood scanned the names. It seemed that all the stores in Syracuse sold pizza, electronics, auto parts, or beer. The people on the streets had changed from African-American to Native American as they got closer to the reservation and once again there was a preponderance of teenaged girls with babies. Syracuse was a fertile place, he guessed. Tom stopped at another store and Drood got out in the heat to stretch his legs. He smoked and leaned on the hood and watched more poor people go by. They headed back north, went up Brighton hill and into the University area through the back way. The houses here were newer, maybe built in the fifties, sixties, and seventies and the neighborhood populations seemed to be mixed fairly well among African-Americans, whites, and Asians. They went over Comstock to get back to Erie Boulevard, the main commercial artery leading into and out of the city to the east. They went from residential, to student housing, a brief startling glimpse of brand new sharply designed and constructed gigantic buildings of the University, and then through another thin strip of poor neighborhood by Genesee and Fayette, and across Erie. Now they were heading back into Eastwood, Drood's familiar neighborhood and Drood surmised they'd be back at the shop again next. They stopped at one of the corner markets in the first floor of a house to grab some lunch. People waited patiently in line and chatted with one another, in good humor, not very much like the New York City of Drood's memory. They got their sandwiches and got back in the car and Drood once again had a good feeling about the people of Syracuse. They might not be fancy, they might not be rich, but they sure were real, he concluded. Nothing but people trying to get by or get over and it didn't get much more basic than that. He thought about the city they had just circled and realized they had not gone through any of the high-priced neighborhoods or the business areas of downtown and he thought about the layout of the city. It seemed there were pockets of affluence around the edges of the city, basically, up in the hills. On the flat parts there were poorer neighborhoods with all the multitude of two-family houses. Closer to downtown were all the crumbling brick factories that had been used and re-used by many companies a thousand times but never rebuilt or restored. Then there were the big commercial buildings downtown and the city proper. If you shot a movie here, Drood concluded, you could have every conceivable setting you wanted without ever leaving the city. Suburbia, decaying urban, commercial downtown, large green parks and lakes, and all kinds of extreme weather at all different times. Newness, oldness, and everything in between. Syracuse, to Drood, represented sanity and reality. The rest of the world was vague, dream-like, and absolutely incorrect, he surmised. Syracuse was the right place. He never felt afraid, ashamed, or anxious in Syracuse. Only affectionate.

This feeling was familiar to Drood and driving around with Tom had caused him to remember another place and time when he had felt this way. It was another valley, similar in geography to Syracuse's, but instead of being filled with a city and a creek, it was filled with a dark lake. The shores of the lake were littered with stones and granite boulders and the hills on the far side of the lake were stark gray, mostly granite and moss, heather and lichens. Drood and his teacher had wandered into the valley when Drood was just a boy, but he had come back over and over because of the feeling of peace that came over him every time he came around the bend in the trail and caught sight of the lake. Time stood still and there were no wars, no teachings, no people, just the birds, the fish, some deer, and occasionally some cattle from a nearby family. Drood walked around and around the valley and the lake until he knew every stone, every blade of grass. He threw stones in the water, he sang, and sometimes he lay down and slept. But mostly, he just walked and looked. Forgot about everything and just looked and walked, looked and walked. The peace. The peace. It was indescribable. And Drood had sighed on the drive through Syracuse, remembering the magic valley of home, and he sighed now in the workshop as he caught just a wisp of that feeling again. Drood wished his time in that valley had been longer and he sighed heavily. No going back.

Drood looked over at his friend and saw that Tom had stopped working and was just sitting at the bench, hands at his sides, and head down, staring at the table. Motionless. The music had stopped too and Drood wondered how long both he and Tom and the music had stopped. They had worked and listened and remembered themselves into a trance. Drood straightened up and coughed a little and Tom looked up. His eyes were wide open, innocent and tired and he just stared at Drood, who said, "Well. I guess I'm done for now. I'm gonna get going."

"O.K." Tom seemed to come back to himself. He stood and turned off the power strip on the side of the table.

"I guess I'm gonna call it a day too." Tom said. And Drood saw that Tom would carry the mystery of his thought home with him and Drood would not disturb that and it made Drood happy that he was old enough and wise enough to understand things like that. And it made him very grateful that he had a friend like Tom. Loyal. Silent. Deep. He would depend on Tom when he had to. And he knew he could depend on Gus too. Even Shiny, in his belligerent, blustery way, would probably come through for Drood. Loyalty to a man who definitely didn't deserve it, that was the way Drood looked at it.

They left the shop together and Drood thought for a second about letting Tom in on his plans to help the boy. He looked at Tom going about the business of locking up and he started to speak but something held him back. It wasn't quite time yet. "Wait, Drood, wait," he told himself. "You know that things develop in their own time and you know you have to match yourself to the universe, not vice versa. Keep your own impatient needs apart and pay close attention and observe," he reminded himself. "Tom's not going anywhere and he'll be there when it's time. Just keep it together Drood." The constant struggle with himself.

Chapter 9

As he got onto 690 once again (who in Syracuse doesn't drive on one of the three highways in the city at least once a day?) and headed west toward Eastwood, Drood merged and smoked. He could feel events begin to coalesce and he could feel the whole future had already happened and been decided somehow, but it was just far enough ahead to be too cloudy for Drood to discern it.

In the apartment: leftovers, cigarette, radio talk show, street light gazing, message check, glance at everything, pick up keys again and go to car for short ride to St. Francis. Drood parked on the wrong side of the street below the hospital on the hill and trudged up the hill, quite winded by the time he arrived. Sidewalks getting slippery now with ice, salt, slush. It was quite a trek to get there. He walked into the lobby and stopped in front of the giant statue of Christ on the cross facing him. The security people, the admissions people, the people sitting in the lobby, all going about their business, none of them showing even the slightest indication that there was a six-foot tall, brightly painted, statue of an almost naked man dripping blood and contorted in agony hovering over all of them. It dominated the lobby and the view of everything and Drood wondered if that was really the image one wanted to see when one came in sick and helpless. Having never been a Christian, Drood wondered how many people were frightened and felt oppressed by the morbid and ghoulish apparition so dominant throughout the building of "healing". Children certainly. Anyway, he'd have to ask Mickey his thoughts on that some day. Drood had never yet met a doctor who believed in God. He suspected it was because they feared competition, but careful thought always led him to blame science instead. Science can't prove or disprove Jesus, and so they ignore and fear it. And in St. Francis' Hospital, at least, they all worked in the shadow of the tortured and murdered man-God.

Mickey was waiting for him, pacing back and forth in front of the bed in the small room.

"Drood! You're here; I knew you'd be coming. Listen, we have to talk right away, but not here." And he pointed to the ceiling and pulled Drood by the arm into the hallway. Drood glanced at the ceiling and wondered if Mickey meant the surveillance that he always feared or a higher power. Free will and fate were nibbling around the edges of the cheese called gray matter in Drood's head.

"You gotta make your move Drood, I don't have much more time. I'm now involved in your plan, the boy, the girl, the people after you, you brought it to me and now Zulu's onto it," Mickey whispered as they shuffled down the hall to the cafeteria."

They sat at a table near the window and looked out on the bricks of the other parts of the hospital. Through a crack Drood caught a glimpse of the reservoir across the valley on the western edge of the city. He thought about people sledding down the giant hill in the back of the reservoir as Mickey fidgeted and glanced quickly around him.

"Zulu's going to interview me today for a new 'program' of his," Mickey confided. He spat the word program sarcastically.

"So the next time you come I may be dead or incoherent from whatever mind-chewing drugs he intends to put me on. I know, I know, I could probably escape, but I think I can outfox him by playing possum."

Drood saw foxes, opossums, and rabbits running through a meadow.

"Here's what you gotta do." And Mickey leaned closer. Drood said nothing for fear of interrupting Mickey's great agitation, which could lead to prophecy.

He lowered his voice so Drood could hardly hear it. "You gotta get the boy out of this world, send him to the west, make him the traveler. He has something very important to do in the world to the west. Don't let Zulu and the others get hold of him. And Drood."

"Yes?" Drood too leaned forward.

"Your work will be all done when you are through with the boy." Mickey paused and held Drood's gaze intently. "You know what I mean, right?"

Drood was stunned and wondered if Mickey was really answering the one question he had been unable to answer since arriving in New York so many years ago. Did Mickey mean that the

Gods would be done torturing him and he could return to the Ireland of the Celts again? Drood's heart skipped a beat.

"You mean I will be free to go?"

"Yes."

"Free to return home?"

"Yes."

"Do you know what you are saying?" Drood's voice rose at the end of the question and the hair on the back of his neck bristled.

"I do. Completely finished." And Mickey sat back suddenly looking very tired, old, and sick. Drood stared carefully at him, his mind racing with thoughts of leaving this world, with marvel at how Mickey's psychoses could match so well with actual events and could even have a predictive value to them. As modern physics had proved, the observer helps to create the observed, and Drood knew that Mickey's talk would be just so much delusion and drivel to so many people, but not to him. Drood wondered how neurons, electricity, and chemicals could possibly be connected to the human, to the supernatural, and to the spiritual. No answers in science. Not yet anyway.

They sat tired and spent in the cafeteria and looked around at the patients, the staff, and the doctors. They were all so very engaged in themselves and their lives and Drood's egocentric childish unconscious mind was agitated by so many people knowing so little about him, knowing so little about the world, the past, about everything. "How could so much be out there and so many people know nothing about it?" To Drood it was as though a whole planet of oxygen-breathing people walked around under water holding their breath without knowing that there was a surface, that their lungs required air, that all they had to do was swim a few feet to the surface. And at the moment, the unknowing general public even had Drood and Mickey's dangling feet treading water in their faces to show them the way to the air, but they simply steered around them and trudged along the seabed, going as far as they could on the meager poisoned air trapped inside their lungs.

Drood felt positively hallucinatory and thought he'd better get the heck out of there. He bought Mickey dinner and left him eating from the tray. Mickey's urgency had exhausted him. He sat back in his chair spent, done with speaking and with no interest at all in Drood. Honesty was dangerous and not because of the consequences of speaking it, but because of the enervated helplessness it induced in the speaker. Drood said good-bye to the listless husk in front of him and left. He glanced at Mickey as he left the cafeteria and wondered if the next day Mickey would even remember having spoken to him. He wondered too if Zulu did indeed have a new program for Mickey. He knew that drugs didn't work after a while and he knew that Mickey was a prime target for experimentation because he was so verbal and had no interested family or friends to consult with or to speak for him. Drood shook his head and lit up a cigarette as the sliding doors released him into the secular and non-medical world. "So, the future is picking up speed," Drood thought.

* * *

I don't know what the point of school is anyway. You don't really learn anything, just a bunch of names of stuff, dates, and useless math. I don't think anybody ever uses the stuff anyway, they just want to keep you somewhere for most of the day, make you sit still and not do anything. If you ask any questions they get mad at you anyway, everything you do turns into something that's your fault. I get picked on and beat up at school and not one person except me knows it. And I get in trouble with the teachers because of it too. I think I'm going to stop going. My mom will be pissed, but I bet I can work it out so she doesn't know. She's always at work when I get home anyway; all I have to do is stay out of trouble and stay out of the house until she goes to work. Then I can come back in and read or watch TV or play Nintendo or whatever. Maybe I can get my own video card somehow. That reminds me, I gotta get some books about playing poker. Drood and Gus say that I'm already pretty good, as good as they are, and I'm only a kid. By the time I'm grown up, eighteen and everything, I can go to Las Vegas and make money playing poker. The only thing is they don't have a professional basketball team in Las Vegas, so maybe I'd have to live in Los Angeles and go to Las Vegas all the time to win money. My uncle was right; this journal is kind of cool. I looked back over the last couple of things I wrote and I can't believe I wrote it. I mean, none of it is like literature, or like poems and stories or anything, but it sounds like somebody who makes sense wrote it. And I know that's not me so it's kind of like reading somebody else's diary. It's like I'm two people, the one writing and living now, and the one writing and living then. It's interesting; I think I'm going to try to write in it all the time. One thing, though, I have to make sure Mom never finds this, because she wouldn't like all of my plans. And she'd probably end up telling them to Charles when she gets high, and then Charles will use them against me, make fun of me, tell me how stupid those plans are, how impossible it is and what the odds are

84

against it. Charles thinks he's helping by giving me little talks about staying in school and not taking drugs. He just watches those dopey public service commercials and then copies them. He even uses the exact same sentences they use in the commercials. Charles and the commercials never tell you anything good that can happen from staying in school or from not doing drugs, they only tell you all the bad things that MIGHT happen if you don't. They either don't remember school and being a kid, or they're just doing it to make themselves feel good and look good to other adults.

Like Charles tells me not to do drugs, but at the same time he smokes pot with my mother and thinks I don't know it, and he works construction, which requires no school whatsoever. He really talks to me like that to act like a bigshot and to pretend to my mother that he cares about me. What he's really interested in is the part where he gets to tell that no white kid like me can make the pros from Syracuse, or that there's no way I'll ever live in L.A. or New York because it's too hard to make it there if you're not from there. Or like now with playing poker he'd probably tell me that there are no professional poker players who actually make any money and they all end up going to jail or something.

Anyway, I wish I had a girlfriend. There's some that are really beautiful but they don't even look at me because I'm only wearing jeans, sneakers, and a regular shirt and I don't know anybody that's really popular so I don't really exist. But sometimes I think I'm just going to die without being really in love with someone like in the movies.

* * *

Tag put down the pen and bounced down the stairs into the kitchen. His mother and Charles were sitting at the kitchen table reading the newspaper. Tag opened the fridge, grabbed a can of soda, and bounced back up the stairs as Charles yelled after him,

"You're gonna put a hole in those stairs jumping like that."

Tag ignored him, but heard Charles begin to complain to his mother as he closed the door to his room. He put his journal away in its hiding place in the hole in the back of his closet and wondered why all his mother's boyfriends had to be exactly the same. He wondered if his father was like that, a bully, a pompous and weak low-life. His Mom always had to be the one working, taking care of everything, making the boyfriend happy, putting up with bull shit, and she didn't like when they picked on Tag, but Tag knew she didn't observe most of it. They were usually sneaky and found ways to pick on him when she wasn't looking or wasn't around. They went through the charade each time there was a new one: his mother tried to convince him that this one was different, she'd try to make them spend time together, she'd end up getting abused and then there'd be a big scene and the guy would leave, sometimes taking money or causing damage to the house before he left. Tag sighed and looked out the window. Here came the evening freight train and he heard the whistle and saw the red and white gate go down on the tracks that crossed the road not far from the house. Tag waited and then he heard and felt the deep rumble and the vibrations and he relaxed unconsciously for a few seconds. He'd been hearing the trains since he was a little kid, and although they bothered most people whose houses backed up to the tracks, Tag always felt at home when he heard them and he loved the whistle, the noise, the clatter, and he loved to track the metal cars as they passed in a steady stream, arresting all motion and attention as they came through town. Tag had no idea what was on the trains or where they were going, they were just sight, sound, and vibration, temporary interruption of everything. Finally, after Tag was deeply in the train-induced trance, the last empty car rattled away and he realized he had his forehead pressed against the window, and he was surprised, as always, at the lightness, the silence, and the emptiness when the train had gone. The physical relief and the return to normal of the senses and the world wore off quickly and Tag felt tired and crawled into bed. "Maybe some day," he thought, "I'll jump on one of those trains and go out to California."

* * *

Well, disaster strikes. I have to go to St. Andrew next year, no matter what I say or what I want, and Mother doesn't even want to discuss it anymore. It's almost like I'm a two year old and I'm not supposed to have any understanding or interest in the life I'm going to live. Lewis is backing her up of course, probably so he can get his hands on her money. It looks like I may have to spend the summer in Iowa too. I mean, I love Gramma and Grampa and all, but there's nothing to do there at all. I mean, I get it that the farm and the fresh air and all that is supposed to be good for you, but really, why is it good for you? You have to get up at four in the morning and you work all day and so you're exhausted all the time. That can't be good for you, the immune system has to be weak from that and you probably can catch all kinds of things from all the dirt and animals and stuff. And as far as the value of work and family and all that, aren't I going to spend the rest of my life working and having a family? Why do I have to waste so much time at age 14? It's not like they won't have time off away from me, I'll be going to school in St. Andrew's and so they won't see me at all, it's not like they need a break. I don't do anything wrong anyway, I don't know why they want to get rid of me. All I do is stay in my room or go out with Rebecca. I don't bother them. Mom and I have arguments some times, but so what? Everyone does. I can't prove it, but I always wonder if it has something to do with my father. I think it makes Mom very nervous and uncomfortable that I never knew him. It seems like she feels very ashamed or angry or something about my father and I can never find out anything. We can talk about pretty much anything else in life except that. Sometimes I've been almost at the point of begging her to talk to me more about him, but I just can't bring myself to do it. I'm afraid to push her too much; I don't want her to get really angry, you know, like forever angry, at me.

If he was Irish, I wonder if he was in the IRA or any of the political stuff in the north. Maybe that's why she won't talk about it, maybe she's keeping some secret about his rebel activities. She said he worked for one of the networks and died just after I was born. That was before she married McGrath. Things must have been wild back then if she had a little kid, a husband who died, married and divorced again in a few years. Before I go to Iowa, I've got to get her to talk about this stuff more. Gramma and Grampa will only tell me what she tells them to say. I can tell it makes them unhappy, that they wish I could know everything, but they're not going to go against mom. Personally, I think everybody would be more relaxed and happy if I knew more about my father, but that's the way it is. Well, I wonder what Philadelphia will be like. St. Andrew's doesn't have boys, but there is a partner school for boys right nearby. I hope I can come back to New York often or that Rebecca can come see me often. Anyway I've got five more months to go here. Might as well just relax, they're going to do whatever they want anyway and I have no say in anything. I'm just like a suitcase, they'll pack me up and load me off to Iowa and Philadelphia, bye bye. I've decided I'm going to be a writer and write on a different subject every week, they have a great journalism program at St. Andrew's. That's all for now.

And Dee Dee Dewar locked her diary and put it in the strongbox in her desk and locked the strongbox with the little silver key on her key chain. She thought about calling Rebecca, but it was getting late. She went to the window and looked out over the roofs and through the cracks in all the buildings on the upper west side of Manhattan. She thought about all the grownups in all the windows throughout all the gray buildings and it just seemed at that moment like there was not one single person her age in the whole city. She was just alone in a world of uncaring grown-ups and cold, hard cement. She crawled into bed and clicked on the remote and thought, "Some day there will be somebody in my life who understands me just perfectly and who will take my side in everything no matter what, right or wrong. And then my life will be completely right and everything will start to take off from there." And as she started to drowse she had the incongruous half-vision of a freight train rumbling over a crossing, whistle blowing, lights flashing, and the vibrations from it were so real she could feel them in the pit of her stomach. She felt curious and relieved as she drifted deeper into sleep.

Chapter 10

"The first thing you have to do is decide for yourself how everything would be if the world were yours to decide. And by that I mean, figure out exactly how you want life to go. Don't listen to yourself about what's possible and what's not possible. This is the first teaching." Drood had to adapt the teaching from his own ancient training, and since there was no cultural context for this peculiar bloom of apprenticeship, the first step would be to set goals.

Tag looked around the empty falling down factory in the dark. Brilliant moonlight fell softly over the beams and through the windows, giving the place a blue fairy sheen. He and Drood were several hours early for the poker game and they had exchanged phone numbers and were definitely now working together.

Tag looked Drood in the eye and said, "It sounds like bullshit to me. All I want to do is get those guys off my back." And he held Drood's gaze.

"I understand that Tag, but there are sixteen thousand ways to go about it, and YOU have to be the one to determine the course of it. It's only common sense."

The boy shrugged and Drood found an intact half-wall of brick to sit on. Tag joined him and they looked up through the remnants of a skylight at the clouds. Cold.

"Whatever."

"Just trust me," he said. "I'm going to show you how to do a bunch of things that might not seem related to the problem you have just now, but in the end, you'll be glad I did, and," he paused significantly, "they'll probably make you a better poker player too."

That seemed to do the trick, the boy sat up and his eyes brightened again. Drood would have to be careful to keep the goals always right in sight, while bringing the boy along slowly. Training and discipline would probably be new in the boy's life and he'd have to feel his way at first.

"O.K., so, it might take a little while to get them out of your life for good, but there are little things we can do along the way," Drood continued.

"Like not go to school," said Tag.

"Well, maybe, but let's not get ahead of ourselves. First, how do you see your life going from this point forward? Be honest, I won't make fun of you, just think for a couple of minutes and tell me what you want."

Tag hopped off the wall and walked to a slanted, rusted, steel girder and walked halfway up it. He jumped off and kicked up a cloud of dust. Drood noted that the boy preferred to think while moving and that was a good sign. It meant that his actions and his words would always be connected.

"I want to live in Los Angeles and go to a lot of professional basketball games. Lakers and Clippers, especially when they play the Knicks." He paused and eyed Drood, who merely nodded, and held his gaze. Tag seemed to be reassured and settled down.

"I want to be a professional poker player, and I want to have a nice house with a pool and lots of friends. I want to have a girlfriend who loves me and I want to be able to give my mother money whenever she needs it."

"Okay, good..." Drood began, but Tag interrupted him,

"How does any of that have anything to do with getting those assholes to leave me alone?"

"We're talking about gaining wisdom, knowledge, and strength. They come from bending the will and training it. They come from focus and concentration. Those three sick boys do not represent the entire picture of your life. They dominate your thoughts right now, but in reality, they are just obstacles in the path of you becoming who you are supposed to be. Let's take it a step further and maybe it will start to make sense to you."

The boy looked sullen and uncertain, but behind those poses Drood detected a growing curiosity and maybe a tinge of hope. The boy's skips and jumps increased in frequency as they spoke until he was practically running around the open spaces. Tag had begun to pick up objects and examine them and then toss them into the shadows where they'd disappear with a clang or a thump. He had stopped looking at Drood and appeared to be ignoring him and trying to show him how disinterested he was, but Drood noted that the boy never left earshot and he paused to listen each time Drood spoke. When Drood stopped speaking the boy immediately turned to him, in spite of himself, to provoke further discussion. Drood smiled.

"Now," Drood went on, "imagine yourself in the future. Imagine what it is like to be the kind of person you want to be. Imagine your house, imagine your pool, and imagine you have the girlfriend, imagine you are a professional poker player. Take a minute to actually see all those things."

Tag paused where he was, about twenty feet from Drood, by a window frame with no glass. He had his hand on the frame and he was looking up through the trees at the moon. The light washed his face and the shadows brushed him as the leaves fluttered in the wind. The boy's eyes gleamed and Drood's breath was taken away by the vivid face and weird light. Tag stayed in the window frame for several moments and then turned to look at Drood. He looked calm and far older than his years.

"Now, without thinking too much or deeply about it, just off the top of your head, tell me what kind of person that future Tag is. Quick now."

"He's strong," Tag answered right away. He paused for a second and then said, "He's strong and he's tough, but he leaves people alone and only tends to his own business. He helps people whenever he can. And he's really, really smart. He's so smart that people can't believe it when they find out, but usually they don't find out because he's so humble and so shrewd. He just keeps it to himself and mostly only uses it for his business, playing poker. Sometimes he wins a lot, sometimes not as much, but he almost never loses. He has nerves of steel."

Drood said, "Good. Now what I want you to do is hold on to that image, hold on to that person. When you are in a tough spot, when you are frightened or need help and no one else is around, talk to that Tag of the future and ask him for advice, ask him what he would do."

Tag frowned and gave Drood a dubious look, but he didn't say anything.

"The qualities you must have to become that person you have described are strength, intelligence, humility, self-control, and guts. These are the qualities we will examine and these are the qualities that we will both develop and use to deal with your current problem. How does that sound?"

"Well, it sounds good, but it's impossible, it's way beyond me. I'm small, I don't do well in school, nobody notices me, and I don't have any money or anything. I don't have any of those qualities."

"Can a small person be strong?"

"Yes."

"Does not doing well in school mean you are not intelligent?"

"No."

"Does being noticed have anything to do with your plan or with those qualities?"

"No."

"Do you need money to have any of those qualities?"

"No."

"By answering these questions correctly you have demonstrated enough of those qualities to begin working toward your goals. You already know far more than you think you know about life, about yourself, and about where you are headed. You just never had anyone tell you know these things or that it is okay to know these things. Trust me, you are in good shape. Now, I think I hear Tom puttering around over there in his workshop. It's almost time for the game. Before we go in there, let me give you a few basic tips to get you by for the next week until we can talk about this some more."

Tag was smiling and hopping now. He couldn't understand all that they were talking about but Drood clearly believed in him and wanted him to get what he wanted out of life and this was so foreign to Tag that it was overwhelming. He couldn't contain himself and jogged in place while Drood finished talking to him.

"Now nothing we've talked about yet gets you through the week without getting beaten up, so I'm going to give you some advice that maybe can help. First, eye contact. Never make eye contact with any of the three of them. It will frustrate them, but it will begin the process of separating yourself from them. They want to see fear in your eyes. Even though you'll still have it, don't let them see it. It incites them to greater violence, it turns them on, so to speak."

Tag nodded. It made sense.

"Second. The presence of adults or the thought of the presence of adults will stop them in their tracks when they are in the school, but outside the school they won't care. So if you have to, in the school, move from adult to adult when they are around, and if caught without one, pretend there is one, talk to the adult right behind them. It might give you a split second to get away. Even when they're not around, always act as if there's a police officer at your side. It will give you confidence."

"Third. Outside the school is more dangerous. Change your behavior every day as far as where you hang around, who you talk to, how you get to and from school."

"Finally. Find others who have been picked on by these kids. Talk to them, get information, find out what happened, find out where they live. Knowing the whole picture will make you feel better and maybe even give you some ideas. If they do catch you, fight like hell. Hurt them. Go for their vital parts. Kick, scream, gouge. Turn into a wild animal. Do it instantly. Yes, it won't prevent you from getting a beating, but it will make them work and suffer for it. It might increase their anger, but this is where the guts part comes in. Avoid getting caught as much as you can, even turn it into a kind of mental cat and mouse game, stalking them too. But if you do finally get caught, you simply have to start doing something. Use your head."

Tag nodded. Here he felt he was the older and the wiser of the two. Drood was telling him survival techniques that he had already instinctively chosen, but he believed Drood was overestimating the effect he could have on those three. Tag was determined not to fight back in any way; playing possum was the only way to survive one of their attacks. They had weapons and Tag was sure they would use them. Drood patted him on the back and they turned the corner from the factory into the clubhouse where they had seen the light come on. Tom was taking beer, poker chips, and potato chips out of a brown grocery bag when they stepped into the light.

* * *

As January hit New York, Dee Dee began to find herself more deeply in trouble with her mother and with the people at school. Even Rebecca got mad at her now, and Dee Dee felt as though she just couldn't help it. She got more miserable and more miserable and everyone was always mad at her and she just couldn't figure out why. She thought there might be something mentally wrong with her, she was so unhappy all the time. She stayed in her room for hours at a time and just read books and watched TV. Sometimes she talked on the phone but it didn't help. The only one she talked to was Rebecca, and even that didn't seem to interest her anymore. She grew more interested in poetry and read all of Emily Dickinson's poems over and over and over. The isolation, the stopped-time quality, the precise and delicate perceptions and observations, and the little tricks and clever plays of words seemed to hit that delicious painful spot right in her center and resonate with all her misery. A lonely, New England spinster locked away but with the sharpest mind in the Western Hemisphere, this was the only thing Dee Dee felt she could relate to. As the winter lost its grip and Manhattan turned slightly brighter, Dee Dee's thoughts turned to the future more and more. She knew she would be leaving her home behind, and she knew that she would be having new experiences and she was frightened and a little curious at the same time. She had lived her whole life in Manhattan and yet she had the strangest dreams at night. She dreamed of green hills and primitive, dirty, ugly people. She would wake up in the middle of the night and feel certain that she was just about to see her dead father's face and then he would vanish again. He came out of the green hills and he was dressed strangely, in robes, and his face was shrouded and he was always trying to come near to her to tell her something, but she always woke up just before his face became clear. In the only picture she had of him he could have been anybody. A white man with brown hair and seemingly smooth features.

On this particular morning in spring Dee Dee went to the park by herself. It was a beautiful day and she took her Dickinson and her notebook. Just before leaving she looked in the mirror and saw a smooth white face with even features, thin eyebrows, framed by black hair, with a high forehead and bright blue eyes. She looked older than her years. She knew it was a pretty face, and let herself feel that for once. She told herself not to carry her torment with her this time, but to just try to enjoy the nice day as if she were a pretty young woman, out in a park on a nice day with no big problems. She refused to look at her body, because she knew it would only be a flat chest with spreading hips and would ruin her fragile but happy mood. She had been told she was a beautiful girl becoming a woman, but that was not the way she saw herself and she was the one who counted and she hated her body.

She was a timid girl and so she chose to sit alone by one of the boulders closer to the southwest end of the Sheep's Meadow. Most of the people were out in the middle of the grass. She sat against the rock and read and watched people. It was warming up and there were a lot of people coming out to the park. Footballs, Frisbees, blankets, dogs, children. Dee Dee tried to read, but found her attention constantly distracted. After twenty minutes of being unable to settle down she decided to go for a walk. She went across the south edge of the meadow and headed for the path in the trees. She thought she might go watch the skaters. Just as she passed the first tree she glanced at the couple sitting on the blanket and almost stopped breathing when she caught a glimpse of the man.

It was McGrath, she was sure of it. She was only a child when he and her mother had gotten divorced but she would never forget the sneer on that face and his rage when Dee Dee had seen him hitting her mother. It was McGrath, the womanizer who hated women from the depths of his soul. Dee Dee was sure he didn't recognize her because he glanced at her when she paused and there was no sign of anything in his face. She walked on, her anger building. He was schmoozing the young woman he was with and had a fake, aggressive smile on his face. He kept leaning in and touching her arm the way a woman does to let a man know she is interested in him. Dee Dee kept her eyes to the path and walked away, disturbed, but not nearly as afraid as she would have thought she would be. She had seen him once on TV several years ago when he had run for mayor. He was polished and slick and he almost looked believable if you didn't know the real truth about him.

Dee Dee approached the skaters and suddenly realized that to him, Dee Dee was just another woman, someone to be automatically despised and manipulated. She knew her mother wouldn't talk about her father, there was still some weird kind of pain or love there, but she would occasionally talk about McGrath and angrily mutter that he was the biggest mistake of her life. Dee Dee wondered what kind of state of mind her mother must have been in to take up with a man like that. She smoldered a little and wondered if McGrath had ever been made to pay for his manipulations. She felt a teenager's intense sense of injustice and wondered what would happen to a guy like that. After all. Something should be done. People shouldn't just be able to walk away from their misdeeds. Her anger rose from an ember to a flame and she began to rehearse what she could say to him. How she could hurt him with words? He had hurt them and he should be hurt. What could be done? Her anger was beginning to take over now, as it had never done before. It torched her depression, her constant unhappiness went up like so much tinder and she began to walk back toward the meadow without even realizing where she was headed. She started to think that there was nothing preventing her from humiliating him right now, right there on this sunny morning in the meadow. She could say whatever she wanted to him. There were plenty of people around so he couldn't do anything, and he'd be restrained but embarrassed and humiliated in front of the woman he was trying to impress. Dee Dee had a little tiny nagging feeling in the back of her brain that it wasn't her business and that she should just let sleeping dogs lie, but this anger thing, it felt so good, and it made one so powerful, it wiped away all doubts and fears and took control of you and made you able to act. The cautionary nagging in the back of her brain got buried in the cacophony of anger in the frontal lobes that made her walk faster and begin to rehearse her speech.

She came around the path and saw them at the far corner of the meadow. They were still there. Now they were holding hands and looking like something out of a commercial for allergy medicine, sitting all lovey in the green field. Dee Dee walked a straight line over the grass toward them and didn't stop until she was standing right at the edge of the blanket. They looked up at her, the young woman with fear in her eyes at this stranger, and McGrath, though obviously still not recognizing her, immediately looked guilty and sneaky. He probably automatically assumed he had somehow screwed over this impatient angry looking young woman.

"You're McGrath, aren't you?" she spat at him.

"Yeeeeessss," he said with his eyebrows lifted.

"You don't know who I am, do you?"

"No. And I don't give a shit, either," said McGrath, and he got to his feet in a swift motion. The woman remained seated looking puzzled, but relieved that it had nothing to do with her.

"Well, my name is Dee Dee Dewar." And McGrath was nonplussed for a moment, before he recovered his sneer. "And you beat my mother and almost put her in the hospital, when I was a little kid."

McGrath looked wistfully at his date, as if he knew he no longer had a chance with the woman, and then turned to address Dee Dee. "I think you're mistaken about that. I don't give a damn who you are, and get the fuck out of here before I have you arrested!" His face got red very quickly, but Dee Dee held her ground.

"Just so you know, asshole, if the police come, I'll tell them you raped me. I just thought maybe your date here would like to know what you really think of women." And Dee Dee could see that it had already worked. If the woman had even half a brain, whether she knew McGrath or not, she would at least have doubts and cause to pull back from McGrath. Women didn't take chances these days and she had probably already gotten at least a glimmer of his real nature. Dee Dee saw the comprehension in the woman's eyes and knew her work was done. She couldn't resist a last shot.

"Bye bye" she called cheerfully over her shoulder as she spun and walked airily away. "Have a nice day." And she chuckled to herself. Her anger had been used so righteously, with such pleasure. She remained high from the release of her scorn and she started to skip. She didn't look back.

When she was twenty yards away, McGrath yelled, "Your mother hasn't told you the truth about your father yet, has she?"

Dee Dee froze and she heard McGrath laugh. He started to yell something else, but she put her hands over her ears and began to run. Whatever it was, she desperately didn't want to hear it from his evil lips. Her triumph was stolen and she felt assaulted and she could feel all the depression and unhappiness rising from its chair in the corner of her mind to take center stage again.

Chapter 11

Tag was headed for English class, on time this morning, for once, and he felt good today. He didn't remember ever feeling like this. He thought about Drood and the poker game. He felt so at home there in the dark with the men. They were all nice to Tag, except Shiny, but even Shiny seemed to be getting used to him. Tag tried to remember all the things that Drood had told him, but it was a lot and he couldn't keep it all in mind as he walked through the crowded, noisy, riotous hallway. As he came around the corner to the English hallway, he caught sight of Loomis' large head by a locker on the other side of the hall, halfway down. Tag hesitated and tried to remember what Drood had told him.

"Look at him with the eyes of the grown-up Tag," he told himself, "no eye contact, act like there's a grown up around." And indeed there was, Mr. Edwards stood with his arms folded, kitty cornered from where Tag had paused. Tag took a deep breath and walked down the hall. He decided to rely on the presence of the security guard at the other end of the hall, and he walked on Loomis' side of the hall. He kept his gaze steadily on Loomis as he approached even though his heart was pounding hard in his chest. Tag thought that if he had to walk just ten extra yards in front of Loomis, he would pass out. He stared into Loomis, as Loomis struggled with the combination to his locker and swore. Loomis pounded the locker with his fist, as Tag got closer. He looked up as he sensed someone approaching and as he did, Tag looked away and slipped by. He heard Loomis mutter, "Fuck!" behind him. He could not have failed to know it was Tag, but there were so many people in the hallway and the bell was about to ring and Mr. Edwards played statue so that there was no way Loomis could do anything. Loomis was taken off guard while struggling with his locker and he couldn't react fast enough and Tag was away and into his classroom.

Tag sat at his desk and the teacher droned on about the reading assignment and Tag couldn't think. He had just been delivered from the lions in the pit and his brain was tingling. The neurons were firing all over the place as triumph, hope, and relief passed through the several cortices and striations in his brain. He began to believe that Drood was actually helping him and that there might be a way out of this whole mess. Now, the question was, would Loomis become more determined to get him, or would things continue to get better from here? Tag didn't know, but he decided he would spend the rest of the class thinking about the future and what might happen. He had spent his whole life worrying and fearing. It was no wonder he was exhausted all the time. To be able to daydream and to want things was a tremendous relief to him, though he didn't of course think in those terms. Denied the ability or opportunity to fantasize and to want things, he had been depressed, but Drood had already helped Tag, even forced him, to do what was good for him.

Tag pictured the pools and mansions of Beverly Hills that he had seen on so many different television shows. He fashioned one for himself, where the pool was kidney shaped and you could look out from it over the hills at the city. The mansion he lived in was white with really high ceilings, glowing fish tanks all over the place and a lot of levels and decks to sit on and look out from. He would do all the work himself, because he didn't want to get lazy and condescending like most rich people, so he'd have a shed for tools and lots of machines for cleaning the house. There'd be a basketball hoop in the driveway, but people wouldn't be able to see the driveway from the street. There'd be huge evergreen trees all over the property, a wall of them closing the place in. The sun would always shine in the day and the city would always twinkle in the night.

His friends would all come over and they'd be tough but kind city people, with jobs like plumbers, cooks, landscapers and things like that. They'd know the value of money, but they'd also know the value of loyalty and friendship. They'd be glad he had money, but they wouldn't resent him for it or try to stab him in the back. He'd go to every Laker's home game and sit courtside like Jack Nicholson, and sometimes he'd go to the Clippers games too, unless he had to work, which would be where and when the big poker games were. Each time he'd go, one of his friends would go with him and they'd enjoy the intricacies of the game and eat cruddy hot dogs and drink flat beer. His friends would be both men and women and he'd be able to talk to all of them. None of them would ever make fun of him and they'd all respect him.

He'd have a bag packed all the time and a regular routine for getting to the airport and going to Las Vegas. There'd be the same driver each time for the car service and they'd sort of be friends too, and he'd always come by whenever the grown-up Tag had a party. He'd always fly the same airline so they'd all know him and the flight attendants would say, "How'd you do this time, Mr. Clifford?" and he'd smile and joke with them and he'd look real calm and confident and that's how he'd always be no matter whether he won or lost.

And in Las Vegas, or anywhere he played poker it would be clear that he had a gift, but the way the cards go you have to lose too and so it wouldn't be like Tiger Woods or Michael Jordan or Wayne Gretzky where no one would want to go against them and they had it easier because the competition choked up against them because they were intimidated. So he could always get a game and he wouldn't have to con anybody or manipulate or cheat, he'd always win fair and square.

And the girlfriend. Tag could see this life so clearly that it amazed him as he looked up and realized the class was almost over. What had they been doing? Still talking about the reading it sounded like. He could see this life so clearly, could smell the chlorine in his pool, could see what his friends would look like. It was so vivid and so beautiful to him that he was sure imagining the girlfriend would be easy, but it wasn't. He could see her coming from the driveway on the walk to the front door and he could see that she was young, that she dressed casually, with jeans and a t-shirt. He could see that she was graceful, though she was tough too, but he just couldn't picture a figure or face. He could only see that she was completely 100% honest and straightforward all the time and he could see that she knew who she was and what she was all about. She could help Tag because she was so good with people and understood so much about life, she'd always be able to give him advice. She was probably an artist or a writer or something because she was very creative and thoughtful.

And as he pictured her coming up the walk to the front door, he pictured her pulling a strand of her long, straight, dark hair behind her ear and smoothing her hair. But he couldn't quite make out her face. Tag tried as hard as he could to imagine her face. He even tried to put a few different faces in there, but none of them was right. Intelligence, honesty, seriousness, deep creativity should all show up easily in an imaginary face, but Tag couldn't quite put it together. It was disappointing and maybe he'd ask Drood about it, but probably not, because he didn't think that Drood had meant he should be daydreaming like this and fantasizing about girls. With that thought, self-consciousness returned and the class seemed to be in a question and answer period again, and so he had better snap to in case he was called on. He did smile, though, as he thought quickly again about his life in L.A. Most young people in frosty Syracuse at one time or another pictured themselves living in California.

* * *

Drood too was pleased with the outcome of his first session with his new apprentice. The boy had just needed a little encouragement and hope and Drood believed his natural intelligence and courage would see him through. The trick was, Drood thought, to get him to become someone extraordinary and exceptional, to give him the tools of a Druid: knowledge of the future, mind-reading, teaching, healing, understanding dreams, and working with souls. Tag's fantasizing about a future life would of course miss in some of the important details: the woman would be human and not perfect, he'd eventually realize that gambling was an unsustainable life-style, and he might not care about his living quarters after a while. But, Drood didn't want to just help him to grow up and become a sane, ordinary, contemporary, human adult. He had to keep the fantasy alive, because it would drive the boy beyond the ordinary. And why, Drood then wondered? To what end had this apprenticeship arrived? Drood sighed because his return to active life meant once again trying to understand, to learn, to investigate. Energy. He didn't know if he had it.

What would they talk about next? Well, he'd see how the boy's week went and then maybe they'd do some more work on the thug problem, and then they should probably talk about poker. Or would that be rushing the boy too soon? Drood knew that adolescent fantasies changed with the wind and the boy could just as well be interested in being a jet pilot the next week, but you had to start with something and see where it took you. Might as well focus on poker, he concluded. The skills involved would stand him well for the rest of his life and they fit well with the training Drood could offer him. Besides, the boy seemed to be a natural at it. He had the math and the percentages down, he wasn't afraid to take risks, and the psychology of it was just a matter of experience.

But Drood had his own situations to face before the next Saturday and he turned his attention back to work on Monday morning. As he sat in his new office, right next door to Mr. Muke, he could hear Muke bustling about, generating importance, shuffling papers wildly so there would be information in the air, making frantic phone calls to be sure there would be some crisis to deal with soon, arguing with his equals, instructing and scolding inferiors, begging and pleading with superiors. Drood read his e-mails and deleted them one by one. Only one person in his new group of eight subordinates hadn't sent him an e-mail between Friday and Monday with a list of complaints. Worker 1 complained that worker 4 didn't listen to him when he told him how to do his job, worker 2 believed they were not following the procedure (that was written six years before to cover a product they no longer supported or even had), worker 3 was supposed to get an engraved invitation to a weekly meeting that never changed time and place, worker 4 was telling him how to do his job and he didn't even know what the job was, worker 5 should get a raise for general overall excellence even though it's only the middle of the year, worker 6 didn't think it was fair that taxes are taken out of the check before he gets it or that the company automatically deducts some money for their pet charity without asking, and worker 7 wanted to know exactly what Drood's plan was for her and she would be unable to do one more lick of work until Drood would explicitly tell her exactly what she should be doing each day and at what time she should be doing it. Drood was momentarily puzzled by the absence of an e-mail from worker 8 until he looked at his calendar and realized worker 8 had the day off on Friday. He chuckled to himself. One week later and he was just like a regular manager and he had no friends in the office and he was responsible for all the workings of the universe.

Drood smiled and thought for a couple of moments as he stared at the listings of the e-mails on his screen. How to reply? He ran through the complaints again in his head as he deleted sixteen e-mails from corporate functionaries without reading them, and checked the "Will Attend" box for all the invitations to meetings, whether or not they conflicted with each other or whether they had anything to do with him. He knew that whether you said you would attend was far more important than whether you attended or not. If they really needed his opinion, ideas, or decisions, they would come in private, in secret anyway. When they asked why you hadn't attended or cancelled, you just said, "Something came up" and it sounded mysterious and important and made you look like you were really valuable. Plus, you didn't have to sit through a bunch of meetings where nobody could decide anything. So anyway, he got back to the e-mails from the people in his group and decided he would answer them, rapid fire, without thinking. This would cause more trouble, but it would be trouble for them, not him, and that's what counted.

He answered the e-mails: Worker 1 should speak louder when telling worker 4 what to do, he may have an attention problem, worker 2 should do a fifteen page report on the procedure and how it applies to the situation today and should send the report around the group and schedule time to explain to each group member what they need to do (not to Drood, of course, he assured worker two that he was already on top of it), worker 3 should try to re-schedule the weekly meeting that was always at the same time and place, that way worker 3 would become in charge of the meeting and would always know where it was, worker 4 should make it a point to ignore worker 1 and avoid worker 1 until she goes away, worker 5's raise has been discussed and is being evaluated right now by Johnson and Johnson (no such thing was occurring), worker 6 can have all the deductions arranged to suit him by just contacting Human Resource and the IRS (that'll fix him, Drood thought), and worker 7 should do exactly what she did before he was made the manager. The e-mails went out and Drood thought, "Hey, I might actually get to like this boss stuff."

Shadow in the doorway, Drood looked up. Johnson. Johnson motioned for Drood to follow him and stepped next door into Mr. Muke's office. Drood got up and went in and sat in the chair Johnson motioned him to. Mr. Muke was on the edge of his seat with shining eyes, clearly delighted to be in the presence of Johnson. If he had a tail, Muke would have been wagging it.

"I need you two to go out to the L.A. office right away. There's a big meeting with one of our biggest customers there and they want to get into the nitty gritty of how the company runs. That's where you guys come in. I want you to show them what we do and really wow them with how on top of things we are, especially with their account. Have all their account information with you and don't leave any stones unturned while you try to find out what they're after and make sure you keep them as our clients."

Drood's shoulders sagged and he tried hard to keep his face from going blank. He looked at Mr. Muke and saw that Muke was about as excited as he could be, half standing and ready to ask about six thousand questions. Being a back office type, Mr. Muke never got to travel for the company or to deal with the customers and he considered this trip to L.A. a great honor. Drood dreaded it. Being a manager seemed to mean that you had to actually do things for the company. Meetings with customers, traveling with Muke, convincing somebody of something. That was all bad enough, Drood considered, but he'd also have to leave his beloved Syracuse and the cold gray, dark beauty of the place, the freedom, and the relaxed casualness for the brown and crowded city with all the hurry, the struggle, the searing bright loud Americanness of the ferocious megalopolis.

He'd probably miss the next poker game and his meeting with Tag as well and that disappointed him most of all. Just when they were getting going. Maybe he'd call the boy and talk to him on the phone. When did he say his mother was at work? Drood didn't want to be a strange man calling her young teenage son. Eventually Tag would have to explain the situation to his mother. Drood almost despaired as Johnson and Muke went over the who's, what's, and where's of the trip. The meeting began to break up and Johnson growled a "Thank you" over his shoulder.

Drood tried to leave but Muke stopped him. "So, Seeeaaann, we hit the road together, eh? Nice to be a manager now, hmm? You get to travel and talk to the customers!"

He seemed to actually be sincere in his enthusiasm, which Drood found all the more disgusting, but all he could manage to say was, "Imagine my excitement." Muke's balloon was punctured and Drood shuffled back to his office, slumped into his chair and wondered, "What kind of power or wisdom can I gain from this?" His own training said there was a way to turn every situation in life into an advantage, but he couldn't quite make it out right now. He had to be in the right frame of mind to be on the lookout for wisdom.

He thought about the airports, the planes, the hotels, the business suits, the dinner and drinking with fat, racist, sexist, money-grubbing depraved businessmen. His mind struggled not to sink. At least he would be going west, he thought, where the sun sets and the magic of twilight and the end of the world was and maybe some strange magic would occur in spite of the inanity of the trip. And L.A. was where young Tag saw himself going. Maybe he could do some scouting for the boy, come back with some ideas, or pictures, or maps or something. Souvenirs. That reminded him of something he had meant to do. Drood clicked onto the Internet and went to The Bookstore. He did a quick search and then ordered seven books on the theory and practice of playing poker. He could read some on the trip and give some to the boy to read.

* * *

Dee Dee ran home crying and thanked the doorman who gave her a tissue. As she waited for the elevator in the lobby, she caught sight of herself in the mirror. Her normally crystal blue eyes were surrounded by red lines and swollen. "Better not let Mom, or Lewis see me, or they'll be all over me." She rode up and tried to compose herself as well as she could. She zoomed through the apartment to her room and closed the door and leaned against it. She breathed deeply for a few minutes and then sat down on the bed, thinking hard.

She wanted to know. She had to know. What was her father like? How old had he been when he died? What was he interested in, what did he think about, how did he grow up, what was his family like?

As she thought of McGrath's sneering face, and Lewis' condescending smugness she contrasted their nasty male faces with that of her mother's. Her mother was still beautiful, still young looking and quite well cared for and well made up. She was still fruity, Dee Dee considered. What had happened between her and her father? She pictured her mother's frown; her perpetually worried and anxious face and wondered if she had always been that way. What had she been like before the tragic death of her first husband, the disaster of her second marriage, the raising of a girl and the annoying Lewis? Dee Dee wondered if her mother had ever been carefree or optimistic and if she could remember being that way. She vowed to reach the young girl in her mother, to get that younger woman to tell her about her father. And maybe she could apply a little guilt to her too, if she told her mother about the encounter with McGrath. She knew her mother would be horrified that Dee Dee had even seen him, let alone taunted him and insulted him. In spite of her mother's clear superiority to McGrath, and in spite of her dismissal of that period of her life as a big mistake, she knew her mother was still afraid of him. McGrath was a politician and he knew powerful people and he knew how to hurt people. Dee Dee cursed herself and wished this day had never happened. She wished someone could come and get her out of her life.

In spite of her mother's experiences, Dee Dee fervently hoped to have a husband some day. Hugging and talking to her Patrick bear, she tried to picture what he would be like. He'd dress sloppy because he'd be into way more important things than clothes. He'd be tall and have light hair and his eyes would be brilliant and brown. He would be unconventional and he would be very sensitive to other people and their suffering. He'd be the center of a group of interesting people and he'd be totally devoted to her. She would bring out the child in him, but with everyone else he'd be serious and tough and smart. He'd be athletic and be able to live his life any way he wanted no matter what other people said. And she would share her life with him. And she would be a free-lance writer, writing about anything she found interesting or compelling. It would be the perfect life and she'd never come back to New York. Her mother was welcome to visit any time but she could never bring Lewis. She'd only be allowed to visit by herself.

Dee Dee heard the front door slam and she knew that her mother and Lewis were home. Time to go confront. She rose, steeled herself, breathed deeply, and pulled open the door to her bedroom.

Chapter 12

Drood pawed through the pile of books in his lap. Muke was in the seat next to him describing in great detail the last Broadway musical he had seen and they were only in the first fifteen minutes of the non-stop five-hour flight to L.A. He had to find a book fast and dive in. Muke, he didn't have to call him Mr. anymore, since they were equals, was one of those people who would not recognize even the most aggressive of social clues and his conversations knew no boundaries. Every subject was part of his talk, whether you liked it or not. And he never let a person off the hook when he wanted to know something about their personal life, asking rapid-fire question after question until he had what he wanted, barely even pausing to hear the answers. Quickly, quickly, Drood pawed and finally settled on a collection of essays by a famous poker player. He dove in and Muke's voice droned on and finally withered away.

By the middle of the flight Drood had finished two of the books and realized that Tag's journey to becoming a professional poker player would be a false start on the long road of life. The skills you learn in playing poker, observing and calculating, were priceless, but they could only be successfully applied in some other endeavor. The odds, it was all in the odds, were against the individual. The assertions to the contrary, the passionate advocacy of certain systems in the poker books by the "experts" were irrational and hollow, justifications for the good luck those particular "experts" had experienced. Drood was convinced they would all lose in the end.

Drood sighed and frowned and tried to decide whether to steer the boy away from the gambling. He realized he had arrived at his first big crossroads in this relationship. Would it be better in the long run or the short run to intervene in the boy's plans? The disillusionment would come and it would be brilliant knowledge for the young man. Should he let tag fail at gambling at a young age while acquiring sharp skills? Or, steer him toward something safer and risk taking away the boy's newfound will to learn and explore? Drood decided it was worth the pain and the risk to let the boy pursue his own path without revealing the boy's obvious future to him. "We only learn by doing, not by listening," Drood remembered from somewhere. He knew Tag, and he knew Tag would succeed in this world eventually. Drood resolved to give him all the skills he could but to make none of the decisions for him. Tough line to hold, he thought.

The boy would need lots of practice and a bankroll. And it would have to be practice against good players. Well, Drood would concentrate on teaching him to bend every part of his will to the task, teach the boy to become obsessed with learning and practice. It almost didn't matter which subject the boy's passion went into. It was the discipline and the practice that was important. Drood knew that never again in life did one have the potential for concentration, endurance, and passion to master something as when in the teens.

He remembered his own teacher explaining this to him on a hilltop. "You must put aside the games, the roughhousing with the other boys, you must try to ignore the impulses that come upon you. Your path has chosen you and you can't avoid it and anything you do to obstruct it will hurt you. If you are to become the man you must become, you will not have a second chance at mastery. Life is short and there are no absolute concrete rules, but the consequences of everything you do will be irreversible. Youth cannot be recaptured."

And Drood had looked up at his old teacher with the white beard and wondered what his teacher had been like as a young man. Had he also struggled with the desire to chase women, to compete with the men, to run away and see the great cities and mountains and seas of the world? His teacher turned his gaze from the sheep grazing on the far hilltop and looked Drood right in the eyes. The sixteen-year-old Drood had no defense against those amazing, brilliant, penetrating eyes. And there was great suffering in old Mylvwyn's face as he stared at Drood and Drood felt the weight of a life fully lived bearing down on him through those eyes.

"Yes, I too was once just like you. I gave my teacher a terrible time trying to get me to focus. And I missed many opportunities by doing so. You cannot fight against the desires of youth and you should not try to. But you must place them second, behind the desire for mastery. In our cases, there are many songs and poems we must learn, there are many medicines, traditions, and laws that we must practice. We must watch the sun, the moon, and the stars and learn their movements and their meanings. But most of all, and the most difficult of all, is that we must learn the hearts and minds of our people, because it is they that we serve, that we exist for, that we create the songs for. We must serve. I cannot stress this enough. We are servants. We gradually become the most knowing, useful, and powerful of our people, but it is above all through our service and our usefulness. Never forget that. It will lead you to consider each situation and learn what you can gain from it. It will help you to sublimate all your selfish desires to the needs of the people. And it will ensure that you are never at a loss for the proper attitude to take. You will always know what to do if you consider yourself a servant."

And on the plane, remembering, Drood smiled at the clouds while a sharp pain pulsed in his heart. He had bristled at the old man's insistence on servitude and he had never listened after that when Mylvwyn would talk on the subject. And perhaps that was why his life had been ruined and so evilly tormented since then. Drood's young man's pride and his pride in his skills and accomplishments led him to despise the idea of servitude. Indeed it was a dirty word among his people and he didn't grasp then, as he did now, he realized with surprise, that his teacher had gone on to expound that no one need ever know you were a servant, that your servitude was your own secret and that was the trick. The ultimate servant is invisible. Drood laughed out loud at his own stupidity and his wasted life. Muke looked quizzically at him.

"A poke-her joke?" Muke asked. "Get it, poker, poke-her?"

"No. Just remembering something."

"Why are you reading all those poker books anyway?" Muke continued.

"A friend of mine is interested in learning poker and so I'm scouting all these books to help him." Drood replied.

"You're reading a bunch of books because a friend is interested in the subject?" Muke's eyebrows raised and he seemed incredulous.

"Mmhm." It was not a big deal to Drood. Drood had learned painfully about friendship and teaching. Muke looked uncomfortable and Drood guessed that he didn't believe Drood was reading the books to help someone else, and so was being deceitful to Muke. Drood figured he'd better get out of the conversation so he dove back into another book. He held the pages, but he was really watching the Rocky Mountains slide by the window. They were so brutal and still and calm and snowy that they were arresting and he stared at them. He could see out of the corner of his eye that the Muke kept shooting dissatisfied looks at him.

As the flight droned on, Drood's mind turned to the past, again. Memories of his former life tormented him. Drood had once betrayed his best friend and it had driven him insane. He was still trying to recover from the betrayal. He couldn't think about it or the old panic and disgust would rise in him again and eat at his mind. Drood was a fugitive and it would take a long time for him to return to some kind of rightful place in life. He had a sudden vision of McGrath's leering face. McGrath. Now, there might be the possibility of correcting things. He pondered atonement for what he had done to Kilty. Could he make up for it by doing unto McGrath? McGrath had turned him in to the police. McGrath had stolen Drood's life, his family. McGrath had manipulated Drood into destroying Kilty. Revenge. It clicked. Drood suddenly smiled at the Muke and the Muke retreated to the rest room, alarmed.

They got to L.A. and all through the terminal the Muke kept talking and marveling at everything he saw, even though they were still in the airport which looked like every other airport, Drood thought. Muke was becoming like nails on the chalkboard and Drood was dying to get away from him. They had to meet the client for dinner and drinks that evening. It was 2 p.m. when they arrived and Drood wanted to lie down and rest his eyes and his ears before they went. He was very eager to get away from Muke.

On the ride from the airport, Muke said, "I can't believe all the poverty here, I always thought L.A. was such a glitzy city," Muke was saying.

"It's a city. That means there is great poverty there. Like every other city on the planet," Drood said a little testily.

"Yes, but..." and Muke went off again.

Finally they arrived at the hotel and got to their rooms, adjoining, to Drood's dismay. Drood dropped off his things and skipped back into the elevator before Muke could come to his room with some observations about the towels or the curtains or something. He got to the lobby and found a bellhop; yes they had bellhops, and pulled him aside.

"I'm a poker player and I'm in town for a few nights. Where do I go?"

The man was Mexican and said that he didn't speak much English, but he held up one finger and hustled through a door in the side of the lobby. He came back with another older Mexican.

"Give me ten dollars and I'll tell you everything you need to know about poker in L.A."

Drood gave him ten dollars and the man smiled.

"Most of the big players of course go to Las Vegas. There are a couple of tourist type games where you can make some money around town and I can tell you where those are."

"No," said Drood. "I'm looking for the real thing."

"Okay, I'll tell you, but they don't like spectators. It's a fifty dollar game and you better be ready to put up."

"Don't worry," said Drood. "I can handle it. Where do I go?"

The man told him the address of a place right down in the city, off Hollywood Boulevard. He told him to use the back door and tell them Osvaldo sent him, and prepare to pay a fifty-dollar house charge. He told him not to park down there, take a cab. Games started at 9:00 p.m., everyone out by 3:00 a.m. Usually three tables.

Drood sat through dinner with the clients - between the clients, Meltocom's own regional sales manager, and the anxious Muke. Drood couldn't really get a word in. Every once in a while he'd try to say something positive about Meltocom and they'd all pause, stare blankly at him, and then continue their conversation. They were all eagerly positioning themselves and pushing themselves and manipulating, negotiating, jockeying for position, and Drood therefore was quite unknown and irrelevant. They were at an expensive French restaurant in Santa Monica and the lighting was low and they were drinking expensive wine. All the people at the dinner seemed to believe that they were in the seat of power, spending the company's money copiously and trying to soak in what they could of "taste" and Drood had no idea what they were talking about. They were speaking the sales/financial jargon common to the business world, and Drood was not privy to the secret lingo and not very interested either. When the meal was eaten and the clients were beginning to get drunk, Drood excused himself as not feeling well and left to go to the poker game. Taxi to Hollywood.

The alley was disgusting by anyone's standards, all garbage and stench, and Drood was a little nervous about getting robbed. He had $2,000 in cash with him, his entire savings, which he was fully prepared to lose, but he'd prefer to learn something about poker while doing so. With a manager's salary Drood was sure he'd make it back in no time. He knocked on the door and it was opened by a skinny boyish fellow with long lanky hair, a pale face, and glasses.

"Yeah?"

"Osvaldo sent me."

The boy simply stuck his hand out and Drood slapped a fifty into it. The boy stepped aside and held the door for Drood without speaking and stared at his feet while Drood slipped past him. It was a long hallway with one door at the end. The boy called after Drood as he went down the hallway,

"Just knock four times, real loud."

Drood reached the door and did so. It was opened by a young woman with a tie-dyed T-shirt and lots of beads and silver. She too was pale with long lank hair. She sized Drood up and said, "You've never been here before?"

Drood shook his head and she smiled and said,

"Fifty dollar ante, fifty dollar limit on the betting. Games over at 2:45, chips and cash go with me. We're kind of light tonight, so there's an empty seat at two of the three tables. Here, take this one." And she guided him to a table. The three tables were spaced twenty feet apart in a huge rectangular room of cinder blocks that looked like it might once have been a warehouse. There was nothing luxurious about the construction of the room itself. It had a dropped ceiling and fluorescent lighting, but the tables and the surroundings had been carefully chosen and constructed for maximum comfort. The green felt on each octagonal table came right to the edge so the table looked and felt expensive, but it was the chairs themselves that were built for comfort. They had leather backs and seats and each arm had a folded out tray with an ashtray and a holder for drinks. Drood settled in.

"Something to drink?" The girl asked sweetly. Drood answered, "Scotch and water. No ice."

She vanished to the darker end of the room and Drood surveyed the other people in the room. All men, all seated. Only one younger than himself, now only one space at one table. Six per table. Drood wondered who could be the owner or the proprietor of these games. The young boy and girl collecting the money and taking care of things clearly could not be in charge. They looked as though they could be robbed with no effort at all. But everyone else appeared to be playing. Drood surmised that there must be more to the situation than he thought. Maybe hidden cameras and people in another nearby room. Maybe there were plants at each table, Drood wasn't sure. But, Osvaldo had assured him that it was a straight game, so Drood had nothing to lose but 2K. Of course, he didn't know Osvaldo well either, but his intuition told him to relax.

The girl came back with his drink and pointed the restroom out to him, a simple door in one wall, and then changed his money for him. Drood changed it all. Why hold back? If you're gonna play, you'd better play. Know when to risk and how much to risk. That applied to everything in life, but it also applied specifically to poker. It was something he had learned from his reading and from experience and from playing poker with his friends. You had to put some action into play or there was no payoff. The game began and Drood examined the other players at his table. From the little comments and motions they made he assumed they were all veterans of the club. They looked completely comfortable. There were two very fat men, two very thin men, and one real old-timer. None of them looked like money, but Drood knew that was not the thing when it came to poker. Some people spent all their extra money on poker. The old-timer and one of the big guys appeared to know each other and talked occasionally about a woman they knew. The other three were mostly silent and concentrating. Drood studied them all for "tells", and as the game went on he was able to pick them up in two of the players. He was surprised. He thought it would be easier to mask thoughts, but it was plain as day. When thin man 1 took a sip from his drink after the deal, he had a great hand. When he didn't and bet hard, he was bluffing. When thin man 2 looked up at the lights before betting, he was bluffing. They lost almost every hand and Drood surmised the others were simply stringing them along to get as much money out of them as they could. They were taking it easy on the thin men while they examined each other and worked each other. Drood, being new to the game, and an amateur, lost most of his bankroll within two hours. He folded once with a good hand, and he bluffed and got caught with a bad hand. He even miscalculated the number of aces on the table once.

By midnight Drood was down to $500 and the other players had ceased showing any curiosity about him. Drood had established himself as a tourist. But he was picking up tips from the old-timer and his partner, who by now had clearly come to the game together, were regulars at the club, and were used to much stiffer competition. They were really just playing each other now, and enjoying the competition. The large man preferred stud poker and the old-timer preferred the much simpler draw. Drood himself was better able to compete in the draw games. He saw that the choice of the game was really the key to how to win; the big man won almost every hand when they played stud. The old-timer won a lot of hands at draw, but the others won a hand in it now and then. Drood wondered if the old-timer was making it a more friendly game, or if it really was his best chance to win. If he were skilled it seemed as though he would choose a more complicated game that would suit his talents better. Drood wanted to talk to the old-timer.

Drood got lucky and picked up enough tips to win some back, and so, by 3 a.m., he had landed enough dough to put him back up to $1200. A loss of $800, not too bad, considering he didn't really have the experience to play for those stakes. After closing, they were filing out into the alley, and Drood saw more of the outfit running the poker game. There were three large, tough looking young men at the door to the alley and one more at the opening of the alley to the street. They looked to be armed and Drood thought it was considerate of the owner of the game to protect his players as they tried to make their way home. Drood found himself next to the old-timer.

"Why do you always play lowball draw?" Drood asked him without preamble.

The old-timer looked out of the sides of his eyes at Drood and frowned.

"I'm just a tourist, I'm going home tomorrow," Drood explained. The man looked at him for a second longer and let a couple of the others pass before he spoke. A wry smile crossed his face.

"That's a very smart question for a tourist."

"Well, I've developed an interest and I'm trying to learn."

"Hmmph." The old man seemed to consider for a minute and then spoke slowly. "I need help to beat Harry. He's much better at a lot of different games, so I need to keep it simple and I need to use the other players at the table to shake it up, introduce a little doubt. No offense, but nobody else at the table was really in Harry's league. Or even mine for that matter."

"None taken, " Drood replied, "That's kind of what I had guessed myself. How did you end up?"

"Up six hundred. Meal money for a few days." The old man shrugged and walked away, leaving Drood with several more questions. The other players had disappeared around the corner but as the old man stepped up to the end of the alley, Drood saw a long black car pull into the opening and the door opened and the old man folded himself in. Drood wondered who he was and where he came from. This encounter had all the mysterious signs of a direct intervention by the Gods. Was the old poker player sent from Mannanan? Would they run into him again?

"Enough," Drood thought to himself, "time to get some sleep for the next round of weirdness with the Muke tomorrow." And as he walked to the main corner, Hollywood and Vine, to find a ride back to his hotel, he wondered what else he could find out in L.A. for his young friend Tag. Perhaps real estate prices? He turned his mind off and traveled back to the hotel.

* * *

Tag had scouted the area in front of the school carefully, and it looked like it was safe to walk and stand at the bus stop. As Drood had taught him, he scanned the area to find the nearest adult. No one but kids at the bus stop, but he knew in the neighborhood across Teall heading east, there would be ladies out walking their dogs and whatnot, in fact, there goes one now, he thought. She was heading north on Teall on the other side of the street with a little froo froo dog in front of her on a leash. Tag didn't relish the thought of standing at the bus stop out in the open, right in the path of Loomis' route home, and so he quickly decided to follow the lady up Teall and make the long walk down Grant or maybe New Court back to his own neighborhood. He left the bus stop and waited for traffic to lighten up. As he did, he saw Loomis and crew heading with purpose toward the corner. He had been spotted and targeted.

Tag sprinted across Teall and jogged half a block to about ten yards behind where the lady was walking her dog. He matched her pace and she heard him and turned to look at him. She looked right through him and continued on walking. Tag threw a quick glance over his shoulder and saw that the demons were still waiting for traffic to let up so they could cross the street. The lady turned right onto a side street and Tag was right behind her. They were blocked from the view down Teall by a big yew hedge and a fence. Tag saw with joy that there was another woman walking her dog on the other side of the street, a man cleaning out his car and, far down the street, on the other side, was a mailman's truck facing this way, which meant the mailman would be working his way down the street toward Tag. He was a little relieved, but knew there were no guarantees. This neighborhood backed up to his neighborhood and so Tag knew he could go home almost in a straight line. He'd have to cross Grant, eventually, and then he'd be on his home turf and he'd be able to hide. He felt he had a chance and that the goons probably would not have the stamina to follow him all the way. He just had to rely on the presence of adults. If the freaks wanted to beat him, there was no guarantee any of these adults wouldn't just run into their houses and hide. Tag wasn't naïve about that, but Drood had said just their presence should be enough to deter the bullies.

Tag was halfway down the block behind the lady now and the mailman was still coming toward them. He was afraid to turn around but he heard shouting down at the end of the street by Teall. They were taunting him. Tag pretended not to hear. He didn't want to inflame them any, but to his great relief he knew they weren't going to follow him through this neighborhood. And by the time they went around to get to Grant, Tag would already be safely across. Okay, he thought, two more points for Drood. It seems like the guy knows what he's talking about. The lady in front of him turned around and gave him a dirty look and so Tag crossed the street and walked on the opposite sidewalk. Didn't need her anymore since they had curved around out of sight of Teall and now he was just a normal kid walking home from school. He began to look forward to some day not having to play these games.

* * *

Dee Dee screamed at her mother, "He's my father!!!!!! Why can't you just tell the truth!!! What are you afraid of??!!!"

And Dee Dee's mother looked down and didn't say anything. Lewis began to speak, but Dee Dee's mom raised her hand to silence him.

"Come with me." And they walked into Dee Dee's bedroom and her mother closed the door.

"First of all, don't you ever scream at me like that in front of Lewis again. It upsets him."

'Who cares about stupid Lewis."

"HEY!!!"

"Sorry. But c'mon Mother, you know, I mean you totally really know that what you're doing to me is wrong. Even a scumbag like McGrath knows the truth about my father and I don't?"

"I told you about your father. Will you believe McGrath or me?"

"Well…. I'd never believe him over you. But you're NOT telling me the truth are you?"

"I…" and her mother put her hand to her forehead and sat heavily on the bed. "I think," she continued, "I think I'm telling you the truth. I really believe your father died shortly after you were born."

"What do you mean you *believe* that? Don't you know for sure, didn't you have a funeral? Where was he?"

"Well, I guess I'm going to have to tell you the whole story, now. You're definitely old enough, mature enough, and smart enough to hear the whole story. I knew this day would come, but I guess I didn't expect it now and so soon."

"Okay," Dee Dee began, "but now you're making me nervous. What is 'The Whole Story'?"

"Well, I'll tell you what. I need to collect my thoughts, and I need to get something from the safe deposit box and I need to really think about how to explain everything to you. So why don't you relax this afternoon, forget about that…. McGrath, and tonight you and I will go out to eat someplace nice, and I'll explain the whole thing to you. Would that be okay? Do you think you can wait that long?"

"Well, yeah. But now I'm going to be really curious for the rest of the day." Dee Dee frowned anxiously.

"Don't worry honey." She patted Dee Dee's knee. "We'll be fine no matter what. I've got to go make Lewis his lunch. You just relax and I'll take care of it."

"Okay."

And Dee Dee lay back in her bed and tried to plan what would be the best way to spend an afternoon while she waited to find out who she really was and the whole story behind her birth, her parentage, and her heritage. She thought about her mother, who had suddenly become three and even four dimensional even though she had tried for many years to just play the role of mother to Dee Dee and to pretend at the same time with her daughter that the rest of her life had not really existed or been important in any way. Dee Dee had her first glimmering that perhaps her mother was a complete person, and perhaps could be seen with some kind of compassion after all. Dee Dee was beginning to grow up and her stomach hurt and kept fluttering the rest of the afternoon, no matter what she did to occupy her time. She went to the chat rooms looking for entertainment. The people in her favorite poetry chat room wanted to talk about slams and raves and she couldn't get into it and signed off. Finally, emotionally exhausted, she lapsed into a deep dreamy sleep. The sun crossed her face and moved over the bed as the day wore on.

Chapter 13

Drood had managed to get a seat away from Muke on the plane back and he was delighted that they were actually going to get back to Syracuse by Saturday afternoon. He'd be tired, but he'd be able to meet with the boy after all and find out what had been going on. Drood pictured the boy's impatience and intelligence and smiled. He wondered if that's what he had been like as a young man. Then he thought again about his never-to-be-known daughter. What would she be like? Deirdre. Deirdre of the myth, Deirdre of the sorrows, condemned to love the wrong man all her life and to be punished in the most brutal ways because of it. What had possessed him to insist on naming her that? He couldn't even remember what the impulse or the reasoning had been. That was back when he believed in Gods. Was there some God he was trying to please back then? Drood thought again about Mannanan and got that feeling in his stomach again, the hard knot, and he was surprised at how much he could hate a god in whom he did not believe. His relationship with Mannanan was much deeper than simple belief or disbelief.

His daughter would be a young woman by now. He had missed her entire childhood and his heart quietly broke again. "When will I quit this life, finally?" he thought again. "How have I been able to stand it for so long?" He didn't want to go down that lane again, so he ordered a drink from the flight attendant, though it was early in the day, and decided instead to try to imagine what she looked like and what she was doing now.

She would probably be tall and she would definitely have blue eyes. She would have inherited both her mother and father's gravity and intelligence, but what else? What would be the things in her DNA and her upbringing that would mark her as different from her parents? Those were the important things with each generation, not the similarities. Maybe she'd be more raucous and outgoing. In that case she'd have a tough struggle with Claire. In fact, as he thought about it, no matter what she was like she would have a tough struggle with Claire. He pictured Claire's stern, unforgiving glare when things weren't going exactly the way she thought they should go. The girl would grow up tough and straight under that influence, Drood was sure. So she'd be tough, smart, and tall. "That's good," he thought, and he tried to picture her face, tried putting parts of his face together with parts of Claire's face. He knew he himself was very Irish looking, with the fair skin, the blue eyes, the high forehead, the prominent nose, and the wiseacre side-of-the-mouth talking mug. And Claire had those perfect made-for-TV looks, nothing uneven or out of place anywhere, pure and straight beauty. He wondered if the girl would have her mother's eyes or his own. Claire's were perfectly round and Drood's were slanted and had a perpetual smiling-look.

Drood got home finally, and took a nap before going to the factory to talk to Tag. After the searing sunshine of southern California, the cold gray sky of Syracuse was a relief and Drood was glad when he woke up and it was snowing outside again. They were big, heavy, wet flakes and they would accumulate quickly. Drood considered walking through the main drag of Eastwood to get to the factory. It was dinnertime on a Saturday. There wouldn't be that many people out, especially with the snow coming down hard. Drood decided to walk it.

As he crossed the street at the little island where Grant came into James, Drood wondered how Tag got to and from school. He wondered about Tag's mother and about how the boy had lived until now. As he understood it, the mother was under duress from several addictions and a string of bad relationships, but he must have gotten something from his mother, because his gifts, his intelligence and his sensitivity, were still so close to the surface. Drood could see them. They had not yet been completely submerged or drowned. Drood passed the first of the stores on Main Street in Eastwood. A long time ago Eastwood had been its own little town, but now it was just another little section of the city. The Syracuse Nationals, an NBA basketball team and NBA champion in the 1950's had been headquartered here in tiny little Eastwood, back in the heyday of Syracuse, when unions and manufacturing companies pulled a lot of people into the area. Eastwood had seen better days, Drood decided, as he passed two boarded up storefronts. Tax preparers, clothing store, pizza place, appliance repair. It was all the same in Syracuse.

122

Behind the main drag were all the 1920's houses that filled the rest of the city. Bowling alley, pool hall, gas station, pizza parlor. The snow was thick in Drood's uncovered hair and he felt the melt running down his neck and over his back and his chest. Just this morning he had been in the West Coast sun and the smog. It was a miracle world.

Drood was cold and wet and he began to feel annoyed by it until he realized he was suffering and, by reflex after years of training, he confronted and accepted his suffering. He turned that little switch in his head that subtracted all the unpleasantness from the cold and the wet and turned them into just more sensations for his mind to take note of. He would have to teach detachment to the boy as well. Drood's experience and his reading told him that all systems of belief and all mystics and ascetics in all faiths and cultures around the world taught the same detachment from the body and from pain that he himself had learned to do. Physical pain was merely one sensation among many, but suffering was entirely optional. Drood had fought that for a long time as well.

Drood's mind went back in time.

"How can you ignore what is happening to your body?" he had challenged his teacher.

"How is simple. You just make up your mind to do it and it's done. It's knowing when to do it that is the trick. When you believe all that is going on around you and allow the events and objects and people to tell you how to think and feel, then you have missed your opportunity to detach yourself from your body and to observe the world. It is observation and perception that are the keys to all the skills I am teaching you. And observation and perception must be done and achieved at all times in all circumstances, regardless of difficulties. This is why we meditate, to understand this. To achieve detachment and to be witness. It will help you with your songs and poems. It will help you with your chief; it will always help you. You must learn this detachment."

Back in Syracuse, as Drood finally turned on Midler to head down towards the old factory, he remembered how he had paid lip service to his teacher, but how he had really not understood and had been unable to proceed with that part of the teaching. Although Drood had been accepted into the Brotherhood, his teacher had acceded to it with misgivings. Drood had never completely finished the training and only he and his teacher had known it. Walking through the blinding, heavy snow in Syracuse on a Saturday night, he smiled and wondered if anybody ever really completed the training, or if it was just a way of getting the most out of you, setting the ideal beyond grasp. And once again, he realized, he had come to the crux of his problem, then and now, and everywhere and every when in between: his inability to fully give himself over to belief. It caused him to always have doubt. During all he had achieved in Ireland, during all he had done in New York, and even today in Syracuse it was causing most of his misery. Doubt, skepticism, and fear. He stopped at the entrance to the parking lot of the old factory and stared at it again, the crumbling red brick now draped with big wet slabs of snow and he realized that facing his doubt and fear was the chore of his life. This time with the boy would be his last chance. It was not a rational conclusion that he had arrived at by linear thinking. It came on him all at once as an accretion of all his previous experience, and his unhappy, random wet, gray thoughts. All had coalesced suddenly to form a clear picture for Drood of what had been so elusive and confusing for him throughout his miserable haunted, tormented existence. It was his doubt and his disbelief that had to be conquered. And how in the name of all that had gone before was he going to do that? He didn't even know what he didn't believe anymore. There was not even any brick wall or backdrop against which he could fling himself to destruction in his attempts to rebel. Drood was baffled and felt raw as though something had been once again taken away from him. He had wakened several times into a different life and this rawness was a similar feeling. Nerves, terror, torment, and weakness.

Something was happening inside him, and yet, he was still standing in the parking lot of the old factory. He hadn't come to in a bed, locked up, or in a rowboat. There was not a strange shore in front of him. He had awakened this time without any dramatic change from what had been. There was the lone street light above him, turning the snow pink as it drifted into and then out of the light. There was the gate where Tag would come through. A car slid through the slush on Midler behind him. Drood was suddenly elated at having a monumental change occur inside him that was not at the same time mirrored by a complete shift in his world. Did this mean he was growing? Did this mean he was going to be better, a real person, finally? Drood walked like one in a trance toward the side entrance of the old factory. The world was absolutely silent.

Fatigue struck him hard as he picked his way around the heaps of junk and stepped over the puddles and ducked under the pipes. He looked into the cold wet gloom and decided he'd be better off by a fireplace with a book. Where was his detachment now? He chuckled. He sat on the brick wall where he and Tag had last talked and closed his eyes and waited. Soon, he heard stamping feet by the door.

The boy looked directly at Drood as he came through the wasted interior of the factory. He kept looking at the older man as he approached and he appeared to be on the verge of speech. Drood was hopeful that the boy's enthusiasm could carry the conversation because he just didn't have it in him. His eyelids were sore, his neck hurt, and he felt heavy. Like carrying around a painful sack of cement. Tag hopped up on to the brick wall next to his teacher.

"It worked. All the stuff you told me worked."

"Which stuff," Drood replied, "the safety tips, or the long-term discipline training?"

"Both. I can't stop thinking about my pool and my house in L.A. It makes me happy all the time. And I've been able to get away from Loomis and his crew." Tag went into further detail about his escapes and about his lack of eye contact and his approaches toward Loomis. He explained how he really thought the whole thing was going to work, and he wanted to hear more, he wanted to know everything Drood could tell him.

"Well," Drood hesitated, "I'm an old man compared to you, there's an awful lot I could teach you. I really don't know where to begin. I was thinking we could focus on poker and how to deal with people for now, and not worry about the rest. There are things you will pick up along the way that will be useful, and you'll learn all kinds of stuff on your own. But I guess there are things we can start with."

"I want to stop Loomis completely. I can't take it anymore. I gotta do something."

"Good," Drood said and he hunched against the wall. He knew the boy's enthusiasm would fade eventually, but they should make the most of his first success and the coming to life of his spirit. They should go for everything while he was on top. Drood felt a little refreshed and paused in silence to sit next to the boy's energy and let it soak in. Tag twitched and fidgeted and Drood listened and felt it all with the sensors in his skin and it woke him up and relieved his exhaustion. Even his eyelids didn't hurt anymore. They sat in silence for a few more moments and then Tag turned and looked directly at Drood without saying anything. He was waiting.

"Well then you have to go after him. Remaining anonymous, of course, is always the best option. Unless you want him to know who it is that did it to you?"

"I'm afraid for him to know I'm getting him. But isn't it kind of wimpy and sleazy to get at somebody without them knowing it's you?"

"What is he doing to you? Is there anything honorable or fair about that? Do you hold any cards that make the game a fair game or is the deck stacked against you?"

Tag considered for a moment. Before he could reply, Drood continued, "Any time you worry about what you are doing, think about what has been done to you and what will be done to you if you don't do something. You don't have to go as far as seriously damaging him if you like, but he's made the choices to get him where he is, he's taken advantage of weakness, and you can give yourself the right to strike back, if you like. Higher morality in many religious systems calls for no retaliation of any kind, but then again there are all kinds of religious persecution and oppression in all systems throughout the world, so why accept their morality that ensures passive weakness?" Drood didn't want to get on a soap box here, but sometimes he felt he might be the only person in the world who knew about a time before all these religions started, a world where religions were more earthen, more brutal, and more honest.

Tag smiled. He stammered, "I guess, that sounds right. It's just not...I'm not used to thinking like that."

"Of course not, you're used to thinking like a victim. That is what you have been taught because you are young and lacking experience and skills and they can get away with teaching you that. Do you want to always be a victim?"

"Hell no. But I don't want to be an outlaw and a savage either!"

"Do you think those are the only two choices, victim or outlaw?"

Tag had no response to that.

"Why don't we put philosophy aside for a while, and give you some time to get used to thinking in new ways. Just remember that what I tell you has to work for you. If it doesn't work, it doesn't matter. You said that so far it's working. Let's continue. Let's make the next plan."

"O.K." said Tag. And he kicked his legs a couple of times. He appeared to be not quite as energetic, but still alert.

"Okay. The best place to trap these kids is at school. They're already half trapped there and that is one of the causes of the problem. Get them out of school and you decrease your exposure. They'll fall out of your life pretty quickly after that. So, what gets kids out of school?"

"Weapons. Hard drugs."

"So?"

"I already know that Loomis carries a knife and probably keeps it in his locker. I could turn him in."

"How do you do that without getting caught?"

"A letter? Maybe a phone call?"

"Try both. I'll write the letter with adult handwriting that can't be traced to a parent. You make the phone call from a pay phone. Don't let anybody see you. It's that simple."

Tag shrugged. Kind of anticlimactic, he thought. He could have done that himself a long time ago, but he was afraid he'd get found out and get in terrible trouble. He was also a little skeptical that it would actually work, but Drood had been right so far. He shot Drood a frown and Drood smiled back at him.

"You have a strong conscience Tag and all this stuff seems wrong to you. Let me ask you again, does the boy have a weapon and has he threatened you with it? Do you believe he might use it some day? Is it against the school rules and against the rules of this society?"

"Yes."

"You are only taking steps to protect yourself and others. We will make sure it doesn't get traced back to you. There are plenty of people who know about that knife. If it doesn't work, we will have at least increased the pressure and there are many other things we can try. In the meantime, keep avoiding eye contact while getting close to him when it's safe. Keep observing him. Get him out and the other two won't have the pure evil that it would take to keep up his work. Trust me. I know this."

"O.K."

"Now, take these books, and start reading them. I've gone through a few of them myself, but they won't do me as much good as they will you."

Tag's eyes went real wide and he grabbed the books and quickly scanned through them. Drood believed he would have sat right there in the filthy wet factory and tried to read them by the faint light from the street lamp if Drood didn't have more to tell him. He told Tag about his trip to L.A. and what he had seen there and he told him everything he could remember about the poker game and his discussion with the old-timer. He figured to be traveling to that office again in the future and he told Tag he would do research on specific questions that Tag might have when he went.

"When do you have to return these books?" Tag asked.

"I bought 'em. They're for you. To keep." Drood grinned.

Tag was frozen and speechless with a stunned, wide-eyed look of terror on his face. He'd never known anyone that actually bought books.

"But...I didn't.... I can't pay... why did you do that? And why would you spend money at a poker game for me?" Tag's eyes narrowed, serious and hard with suspicion. Drood feared he might run. Drood sighed and considered carefully what he should say.

"You probably have no experience of this and will have a hard time believing it. But when someone decides to teach someone or train someone, they have to put in a great deal of effort, risk, and resources. If they really mean to do it right. And what the teacher receives in return is the effort and the knowledge of the achievement of the student. That's it. I know it's almost never done that way in your world, but that is the way it used to be and the way it ought to be. I want nothing from you but the satisfaction of your success. Really."

Tag looked somewhat mollified, this was not the way grownups operated and he still found it impossible to believe. When would the other shoe drop? When would Drood reveal himself to be a pervert, or a criminal who was looking to use someone, or mentally ill, or just someone who got violent when you didn't do what they wanted? He held the books in his hands and walked in a slow

128

meandering path around the factory. Drood stayed on the brick wall with his head hanging down.

A loud bang announced Tom opening the workshop and Tag looked over his shoulder at Drood. Drood's head raised and looked toward the open end of the clubhouse. He slowly lifted himself by his hands off the brick wall and looked at Tag.

"I'll be back in a little while," Tag said, "I gotta take a leak. I'm gonna leave the books out here for now." He didn't want Shiny pawing through them and making fun of him or asking Drood why he would spend so much money on books for a kid he didn't even know.

Drood walked away and Tag put the books down on an old washing machine. Tag wandered through the factory complex in the dark. He had to calm down before he went into the gathering of poker playing men. He crouched and scooted under a giant duct that had collapsed from the ceiling and found a little door on the wall furthest from Tom's workshop. He had never noticed the door before. It was blocked from view by the twisted and crumpled ductwork. The door was ajar and Tag pushed it a little and went through. It was pitch black inside, so he waited a minute for his eyes to adjust. To his surprise, there were two staircases, one going up and one going down. The staircase going up was open, but the staircase going down had piles of wood stacked on the steps and there were boards leaning over the entrance to it. It was stuffed full of junk. In the gloom, Tag could just make out the stairwell at the bottom and he could see more boards sticking out from what must have been another set of stairs below. "Must be packed all the way down, but that meant there must be a basement here. That would be odd for a factory wouldn't it?" he wondered. Maybe some time he'd climb over all this stuff and move some of it and see what was down there. Something told him there was something important to be found down there in the gloom.

He turned his attention to the stairs going up and tried putting his weight on the steps. It seemed to be okay and so he clambered up the metal steps to the door at the top. It was a metal door painted red. It was bolted and padlocked. He was about to turn around to go back to the poker game, when his hand brushed the padlock and it swung away from the door. The screws in the hinge for the padlock were gone. Someone must have done that on purpose. He pulled the bolt and pushed on the door. It wouldn't give, so he pushed his shoulder hard into the door and it swung open a few inches. Cold, wet air streamed over his face. He stepped back and rammed the door with his shoulder and it opened enough to let him step out.

Tag stepped out into the snowy night and steadied himself. He was astonished to find that outside the door he was close to the roof edge and there was no railing. He looked around and saw the vast reaches of the factory roof, covered with an untouched blanket of snow. He saw dark swirls that were holes in the snow and he surmised that crossing it would be like crossing a glacier, like he had seen on TV one time, with dangerous crevasses everywhere, but lots of open space and beautiful white fields and formations. Tag was excited by his discovery. A private place to be alone. There was a pile of old beer bottles and cigarette butts next to the door. Somebody, years before, had come up here to drink and smoke. A lonely sentinel. Tag claimed this place as his own and resolved to come back soon.

Drood and Tag both cleaned up that night at the table. Tag actually had a stake now every time he came to play and he never went home completely broke, as Shiny often did, and Tom sometimes. As he stooped through the hole in the fence he wanted to take credit for his luck, to believe that he and Drood were on the right path of learning how to win at poker, but he couldn't trick himself. He had to remind himself that the cards had been lucky and that they could turn against him at any time.

Chapter 14

Finally, they were at a table at Mojumbo's, the only Ethiopian-Cuban-Mexican-American restaurant in Manhattan that also served sushi. The waitress brought her mother a Manhattan and Dee Dee had a gigantic round goblet of fruit punch and her mouth was watering to try it. As the waitress disappeared, Dee Dee sucked on the straw and took a huge mouthful of liquid, sucked it down, and kept going; getting the sugar into her as quickly as she could. It wasn't chocolate, but it was close enough. She needed it. She had sworn to herself that she would let her mother tell the story her own way, but she couldn't contain herself.

"So is he dead or isn't he?"

Her mother sighed and sat back in her chair and held her glass to her lips and just kept it there. Claire seemed to be savoring the feel of the glass against her lip, or perhaps she was enjoying the sweet chemical aroma of the alcohol. Dee Dee tried to force herself to keep her mouth shut. Her mother was finally going to talk and she didn't want to push her but she couldn't help it. When she wanted to know something, she wanted to know it.

"I don't know for sure that he is dead, but I believe he is."

"Why?"

"It's a really long story and I'm not sure where to begin. But let me tell you a little about your father."

Dee Dee sat back and folded her arms. She was really scared. The phantom was about to become real and her eagerness suddenly changed to near panic. She forced herself to be calm, but she could hardly breathe. She finished off her juice and leaned forward again. Her mother leaned forward also and continued.

"Your father and I met at a party, but he had known who I was for a couple of years before that. Apparently, he had caught sight of me at the public library and had spent two years trying to find out who I was and how to get to know me. When he first saw me, he had just come to New York from Ireland with a friend of his, and he didn't have a job or anything. By the time we met, he was in the management of XBC."

"Wow," Dee Dee said. That was something! And apparently it was only the beginning of the story.

"After a brief courtship," (Dee Dee noted the flush of pleasure in her mother's cheeks,) "your father and I were married and were pretty happy for about two years." Claire paused to take a sip of her drink.

"Right around the time I got pregnant with you, something happened to him and he began to change. I'd catch him staring out windows all the time, and he didn't even hear me when I spoke to him. He started getting secretive phone calls and he'd have to go out late at night. He told me they were having problems at the office and I sort of believed him, and I sort of didn't."

The waitress interrupted them and Claire fussed about her order, while Dee Dee ordered the first thing her eye caught on the menu. Finally she was gone and Claire went back to telling the story.

"Well, it turned out that his friend, the one he came over from Ireland with, had risen through the ranks of the Irish mafia down in Hell's Kitchen. He was threatening and extorting your father and your father was going along with it. In effect, your father was part of the Irish mob at the same time he was becoming an executive in XBC." Claire noticed Dee Dee's frozen incredulity. "I know," she continued, "but that's not even really the weird part of the story. Well, while you were busy being born in the hospital..." Here Claire paused to give her daughter a maternal, loving smile. Dee Dee quickly smirked to get it over with and Claire continued. "While you were busy being born, your father's friend was arrested for murder. It was very alarming. Now remember, at this time, I had no idea your father was involved with him to any great extent. So anyway, the police came to our apartment when your father was out and started asking me a bunch of questions about your father's whereabouts on certain dates and what was his connection to the mobster and things like that. I thought they were doing background checks, you know just trying to build a better case against the mobster. I later put two and two together and realized that many of the times they asked me about were times that your father had been called away in the middle of the night. I told them he knew the mobster from the old country and that they had lunch together once in a while, but that was it." She paused to drink more.

"Well, a smart reporter broke the story ahead of the police that your father was a suspect. They said that he had betrayed the mobster and turned him over to the police in exchange for money. They said the police were looking for your father. And that was the last I ever saw of your father. He tried to talk to me now and then on the phone, but the whole thing was such a shock, such an awful disgraceful surprise to me, that I handled it badly. I shut him out. I couldn't believe he had done all they said he had done. I felt like he wasn't the person I thought he was. I was very angry. And I still haven't gotten to the really weird part of it yet, the part that nobody but me knows about." She looked down. "It's disturbing."

"Well, did they ever catch him? The police, I mean?"

"No. Disappeared without a trace. For a while they would find clues and signs that he had been places like Long Island and New England, but then he just vanished off the face of the earth. That was ten years ago, nobody's seen hide nor hair of him since. The last place he was, they found a sort of a rambling, incoherent suicide note from somebody that could have been him, but they've never found his body or any evidence."

"Oh my god." Dee Dee didn't know what to think. She was overwhelmed and just sat staring at her mother. The food came and she didn't even glance at it, she just trembled and stared. My father: Irish Mafia, executive, fugitive, and suicide? Jesus, no wonder she didn't want to tell me all that. And this is not the weird part? What else could there be? She wondered.

"Eat, Dee Dee. I need to take a rest. I'll tell you more after we eat a little bit."

"Uhhuh" she said, in a trance. She picked up her utensils with hands that couldn't feel them. She cut the steak and put pieces in her mouth and chewed, but she didn't taste anything. She waited and watched her mother. What must her mother have put up with in her life? What pain it must have been for her to try not to tell her daughter all this. And this saga was followed closely by McGrath? Why had she told McGrath the story? Or did McGrath know on his own? Dee Dee suddenly was coming back into herself and she had sixteen thousand questions, at least.

"O.K. Mom." She rarely used the familiar address, but she thought she'd probably use it all the time now. This dinner, this conversation changed everything. "O.K., so now you have to tell me what the weird part is. I don't think I can stand to hear you say one more time that that's not the weird part."

Claire smiled and set down her utensils. It was a fake, trying-to-keep-a-grip smile.

"Well, after your father disappeared, I did a bunch of things to get over it. I changed our names, I cleaned out his stuff, I wanted him gone with a vengeance. I did love him, but…" and she paused and her eyes teared. "Anyway, one of the things I had to do was get the contents of the safe deposit box from the bank. I did." And she pulled from her pocket a crumpled and folded typewritten letter.

"And this was in the box. I think it proves he was mentally ill. I didn't know. I had no way of knowing."

Dee Dee took the letter and held it in front of her. She didn't know what to think or what to do. Now, a communication from the father that had been hidden from her for so long. In his own words? She trembled and looked down. Her stomach hurt. She placed it carefully beside her plate and took a long sip of water. She looked at her mother. Her mother looked spent. Claire picked at her food and looked very much older than she had been when they sat down. The wrinkles around her eyes seemed darker and more pronounced, her posture was worse and she seemed to have lost some color. Dee Dee noticed she had a couple of age spots on her temple.

"I don't know what to do. Should I read it now?"

"Yes. Or maybe wait at least until you finish eating."

Dee Dee watched her mother for a moment and then stared at the writing showing through the outside of the letter. It was a treasure beyond belief and she couldn't bring herself to look, to expose herself, to change everything. Her father was mentally ill, a mobster, an executive, a fugitive, what else? What could be so weird about this letter? She held herself in suspense and forced herself to focus on her meal. She ate slowly at first and then quickly as her senses came flooding back to her and with joy she woke up to the meal, to her mother's love and sorrow, to the passion in all the people surrounding her in the restaurant, to herself and her own future and her potential.

Dee Dee was about to give birth to a father, a real person, one that would probably cause her pain, an interesting person clearly, a difficult person. She felt all the expectation and anticipatory pleasure of a soon-to-be mother. As she ate and drank and took in everything around her with suddenly voracious eyes, she concluded that any father, even a notorious or infamous one, was better than a phantom or a shadow. She almost couldn't contain the strange tingling, bursting, painful pleasure she felt inside her. As she finished cleaning her plate, she noticed her mother staring at her quizzically.

"It's not a happy story, is it?" her mother asked.

"No. It must have been awful. And frightening. And sad," Dee Dee responded.

"Yes. I still don't know what to make of it all. And you'll know what I mean when you read the letter."

Dee Dee patted the letter. A thought occurred to her.

"Would you mind terribly if I didn't read it just now, but carried it around with me for a while? I want to think about it and get used to the idea before I read it."

"Well. Okay. Let me make a copy though. I don't want it lost."

Dee Dee nodded. Correspondence from her father. It would be her lucky rabbit's foot. She would carry it with her everywhere she went and touch it once in a while so she would be able to draw strength from it. Because of this letter she was going to become a whole person with two parents. That was the power and magic in the piece of paper. She had a spasm of fear in her stomach, that the letter would hurt her or somehow make her worse, but her mind came back and reassured her. "Any father is better than no father. And if he was dead, it's not like he would be influencing me, I'll just be filling in my past, not my present or future. I'm safe," she told herself.

Claire and Dee Dee ordered dessert, coming at relief and pleasure from two different angles: one of long-contained pain and anger being eased, the other from an entire lifetime of uncertainty and need that was about to be fulfilled.

Dee Dee spent the next several weeks in a daze as the weather turned warm and spring finally made its way down through the crevices and alleys into the ground of Manhattan. She fondled

135

the letter and forgot about her studies and she looked like any other fourteen year old in love, only she was in love with possibility and redemption, not with some awkward, aggressive, confused boy, but with the whole world. She took a walk down Park Avenue to Grand Central, but she walked on the edges of the medians, looking at all the beautiful tulips in bloom and barely noticing the cars soaring past, inches from her legs. When she did notice them it was nothing but the pleasant sensation of wind and a humming and the honks of horns sounded funny and irreverent, rather than impatient and angry as they usually did.

The people walking the streets of the city all seemed to her to be earnest and decent people, deep down. She noticed everything and everyone as she rode the subway and for once she enjoyed watching people.

Her mother didn't know what to make of her new attitude. Claire was terrified that she had created a strange hope or expectation in the girl and that when Dee Dee read the letter she'd be very disappointed. Claire considered that she would instantly know when her daughter had read the letter by the look on her face. After the first week she began to get a little amused at the dreaminess of Dee Dee, but by the third week she was beginning to become alarmed. She tried a couple of times to reason with her, but it was not going to happen. She gave up; she would be there to help if it all got out of hand.

Dee Dee tried to explain her feelings to Rebecca, but Rebecca just wanted her to read the letter, she wanted to know what the father had said, what he was like. Dee Dee was in no hurry; she had waited all this time. The end of the school year was coming, and she would be going out to Iowa, and that meant really the end of her life here in New York. She'd be living at St. Andrew's in Philadelphia. She calculated and decided that she'd read the letter the weekend before she left for her grandparent's house. She'd save it until the last minute and then leave her mother and almost all of her old life behind in one big flourish. It seemed appropriate to her to start her new life with a new outlook; with words from a father she had never heard from, spoken to, or seen.

She held on, while her mother watched and hovered and Rebecca pestered. Finally, the last weekend was there and it was time to read the letter. The paper had quite a bit of grime on it now, from constant handling and as she had unconsciously planned it, her curiosity had grown, and the letter's magic power had worn off and it was time to read the darn thing. Still, she wanted to do it right and she wanted to be careful. She was very afraid of spoiling something, of jinxing it, of somehow making a mistake. She would only get to meet her father for the first time once, everything after that would be reacquaintance. She thought about the best way to manage it, to set it all up and thought about what rituals were important to her. She finally decided on a plan and she told it to Rebecca and her mother, who were both disappointed that the plan didn't involve more participation or presence from them.

For a few years Dee Dee and her mother had attended mass regularly at St. Patrick's Cathedral. It was out of the way for them, and neither of them had been baptized or spent much time being Catholic, but they loved the old church and the plaza surrounding it. It did strike them as a holy place, THE holy place, in the middle of all those commercial buildings and tourist trap shopping venues. They liked to sit on the sidewalk outside the church after the sermon and talk over things about God. Dee Dee's plan was to go to confession on Saturday afternoon, stay for the mass, and then sit on the sidewalk afterward and read the letter. She felt this would get her in the proper frame of mind, would calm her down, make her feel small and protected and safe, and give her the right humility and balance with which to begin her new life. She didn't tell her mother and Rebecca that it would be the beginning of a new life, because she didn't want to alarm them or have them suffer or pester or hover, but she knew. She had a certainty deep in her that this was the initiation, the first step of her life as an adult, and unlike 99.99% of humans on the planet, she was fully aware of it as it was happening, she was prepared for it, and she wanted to take charge of the giant leap into adulthood. Nothing haphazard about it.

Dee Dee went through the giant wooden doors that were chained back with metal bolts to keep them open for the tourists and the worshippers. It was just four o'clock and she could see one line of penitents on the other side of the columns, by the edge of the pews. They were lined up for two confessional boxes and it was dark inside although it was bright outside. The votive candles in their little red jars flickered all along the sides of the church. Blue, red, yellow, and green light streamed in from the glorious stained glass overhead. Dee Dee breathed deep and caught a whiff of incense, some candle smoke, and the odor of floor wax or maybe it was wood polish. She began to relax right away and she tried to hold still in the vestibule for a few moments and soak in the serenity. She never thought about religion or theology or Jesus Christ or the Gospel and all that when she was in a church, she just felt the peace and the joy of God. She sometimes wished only she herself were allowed in churches.

Dee Dee finally took her place at the end of the line and watched the people in front of her. There were three young women, maybe in their twenties or thirties, and the rest were much older men and women. The penitents were silent with their sins and they waited patiently and did not speak to each other. This was a serious matter. Dee Dee wondered what their sins might be, these staid and solemn mumblers. They didn't look like they had enough life in them to cause any harm. She mused that maybe only the people who didn't need it were really religious. After a short time, it was her turn and she went in and closed the door. She knelt.

"Bless me father," she had learned to say, "It's been about three months." She could never remember the rest and they never seemed to care.

"Yes," said the old, dry-looking priest through the grate. "And what do you have to confess?"

"I have been selfish. I haven't paid much attention to my mother." Dee Dee was surprised that these words came out of her. She hadn't realized she felt guilty about her relationship with her mother.

"That's very sad. Do you understand how your mother needs you? Are you sorry for the condition you have been in?"

"Yes, I think so."

"Good. God forgives you and I forgive you in his name. To atone, be good and kind to your mother the best you can, for as long as you can. And to think more on what your mother has done for you, say five Hail Mary's today, and each time you feel yourself slipping back into your old attitudes. God bless you my child."

And that was it. Dee Dee was relieved and she felt tears for her mother welling up in her eyes. She went to the altar to release the tears, and she knelt on the cold white marble, ignoring the kneelers and she said her prayers and she cried quietly to herself in the beautiful old church. She got up stiffly and retreated to a pew three quarters of the way to the back and sat down to wait for the five o'clock mass. Most of the other penitents appeared to be staying for mass and she wondered if they all lived in the city. It was not a big residential neighborhood, at least not for the kind of people she saw around her. They looked more working class, old Irish, maybe. They probably came for the same reason she had, attracted by the haven, the rest, and the stately presence of the old place. If you can't get to God through that place, well there's probably no getting there, she thought.

The mass began and she stood and she kneeled and she sat and she stood and she muttered the prayers, and the longer the mass went, the older she felt. Something in her spirit tuned in with the other worshippers, with the old cathedral, with the ancient rituals. And in her pocket she had an old letter from the father from out of time. And she was on the verge of growing up. It all fit together and Dee Dee felt peaceful and she felt reverent. Life made sense to her and she made sense to herself and the smells and the lights and the rituals made sense to her and she knew everything was going to be okay. She didn't understand the sermon, it was something about charity, she guessed, but that was okay too. She didn't take communion but she watched with fascination as the old folks filed to the front, and then returned quietly and seriously back to their seats. Their faces were like stone, their motions were those of people in a trance and Dee Dee felt great love toward them. Their gentle piety moved her.

As the mass ended and the loud and weirdly angry organ music tormented them and they shuffled out of the church, Dee Dee slipped into the center aisle among the other people. She noted that the young women who had been ahead of her in line for confession were long gone and it was just herself and the ancients. She walked with her head down - eyes on the floor - until they passed the wooden doors again and she found herself in the honks and screeches and exhaust of Manhattan on a warm Saturday night at the beginning of summer. It was time. She looked to the left and the right and saw a corner of the steps where they curved away from Fifth Avenue and it seemed like a good spot to be alone but safe. Out of the way of pedestrians, off the road, but not out of sight enough to be dangerously isolated. She sat down on a step, put her back against a higher step, stretched her legs out in front of her and crossed them, and pulled the letter from her pocket.

The letter read:

"Dear Claire,

I don't know when you are reading this or under what circumstances, but I know what I say will come as a shock to you. You have been the best wife, and I love you completely, as you know. But you do not really know who I am, and I have taken no steps to show you and have gone to no little trouble to keep from you who I am.

Please remember me as you have known me. Do it now. Fix it in your mind, because what you have known has been as honestly me as there is any truth in the world. My wants, my desires, my failings, these you have known, and they have all been real. They have all been mine, not somebody else's.

But there is more. I have training that you do not know about; I have a history you do not know about. Do you remember all the times I explained the movements of the clouds and the wind to you? Do you remember what I told you about the trees when we were camping upstate? Have you ever noticed how I know what people are thinking? Have you ever wondered about my strange perspective on things, how I stand apart from life and look at things as if I came from somewhere else? There is a reason for all these things. My moods. My daydreaming. It made you curious. Did you ever wonder why I questioned you in detail about the dreams you had? Did you ever see me mumbling to myself? Did you ever see me looking strangely at trees, at people? Did you ever wonder why I started and stared at ordinary things people said or at clouds or birds? There is a reason for all this. I know you have wondered about my friend Kilty, why he is my friend, why he is still my friend, why I let him tell me what to do when there is no one else I allow to have so much influence over me.

Well, I have put this off as long as I can. I may even be dead as you are reading this, in which case you will hate me for keeping this from you. But I will ask you again to keep me, the me you know, with you, because it has been the best part of my life, and all that I could ever have wanted out of life, you have given me. So. Here it is.

Kilty and I were born in Ireland some time between the years 500 a.d. and 550 a.d. We don't know exactly when because we didn't keep a Christian calendar then. I later traced the dates by the fact that we had heard of the saint Patricius, but had not heard of Columcille.

Kilty was the son of a chieftain and became a chieftain himself. I was the son of nobody, I never knew my parents, but I was raised in Kilty's clan, with my brother. Because of natural intelligence and some favorable signs from the Gods, I entered into training to become a Druid, priest, judge, and teacher.

At the age of 35, Kilty and I left the mainland in a small curragh for what are now called the Aran Islands off the west coast of Ireland. We were going there to seek counsel with my former teacher Mylvwyn and to rest and hide temporarily from the Ulstermen with whom we had been having constant troubles. As we rowed toward the great rock, a wind rose up and a squall followed shortly after. We were driven south at a rapid pace and soon found ourselves adrift in the wild Atlantic. I don't know how many days we were at sea, but we were near dead when we finally spied land.

And what else can I tell you? It was Long Island, 1990 when we landed. In the years since, Kilty and I have built new lives and new identities. But he is still my king and I am bound to obey him.

Having read this, you will surely think I was mad or am mad. And I can offer you nothing as proof; if I were telling a story or having a joke with you I can not even give a good reason for it. But I want you to think about me as you have known me, and until the time you are reading this have you seen anything in me to suggest madness? Anything to suggest a warped personality, or a significant change in my character? No. You have not. So I can offer you nothing except this as an explanation. It makes as little sense to Kilty and me as it does to you. We cannot explain it nor can we change it. For years we tried to think of some way to reverse it. Kilty still does, I think. He sees this world as temporary and refers everything in it to our home in Ireland. I gave that up the day I saw you in front of the library. You have been the ultimate achievement of my life. When I first made love to you, I knew I was done forever with what had gone before, and I resolved to become a man of this time.

But Kilty is still my chief, and he is becoming insistent that I obey him and help him with his plans. And this is causing me heartache. I feel as though I am being forced to choose between this life and the old one. And I have already made my choice. So, for now, I will try to blend the two, and keep them separate and yet both real.

As you read this, many things will undoubtedly have happened. I do not know where Kilty's plans will have taken me. But, if it has to come down to it, you will have no doubt as to what my choice has been. My actions will have shown you where I stand. And you will know that I love you more than I have loved anyone. I don't expect you to understand or believe any of this. But you will know what I have chosen, and you will know what you are to me. That is all that matters to me."

It was signed with an illegible scrawl.

Chapter 15

"Dear Principal Barkley-Jones,

I am a concerned parent who will not sign my name to this letter due to potential repercussions for my child. My child is a student in your school and reports to me that weapons and drugs are regularly seen in the hallways. What kind of a place is that for a kid to grow up and try to learn? My child would not be willing to testify and thus be put in danger, but states clearly that the school has a big problem with it. I demand that you do something. The parents of the school will be getting a clandestine group together to deal with the problem if you don't do something soon, and do it publicly. I can give you one specific example; a student named Timothy Loomis has been seen with a hunting knife in his locker. He has showed it to several students, and has boasted of how he will use it to kill teachers and students. Sorry to be so secretive, but you leave us no other choice."

The phone rang in the principal's secretary's office one week after the letter had been sent. Tag looked at the piece of paper Drood had written out for him. When the secretary answered, Tag spoke softly and quickly:

"Reggie Nickel said he's gonna use Loomis' knife to kill Mr. Edwards, the security guard, tomorrow."

Click. Reggie Nickel was one of Loomis' accomplices. Tag looked over his shoulder, saw that no one in the grocery store had seen him at the phone, and slipped around the corner into the expanding possibility of the afternoon. Hundreds of kids passed the store on their way to and from school and Tag was still a non-descript kid who was getting good at avoiding notice. Drood had also begun to teach him little tricks to keep himself out of the notice of people. Drood's strategies were working: silence, constant

143

movement, meeting all the schedules and assignments in the school. His improvement in attendance and performance over the spring had raised a few eyebrows at first, but it wasn't enough to make him really stand out and wasn't worthy of a call to let his mother know

The campaign against his bullies had been escalated and Loomis and company had begun to find themselves the objects of suspicions by the adults. Somebody was playing tricks on them. Little things, chewed gum stuck in their locker combinations, forged notes to girls from them, and even ink surreptitiously sprayed on their clothes. Some of the other kids seemed to be lipping off to them all of a sudden, and they seemed to be organized about it. The bullies were on the defensive. Tag had been walking a fine line, but he had been very careful and Drood had taught him well. The whole thing hinged on concealment.

Their persecution of Tag had slackened because he was less available to them than before, but they still chased him when they saw him, and over the spring months there had been two more encounters of great threat, but Tag had managed to escape them without physical harm. The campaign was confusing them, introducing self-doubt into their terrorism, and it definitely seemed to be coming from more than one direction at once. Mr. Edwards, the security guard, was on their case now and it was only a matter of time before something happened. Tag had stumbled into the perfect situation by overhearing two kids in the lunchroom repeating what Reggie Nickel had said. Violence against other kids was still tolerated by the adults as "just a part of growing up", but when an adult was threatened, that was a different story. Tag knew that the timing was right. The letter had just been sent last week, and now things would begin to happen quickly. Tag's fear was gone. He knew he had won.

The next day Loomis and Nickel were expelled from the school and reporters came and everyone was all in an uproar. Tag watched the whole scene as just another face in the crowd. Silently, he thanked Drood, who continued to teach him while asking nothing in return. Tag was standing with a couple of other boys during the lunch hour, and they watched as the reporters gathered outside the school. Loomis was gone and the police had come and were now taking Nickel away. Tag believed that whatever the police did with the bullies, of course there would be no real consequences, but they would be out of this school. He kept his fingers crossed that they would never know why. His new friends knew nothing about how the bullies had persecuted Tag. He had been careful not to tell them, on Drood's instructions. When the bell rang, and he meandered toward English class, late for the first time in three months, deliciously late, he realized that he had engineered a justice here. He had taken two people who were doing bad things, and he had gotten them removed. He had created a perception, orchestrated incidents, and he had brought the whole thing to a close, without doing any further damage to himself. He didn't have to fight back directly. There hadn't even been a ripple in the water. This was Tag's first victory in life, his first accomplishment. He knew it would be misunderstood if he shared it with his mother or Charles or if he let anyone in the school know. He would be seen as a sneak and a snitch, but he had no other weapons. He was really trusting Drood here that it was O.K. to do this and he worried briefly that he had done something wrong. But Drood's logic kept coming back at him. No one was going to help him, and direct combat would have been suicide. He did the only smart thing and he had won and now he could turn his attention to other things. He could concentrate on poker, girls, making friends. Maybe he could even learn something in school, while he was there, although he didn't plan to be there much longer. He was almost fifteen now and soon he would be able to drop out and go to L.A. and pursue his dreams. And with a teacher like Drood, he felt that he was going to end up owning the whole world. He couldn't wait to tell Drood what had happened.

* * *

Deirdre had been at her new school in Philadelphia for two weeks already and this was the fifth all-class assembly she had to attend. Dee Dee, who had decided to use her full name, Deirdre, in her new school, didn't think she could make it through another one. She thought, they really go after you here about discipline, about "values", and about teamwork and all that. I get the point, I understand what they mean; can't they move on? She had spent the last assembly thinking about her father and all that her mother had revealed about him before she had left New York. As she slowly mounted the steps to the assembly hall, she sighed and felt the other girls swarming around her. They were chattering and pushing each other. When she was just at the top of the stairs she was shoved roughly into the balustrade and the air went out of her with a rush.

"Hey!" she snarled without thinking.

A beautiful black-haired girl turned and glared icy daggers at her.

"Yeah? You got a problem?" the girl said.

Deirdre just stared in open-mouthed fear until the other girl snorted and whirled away, dismissing Deirdre as so much inarticulate furniture that had gotten in the way. Deirdre sighed again.

The school was very "right" and most of the girls there seemed to know a secret code, expected to be in tune and agree with each other. It was lonely for Deirdre. She noticed there were a few other girls like her, looking doubtful most of the time, spending their free time alone, looking soulful. She wanted to reach out to them, but the "girl system," as she called it, forbade it. She was to suffer by herself and she would only be more scorned if she allied with another outsider. She feared attack. She didn't know what to do. Her mother had called just once and Rebecca had only sent two e-mails. Every moment she was awake there was a deep, hollow pain in her stomach.

Without noticing where she was, she sat in a chair behind the beautiful girl who had elbowed her and listened to the head mistress drone out the introduction to today's speaker: a female CEO on Madison Avenue. Deirdre hoped it wouldn't be four years of this kind of "training". She wanted to be a writer, alone with her thoughts. She knew she wasn't meant to be a CEO or a power driving anything. She didn't want to push anybody, didn't want to fight with people. She wanted to daydream and to think and be able to go and do as she wanted. She couldn't imagine herself being determined enough to fight through obstacles. Fighting through obstacles seemed to be the entire inspirational message the school had for these very well off girls who had so few obstacles compared to the rest of the population of the world. Deirdre considered that you had to fight through obstacles if you wanted to go in a straight line, but what if you wanted to meander around and find things out? Couldn't you just go around obstacles and look somewhere else? She thought of Emily Dickinson becoming a CEO and snorted. The beautiful girl's head turned and glared at her.

146

"Shut up, slut!" The girl hissed at her, and Deirdre was startled. As far as she knew she had done nothing to provoke the girl. She didn't know what to think and looked around her in confusion. Nobody else seemed to be paying any attention.

The speaker went on about her life and herself, and it was pretty clear that the promise and reward of overcoming obstacles was being able to blab to other people about how great you were. Deirdre was turned off and quickly lost focus. She began to daydream about her father again. She could see his face from the one picture her mother had given her and she re-read his letter again in her mind. What would he think of his daughter if he could know her and what would he tell her? She imagined he wouldn't even want her in a place like this. She imagined him taking walks with her in Central Park. He'd be quiet and thoughtful and would listen carefully to her and occasionally say something very gentle and intelligent. He'd always be on her side, no matter what.

The beautiful girl turned around again, although Deirdre was pretty sure she had made no sound or motion. The girl snarled, "We heard all about you, you stuck-up bitch. We're gonna tell everyone about you. You better watch out when you're alone." And she turned her spectacular glossy hair around and her head stayed perfectly still and attentive to the speaker.

Deirdre was again stunned and she didn't know what to do. Why was this girl suddenly persecuting her? She hated this place and the beautiful girl and the lectures and all the rules. She wanted to die. Her mother didn't care about her and Rebecca was gone. There was no one. She felt the tears welling up in her eyes. Why was this girl picking on her? What had she heard, and who was "we"? She clenched her fists in frustration and fantasized about punching the beautiful girl's beautiful head. As she took a deep breath, as quietly as she could, the image of her father from the old photograph came into her view. She imagined him turning to look at her, with deep concern in his face. He spoke to her,

"She's not for real. Ignore her. Some people are for real and are dangerous, some are not. This one is not. Find some friends, do your reading, learn what you want. You'll be okay. You have too much talent and presence not to be noticed and envied. Don't fight back unless you are physically attacked. Let it all go. Girls usually fight with words and words are easy to deal with. This girl has no

147

power in her words. If you pick up the words and carry them with you, she has won. Let them drop and be unconcerned. By not giving her importance you will win this battle. You'll be O.K." And with that speech, the face turned back to its photograph and became two-dimensional again.

Deirdre looked around her in wonder. Was she going mad? A memory of a photograph talking to her? She fumbled in her backpack for the picture. She decided she'd have to have it laminated. She didn't question the advice she had just received, didn't care if it came from her unconscious or somewhere else. She knew the advice was sound the moment she heard it. She thanked him and reminded herself to seek his help again when she needed it.

Deirdre looked at Miss Glossy's head and smiled. She faked a cough, loudly, and when Miss Glossy turned around to glare, Deirdre looked at her with feigned indifference. And then looked away as if she had seen no more than a gnat. Miss Glossy fumed and glared and waited for Deirdre to look at her again, but Deirdre kept her gaze focused on the speaker.

"Hey. I'm talking to you! Bitch!"

Deirdre smiled back at her. Finally, Miss Glossy turned around and folded her arms and breathed hard. The girl passed from Deirdre's consciousness and became a problem no longer. The pain in Deirdre's stomach eased and she caught the eye of another lonely girl. They smiled. She'd introduce herself after the assembly. Deirdre was going to take hold and move forward.

*　*　*

Drood sat on a stone bench and everything around him was lush. There were large gray birds sitting on the branches around him and they sang into the sky. It was dark overhead, but somehow he could still see the outlines of navy blue clouds. They were in a perfectly symmetrical pattern, like wallpaper, and they spread out as far as Drood could see. There were no stars or moon, just navy blue clouds with black space between. In spite of the darkness Drood could see the gray birds clearly. They were about a foot long, with black bills, and their songs were sweet and melodious, burbling into the air like a magic brook. Drood listened in awe, and he wanted to sit there forever, with the marvelous pattern in the sky and the lilting of the birds in his ears. He spread his arms over the back of the bench and leaned back and felt the first peace he could remember ever feeling. His whole body, every muscle, every nerve was loose, and there was a slight rhythm flowing through him each time the breeze blew. As he wondered if the world could get any more perfect, the breeze began to give him at first just a little whiff, and then a little stronger, the sharp and earthy smell of a turf fire, and Drood realized that Ireland still had turf fires in some places.

The stone was cold to his hands, but he relished it. It was a dark wholesome, ancient and immovable cold and he kept his hands on it. Drood was feeling ecstasy; his whole body was in love. He wondered if he had been drugged, but then he didn't care, because now he had a feeling that his life was being given meaning and he was being rewarded for his suffering. He didn't know why and he didn't know how, but Drood knew that this feeling of enchanted peace was in his future again, he was being given a taste of it so that he would know, so that he could keep going. One God, two Gods, a thousand, a cosmic wind, a collective unconscious, whatever it was, it was real. Even if the presence that was creating this moment for him was simply an unconscious conglomeration of all the thoughts and wills of all the infinite numbers of souls that had ever existed, it was still real. And it wanted him to live on.

Drood waited in suspense, all his cells quivering with joyful anticipation when, from the clearing in front of him, a hand brushed away a low-hanging branch from the hoary old oak tree, and a young woman stepped into the clearing. She was unfamiliar to him, but he knew it was his daughter, Deirdre, just like he had known his wife the first time he had seen her. His daughter came further into the clearing without looking at him, and she stopped and appeared to be waiting for something. Drood felt an outpouring of love, and grief, and sorrow, and joy for the young woman. Her beauty, strength and the peace he could read in her eyes stunned him as she gazed quietly at the oak tree on the opposite side of the clearing. Delicious tears ran down his cheeks, and he took a long, loving look at her. She was tall with black hair and sparkling blue eyes. She had a high forehead and a graceful womanly figure, but above all he saw a clear gaze and intelligence and confident presence in the eyes. Though he had given her no teachings she had become everything he would have wished. She was dressed in the tartan drapery of ancient Ireland, and she wore a beautiful gold brooch on her breast. The giant stone in the middle of the brooch looked to be a sapphire and Drood realized if he were given the chance all over again he would name his daughter Sapphire.

Another hand brushed aside a low-hanging branch on the other side of the clearing, and Drood suddenly noticed that the branch was an exact symmetrical copy to the branch his daughter had brushed aside. Before Drood had time to wonder what kind of a magic place this was, a young man stepped into the clearing. He was slightly larger than average height and he had pale hair and high cheekbones. It was Tag, and Drood wondered why he hadn't recognized him immediately. Tag too was dressed in the kilts and leggings of the old days, and he carried a single lily in his hand. He crossed the clearing with a tender look in his eye, and he moved very gracefully, giving the impression of athletic strength and ease of movement. He came forward and silently extended the lily to Drood's daughter. Drood had a moment of confusion about the lily. What did it mean, usually death, but whose? And then he forgot it as Tag extended his hand to Deirdre. She took it and smiled, and Drood held his breath. During these moments he retained a vivid awareness of the birds, the trees, the sky, and the wind. The feeling of peace and joy never left him.

Tag and Deirdre began to dance, a stately waltz, and there was no music but the birdsong. Drood watched and the tears stood on his cheeks and his mouth dropped open as he saw them move in perfect harmony, perfect synchronization. The dance was so completely done, so perfect, with not a step or a finger out of place, and the two dancers looked with such loving smiles into each other's eyes, that Drood suddenly realized he was having some kind of hallucination.

He waited, now sitting on the edge of his seat, for the dance to end. The feeling of peace began to ebb, slightly, and the dancers somehow seemed to become more aware of him in their motions, and they seemed to be edging closer to him, and somehow aiming the dance at him. Finally they finished and bowed to each other. They turned to Drood and bowed deeply to him. Then they stood up straight and both looked directly in his eyes with brilliant, laughing smiles on their faces. Drood slammed back against the stone bench as if he had been struck. Morning came and Drood awoke.

Part II

Chapter 16
Several Years Later

"Tag, what're you gonna do man, just split out there with no job or nothin' just head out west and find a job or something when you get there?"

"I got connections. I'm gonna have help, don't worry about it." Tag flipped his hair out of his eyes and reached over and took a long pull from the cold beer sitting on the hood of the car. He wiped his brow and looked over the car. It wasn't all that much to look at, being an old junker and having lived in Syracuse its whole life, but it was dark and it was powerful and fast. Tag's car was the envy of his friends. They called it "The Monster" and they drove all over the city in it. Most of Tag's friends didn't have cars.

"What kind of connections? What do you mean?"

"Don't worry about it. You sound like my mother," Tag rejoined.

"Hey, I don't care, I'm just curious, that's all."

Tag chuckled and crouched down with the rag and resumed buffing the body of the Camaro. He caught sight of himself in the chrome around the rim of the headlight and stared for a second. He had shaggy straight pale hair hanging in his eyes and a scraggly beard all over his face. Shattering his own meager expectations, he had grown strong, handsome, and manly. His St. Christopher's medal gleamed at his throat, and his brown eyes looked foreign to him for a second. Pale Syracuse skin. He resumed wiping and occasionally he patted the car. Two of his friends sat on barrels and watched. They didn't know about Tag's weekly poker games, his apprenticeship, or even that sardonic Tom's workshop was fifteen feet away from them, behind Tag's car. It was a sunny Saturday afternoon in August. Tag was seventeen and had just announced that he wasn't going back to school, but was taking off for L.A. instead.

He had spoken as if he was going around the corner to buy a pack of cigarettes.

"Yeah, I'm going to go to L.A. next year too, after I graduate. I think college is free out there, that's what I'm going to do," said one friend.

"Yeah. My father lives in Florida. He said I can come down there and work landscaping with him any time I want to. I might do that next winter. I don't know," the other friend said. They looked at each other and Tag looked at them. He knew they would never leave Syracuse, or if they did, they'd come back eventually. They just didn't have it in them. To Tag, his departure was fact, neither positive nor negative, but there was a big thing between him and his friends about getting the hell out of Syracuse. They all talked about it.

Tag didn't expect great things from his friends. They were followers and Tag was their unacknowledged leader. He was good-natured, calm and quiet. He had a self-assurance the other kids didn't have. He stood out by standing back and by seeming to know what he was doing. The girls had begun to chase him and he had dated a few, off and on. His grades had improved dramatically to the point where teachers and guidance counselors had begun to ask him about his plans for after graduation, and had each suggested their favorite colleges to him. Tag was polite, but evasive. He was going in another direction and the time for them to capture his interest would have been several years ago, "When no one cared but Drood," he now thought. His loyalty and respect for the older man had increased almost to the point of idol worship and he occasionally found himself wondering what he would do if Drood moved away or if something happened to him.

"You guys should come out and visit me," Tag said. "I'm going to have a pool and a giant house in Beverly Hills, with beautiful people around me all the time, and the sun will be always shining." They all laughed, Tag too. He laughed because he already knew he really was going to have this dream life. "It will be cool," he thought, "when I remind them of this conversation a few years from now when they come out and visit me and we laugh about how we laughed about it now. And they will be amazed at how I had described it so accurately." Tag looked at his two friends again and thought he would miss them, but there was no way they could travel the road he was going and there was no way he could travel the road they were going. But only he was aware of it. And he hadn't told them he was actually leaving the next week and not at the end of the school year. They wouldn't believe he was going until he was gone. Tag finished the car and stood and wiped his hands on his jeans. His black Converse sneakers were soaked. He stared at a soap bubble on his toe. Tag was pursuing what he wanted and that didn't happen to coincide with what his friends thought or did, and that was fine with him.

He hadn't told his mother about leaving yet either. He wanted to give her only a week to whine and beg, but he didn't feel it was fair to just split without giving her any chance. He knew she had given up a couple of years ago, when Tag took control of his life, and she was too much absorbed in her death struggle with liquor and with Charles to notice Tag's leaving. He would have liked some support or some kind of relationship with her, but it wasn't possible. Drood told him to let it hurt if he had to, but he'd probably just have to get over it. Drood told Tag that his mother would regret it when she was older. Tag again worried about taking so much advice about people from a lonely old miscreant like Drood, but the man made sense, and almost everything he told Tag worked. Tag wasn't quite naïve, if something didn't work or jibe, he'd reject it. "The litmus test," he thought, "of all speech is result. It either works or it doesn't." This was his corollary to "actions speak louder than words."

As he pulled the Monster to the curb in front of his house, he wondered if he should give his mother something, or make some kind of speech or something. He had meant to ask Drood about that, but had forgotten. Well, he didn't have to ask Drood about everything, did he? He went in and there she was in the kitchen, red-faced and wild-eyed. She'd been drinking hard and it was noon, and her behavior lately made Tag wonder if she hadn't also gotten into the crack.

"Do you know what the fucker did this time?" She got right in Tag's face and her chemical breath made him step back quickly. He thought "Some day, I'd like to walk into a house that is completely silent and empty." His mother was currently "between" waitressing jobs, as she was more and more lately.

"Who, Charles?" he answered.

"Of course, the evil crookedy quack quack!" she howled. Tag smiled, his mother's speech was getting funnier over the years as her brain slowly fried to mush.

"He gave Donna a ride home last night. That son-of-a-bitch, he fucked her, for sure he played the old slap and tickle with her, hide the salami, snapper and wieners for hors d'oeuvres." She hopped and went back to the table and sat down heavily. Tag believed she was almost insane. He didn't care any more what Charles had done or what she imagined he had done, but he didn't know what to say to his mother. He wanted to help, he always wanted to be her son, for her to be his mother, it wouldn't go away, but he had just run out of any way for him to deal with her. He said nothing, but slid dejectedly into the seat across the table from her. "How long will this rant last," he wondered without really caring.

"Donna's always after everything I got. Surprised she hasn't tried to adopt you. You'd like that wouldn't you, Donna for a mother? She'd probably tuck you in at night and bake you pies, wouldn't you like that, you'd love her as your mother!" She was practically yelling at him, accusing him.

"No ma, of course I wouldn't. Where's the asshole now?" Get her back on Charles and out of his face.

"Who knows? I kicked him out. It's for good this time. Goddammit I'm going to get cigarettes, I'd better not see him skulking around this neighborhood."

Tag wondered if she had really kicked him out again for the hundredth time, or only imagined that she had, for the thousandth time. She rummaged around the kitchen, found some money, and stomped out the side door. Tag heard her stumble and swear. Some day he'd come back and help her, if she lived until some day, which he doubted. "Well," he concluded and headed up stairs to take a nap before Drood and poker. "I guess that about wraps it up for me, talk about saying your good-byes." He had thought it would be an emotional buildup to a dramatic send-off. That's the way it was in the movies, but really it was more like his life here was running out on him, ending, no matter whether he stayed or went. There was already nothing left. One last lesson with Drood, one last poker game with the guys, he'd take it easy on them, and then his physical presence would be gone and he'd be nothing but a memory, practically was already. When his mother got good and drunk she moaned and cried about what a beautiful baby he had been. And as pathetic as she was, Tag found it reassuring because he didn't remember any time when she had been loving and sentimental with him. It proved to him that she was his mother and not just some tragedy he happened into.

* * *

Deirdre had her bags packed and she couldn't wait to go. It was a tricky plan, but she was all set. Gramma and Grampa would drop her off at the bus station. She'd get on the bus for Philadelphia; she'd get to the first stop, get out and get the next bus in the opposite direction to L.A. She'd been on her own at school for two years now and she didn't need her mother and Lewis to run her life. She didn't think Gramma and Grampa had ever really been on this planet, except as these kindly weird aliens from planet corn-Iowa. "Nice people from that planet, but really. Not much to write about."

She wondered whether to pack all of her journals in one bag, or split them up in case the bags got separated and lost. They had accumulated into quite a stack of paper and she was on the verge of burning them all the time, but she was also on the verge of using them all to write a book of memoirs. She hadn't lived an extraordinary life, but she did think her thoughts and feelings over the last several years had to be worth something. She knew a lot about New York, Philadelphia, and Iowa. She'd had jobs castrating sheep, waiting tables, writing for a magazine, cleaning stables, modeling, and tutoring foreign exchange students in English. She knew a lot about men. She was blessed with good looks and the way she carried herself it was inevitable, and she'd have to be an idiot not to know what the game was. All that had to count for something, didn't it? She'd speak the truth by god; she'd be a great writer. And she had an interesting, funny way of looking at things, a curious way of using words. All her friends said so.

"Time for dinner dear," came her sweet, harmless Gramma's voice from the stairway.

"I'll be there in a minute, Gram." She stuffed the books into one bag and decided she'd carry it with her. It would be a long trip and she wanted to record her observations anyway. There were always a few blank pages at the end of them. She could stretch her trip out through all the books that way, and it would be like a code if the original books were ever discovered. They'd have to be pieced together to describe this trip, the final punctuation point of this phase of her life. She was only seventeen, but she was about to come out, to announce herself as a full-scale adult and take all the responsibilities. She could pass for eighteen easily, physically, and she'd figure out how to get around working papers or whatever they had in California. She hustled down the stairs, couldn't keep Gram waiting.

"My God," she thought, "more freaking fabulous fat-ified farm food. It's a wonder I'm not three hundred pounds." And she felt heavy and sick just from smelling all the butter and the weight of the food that was prepared every night. And bacon and eggs in the morning. Deirdre was in an all-out death struggle with her grandmother for control of her arteries. She came into the room and her grandmother beamed at her. "You have to give her credit for that smile," she thought, and she was grateful for the love, in spite of the weirdness and the old values and the starch.

"Ready for the trip, dear?" her grandmother asked.

"Yes, ma'am," she replied.

"Your mother will be so happy to see you again. She misses you so much."

"Well, Gram, Philadelphia is only an hour and a half drive from New York and she never made it once. She couldn't have missed me that much."

Her grandmother scowled and went back into the kitchen to bring seven or eight more plates of food. The door banged open and her grandfather came in. He was ready to eat, by God, and Deirdre had never seen such gusto with a fork. She admired it terrifically, but it sort of frightened her because she wondered what made that gusto, where it came from, and what torment compelled it to be like that. "There's enough food there for a thousand people," she thought, "but it's just the three of us." She wondered if they ate like this when she wasn't around and what in the world happened to the leftovers? She didn't see them in the freezer or the fridge and they never ate leftovers and they didn't feed them to any of the animals. Further proof they were aliens and Deirdre was too shy to ask. She was always afraid of hurting their feelings, though she never had, and they seemed like the real forgiving type. "And," she reminded herself, "I am the only granddaughter among all those grandsons. Confuses 'em, they don't know how to treat me. I would've thought

Granmma might have been a girl once herself, but what could that mean in a place like this?" She just couldn't see her mother growing up here, the urbane and charming Claire. How had she come from here? These people were charming and gracious in their own right, but there was some kind of a disconnect, a huge chasm. Deirdre stopped bothering herself about it and made ready to dig in. She ate strategically, maximizing the space of the food on the plate, while minimizing the intake of the calories. It was a challenging game and one that she was getting tired of playing.

"Has your mother ever talked to you about your father, Deirdre?" her grandmother asked quietly in her sweet voice. Deirdre almost choked and froze. Her grandparents had carefully avoided any hint of controversial subjects and had been so dainty and cautious around her that she was startled that on the last day of her stay her grandmother would bring up such a vast subject.

"Well, a couple of years ago, she told me about what had happened at the end there. And she told me some private things about him that no one else knows." Dee Dee looked at her grandmother with her eyebrows raised and the sides of her lips pulled up in a half-questioning smile. "Why do you ask, Gram?"

"Well, your mother had always told us not to speak about him to you. We thought at first it was because of her second marriage," and Dee Dee noticed her grandfather frown. "But then, she repeated her wishes to us a few years ago. And we feel now that…well, we just don't know how long it will be before we see you again, and it doesn't seem right to us. We wanted to make sure you knew. You're almost grown up now."

Deirdre was touched and tears started in the corners of her eyes.

"Thank you Gramma," and she looked at her and then at her grandfather and they were both looking at her with deep emotion and concern. It was startling after all the caution and politeness; she didn't know they had this depth of caring in them.

"Well, it was very surprising to us and we were very worried about you and your mother, but she was very determined. He seemed like a good man, dear. Your father was very kind in some ways, very talented, very charming. I think he kind of…well, we think he just got lost."

"New York City did it to him. He didn't belong there," Grampa chimed in. "There was something different about him. You could feel it. Unusual man." And this was high praise from Grampa. Deirdre almost swooned she was so grateful to get somebody else's perspective on her father. Her mother had such pain over it, and she had read all the newspaper articles and a couple of books about her father's friend, Kilty O'Neill, the Irish mobster, but there wasn't much in any of it about her father. Just a name. A name which didn't match a certain scrawled signature she knew about.

"How long did you know him before everything happened?" she asked.

"A little over two years. We felt like they were really just getting started, before he made all those mistakes."

Deirdre could see that they didn't have any of the anger her mother had, just loss and concern. This was a great way to end her visit here, to get ready for the trip. She had closed the book on her father, there was nothing more to find, and it made an interesting story, but not one in which she was personally involved. She had used it to impress friends at boarding school when they would talk about how bad they were, all those really good girls from good families, and Dee Dee's story was somewhat sensational, but it was just a story to her. Her grandparents were certainly giving her something to think about on this trip.

"Well, thank you for caring so much. I could never understand why my mother wouldn't tell me anything about him. She acts so weird about it. I'm glad you guys liked him."

"You don't understand honey. Your mother still loves him. She wishes she had stood by him. She'll never tell you that, but she feels that she was ruined by the whole thing, and she thinks the only thing she has left to look forward to in this world is you."

Dee Dee was stunned and had to fight this off. "What about Lewis?"

Her grandfather snorted. "He just pays the bills. If she really cared about him, we'd see the both of them out here every summer. She sends you by yourself because she loves you. She would like to come herself but she doesn't feel worthy. Lewis is just an excuse to keep punishing herself."

"I...I ....I don't know what to say."

"Well, don't worry about it dear. You've got a big trip tomorrow, and we just wanted to try to help. Ask your mother about it when you get back, and because you're a grown-up now, maybe you can help her get over it and forgive herself."

She had been so angry with her mother - the guilt overwhelmed her and she dropped her fork and excused herself. She went upstairs thinking about how her mother was going to lose her for good just when Deirdre was finding out how much her mother needed her. She cried.

Chapter 17

Drood was working on a Saturday again, hunched over at his computer table and his neck was killing him. He was typing data into a report that somebody who worked beneath him was supposed to do. Muke was hard at work in the office next to him. There was a big sales meeting coming up and the two of them had to be ready in self-defense. Drood would have liked to get some fresh air, walk in the park before Tag and the poker game, but he couldn't. Tag's final lesson. It was too soon, and of course Drood hadn't been able to teach him anywhere near what he knew or what Tag was going to need to know, but Tag wasn't going to become a Druid after all, was he? He had enough to get on his way and he was more than ready to strike out.

The walls of his office seemed to close in and Drood grew increasingly agitated. He coughed suddenly and got dizzy as his heart skipped a beat and then went out of rhythm. It had been happening more frequently lately and he was afraid he was going to have to have something done about it. He thought about Mannanan and suddenly remembered this tedious life and his promising dreams were brought on him from somewhere else and he had no control over any of it. Tag was leaving and life was intolerable. His daughter was lost and Tag was going to find her and what was Drood doing? He was typing inanity after inanity while the sun shone outside and he couldn't breathe all of a sudden. His heart rhythm went wild, and he stood unsteadily. He staggered. His agitation and distress suddenly became rage and he felt trapped. He took a deep breath and looked around him. The computer beeped at him and he kicked at it and missed. He backed up and aimed more carefully and he kicked over the computer monitor and came around the desk and stood panting over the broken plastic. He walked out of his office and slammed the door. Muke began to say something, but Drood cut him off, "SCREW YOU!"

He had to get outside. He had to think. His heart wasn't right and his mind wasn't right, and his life, as usual and forever, wasn't right and it was becoming a crisis again. His lessons with Tag had brought him back to life, stirred up the teachings and the feelings and memories. The boy's nobility inspired Drood; but his waking dreams were coming with more frequency and more power lately. He desperately didn't want to live again, to care, to campaign and do battle, but it was happening anyway. He staggered into the parking lot and had an image of a white beard and a laughing face and he knew it was Mannanan. His chest was very tight and he couldn't breathe and he began to fear this might be the end. He saw Tag's face and he made it to his car and sat on the hood. The sun beat down on his head and he began to sweat. He lay back on the hood and tried to concentrate on breathing. He closed his eyes and the world around him vanished.

As his breathing steadied, he realized it was time to set everything straight. Tag was leaving, a big change, and it was time for Drood to go to New York. He thought of McGrath, of Claire, of his daughter. He had tried to put it all behind him, but now his past was back and it was more vivid and unfinished than ever. In the back of his mind, he had been forming a plan for some time. Like all good plans, it had started out as a fantasy, and now everything in the path of his fantasy was removing itself. How would he complete this plan, what help would he need, where would it take him? As he thought about taking action, his heartbeat steadied and his mind focused. His ideas began to be familiar to him and the panic subsided. The awakening of self-interest and self-concern stirred in his solar plexus and he smiled as he sat on his car.

Drood lit a cigarette and sat up on the hood of the car and looked at the Meltocom building. "Yes," he thought, "it was time to take some action." All the signs were there. There was one thing left to do - run it all by Mickey and see what he had to say. Drood felt both good and evil rising in him again and he felt once again that he was a child of the Gods, and the old feelings and the old madness for power began to steal over him. He had never thought he would feel this way again. He was becoming a Druid again and it had taken years of darkness and misery to bring him to this point. He looked up at the clouds coming in from the west. The shape and color of the

164

clouds meant that it would be a good time to hunt the deer and that the harvest was almost here.

Drood spread his arms out wide and smiled and he welcomed the sun and then the clouds as they brushed over and the sky turned gray. He smoked and felt power surging through him and he knew that his plan was the right one.

He spoke to the sky, although he knew damn well that the one he was speaking to was anywhere but in the sky.

"Okay, old warrior," Drood said to the sky. "I know you can hear me and I know you've been watching me, and I think I know now why you tricked me into coming to this world. You were arranging destinies and now it's almost complete isn't it? The boy is one of yours, I believe, and it was your hand that brought me across the ocean. You rode your chariot out to sea to retrieve us, to deceive us, to ensure the survival of your line into the far-off future. I suspected there was something special about this boy, but now I'm convinced of it. And you should know, he's going to live by the western ocean, what do you think of that? Do you have any pull over there, or are all the gods out there Indian, Hawaiian, Japanese?" Drood chuckled, feeling good about the plan. He continued, "And that dream I had. That was my daughter, right; she is the princess for your son? You had this planned all along, Manannan, didn't you?" No reply.

"Well, I'm satisfied. It's been a long journey, but I see it's all going to work out now. Was it kept from me, because it wouldn't have happened if I knew about it? You have given me immense suffering to satisfy your own desires. Do you think it will be worth it? Did you give me the dream to keep me going or to relieve me? Was the dream some kind of promise? Will I feel that way some day, that joy, beauty and love? Am I bringing together the two perfect mates that will create magic and revive the Gods in this world? You have been mysterious, old fish chief, and now I think I'm going to finish it all off and meet you in person. I know, I tried that many years ago, the whole rowboat and death trip, but it wasn't time and you guided me back, to shore again. I knew that gleaming chariot wasn't a hallucination. I knew I'd seen you. Well, I'm back inside myself now and you don't have to hide anymore. I see where it's going and I'm going to finish it out right. You'll see. I'll get a ride in that chariot yet. Since you are the one making the rules of this game, I think it's time for you to lend me that famous cloak of mist of yours so that I can be invisible and get the job done, and finish off the master plan."

Fifteen minutes later Drood was still sitting on the hood of his car when Muke came out, looking concerned. He was probably looking to see if in his fit of anger, Drood might have vandalized Muke's car.

"Are you O.K.?" a frightened and wildly curious Muke wanted to know. He was leaning into Drood's face.

"Couldn't be better, Mukie, couldn't be better. I'm going to heaven by virtue of my sacrifice and my suffering. Gotta go." And the promise of action and redemption changed Drood into a different person.

Drood rose and brushed Mr. Muke aside and got into his car. It was time to get moving.

Muke stood in a cloud of dust, staring open-mouthed at the departing lunatic. Drood was gone.

Chapter 18

Tag's mind recorded blurred images all across America. He was by himself so he didn't have anyone to bounce things off to strengthen or refine his impressions. He just took them all in, experienced them, and let them all go. He wasn't no damn tourist anyway, he said to himself, he was on a mission. He figured if he saw something he liked, he'd have plenty of time to go back and check it out when he was older, when he had time and money, when he was in complete charge of his fate.

Tag's car had rolled down the flat and straight New York Thruway to Buffalo and then he was down around the Great Lakes on the four lanes, seeing nothing but green road signs, cars, factories and buildings, open stretches or flat farmland, occasional glimpses of lakes. He got out to just south of Chicago the first night and slept in a cheap motel. By the next night he was out into the cornfields, then the following night it was the plateaus gradually rising toward the Continental divide. Finally he went down into Texas and the heat was unbelievable, and it was all four lanes and cheap motels and truck stops and gas stations. Tag checked out a little landscape, but America wasn't localized any more, was it? He figured every highway, every truck stop, every radio station, every TV show, every motel room all across the country was the same and so he never really left anywhere. He wasn't going out to another world, he was going out to the other side of the house, and everything would be almost the same there, a little different weather, a little different culture, but mostly the same.

Tag became exhausted as he drove long days and into nights. He was young and strong and his body felt fine, but his mind got sore, and he didn't enjoy the trip. It was all in front of him, his whole life, and it was a big blank and he couldn't see it in any direction. Sure, he had his vision, and Drood had taught him to hold on to it, but when you're seventeen you don't have any clue how much a vision is worth and how far it can take you and what it takes to make the vision real. There was not enough to distract Tag on this trip and he needed to be distracted, because the plan was all set and what more was there to do once the plan was all set? More thinking about the future was potentially dangerous, could make him fearful; thinking about the past was not really important unless he wanted to review Drood's teachings. He decided on the first day that he'd review all Drood's teachings on the last day of the trip so he would have them fresh in his mind when he arrived. The present was only road, map, car and logistics. So, that left him only one important thing to think about while he drove, and that was her. He couldn't see her yet, but he knew she would be in L.A.

He still couldn't see her face and nothing about his experience with girls encouraged him to think that he had any special talent at discovering what the inside of a person was like so that he could know her when he found her. Drood had become increasingly interested in this part of his vision, about the girl, and kept asking him if he saw her in dreams. It seemed to be the one thing they talked about that made Drood lose his teacherly tone and become avidly interested in Tag's experience. Tag didn't kid himself. He knew Drood had affection for him, but they were teacher and student, not family, and Drood had always retained a certain amount of distance. But when they talked about the future girlfriend, Drood got very shrewd and intent on him, and it was almost like he wanted Tag's vision for himself. He kept asking Tag to describe her, over and over, and he always said it was to clarify the vision for Tag, but it always seemed to Tag that there was more to it than that, like he wanted to see the vision himself.

Tag tried to visualize her again as the desert dragged past outside and the only thought he had about his surroundings was the occasional, "Man I hope the car doesn't break down out here." He thought about her again and saw a lean, dark-haired, beautiful woman his age, with a great smile but somehow he still couldn't put the face together. He could see how she moved though; she was graceful and awkward at the same time, modest and confident, beautiful and strange. She came right into his heart in an embrace every time he tried to visualize her. And it always ended in frustration as he came back to himself wherever he was, because she wasn't real, he couldn't have her, and he didn't know if she even existed anywhere.

Tag speculated on this and wondered again about Drood's interest. Could Drood be just plain wrong here? Drood had made him scrutinize the media and taught him all about how to read popular culture and about how to defy it and defend against it. But with this vision of the woman, or the goddess, as Drood had once called her, Tag thought Drood was teaching him to accept the most patently false modern myth, that of "one true love" and that destiny, with stars, determined with whom you fell in love. Hadn't Drood once told him that love was a modern concept of what had once been just a whimsical feeling? It just didn't make any sense and Tag couldn't reconcile that teaching with the rest of the tricks and skills Drood had taught him to use. The emphasis on the vision of the woman came from something more personal inside of Drood. Tag wondered what drove the old man. And with a start, he realized that Drood was old and he wondered when that had happened. When they had met Drood was middle aged, and now a few years later, Drood was an old man.

In the end, it was Tag's vision, not Drood's, and he would like to have given it up long ago, but it kept coming back, even without Drood's prompting. Tag loved the girl and he wouldn't give her up until he found the real thing or something better. He wanted love and faith and he was going to find it as a card player in L.A. and Las Vegas, by God.

The final day of the drive Tag woke in the motel excited and ready for action. He would be in Los Angeles that evening and his life would begin, his apprenticeship served. He would also be scanning the outlying areas carefully, potential homes and day trips, and he was also excited that today was the day he had chosen to review Drood's teachings as he drove. He remembered the final lesson the Saturday before he had left.

Drood had handed tag an envelope and Tag looked inside. It was filled with cash.

"I can't take this," he said.

"Of course you can take it. I don't have any use for it." Drood had smiled.

Tag put the money in his pocket and thanked Drood. They looked at each other and Drood said,
"Let's walk."

They went outside in the afternoon air and walked around the crazed and rotted buildings of the old factory complex. They hopped up on loading docks, walked the length of them and hopped down again. They tried doors they knew were locked and they picked up broken bricks and hurled them over the fence into the old waste storage area. They were sad and quiet although they told themselves they had no regrets.

"Well Drood, I don't know what to say. I still can't believe all you've done for me. I'm grateful. And I love you, y'know?" Tag was embarrassed to say all this, but he meant it, and he just knew he had to say it. He couldn't believe he wasn't going to see the old guy. "You're going to come out to L.A. once in a while, right, just to relax and catch up, right?"

"Sure," said Drood, "the company will still send me out there once in a while, and I'll probably come out just for the hell of it too. Might even play a little poker myself." Drood looked away quickly and Tag caught it. Was there something Drood wasn't telling him? Was he not planning to come to L.A.?

"Anyway," Drood said. "There's just a couple more things I want to tell you. And they're big picture things. I feel like a father sending his son off to war." And he suddenly looked sheepish and self-conscious.

"So here goes. One side of things, on a human level, is that we need people in our lives. We need love and affection like we need air and water. We need support, we need help, we need backup, we need a lot of it to survive. If we don't get those things, we wither and die inside. We become shells walking around, and who knows what form of weirdness or evil a shell can attach itself to or become filled up with? Anyway, this need is our fatal flaw. Our humanness has nothing to do with logic, the laws of nature, the laws of physics. We can be squashed by trying to protect and nurture those that we need. Now, what else do we need? We need satisfaction. It can be gotten in so many ways - money, achievement, sex, music, art, and on and on. This is a need that can come in direct conflict with our need for love and support. Or they can work together, which is a difficult trick. The skills of love and family are not the skills of competition for satisfaction.

"So, how do we deal with these contradictions? Look at yourself. Your expertise is in cards, using other people's minds to get what you want. You used my teachings to transform yourself, to get out of tight situations, to learn what to do, to practice useful ways of thinking. You used your friends to feel good about yourself and to get some experience in life. Human beings are using, consuming animals. This is clear and it makes most people jump to the wrong conclusion, because they get the natures of the two needs mixed up.

"In trying to meet the needs of Family and Love, many people use the weapons of manipulation and strategy to gain power over other people. In trying to meet the needs of Satisfaction, they try to bargain with their own personal strength. These needs and tactics should be reversed. Personal quality should be used with the people close to us, where personal qualities retain their value. In the competition for satisfaction, people should use manipulation, strategy and a deft touch. Your personal power, no matter who you may be, must be cherished, herded, and marshaled for the personal arena, where it is precious and rare. Your maneuvering and trickster behavior must be used for the world at large."

Tag had stopped Drood there with a raised hand. It had become the signal between them when Tag wanted to think about things and absorb things. He ran it through in his mind, and found that what Drood said made sense. He dropped his hand and told Drood to go on. They came to the back of the warehouse section and sat on cement steps with their backs against a rusted railing. They looked out at the chain link fence that was barely visible because of the vines smothering it. Drood continued.

"It's just like playing poker. You've got the cards held up to your chest, you know what they are, you know what they're worth. But, as you know, the betting is not based on what you have; it's based on what other people are thinking. The betting is based on the size of the pot, it's based on the hour of the game, it's based on a thousand factors that have nothing to do with the strength of your hand. Whether you win or lose has nothing to do with the strength of your hand. How much you win or lose has nothing to do with the strength of your hand. And conversely, no matter whether you win or lose, no matter how the betting goes or how the game ends up, you feel comfortable and secure when you have a straight flush, and you feel nervous and worried when you have a pair of tens. The cards are important to how you feel about yourself and the game, but they don't always relate to winning and losing. And one more point.

You don't control the cards that you are dealt, and so you can't really take credit for them, even though you feel on top of the world when you see that fourth ace."

Tag smiled. He was getting it and it was interesting and really cool to him the way Drood was explaining the whole thing in terms of poker.

"Okay," Drood continued, " so what does all this mean that you personally should do?"

And just then two kids walked around the corner and started when they saw Tag and Drood sitting on the steps. They recovered themselves and continued walking. They swore at each other and smoked and swaggered by and disappeared around the next corner, walking in the parallel ruts of the old road. Tag watched them go and sighed. He was leaving Syracuse. Those boys, probably thirteen or fourteen, were from his hometown and he knew them so well, though he didn't know them personally. They were so pale they were almost yellow. They had no shirts on and baggy shorts hanging down. They had piercings all over and scraggly facial hair. Tag could count their ribs and their stomach muscles. They had crew cuts and bad teeth and bad attitudes and they smoked and drank and got high and they were young and probably one of them had a baby and thought of himself as a man. Would it be like this in L.A? It was almost poetry, he thought, to see the two of them stride by as he was saying goodbye to Drood and to the magic factory all at once. He had shown Drood the door to the roof and he realized that he hadn't ever explored the other stairway, the one to the basement. Well, that would be for some other kid, he guessed, or maybe for Drood if he got bored. What was in the basement of the lost factory?

"It means that you should be anonymous but efficient in all your dealings outside of your heart. Be independent, be careful, and be very observant. Watch which way the wind is blowing. Line yourself up with the right powers keeping as many of your values and principles as you can with you. Don't confront huge powers and try to be bigger than them. Be smaller than them, work around them, let evil destroy itself when you can, and when you can't and are confronted with it directly, be dispassionate about it. Do what's right but don't be righteous. Know what your personal characteristics are, regardless of how you are perceived or portrayed by others who do not belong to your heart. Let things go the way they go, and make sure you go the way you're supposed to go. Consider carefully who becomes part of your heart. Open the door slowly and carefully, learn quickly from mistakes. Outside your heart, be an expert, efficient sharpshooter, play poker for the money, not for the fame or the respect. Never let them know who you are or where you live. Inside your heart, when you trust and love, do it with all your might. Be greedy and in pain, if you have to. Ask for things; be willing to die for things. Live like you will never see those inside your heart again after today, because you might not. Trust me, I know. Let all your dreams and talents out, pull out all the stops. Turn on a dime when you go out into the world and become the robot you need to be out there." Drood put a hand to his forehead. He was getting a little lost, a little confused here. Maybe it was time to finish.

"Finally. No matter what happens, keep going. Something will change. If you are in despair, if you have lost everything, if you despise yourself, if the whole world hates you, keep going. Everything changes, all the time. One day you may wake up in a new world and you have no idea when or how that will happen. Have faith in change. Because it will happen. Watch change, observe it, and think about it. Remember it."

* * *

Deirdre's plan had gone off without a hitch and she had a long bus ride out to L.A. She thought about all the stories of seventeen-year-old girls going out to Los Angeles and ending up as hookers or worse. She didn't worry because she knew she'd be out of trouble in an instant with a call to her mother or the grandparents. As soon as she got to L.A. she'd let them know where she was. The bus going to L.A. had arrived before the bus going to New York. Just a bus ride to go and she'd be there. She had her credit, her accounts, (she did thank Lewis for that much anyway,) and nothing to worry about. She'd stay in youth hostels, find an apartment that was safe and clean and hopefully not too expensive and then go looking for work. She could rent a computer or use the libraries for her first few pieces while she worked some waitress job or something. "Nothing to it," she thought, "just a little inconvenience and a little persistence and patience and I'll be where I want to be."

The bus pulled into a tiny cinderblock building in the middle of the desert. Deirdre got out to stretch her legs and buy herself some caffeine. She wandered around the asphalt in the blazing heat for a few minutes, letting it soak in. The air conditioning on the bus had been nice but it was good to feel her blood begin to heat up and her skin begin to sting. She smelled pine from somewhere and she hugged herself and then went into the building that held the ticket counter, an office, plastic chairs, and vending machines.

Deirdre put money in, poked the buttons and came out with two ice-cold cans of soda. She sat down in a plastic chair, the bus driver had said it would be thirty minutes before they would leave again. She contemplated the middle of nowhere. No-name bus stop, she didn't even want to ask. She sucked down the first can and was working on the second and wondering about the restrooms when the door to the outside opened and a bum walked in. He looked O.K., she thought, for a bum, but he definitely lived outdoors. He had a long gray ponytail, a gray grizzly beard, and a huge backpack with all kinds of little pouches dangling off it. He carried himself as if he knew what he was doing and he must be traveling so she guessed he was maybe a former hippy, traveling around selling and buying things, maybe drugs, maybe jewelry, maybe soap. He had a very used look yet his worn clothes looked carefully cared for. He had the gray-black skin of a white person who never slept indoors. She was staring at him when she noticed with a start that he was staring back at her. "Oops, shouldn't have made eye contact," she thought.

The bum/hippy came right over to her and sat down next to her and introduced himself. "How're ya? I'm David."

"Hi." She said and sort of half smiled. She didn't know what else to say or do. He didn't smell too bad.

"Going to L.A., right?"

"Yes, how did you know?"

"Just have that going-off-to-start-a-new-life look about you. You know, you're obviously not from here. You're off some bus from some eastern place and you're going out to the land of sunshine on the western sea. You're young and full of dreams and hopes. I've seen a thousand like you; see 'em almost every day. Always wonder what happens to them when they get there, but I could probably guess. Not as interesting to me as seeing them in this beautiful, pristine state of anticipation. Say, you're kind of young, aint you?"

"Depends how you look at it. You're right about the rest though." She had decided he meant no harm and held out her hand, "I'm Deirdre."

"Nice to meet you Deirdre."

"Where are you going?" she asked him.

"Up to Bakersfield. Friend of mine says he'll put me up for a few weeks while I work on a project there."

"What kind of project?"

His answer exaggerated one word,

"A SSSSSSEEEEEEECREEEETTTT project!!!!" and he giggled like a little boy. Deirdre was amused but wondered if David was mentally ill. He glanced out the window as a bus pulled in and opened its door.

"That's mine. Gotta go. Nice to meet you Deirdre." He heaved himself out of the chair and headed to the swinging glass doors and pulled one open. Deirdre felt a blast of heat. She started to say nice to meet you to, but he interrupted her,

"Oh, by the way. I'm gifted with sight. You will find your father, but it may not be in the person you thought. Just so you know. You be careful now." And he turned on his heel and went out.

Deirdre stared after him. She was too stunned to move and watched him get on the bus and wanted to hop on after him. She could always find a way to get from Bakersfield to L.A, but she froze. "What on earth did he mean, how on earth did he know that, and am I really looking for my father?" It was inconceivable. She hugged herself again and tried to get a grip on her reeling thoughts as the bus for Bakersfield pulled out and she suddenly felt alone and small and nervous. Some kind of crazy Willie Nelson-looking old hippy in the middle of nowhere says that to her?

She wandered to the ticket counter, dropped some money in a jar that said something about "benevolent" and "kids" and went back out to her bus. As the bus pulled out and she felt the surge of power and watched the dirt and the rocks slide by, she tried to picture her father's face from the one photograph she had and from the wedding pictures her grandmother had kept. He'd be in his late fifties now. Weird. She'd never thought of that before. He was always the interesting-looking young man looking away from the camera, a mystery, a puzzle. She suddenly realized she'd been getting clues and information about her father since she had the talk with her mother. She hadn't been actively searching for them either, but they kept presenting themselves to her. She would have thought

L.A. would be the exact wrong place to look for her father- far from the east and from New York and Ireland, the places where most of his life had been spent. And if he was dead, what did she think she was going to find anyway? David's words and her father's face kept tumbling over and over in her mind as the scenery rolled by. She sighed and closed her eyes.

Deirdre slept through the rest of the trip and woke up to the setting sun as they came out of the hills and down into the great city of lights. The purple and magenta and rouge sky over the ocean was unbelievable and she felt herself to be entering Shangri La, all of life behind her lost now, nothing here but colors and moods and mysteries and magic. She felt the weariness of the trip and it surged into the promise of the night and she felt delightfully melancholy and certain and peaceful all at the same time. L.A. was where she would find the beauty her soul craved, and she would live in art and love and mystery here. She felt herself going a little crazy as the lights began to twinkle on and she saw palm trees, and the purple turned a bluish dark that was even more beautiful. She knew she had to get to the beach right away and the next sunset she saw would be at the edge of the Pacific Ocean. She felt that she had come home to the place she'd only been once and she felt that L.A. was her place. The bus wheezed into the station and she was very reluctant to stop dreaming and enter the streets, but it was time. It was time to get gritty and tough. "Here I go," she thought, "the seventeen-year-old blue-eyed writer from New York about to make landfall in the western capitol of America to try my luck." And the doors opened and down she stepped into the breeze. There was a delicious smell of salt water, frying food, and smoke in the air.

Chapter 19

Finally, Johnson hung up the phone, crossed his legs, clasped his hands, and said, "Now, what can I do for you Mr. Drood?" and he sat back with a smug, bemused grin. Drood wondered if Johnson had actually got a running bet going with all the other big shots in the company to see how long they could keep someone waiting while they stayed on the phone.

Drood shrugged and leaned forward and said, "I'm quitting Meltocom. After today, you'll never see me again."

Johnson lurched forward. His forearms thumped on the desk. "What?!!! We just gave you a good review. You've done the best anyone's ever done managing that group."

Drood considered just cutting and running from the scene, but after all, how many times in life does one get a chance to turn the table? "Yes, you gave me a good review, yes I've done better than anyone. So what? What does that inspire you to do?"

"Well..." Johnson suddenly exhaled and looked defeated. Drood had ripped away the veil and exposed the way things really were. Johnson was just a silly man playing silly games and had totally misread Drood.

"Do a good review and good performance suggest any particular action to you?" Drood waited for a second and when Johnson couldn't answer, Drood continued, "No. They don't."

"Well now wait Drood. Wherever you're going isn't going to be any better than it is here. All these companies and kinds of jobs are the same. Don't think it's going to be better somewhere else." And Johnson was aggressive again for a second. No response from Drood.

"Will you wait until we make a counter offer?" Drood was surprised at how quickly Johnson fell back on reality and dropped the bullshit.

"Actually, I was thinking of doing some traveling, looking up some family. Bumming around for a few years."

Johnson glared at Drood and his face suddenly turned purple. Johnson had the distinct feeling that he was being made fun of. "You'll be sorry Drood. This is the best you'll ever do. We can make sure you don't get a good reference that you never work in this industry again." And he sat back, certain he had scored.

"Oh, if you could do that, I would be really grateful." Drood replied and Johnson looked further baffled and stared at Drood. Was it the first time he had ever encountered an independent person, not owned and beholden to Meltocom? Johnson had probably never seen somebody behave this way before, and he had no frame of reference. He seemed to grab at straws.

"You can't leave without two weeks' notice. And you can't leave without an exit interview. It's in the employment agreement. We can withhold your last check and your remaining vacation pay."

"Oh," said Drood. And Johnson smiled and began to nod his head, looking relieved that he was regaining a toehold.

"In that case," Drood said, "if that's the only worry, I guess I'll just say good-bye to a couple of people now and then leave."

"What?!!!" Johnson was apoplectic. "Drood…wait…wait let's talk about this. How can you do this to the people who work for you? They depend on you!"

"It's touching that you care so much about them," Drood replied. "I'll just tell them that you're going to be looking after them yourself after today." And Drood smiled. His work was done here; it was time to leave.

* * *

There was a message on Drood's answering machine from Tag's mother. She said she had to talk to him immediately. Drood dreaded it. Without dropping his keys he turned around and went back out the door to go over to her apartment. He wanted to get it over with. He'd try to make it a quick stop, but from what Tag had told him, the woman might make a pest of herself. "She's losing her only son," he reasoned, "but then again, I had less to do with it than she probably thinks. It's his vision and he made all the decisions. I didn't talk him into or out of anything." He sighed as he turned the car onto Midler.

He got out of the car and here she came, by the Gods, right out the door at him.

"You Drood?" she yelled across the yard.

"Yes."

"You motherfucking pervert son-of-a-bitch" and she lunged at him with a roundhouse right.

He struggled briefly with her and got her under control quickly. She panted and he begged her to calm down and talk about it with him. He told her he didn't have anything to do with Tag leaving and she slumped over and went limp. He walked into the kitchen with her under his arm and made cooing sounds to her. She collapsed on a chair, crying, exhausted, and to Drood she looked like to be about eighty years old...sallow skin, bad breathing, clumsy movements, missing teeth, thin scraggly hair, and wrinkled eyes.

"Listen," he said to her, and he sat down across from her. "Tag is gone. He went to L.A. to make a life for himself. He's a smart kid and he'll be fine out there. Let's not pretend it's him you're worried about. It's you we're talking about. You're in a lot of pain, aren't you?"

Tag's mother looked at Drood in shocked uncomprehending surprise for a few moments. Finally, as it sank in, she burst into fresh sobs and banged her head on the kitchen table. What he was saying was all true.

"My boy. I never took care of him and now it's too late..." she wailed. She began to punch herself in the head and Drood grabbed her arm and held it. He came out of his chair and put his arm around her.

"You have to take care of yourself now, O.K.? I can't help you and Tag can't help you. You have to get clean and sober and get your life together. And nobody can do that for you. Not Charles, not Tag. You alone can do it. And there's plenty of help when you decide to ask for it. I won't be here, but you will be okay if you really want to be." She stared at him and snuffled. Drood waited for her to reply, but she only moaned. He patted her on the back. She quieted slightly and Drood couldn't think of what else to do. He stood looking down at her. How could such a fine student come from such a wreck? "Well," he thought, "that's another story altogether, and I don't have time to pursue that." And Drood spun on his heel and pushed out the kitchen door. He walked quickly to his car and he heard the door bang behind him. She must have followed him out. He got in his car, still waiting to hear her whining, pleading voice, but it was silent. As he pulled away, he risked a glance at her. She was standing holding the door and she had stopped crying. She looked very weak and still, but she was staring off over the yard to the train tracks as the sound of a train approached. She looked almost peaceful to Drood and he hoped something had changed in her, the pain transforming and deciding her. She was gone from his sight.

And now one last thing before leaving town: Mickey. Down James Street into the city, right over to the hospital, up the hill, through the sliding doors, elevator, and finally up to the floor. Mickey was in the lounge and his bathrobe was open and he had only one slipper on. Drood had never seen Mickey in his bathrobe in the middle of the day before. Something was wrong. And his hair was all disheveled, a first. Even in the depths of his sickness, even when just getting out of bed, Mickey's hair was perfect.

"Mickey, what happened?" Drood asked as he sat on the couch next to him and took his hand. It was limp and cold.

"Uh?" Mickey wiped drool from his mouth and tried to make his eyes focus on Drood. Nobody in the lounge paid any attention to them.

"Are you O.K.? What have they got you on?"

Mickey struggled and finally managed to make his eyes work and he gazed at Drood from far away for a moment, and then closed his eyes and sighed.

"Drud. Iss Zulu. They got me....on.....new sperimental drug. Try'n a kill me. Know too much. Give way too many secrets. Y'better get out here quick."

"Bullshit Mickey. This isn't right."

"Too late for me Drud. Wass the point anyway." And Mickey slumped back in the chair and his head rolled away from Drood.

Almost instantly he snapped his head back up and looked at Drood with alarm, as if some synaptic sting had just occurred, and said, "Use medicines to solve your problems. You know all about medicines from the old days. They'll solve everything everywhere you go. That's the answer. Medicines." And Mickey was gone again. Back into somnolent torpor where the porpoises jumped and the birds dipped and sang. A slight smile wobbled over his face and Drood pumped his hand for a minute to no avail. Drood was angry and resolved to find the doctor and let him have it.

"Is he in?" Drood said, pushing past the receptionist to the doctor's rooms behind. She tried to stop him but he didn't even pause. He caught the doctor reading a chart. The man was engrossed and looked intelligent and even kindly. He was in his fifties, maybe sixties and wore conservative clothes and moved carefully. He looked up as Drood approached him and frowned at the unexpected person.

"Can I help you?" He wondered.

"I came here about your patient Mickey. What are you doing to him? He's almost comatose. You have no right to experiment with him."

The doctor didn't hide behind protocol or pretend he didn't know whom Drood was talking about. He just looked squarely at Drood and said, "You family?" Drood kind of admired the guy for that.

"A friend. I've been through the mental health professions, and I know for sure nobody is supposed to be in the condition he's in right now unless they're dangerous. And Mickey's never been dangerous a day in his life. What are you doing to him?"

"Well, I don't really have to tell you anything, but I will. Mickey volunteered for a drug-testing program. He went through a rigorous education process, signed several waivers, and assured me personally that he wanted to go through the trials. As to his condition now, his body is adjusting to the new stuff; he'll come around in another 15 to 20 hours. They're keeping a careful eye on him and he's really in no danger at all. He'll just be a little groggy for a while. It only started this morning. You have a problem with any of that?"

Drood looked at the man and folded his arms. Was Mickey confused and why did his paranoia involve this man, and why did he also cooperate and work so closely with this man if he had such great paranoia about him? It was a snap decision and he had to get out of town. He made the decision.

"All right. Well thank you for telling me all that. But nobody's watching him at all up there. Can you call and make sure somebody knows where he is and how he's doing?"

"Sure. I'll do that right now. Don't worry. Mickey's in good hands." Did Drood see a gleam in the good doctor's eyes? He couldn't be sure, but this doctor was not one that Drood had the time and resources to fight. He'd put Tom on the case of taking care of Mickey, and maybe Mannanan was involved here, in which case Drood believed all was lost for Mickey.

He'd have to write Mickey and lecture him about volunteering for drug trials and about getting to paranoid and too involved in the medical system. Maybe he'd be better in a halfway house. "Mickey keeps telling me truths," Drood thought, "I've got to keep that pipeline open."

Chapter 20

"You have to go down to the Labor Department for that kind of thing. We don't do that here. We only teach English. There's no job service here." Tag was repeating this for the third time to the man who stood in front of him. He knew the man spoke a little English and he was sure the man had been to the Labor Department because he actually had a green card and everything. It was the first green card Tag had seen. Most of their clients were illegals, he assumed, and they paid the five dollars weekly in cash. Tag looked around but Mrs. DiTomasi was nowhere in sight. She was fluent in Spanish and could have solved the problem right away.

"Un momento," he said to the man and excused himself.

He went into the adjoining room where the waiting room was and where all the people were and he scanned the room for Mrs. D. No sign of her. He turned back and was crossing the hall into the "teaching" room, when the door at the end of the hall opened and Mrs. D. came in followed by a young woman. She was behind Mrs. D. so Tag couldn't see her, but when Mrs. D came up to him she stepped aside so the two could be face to face.

"Tag, this is Deirdre. She's going to be working with us now. She'll have twenty hours a week, in the mornings, and she'll probably be at the desk next to yours. Deirdre, this is Tag, he's been with us for three months now, and he has a gift for teaching. We love this guy." And she patted Tag's shoulder clumsily. Mrs. D. was the only full-time employee. Most of the grant money went to her salary, and the small hourly wages of the "instructors" came out of what was left over and the pittance brought in by the clients. She was an old civil servant, came of age in the early sixties and somehow managed to remain idealistic and activist through the whole ensuing madness of American life in the second half of the twentieth century and the first few years of the twenty-first. In the interview she liked Deirdre immediately and she had always been fond of Tag. She hoped they would get along. When she glanced from one to the other she saw she needn't have worried about that.

Tag and Deirdre looked at each other and smiled and then the two of them couldn't stop smiling. They didn't look at each other while Mrs. D. babbled along, but the attraction was instantaneous and deep and felt more like recognition or reconciliation than a meeting. They were both delighted to have found each other instantly, and they saw into each other, and each saw what the other one saw and they giggled and they each knew that the other had felt the same thing.

Tag said, "Nice to meet you." And instead of offering his hand, he patted her on the forearm. Shivers went up her arm and she thought, "Awesome."

Tag asked Mrs. D. to take care of his client, and offered to show Deirdre her desk and materials. Mrs. D. smiled and left them alone. Tag went into the teaching room and walked to the empty desk. He pulled the chair out and smiled a joyous grin and said, "Boy am I glad you're here." And she smiled shyly back and said, "Me too."

"They come in pretty fast and furious and to not lose too much money we're supposed to see as many as possible, twenty minute lessons each. Clock them; take notes on the times, the number on the card, and the name. Obviously we focus on the survival stuff, food, transportation, jobs, and money, stuff like that. Once they get enough of those words, we start putting them together in sentences. Ever do this kind of thing before?"

"I have, as a matter of fact," she said. "Thanks. It looks like you have another client." And indeed he did. He started backing toward the client, keeping his face to her and said, "Let's talk later, and don't go away, O.K.?"

And Deirdre replied, "No chance of that." His eyes were so deep and brown and his smile was so strong and his features so chiseled she thought she could stare at him for hours. She didn't mind being forward with someone so beautiful. She was almost all the way in love already. He had gotten right to business, no need to flirt or hit on her, he knew his feelings and could read hers. She liked that. "Priorities straight. And those brown eyes, my god. And he works helping people." Dee Dee was very glad to be where she was.

Tag seated his client at his desk and stepped back to Deirdre's desk. He told her to ask Mrs. D or himself when she had any questions at all. He told her they'd probably be sending someone back to her within a couple of minutes. In the meantime she should just relax. He pointed to the restroom, straightened everything on the desk, told her to take a walk around the place if she liked. He acted as though he owned the place, but not in a pushy way, in a helpful, commanding way. Tag then went back to his client, a Viet Namese woman. He made symbols with his hands, repeating the words, correcting her carefully, encouraging her, smiling. She got the pronunciation of the words right on the first try each time, but seemed to have no short term memory. She couldn't remember any of them a moment after she had learned them. Tag surmised that she was probably nervous, scared, or perhaps even traumatized. Something had overwhelmed the short-term memory and she was functional in all other aspects so probably not brain damaged. Well, one rarely got to the sources of learning problems in a job like this. Give them the words they need, move on. Next. This was band-aid social work, not problem solving.

He watched Deirdre and saw her move slowly, quietly around the room. She read everything posted on the walls. She looked thoughtful and serious. Her beautiful blue eyes checked him out every now and then and she smiled when she caught him looking at her. She seemed honest and open and he liked that. He hoped it was real. It was weird how her presence and her carriage matched his vision perfectly and at the same time he'd never imagined her face. He'd have to write or call Drood and tell him it only took three months in L.A. to fulfill this part of his dream, to find the girl. Tag was excited and he lost the fatigue of day-to-day big city life that had built up in him and he was starting life over again in that moment when she walked in.

Chapter 21

It was Drood's fourth week of stalking the streets of New York and he hadn't lost the slightest spark from the soul-fire that drove him there from Syracuse. He'd sent more money to Tag, sold everything he had, quit his job, and headed down the road. He had a last fond look at Syracuse as the truck pulled out onto 81 and headed south for New York, and he hoped to come back there some day. He had some things to do and he didn't know what would become of him, but if he could, he wanted to get back to see Shiny and Gus and Tom. He wanted to go up on the roof of the old magic factory one last time, where Tag had shown him, and where they had gone for so many of their talks. He remembered sitting on the roof with Tag, the two of them talking and sometimes arguing, sometimes laughing. The expanse of tar and metal and glass stretched away from them in so many different directions. He had to get back there. There was something more he hoped to do there, if everything else went right. He had a sudden vision of the stairway into the dark unknown basement and felt an urge to go there. There was something important down there

But Drood's resurrection continued with a fierce downhill rush of momentum. He was on the streets of New York stalking his prey, the inimitable McGrath, and he was totally incognito. A few weeks of not shaving and living on the streets could make a person invisible to others. Drood was free to roam the city invisible, his Druidic teaching and powers coming back to him. He mumbled prayers out loud, he stared, and he recited songs and poems. To the New Yorkers who passed him he was quite mad, a ragged homeless man who was hallucinating and full of electric energy.

Drood sat on the bench watching the pigeons outside City Hall. "The Brooklyn Bridge is right over there," he thought, "and maybe I'll take a swing over there and walk across tonight and look around and look down." Drood wasn't nostalgic about New York. He had left there in misery and pain and he was seeing it as a new place, through the eyes of a predator. He'd heard that it was a safer and more prosperous city than it had been when he lived there, but he couldn't see any difference. It was gray and black, it was hard, and it was competitive. He watched the people come and go from the front of City Hall; lunch hour was especially important for stalking, because everyone went out for a walk, or some food, or to the bank, or whatever, during lunch time. He knew who he was looking for and he knew that enough days of waiting and he'd find his quarry eventually. Drood had a flashback and remembered his days wandering the streets of New York so many years before. A lonely and lost immigrant who had no idea how or why he had come there or what the big city meant, or how you lived in it.

He watched the secretaries come and go, looking worried and nervous, and he watched all the men in their blue suits, white shirts, and black shoes. They were all talking. Talking, talking, talking. New York is all about talking, he thought. Well, he was all about silence now, Drood thought. And he was going to bring a little silence into New York if he could. And then he'd speak to someone else, and Claire's face swam into view, and he'd spread some more silence, if he could find her. And then he'd go out to L.A. to see Tag and to meet the daughter he had dreamed about. Tag didn't know yet that he was going to fall in love with Drood's daughter, but who else could it be? Drood kept himself going through the weeks of waiting by imagining the two of them together and remembering the dream. When he was weary or depressed or despairing, he recalled the dream in exquisite detail and it got him through. He could almost retrieve some of the feelings of deep peace that had washed over him in the dream.

Drood was thinking about it as he sat on the bench in the heat. He figured that anyone who looked closely would see a homeless man who looked unusually composed and self-possessed. He looked grungy, but his arms were spread on the back of the bench, legs crossed, foot gently swinging, a bon vivant, or perhaps a man of leisure, an intellectual. A graceful bum. He sat, unselfconscious, thinking about his daughter and then he stiffened and craned his neck. A familiar walk and some funny ears. Could it be his quarry? He got up off the bench and followed the man down Broadway and into a pizza shop. He got behind him and got a good look at him and there could be no doubt. It was him. He had found the man he was compelled to silence. McGrath.

Drood went to the back of the store and ordered a slice and sat in a booth facing the street. McGrath stood at one of the standing counters and wolfed down a slice of pizza. He hadn't recognized Drood, although he had been the one who had betrayed Drood to the police so many years ago, fingered him as an accomplice of a famous Irish mobster, and turned them on to his trail. He had promised Drood immunity and Drood had fallen for it and the result was exile, banishment, a fugitive existence, loss of family, and ultimately, madness. He remembered McGrath's smugness and his assurance and he remembered how McGrath had coveted his own wife. He began to boil inside and when McGrath walked out, Drood had to take a second to compose himself before following.

McGrath crossed to the west side of Broadway and headed downtown. Drood stayed on the east side of the street and tailed him. McGrath went down the slight hill toward Bowling Green and Drood remembered that a bar right down here was where he had last seen McGrath. "So, the ghoul still haunts the same world," Drood mused. "Good. It shouldn't be too hard to figure out how to handle him." Drood counted his own assets: anonymity, he was sure he had long ago been forgotten or given up as dead, the advantage of a surprise attack, and a full knowledge of McGrath and his world. Whereas, McGrath had no understanding at all of Drood and Drood's life, and he had everything to lose. Drood had nothing to lose. And McGrath was going to lose. Of that, Drood was determined. But to set him up, Drood had to use something that McGrath wanted; McGrath only operated on greed and pure self-interest. People like that were easy to trap, but you had to have bait. Money, position, fame, sex, Drood had nothing to use. He had some thinking to do.

Drood followed McGrath and watched as he went into a building directly across from the benches of the Bowling Green. Drood sprinted across the street and pushed through the revolving doors just in time to see which elevator McGrath had gotten on. Drood knew he'd be hustled out of there quick because of his appearance. The security guard rose from his chair and came around the desk to greet him. Drood didn't even listen as the man instructed him, ordered him, and then put an arm on his shoulder. His eyes were locked on the elevator indicator and it stopped at 5th floor and stayed there. Drood would come back when there was a different security guard on duty and would look at the lobby directory in his fifteen seconds before getting thrown out again. He'd take a chance that it was McGrath getting off on the fifth floor and find the names of the companies there. He'd know where McGrath worked and what he did and then payback shouldn't be a difficult thing to plan.

* * *

Some months after they had met, Tag hung up the phone and sat frowning at his desk. Deirdre had a client and he watched her for a moment. She leaned in toward the person, trying desperately to put the language into the man's head, make him get it. She patted his shoulder, she cooed, she repeated motions and words carefully, she was trying as hard as she could. Tag was impressed with the effort, the seriousness, and the passion and he wondered how long it would last. Day after day of trying to make tired, frightened, uneducated, half-desperate people learn a difficult language tended to make you numb and Tag had to remind himself all the time not to just go through the motions. Having Deirdre next to him was an inspiration. She was so perfect, he thought. She brushed a strand of dark hair behind her ear and caught his eye for a second. She moved just the corner of her mouth in acknowledgement - she was always alert to him- and kept right on going with her explanation. The client's tongue seemed to be too thick and he couldn't handle the pronunciation. His eastern European nativity caused him to swallow the vowels and squash the consonants.

Tag leaned back and put his hands behind his head. He looked at the ceiling. "Where the hell is Drood?" he wondered. He had just left another message with Tom and now he was beginning to wonder what had really happened. He was making it O.K. on his own. He had two jobs and he was finding the card games and learning the rules of each house, figuring out which games he was good at, which games he should avoid. His bankroll was still intact; he was about breaking even. But there were some things he wanted to talk over with Drood. He didn't come out here to break even. He had places to go and he had a lot to learn, but he had to start making money at cards, like now. He hoped that Drood was getting his messages anyway, wherever he was.

Tag went to the front desk and asked them not send him any more clients; he had some errands to run. Since it was practically a volunteer job nobody gave him a hard time about his hours unless he was the only one working that day. He went back inside and waited as Deirdre finished with her client and turned to him.

"I'm taking off, I have some things to do. You want to go to the beach later?"

"Yeah. I'll be home. I've only got a half hour here, and then I'm going to eat and head back."

"O.K., I'll get Digger's car and come by around 3:30. How's that?"

"Good." A peck on the cheek for good luck and Tag was out on the street and man it was hot today.

He walked down to Hollywood Boulevard and stood on a corner. He had some thinking to do and he wanted to see some people and observe. It was something Drood taught him. Stand still someplace where there are a lot of people and a person could learn more in an hour than from a year of studying psychology. Searching for the roots and underlying causes of human behavior was not nearly as important, practical, or sensible as studying the behavior itself. Tag really missed Drood and had begun to smoke like Drood. He had begun even to dress like him, giving up adolescent clothes for faded jeans and colored t-shirts. He kept his high-tops though, had to be himself. He didn't realize it at first, but being seventeen, dressing down, and standing on a corner in Hollywood identified you as a prostitute and he'd had to fend off advances and cops whenever he stood on the wrong corner. He saw how the weak and the desperate could easily get trapped. Somebody offers you $150 bucks for ten minutes, you measure your disgust. Once you've given up that much, there's not a whole lot left to give up, but you don't realize it at the time.

Tag watched a Mexican couple arguing their way down the street. "About time I learn Spanish, living in this city," he thought. He wanted to know what they were arguing about, but he saw from their body language and their facial expressions that they would stay together. They were arguing passionately, but they had a whole system of rules worked out, so there was no danger in it. He watched an elderly Asian man walking with a cane and occasionally turning stiffly to assess the cars passing him in the busy street. Where was the old man going? The man moved thoughtfully but also uncertainly. Tag surmised that it wouldn't be long before the man had to be kept in or watched. A black man walked by in the other direction, looking in all the windows and singing to himself. He looked to Tag like he had had sex this morning or maybe late into the night. He had the loose-jointed casual saunter of a satisfied man. A homeless man rounded the corner where Tag stood and looked him right in the eye. He was muttering to himself and Tag couldn't tell if the man had hands or not, since they were hidden in an army fatigue jacket, Viet Nam or what? For no reason at all, Tag expected to find Drood here. And he decided he'd make it a regular thing, hanging out on this corner waiting for Drood. Drood wouldn't just vanish, he'd contact him and Tag knew Drood was coming, sooner or later. Nothing to worry about. He knew they weren't done just yet. There was something big they had to do yet. He didn't know what it was, but there was something big still to come. In the meantime, how could he make more money at cards? He came up with the rookie's idea: he had to get into the bigger games. Drood had warned him against rushing into this, but Tag felt he was ready and what did he have to lose but money? He' make it somehow. He resolved to try the Sunset Lucky Card Club again. There was a big game there and he'd have to eventually win it. Then, he could head to Vegas, having earned his stripes.

* * *

Deirdre watched Tag go and waited for her last client of the day. Tag was brooding today, being a little mysterious and she felt a spasm of concern, but she had her own problems as well. At least they would hit the beach and not have to live in the harsh, ugly world for a while. They could dream and swim and stare at all the people and smoke and drink and not be ambitious. It would be relaxed and his only L.A. friend, Digger, might come later with his music and his sayings and his stories. And Tag would probably be more lighthearted then too. They had a tacit agreement to put aside all other thoughts for a few hours a day when they went to the beach. There usually weren't a lot of people at the beach during the week, which surprised Deirdre. She couldn't understand why anyone would want to live in this city without spending a significant amount of time at the beach.

The arrival of her client brought her back to the present. She repeated words, she smiled, she coaxed, she showed how the tongue and the lips worked to form the right sounds, and she pointed to things. She used all the pictures and books and props she had and she put her heart into it while at the same time she thought about all the articles she should be writing. Life was all happening at once and it was very fast and sometimes it was overwhelming, but most of the time it was just a delight to her to be able to do so many things at once, to have such a full life, to find out what her limits were. Deirdre was eager to know. She knew that people didn't have this kind of energy forever and she burned to live it all and to push and stretch everything until life told her otherwise. Her mother, her school, New York, her mysterious father; it was all beginning to slough off her like an old skin and she felt raw and tingly, alive for the first time.

She dipped her head down to try to demonstrate the concept of "under" to her client. It was amazing the difference in how different languages handled prepositions, but a significant part of her mind was concerned with why she hadn't been able to sell her articles. She thought they were sharp, perceptive, and detailed, without being too smart. Vivid. She thought she had captured unique but recognizable angles and made them come alive for a reader. In fact, she had, but she had no readers, no editors, no anybody to get back to her, to help her learn what worked and what didn't work. All her work was returned with form letters and she seemed unable to get past the guard dogs at each of the publications. She learned what every writer eventually learns: the quality of your work is between you and whatever Gods you have. The rest is chance, birth, and compromise.

She had written an article on the quality of the water in the ocean, a descriptive tour of the all parts of the city, a mid-westerner's perspective on the city (she'd had to stretch the truth a little on that one), an article on the bug life of the beach, an article on clubbing, an article on English as a Second Language options in the city, an article on gambling (thanks to Tag), an article on the family structure of the Mexican-American, an article on the differences between the cultural experiences in New York vs. L.A. (she'd really enjoyed thinking and investigating that one), an article on two retired area baseball players and what they were doing now, and she was in the process of doing an article on the profession of Funeral Directing (with assistance from Digger). It was really a prodigious amount of legwork and writing for someone who had only been in the city and on the job for a few short months. She was convinced the writing was good, Tag confirmed it, and she wondered what it took to make it as a freelance writer. Sometimes she wanted to scream. Her last client of the day left and her mind instantly seized the issue of freelance writing again. It was a bone she couldn't let go of, just like Tag with his obsession for the best poker games. She had to make it. There was no fallback plan and she couldn't stand living in near poverty too much longer. She just wouldn't have it.

After a steamy, maddeningly sunny and depressive bus ride home, she slugged up the stairs and into her afternoon apartment. There were three messages on her machine. The last one said.

"Deirdre, this is Johnny Morew" a woman's voice said, "and we'd like to talk to you about an upcoming assignment. We can't use the samples you sent us, but we have an idea for a story that we're hoping you're right for and available for, please call me back...."

"YES!!! YES YES YES!!!!" She jumped and spun in the air and tripped over a coffee mug on the floor. She went down to one knee and then flat on her stomach, laughing. She rolled over on her back and smiled and breathed deeply. Her first story assignment, and it was a major newspaper too! This was it; this was the break she wanted. She was very curious about the assignment and she was dying to find out what she'd be paid. How could she get more information on what she could expect? Her mind raced and she began to calculate. How could she disguise her age in the interview? She had presented herself in the portfolio as being older than she really was, and she knew her work came off as being that of an older reporter. She ran to the mirror to look at herself. "Nope," she thought, "I'm still a teenager, definitely. I'll never be able to pull it off." And then she thought about the clothes she must wear and the posture and oh there was too much to do. First she'd have to calm down enough to return the call and set up the meeting.

Deirdre wandered around her apartment looking out the windows and feeling great about herself and her life and she couldn't wait to tell Tag and she even thought about calling her mother, but it was way too premature for that. She was going to stick to her plan of mailing her mother nothing but a copy of the first published work. Her mother had tried to get her to come back to New York and had said some negative things. Deirdre knew her mother was critical out of fear and worry, but still she wanted to prove to her mother that her doubts were baseless. Yes, telling her mother would be the sweetest part of the whole thing. Deirdre was going to get her flask out and fill it with whiskey to bring to the beach. They needed to celebrate this. She just knew this would get Tag in a better mood.

Chapter 22

The famous Venice Beach. Tag and Deirdre were still tourists, in a way, and they had never even tried to go to any other beach. It was L.A.'s showcase for weirdoes, musclemen, thongs, hippies, skates and boards, costumes, sunshine, drugs and alcohol, art, food, mental illness and homelessness, and selling. They enjoyed wandering up and down the sidewalk and they looked at favorite beach houses they would rent when they got enough money. They liked to sit in the little restaurants that changed names every week. They ate bean sprouts and mushrooms and drank juice. They sat in the sand and read books. Tag went swimming occasionally, which really made him a tourist, and they looked at all the people. The beach was where they had met Digger, their new friend. They watched as many sunsets as they could. They never got cold and they never got bored. They held hands and sometimes they had long passionate kisses in the twilight. Every night they were there, when it was finally dark, they left, walking slowly, with heads down, back into the city of cars and roads. They always left with a feeling of fullness, completeness, and a little sadness. They were quiet and gentle with each other and each time they walked away from the beach they both thought they were living in a dream of rare beauty and strangeness. If they never reached their dreams, they at least had this time of hope and purple night. They reveled in each other's youth and beauty and they had long talks about the future and about what they loved about each other. If Digger was with them, it was the same. He saved all his frenetic chatter for when they were in the real city. He too seemed to calm down by the water.

This afternoon Deirdre had shared her good news and they were in a happier than usual mood. Tag's moodiness had left him instantly when he heard about her assignment. He watched her move about the sand and the blanket with her quiet joy, a half smile ready to burst into full bloom at any time. Digger had some news too.

"Tag I found out where there's a big game this weekend. You can get into it for $1,000 and it's gonna have some weak players in it. You can really clean up. Also, I heard there was gonna be this big player there from Vegas. The couple of guys that I heard are playing want to see how good they are against a pro. Might be a good game for you to get into."

"Where is it?"

"Down in some guy's house, down in Huntington Beach."

"Huntington Beach?"

"Yeah, I guess the guy who's holding the game is some kind of corporate lawyer."

"Hook me up?"

"Sure."

And Tag too had a reason to be excited about his future. Maybe this would be his big break. They drank some more whiskey, and soon the three of them were quite drunk. It was a new experience for Deirdre and Tag. They hugged and held onto each other and were playful with Digger. If anybody had been sitting right nearby they would have been either amused or nauseated by the full expression of awkward, loving, energetic, crazy youth. The sun began to go down and they were all three changing, metamorphosis, from tanned brown skins to a dusky pink in the sunset's glow. Digger was singing an old Beatles tune under his breath, "Love Me Do", and Tag and Deirdre had gotten tired and were just staring out to sea.

Deirdre thought the Pacific Ocean looked more colorful and exotic than the Atlantic and it had a glorious western wildness that you couldn't find in the east. The eastern ocean appeared in her memory as colder, greener and grayer, more full of fish and boats and traffic, less open and fanciful. They watched the waves pound slowly, hissing, and they reveled in the salt breeze. Digger noticed none of it, but Tag and Deirdre were entranced and felt the stirrings of a God. Digger's singing was at the fringe of their minds, when his voice stopped abruptly,"Oh shit."

And they turned to follow his gaze and saw a man coming straight towards them over the sand from the sidewalk. He was homeless, filthy, wearing several layers of rotten clothes in the summer of L.A. His gray hair fanned out in a perfect circle around his entire head, including a grizzly gray beard. He carried a plastic shopping bag in each hand, filled with an indeterminable swirl of stuff. He had shorts on and taped up old sneakers. His legs, by contrast, were completely hairless and smooth and tanned to leather. They were lean and sinewy and they gave the appearance of belonging to a different torso altogether.

Digger was annoyed. He had lived in L.A. all his life and knew this was going to be some kind of aggressive panhandling that might cause a scene and ruin their peace on the beach. Deirdre was cautious and kept a close eye on him. Tag, who had lived in neither L.A. nor New York, saw only an individual as the man came right up to the blanket. He wondered what could have brought the man to this condition, what kind of tragedy or weakness. He looked the man right in the eye as he came up. Digger and Deirdre edged cautiously away and left Tag sitting, looking up directly at the man, who now hunched over from the waist to address Tag.

"Your teacher is the father of your love. Learn everything you can now, before the whole thing goes out the window. The evil doctor has slain the oracle and your teacher is bent on revenge."

Tag started to reply but the man left just as abruptly as he had come and walked straight back to the sidewalk. They stared at him as he made a beeline down the sidewalk and eventually disappeared around a bend, heading south. Deirdre and Digger edged back onto the blanket.

"What did he say?" she wanted to know.

"Some babbling. But it was weird, some of it sort of applied to me. He talked about my teacher being the father of my love, and some other stuff about a doctor and an oracle."

"Have you seen him before?" Deirdre wanted to know.

"Nope. Just some nut-job."

Deirdre teased him, "Well, if I'm your love, that means your teacher is my father. And since my father has been dead since you were one, your teacher is a ghost." She giggled.

Tag shrugged, "Whatever."

They left the beach and the drunkenness began to wear off and Tag and Deirdre thought about the big week ahead of them. Digger steered the car through the highways and they ended up back in shitty old Hollywood, Deirdre dropped off first, then Tag. Digger drove away and disappeared into the traffic and the lights of the city. Tag opened the outer door to his building and climbed the beat-up old stairs and put his key into the lock. He turned and looked down the stairway into the little pool of light on the floor coming from the street. He sighed. Big week coming up. His apartment sat heavy and empty and he on the sagging sofa. He picked up his deck of cards and dealt out four hands. This was how he had learned to think and to work.

*　*　*

By Saturday, Tag was anxious about the game. He knew Digger was susceptible to rumors and Tag had been on wild goose chases with him before. Digger was the kind of guy who wasn't happy unless he felt that he was part of something spectacular, and since he wasn't the kind of guy to ever be part of something spectacular, he made it all up. The game was supposed to be in somebody's house and Tag didn't like that. He'd be in hostile territory and he'd have relied on Digger to get him into the game. Tag got dressed up anyway and tried to look as much like a tourist as he could. His youth would cause them to underestimate him anyway, but he wanted to make sure. He thought about Deirdre and smiled. Her big meeting was Monday. By that time he'd either have won and would be on his way to the big time, or he'd be struggling worse than before. Tag had decided that he couldn't waste this opportunity; he really needed to go for it. No more learning, no more aiming for breaking even, he had to hit hard this time. He was going to bring his whole bankroll and go until it was gone or until the game broke up. "Got to have the boundaries straight before going into the game," he told himself.

Digger drove him south down the coast through the small beach mini cities. Tag watched the houses and the lawns get cleaner and nicer and the streets get a little quieter as they left the main city. Digger seemed to know exactly where he was going and made the turns quickly and efficiently.

"You nervous?" he asked Tag.

Tag looked at him and smiled. "Nah," he said. He was, but Drood had taught him to be very careful about showing his feelings anytime he was near a game or in a tough spot. Tag was practicing his game face, getting himself up for the cards. He worked on getting the butterflies under control. The self-doubts had to go. He stared out the window, and said to Digger, "Just another game you know. I'll either win or lose. Tomorrow I'll get up and have breakfast. You know what I'm saying?" He held his hand out steady, palm down, to show Digger that he wasn't nervous.

Digger finally pulled into a driveway in a row of houses that looked as though they'd all been poured from the same plastic mold. They were wealthy-looking and they were all immaculate and no cars were parked in the driveways. "In the garages under lock and key. Porsches I bet," thought Tag.

"Just go up to that door and knock. When they answer tell them that you're the friend of Digger's, that it's all arranged for you to be there. Good luck man. I'll wait here until you get in. Give me a call on my cell when you want me to pick you up. Doesn't matter what time, man, I'll come."

Tag stood at the door and looked at the gilt fittings on the doorknocker. He took a deep breath. He knocked and after a moment the door opened and there was psychedelic swirling music and warmth coming from inside. The man who opened the door looked a little drunk. Tag said what Digger had told him and he was shown in. The music was really loud and there were a lot more people there than Tag had expected. It was kind of like a party was in full swing. Tag could smell booze and pot. Tag didn't like this. It was too distracting and Drood had taught him to be very wary when drugs and alcohol surrounded money. It was a bad combination. The man who had shown him in had felt no obligation to do anything further and Tag stood in the middle of a large room that had huge windows looking out over the ocean. It was the background of the party and it looked enticingly white and peaceful. Nobody paid any attention to him or to the beach and he began to wonder if he was in the right place after all.

Finally, a woman came up behind him and whispered in his ear, "Drink, young man?" She put her hand on his hip at the same time. Tag started and turned to her, "No, I'm just here to play cards. Thank you."

"Well you better get on upstairs, then, I think they're getting ready to start." And she nodded to the stairway at the back of the room. Tag smiled and breathed a sigh of relief and immediately made his way through the party to the stairs. Nobody guarded the door and it was unlocked. Tag went in and found himself in the middle of a by-now-familiar scene. There were two tables set up, smoke in the air, a wet bar, and the chips and cards. The room was all male and nobody seemed to be organizing the games. As Tag stood there, motionless, eventually all eyes came to rest on him. He repeated his entrance line about being sent by Digger.

A bald, fat man with a cigar came around the table and introduced himself as Wazzy. He didn't look much like a corporate lawyer.

"You got $1,000?" Wazzy asked.

"Yeah."

"Well, hand it over." And Tag gave him the money and he was in. Tag had $3500 more with him, all the money he had. If it didn't go well tonight, he figured maybe his poker-playing dream would end. He gritted his teeth. "Dammit, I will do it." And the first game called was seven-card stud and Tag smiled and relaxed. That was his game.

Tag's table had three other players, a Mexican, and two Italian looking guys in Armani suits. Tag wondered which one was the big player from Vegas, but then he had to consider that Digger might have had the details all wrong. He glanced over at the other table and saw that it was larger, six players, probably the regulars, and he was at the "extras" table.

They got down to the game right away and Tag was dealt two tens and two fives before he even had a chance to think. He was here to make big bucks, and he decided to push it. He bet $100, the two Italians checked and the Mexican raised him fifty. Tag heard one of the other players call the Mexican Emilio and Emilio looked hard at Tag as he raised. Tag threw his chips in and returned Emilio's stare. The man was trying to psyche him out. One of the other players folded, the other stayed in. With the next card, Tag made the full house, three tens, two fives and he folded his cards down. He could feel Emilio trying to stare into him and so he looked over at the other table, wishing he could be there where there would be more money and where Emilio wasn't. The betting went around again and Tag and Emilio were in it against each other in earnest. Tag watched him closely when he could, Emilio didn't give him much opportunity. He kept his eyes glued to Tag's until Tag could see the black pupils even when he wasn't looking at him. Emilio had long curly, lustrous black hair, and a little bit of Indian in the eyes, but his mouth was a thin slit and his nose was sharp and everything about him was alert, birdlike, predatory. He wore all black with turquoise jewelry. He said very little, but he jerked his head toward Tag once and spoke in Spanish to Wazzy as he wandered by. Emilio looked perpetually tense and Tag couldn't tell if that was the way he was or if he was uptight because he was playing cards.

Tag's full house took the hand over Emilio's aces and sevens, and he raked the chips in and tried hard not to smile, but he was sure his glee was showing on his face. Emilio glared at him. Emilio had played as if he was certain Tag was bluffing or as if Tag might not know completely how to play. Digger had assured him this was a big-time game, so Tag tried to look as professional as he could. He returned Emilio's gaze for brief periods, just to show he wasn't intimidated, but he also looked away from the gaze as if it was a thing of no importance. Tag's tourist act was to get the other players' money. He picked Emilio as the pro, the man to beat. The other players wouldn't notice him facing Emilio down and would try stupid tricks on the young boy-tourist. Tag could envision it all and marveled at the many levels of perception involved in the game.

Tag ran through Drood's teachings as the hands were played and folded and remembered what Drood had taught him about neuroscience. When the eyes go up and to the left the person is trying to imagine something, when the eyes go up and to the right the person is trying to invent something. It helped with bluffing. The two Italians were decent players, but they were conservative and after a while Tag knew when they bet that they had a good hand and he began to know how good their hands were each time because they bet predictably.

The game was between Tag and Emilio. Emilio was increasingly nervous and blew out through his nose each time Tag won. He occasionally muttered to himself and he seemed to bet and play exclusively against Tag. He was aggressive, he was pushing, and he was looking for Tag's weak spot. Tag was a little unnerved by the man's glare. He felt unsure of himself briefly and he tried to picture Drood's face and Deirdre's face and they calmed him down. Emilio got more and more agitated as Tag took many of the first several hands. One of the Italians took a hand and Emilio took one, but Tag was on a roll and he was bringing in the chips. He quickly got to the point where he thought he'd be able to last to the end of the game without going bust. Tag estimated his bankroll must have been $7 or $8 K after the first two hours.

After a while Emilio began to get some back by easing off Tag and looking to keep the Italians in each hand by betting low. Tag's string of luck faded and he got mediocre cards and his pot dwindled a little and Emilio's began to build. One of the Italians was near his end by 2:00 and Tag was exhausted. The constant smoke in the room was irritating his eyes and making him impatient. With his fatigue, Tag knew he was in danger of missing some clues or possibly misplaying a hand, miscalculating the odds. And, he figured, Emilio didn't seem to be the type who could walk away happy from a game. If he won he was sure to be angry at Tag for not rolling over more easily; if he lost he'd be furious. His hands twitched and Tag wondered how he could maintain such a high energy level for so long. There was only about an hour to go and Tag was still in the dollars, but he hadn't made a smash, a big score. It was time to start raising the betting. He sensed Emilio felt the same way. Since none of the men at the table knew each other, it was dead quiet. The cards slapped on the table, the chips clinked on each other and grunts were uttered. The play was fast, no pondering. Tag's adrenaline began to pump as the stakes rose and the time limit approached.

Emilio won a big hand and let out his only smile of the night. Tag finally thought he picked up a "tell". When Emilio had a great hand, not just a good one, he'd look up quickly from his cards and glare at Tag, as if challenging him. He wanted a fight; poker seemed to be manhood to Emilio. Emilio had quickly picked Tag as his adversary and he played not just for the money, but also to dominate. Tag figured he looked like a naïve young gringo tourist; just the kind of person Emilio would be able to push around. That Tag had been able to hold his own in the game had probably insulted Emilio, who would think he couldn't be beaten by a wet-behind-the-ears white boy with a flat upstate New York accent. But Tag continued to hold his own under Emilio's assault and by 2:00 a.m. Emilio could no longer hide his animosity. Tag caught the looks. When Emilio had only a good hand or a mediocre hand, he looked at the Italians first. When he had a killer hand he tried to stare Tag down.

Tag won two big hands and the money was getting large. Another hand was dealt and Emilio instantly glared at Tag with fury in his eyes. Tag looked at his own cards and saw that he had a potential flush and a potential straight flush. Emilio was blazing across the table from him and Tag smiled at him for the first time all night. He probably should not have advertised that he had discovered a tell, but he was young and not immune to Emilio's unspoken challenges to his manhood. Tag looked Emilio right in the eye and folded his cards. Emilio stared at the cards on the table and muttered under his breath. He turned his attention to the Italians, but they quickly folded too and Emilio won a pretty measly pot. For the rest of the game, Tag owned the table. He never played when Emilio had the big hand and this frustrated Emilio so much that he made mistakes even when he didn't have the big hand. Tag had cracked the code and he began to play Emilio, carefully, and managed the man's rage to make money. The chips piled up fast and furious and Tag kept telling himself to hold on, to pay attention, to keep it together, it was almost over.

Finally, three o'clock came and Wazzy announced in a loud voice from the other table.

"That's it. Last hand."

And they played out the final hand and Tag took a lot of Emilio's money in a game of high betting. He knew Emilio didn't have the hand, but he pretended to be nervous and uncertain and Emilio kept recklessly raising his bets. Tag tried to look as young and as innocent as he could as he kept up with the betting. One of the Italians was out, the other was foolishly betting with the other two, and the pot grew enormous. The other table ended their game and raked in their chips. One of Wazzy's people was distributing the cash and another was cleaning up. Wazzy and the other players gathered around Tag's table to watch the end of the final hand. They seemed surprised that the young man had such a huge pile of chips.

Emilio bet and Tag raised and Emilio raised again. Tag called and they laid their cards down.

Straight for Emilio, ten high. He smiled at Tag and muttered something in Spanish. Tag laid his cards down. Straight flush, spades, jack high.

"Whoa!" said Wazzy. There were exclamations from the gathered crowd. There was a hum around the room as Emilio stood up and knocked the folding chair backwards.

"Puta!" he spat at the boy. And he let loose a torrent of abuse directed not at Tag but at Wazzy, in sharp and rapid Spanish.

Wazzy turned red and kept his mouth shut until Emilio had finished. Then he motioned for Emilio to follow him through a side door. They disappeared.

Tag stacked and counted his chips and almost fainted. Unless he miscounted, he was going to walk away from the table with $20,000. A big stake, a huge victory, the beginning of a wonderful career. He sat still at the table, not knowing what to do. One of Wazzy's people sat down at the seat vacated by Wazzy and paid the Italian and left a small stack of bills in front of Emilio's chair. Then he looked across at Tag's stack and counted it quickly. He handed two stacks of money to Tag and smiled.

"Be careful with that now. Don't advertise and don't spend it all in one place." The man was serious. Suddenly Tag had a quiver of nerves. There was a whole house full of people here and they probably all knew he was a young man by himself with $20,000. How was he going to get out of there and get home? A couple of the other players congratulated him and asked him his name. He told them just "Tag." It fit. He decided then and there that he would be known in the card-playing world by just the one name, Tag.

Tag was sure he was going to be a force in the world of cards, and he was now full of confidence and he looked forward to savoring his victory. But Drood had taught him well, and he kept his feelings under control and to himself, and he would wait until he was alone and safe with Deirdre to enjoy the moment. Wazzy's man gave him a zip bag to put the cash in and Tag thanked him. He got out his cell phone and dialed.

"Yo. Whosit?" "

"It's me Tag. Get your ass over here. Quick."

"Where are you?"

"I'm at the poker game where you dropped me off, dammit! Are you high?"

"Little bit Tag. Little bit. Where was that place, Huntington Beach right?"

"Digger." And Tag turned away from the other card players who were beginning to file out of the room into the party below.

"Get your ass over here now. It's urgent, man, I won a lot of money and I don't feel safe with it. Get here quick."

"Right man, don't worry. I'm on the case. I'll be there in a half hour."

206

"Be here in fifteen minutes man! I'm tellin' ya. And look. If I'm not right at the front door, drive by the house and look for me at one of the houses two blocks down the hill from there.

"Right."

Tag turned to the door as Wazzy and Emilio came back into the room. Emilio stuffed his money into a pocket and turned to go. Wazzy put a hand on his arm and Emilio stopped. Without looking at Tag, Emilio extended his hand to him. Tag shook it and Wazzy said, "There. No bullshit in my house."

They all turned to leave and as Emilio got to the door, he turned and looked once at Tag. The menace in his dark eyes froze Tag in his shoes and stopped his breathing for a moment. They stared at each other, frozen. Tag moved first and reminded himself that he had won fair and square and had done nothing wrong. He smiled at Emilio and immediately knew it was a mistake. Emilio's eyes shrank to slits and he left the room

Wazzy said, "Watch out for him kid. You've made an enemy." And so he had, Tag considered. He'd made his first serious enemy in gambling. He knew nothing about Emilio or where he came from, but he would have to keep an eye out for him. The man had ill will toward him. Tag had taken his money and had shown him up.

They came down into the party that was now going at full swing. People were very drunk and very high and the haze in the room was redolent of hash and pot. Tag came down the stairs and someone said, "There he is!" And a cheer went up. Word of his winning had spread and Tag was horrified to see all the faces turned toward him and looking at him, most applauding, but some were sizing him up. He wondered how many of them were considering ripping him off. This was a nice house, nice neighborhood, and if it was a well-known regular game then there would probably be no nonsense but it was a party and people were high and it was three in the morning. Tag smiled and waved and the party went back to being raucous. One woman was naked from the waist up and Tag stared at her globules in amazement.

Several people urged Tag to have a drink and relax, enjoy the moment; they wanted to get to know him. One woman took him in hand and brought him around to other groups of people, and she had her hands all over him. Tag was very uncomfortable and the whole thing became surreal as his exhaustion and anxiety began to get the better of him. He felt as though he was going to pass out and he couldn't breathe. The woman looked at him and asked him if he was okay. He said he needed some air and she dragged him to the sliding glass doors that led out to the deck. There were more people partying out there, but Tag went to the farthest corner of the deck and leaned over. The woman tried pawing him and talking to him some more, but Tag remained motionless and eventually she wandered away.

The moon was full and there were no clouds and Tag calmed down after a couple more minutes. It would be about twenty minutes now since he called Digger. He looked at the bright moon and asked its blessing, as Drood had taught him to do. The white circle of reliable, dispassionate light could always be an ally. The party created mayhem inside. He could hear the surf pounding on the other side of the dunes behind the house. If only he could be walking in the moonlight on the beach, with no money in his pockets. Drood had told him that having money was a lot of pressure and a difficult skill to acquire and Tag had thought he was speaking metaphorically, but he realized now that Drood had meant it literally. He was scared over the money. He glanced again at the party and decided he couldn't face going through there, telling people he was leaving, and being seen going. He just wanted to slink away.

There was only one sloppy and amorous huddled couple on the deck now, exploring esophageal anatomy, and so Tag swung up on the railing and climbed over the side of the deck. It was about fifteen feet high, and Tag let go of the railing and fell into the sand. He checked the moneybag, still secure in his pocket, and got to his feet. His ankles now hurt. He walked around the side of the house, and had to maneuver through a gate and climb a fence. Finally, he came to the front corner of the house and peered around. No sign of Digger's car. Somebody else was leaving and he took his time and made a lot of noise getting into his car. Tag stayed by the side of the house until they left. He was just about to walk out to the curb to wait when he saw a little red light go on in a car parked across the street facing up the hill. He could see Emilio in the car cupping a cigarette lighter around a cigarette. The light went out and the window went dark again and the car just sat there and didn't move. Tag couldn't see if there was anyone else in the car, but he didn't

208

care. He didn't want to take any chances. He slipped back around the house and leaned against the wall and tried to figure out a way to get down the street to where Digger could pick him up.

The houses were like town houses, close together, but they all had fences, dogs, and security systems in the back yards and Tag didn't want to risk that. Emilio might be watching the front door, but in the bright moonlight it would be pretty easy to spot someone sliding from the front of one house to the next. He could wait where he was and then just run to the car when Digger pulled up, but there was no guarantee that Emilio wasn't a killer. He certainly looked mean, and $20K was a lot of money, and maybe he'd follow them. And then he'd know what kind of car Digger drove. No, he'd have to go out to the beach and run down to the next block. Then he'd have to trespass to get back to the street, but it would be just one house and hopefully, Digger wouldn't be long after that.

Tag went back the way he had come and went under and around Wazzy's deck. He climbed the wooden stairs over the dune leading to the beach and looked behind him. Someone from the party might have seen him, but they wouldn't think anything of it. Tag saw two huddles of people on the beach, ignored them, and turned quickly south. There was an inlet about a half-mile ahead. Maybe he could walk that far and find a good way out to the street. There was a sidewalk between the houses and the beach and Tag walked quickly. He saw what looked like a sand walkway between two houses and quickly steered into it without thinking. No trespassing, good luck. He came out on the street about where he told Digger to be. Tag sat on the curb. He was slightly around a curve and out of sight from Wazzy's house. He remembered that Emilio had been parked the other way, certainly going back to L.A.

Tag sat breathing quietly for a moment, wishing with all his might that Digger would show up. He replayed all the hands carefully, trying to remember his best plays and to learn something from the experience. He kept a wary eye on the street, and finally, after what seemed like ages, Digger's car came around the curve. Tag hopped in quickly and they took a roundabout way to get out to the freeway. He gave Digger a $100 bill.

"Thanks for driving." Tag smiled.

Digger was high, but looked tired and like he was beginning to sober up.

"Hey thanks man. Wow, you must have done real good."

"I did okay."

"How much did you win?"

"I did okay."

And they both turned around to look as headlights blazed up behind them from the neighborhood as they paused at the on ramp to the freeway. They couldn't tell from the glare, but Tag was sure it had to be Emilio. The car was clearly pursuing them. Digger hit the gas. They roared onto the freeway with Emilio behind them and Digger came alive, his red eyes blazing with fear and adrenaline and Tag held on for dear life. He looked behind and saw Emilio's Cadillac emerge onto the freeway and hesitate. They went around a curve and Digger floored it. They stared straight ahead and they flew back into the city passing cars and swerving into and out of lanes. A mile before their exit they lost sight of the pursuer in the traffic. It seemed like hours by the time they slammed onto the off-ramp and went through a red light. When they got to their neighborhood, there was still no sign of the ominous Cadillac and neither Tag nor Digger could tell where exactly they had lost him. Tag began to wonder if they, in their exhaustion and altered states, had imagined the evil Cadillac in the dark. But he doubted he'd seen the last of Emilio.

* * *

"Weapons," Jonnie Morew said to Deirdre.

Deirdre straightened in her chair. There wasn't enough in the one word to guess what the assignment was and so there had to be more coming. She wanted to make a good impression on the editor, but she didn't know what to say. She felt that any response she made would come off as ignorant. She smiled at Morew, and opened her brief case and took out a pen and pad. She screwed the cap off and put it on the other end of the pen and she made a show of writing the date on her pad, the editor's name, and then just the one word at the top of the page, as a heading. She raised her eyebrows and looked at Morew as if to say, "And?" Morew grinned at her and continued. She liked the way the girl handled herself but she was pretty sure the girl wasn't as old as she claimed to be.

"How old are you?"

Deirdre said, "I was expecting this, I get it all the time." And she pulled out her fake license showing her to be twenty-five. Morew examined it and passed it back to her.

"We want to do a whole series on weapons. You know, violence is a big controversy in this society and everyone wants to know how to solve it. We want to take a different approach. We think people will be fascinated to learn about the weapons that exist in this country for private citizens, and about the history of them and about the psychology of them. We think you can do a good job. It'll be a series, so we will want so many words per week, and we've only got two weeks before the first one is due. We'll pay you $10,000 for the whole thing. What do you think?"

"Yes. I want to use credentials from your company."

"Done."

And the rest of the meeting was a get-to-know you thing where Deirdre banked on being from New York and having gone to prep school to make points while Morew played professional woman and mentor and tried to figure out if Deirdre was gay or not and how she felt about older women.

Deirdre's mind was whirling when she got back to the street. She walked around the corner and stopped to re-read the briefing material the editor had given her. "Weapons," she thought. "That means I've got to go to law enforcement, I've got to go to politicians, gun shows, historians, magazines, and probably to criminals. Hobbyists and lobbyists. They want the cultural angle. I'll have to check out who uses what, when, why. The Constitution. A little world history of weapons for comparison. And I have no time to lose."

She made her way home and her mind never ceased working, trying to figure out every possible angle and then to make a plan of attack. She'd choose the specific approach after she got halfway into the project. She wondered, "how can you have a perspective and share it on something you know nothing about?" It was education time and this was the first fun part about being a freelance journalist. She loved to learn and every subject she wrote about required her to get a thorough education first. She wasn't yet jaded and didn't know that most journalists didn't really want to know much about their subjects. They focused on the story that sold rather than on the story that needed to be written.

Chapter 23

Drood had visited every herbalist and New Age store he could find in the phone book in Manhattan. He was looking for just the right ingredients. Tasteless, colorless, and potent without being lethal or causing any long-term consequences. A dash of Thorn Apple, a grain of hemlock, some monk's head, and some hemp. He couldn't find them in exactly the form he wanted, but he knew enough about the chemical components to make a combination close enough. He'd add a little Ecstasy gotten from one of the street dealers and that should be enough to send McGrath out of his mind for a while. Of course there might be vomiting and sickness, but that was a chance he had to take. He'd prefer it if McGrath just suddenly found himself chemically transported to another world with no warning. McGrath, former advisor to the mayor, big shot in New York, betrayer of Drood.

Drood caught sight of himself in the mirror and he saw a madman with unkempt hair and beard, dirty clothes and gleaming, eager blue eyes. He hoped McGrath would not recognize him, because he'd have to get very close to be able to put his plan into effect. Upset the equilibrium, push him out of himself, then confront him, incite him, make him go wild. Have the police and the white coats ready.

He followed McGrath everywhere, learning his habits. McGrath was a business consultant working downtown, specializing in Public Relations and catering to brokerage houses and e-businesses. He lived on the Upper East Side and he took a car service to work every day. Drood could follow him without trouble because McGrath didn't see homeless people. He was only capable of seeing attractive young women and older men with money. Drood noticed that McGrath had gotten older too. He no longer had that weird energy about him, but his body seemed to be getting sucked inward, no flesh on his arms and legs and abdomen swelling. He looked sick. When Drood had first known him, McGrath was

213

after power and he was dangerous. Now, he had progressed to evil, fully embraced it, and as Drood could see, was being destroyed by it. Drood knew that McGrath was a fully formed person, rigid, and could by conventional means be shaken from his worship of evil. The drug would start the process, Drood would help it along, and then the institutions of mental health would take over and complete the task. "Welcome to the rest of the universe, McGrath, courtesy of me," Drood thought.

Drood became a fixture outside McGrath's building on the Upper East Side. Rain or shine, Drood woke himself from the grating and stood sentinel, put a hat out so people would give him money. The police rousted him several times and drove him to a shelter, but he kept coming back. McGrath even noticed him once and shouted, "Get lost, you bum. Go bother somebody else. We don't need your filth here."

Careful observations showed him that McGrath drank coffee in the limousine on the way to work every day. The driver had it waiting for him in a pot in the holder in the back seat. Drood decided to sneak into that car and that pot for just a few seconds before McGrath came down. The driver was typically ten minutes early, and waited until McGrath came out. Once in a while, McGrath was fifteen or twenty minutes before coming out. In that case, the driver would sometimes get out and go into the deli across the street, and Drood figured that was his chance. He couldn't tell if the driver locked the car or not, but maybe he'd leave it open in case McGrath came down while he was across the street.

As Drood had mixed the ingredients in an alley, behind a dumpster, he had said invocations to Lugh and to Mannanan and to the sun and to the moon to give his potion strength, to set right a wrong, to bring a little justice into the world. He didn't think McGrath was working for any of the major deities. Otherwise he'd have played a far more dramatic role in the world by now. He was a minor criminal, behind the scenes operator, and the man who had betrayed Drood to the police. Drood got the potion together and poured it from the Styrofoam cup into three glass vials. He'd have at least two chances if it didn't work the first time.

Drood had lowered his eyes when McGrath yelled at him, to avoid recognition. It would make the plan even more satisfying. He watched the same people come and go from the building, day after

214

day, and he got to know them and their habits. Single women, full of angst and verve, old men wondering what had happened to their lives, mothers struggling unsuccessfully to make the world a decent place, kids locked in the cement world with no idea of a world beyond New York, working men tired and drowning, arrogant and eager yuppies lost in a totally mistaken understanding of the world, immigrants dragging their countries around with them trying to make them part of this new world. He wished he could get to know all of them and help them. Although he kept his focus on McGrath, something in him started to crumble. He could feel all his old self returning: the passion, the ecstasy and the misery. Watching the stream of humanity was like meditation and his spirit began to wake up. Sometimes he just stood with the tears pouring down his grimy face, his emotions totally rampant. The pain of life, the confusion of it all, the never-ending effort and struggle, all was like one long bad dream that never ended. He never knew where he really was, never knew what would happen next and he felt guilty all the time for not knowing anything. Buffeted about at the mercy of the winds, the fates, and the Gods, Drood felt pity for his fellow man, and it was in these crying times that he almost abandoned his mission. While loving all these strangers from the sidewalk, it was hard to manufacture the anger necessary to carry out his plan. Drood had more knowledge and more experience than any man alive and all it did was make him old, exhausted, and confused. He shrank onto his patch of sidewalk in tears and nobody noticed him.

One cool Thursday, as fall approached, Drood got his chance. The driver looked at his watch and walked across the street to the deli. Drood looked both ways and nobody was near. Somebody would probably see him, but they'd figure he was stealing something from the car, and they'd figure that he was the homeless guy that was there every day, so there'd be no need to worry about finding him, so they'd be in no rush to report anything. If caught, he could always just say he didn't do anything, just wanted to see what rich people lived like. They'd buy that. Until the sickness struck McGrath, of course, and he became a frothing, raving lunatic. Eventually they'd trace it to the coffee and the homeless man, but Drood would be long gone by then.

Drood scooted to the passenger door and it was unlocked. He pulled it open, slipped a vial from his pocket and stepped in. He knelt in the back seat, unscrewed the top of the coffee pot, dumped the vial in, backed out, closed the door, and sat down on the sidewalk. Looked around. Nobody saw. Driver returned, McGrath came down, off they went. Drood had to hustle downtown, put the rest of the plan in action. He figured he had about one hour to get in position.

One hour later. No sign of McGrath yet. Drood sat on the bench outside Bowling Green. He watched all the suits strutting by and he remembered his old days in New York. He remembered how he and Kilty had arrived and tried to take it all in. "This one's for you Kilty," he thought illogically, for McGrath had done nothing to Kilty. Drood was shivering, anxious, as he stared at the front door of McGrath's building and waited and mumbled to Mannanan, "You old devil, I'm going to finish your plans once and for all and then you'll have to let me go!" Pedestrians passed him without comment or without looking at him, just another madman. The perfect disguise. He was sure McGrath would come out soon. Drood looked around for police and saw a patrolman coming around the corner of the customs house on foot. This could be almost too perfect.

Sure enough, McGrath came out, looking pale and unsteady. Drood had never seen doubt in McGrath's eyes before and he savored it. McGrath looked the wrong way down the street for a cab, and Drood knew his potion was working. McGrath moved slowly and stared at everything around him. He yanked at his tie and sat down heavily on the steps in front of the building when a cab did not present itself. The traffic blocked Drood's view for a moment and when it cleared again he saw McGrath leaning forward with his head in his hands, breathing heavily. "Time to confront," Drood thought as he rose from the bench.

Drood crossed the street and carefully sat down next to McGrath.

"You're the ...the guy...outside my building." McGrath panted. His eyes were wild and he was sweating greasy droplets. "What are you doing here?"

Drood smiled and looked at the sky and sighed. He'd been waiting for this moment for several months, many years really if he were honest with himself.

"I'm more than the guy outside your building, McGrath." He saw the policeman looking at him from across the street. Had to be careful not to be the crazy homeless man harassing the citizen. Had to be seen walking away at just the right peak of terror and rage. He smiled at McGrath and said nothing for a moment. McGrath stared at him and gasped some more. He twitched and flinched when some pigeons flew overhead. McGrath's eyes were wide and he seemed to be approaching terror.

"Don't you recognize me McGrath? It's me. The ghost of Sean. Your old 'partner' and friend. I'm not really here right now. You're hallucinating. But I came to tell you that I'll be haunting you from now on. You don't actually have much longer to live. All the weirdness and stuff you're seeing is because of a tumor in your head. But the police are on to you and they're after you."

McGrath shrank back against the steps and his mouth opened as the drugs stretched the veins in his head and twisted them around each other. His mouth finally closed without a sound. Drood saw the policeman heading toward them. He stood up and said to McGrath, "You're going to die because of what you did to me."

McGrath screamed. All the pedestrians stopped and stared as Drood turned and walked away and raised his hands in the air as if to say, "I can do nothing further, I'm washing my hands of the whole thing." The policeman quickened his pace, but hesitated as he reached the curb, not knowing whether to go after Drood or McGrath. McGrath screamed "No!" at the policeman and bolted running toward Battery Park. By instinct, the policeman ran after the man who fled and Drood hustled in the opposite direction, to the subway entrance in Liberty Plaza. Plan A in motion, clean getaway.

Drood could picture what happened next in fine detail. McGrath would spring from the bushes onto the policeman's back and begin ripping hair out. A long, violent struggle would ensue, with grunting and shouting, and finally three cops would handcuff McGrath and put him, huffing, in the back of a patrol car. Every once in a while as they sat discussing the incident and what they should do with him, McGrath would let out a blood-curdling scream and spit and slam his head against the patrol car window.

Bellevue, they would decide. Nut house.

Later, Drood was humming to himself as he went into the Museum of Natural History. The cleanest, safest restrooms in the city. He made his donation and although they were very suspicious of him because of the way he looked, they let him in. A guard said something into a walkie-talkie, but Drood went off to pretend to see the dinosaur bones and then to find a bathroom unnoticed. He slipped in and took the bag from the front of his shirt. He dumped the soap, the shaving cream, disposable razor and scissors into the sink. Time to move into the next phase of his plan. He smiled as he remembered McGrath's wild eyes and his incoherent terror. Drood had no such religion as Christianity in him, and the wrongs that had been done him justified everything he was doing to McGrath. After all, he wasn't going to do any long-term physical damage to the man. It was merely a battle of wills and wits, one he had taken far too lightly the first time. As he cut his matted hair he remembered the dinner he had had with McGrath and the mayor, when he had turned Kilty over to them, and they had sworn to protect him for it. He wondered how many minutes it was before McGrath gave the police Drood's own name.

It was weeks since Drood had been clean and shaven and he expected when the job was done he would see the same old resigned and miserable face; the crushed spirit and dreading eyes, the slack skin, and the sideways-talking bitter mouth. As the whiskers fell away and the soap sluiced all the grime from his features, Drood was startled to introduce himself to the face of a stranger, a much wiser man. The new plan was transforming him. His eyes were sparkling and his skin was smooth on the cheeks, with a network of fine lines around the eyes and the mouth. The forehead was clean and strong and the nose was thin, prominent and noble. The face he presented to himself in the mirror was alert, eager, and intelligent, barely suppressing the vivid life behind it.

He spoke to himself.

"O.K. old man, what's going to happen to you now? Why have you been brought back to life?" And he glanced at the ceiling and raised his fist. Premonition of his fate crept into his mind as he shook his fist at Mannanan.

"It's almost time for me to return, isn't it? You're almost done with me, aren't you? I can almost see the end of your game now. You owe me. You have to send me back." Drood looked into his own eyes again and butterflies fluttered in his stomach. There was a plan, after all! It all meant something and he was almost there! All those years of confusion and misery and now, he didn't know how he knew but he knew, it was almost all over. He sighed and smiled and felt a whiff of the peace and clarity he had achieved in his dream.

He saluted himself in the mirror and then checked his watch. McGrath would be peaking right about now. Drood chuckled and felt like a man. He was getting some back, taking it to the enemy, evening the tally. He was no warrior, like Kilty had been, but he had his victories and his battles nonetheless. McGrath would fall. Drood would find his daughter and his apprentice would make his mark in the world. Drood mattered in this strange place after all. He was shedding the bonds of the Otherworld like the skin off a snake. He was going to outlast it all, the pain and the injustice. The Druid in him was beginning to shine through. Again.

Drood left the museum and glanced at the clouds high above the buildings. They were circular and puffy and moving from the northwest to the southeast, out to the sea. This was unusual. He studied them for a moment until he saw the shape of a heron in them. Wisdom and long life heading east. "That's the way it should be," he thought. He'd achieved wisdom in this long life through betrayal, loss, pain, injustice and he was heading back to the sunrise, to his birth. "All right." He clapped his hands together loudly and a flutter of cooings and flappings left the fence and headed for the trees. Drood smiled. Now he would head to Grand Central and the lockers that held his change of clothes. Time to get rid of the bum's rags and get the casual togs of a Manhattan yuppie. He was about to become a McGrath family member.

Drood knew that McGrath would probably be quickly released to the care of his private doctor. His instincts also told him there would be no one but McGrath's business partner to interfere with Drood's visit to the patient. No family or friends. Drood made his way through the city to the mental hospital and negotiated the lobbies and elevators until he was at the right ward. Because of his forged identification, his trendy t-shirt, black jeans, and expensive sneakers and watch, and a brief discussion with the doctor in which he convinced the doctor that McGrath and he were cousins and he had been called by the business partner, Drood found himself alone at the door to McGrath's room. It was a double room, but the other bed was empty. Drood had been informed that McGrath had had a psychotic episode, possibly brought on by drugs, but that they wouldn't know much more until the blood tests came back. He was sedated and drifting in and out of sleep. Drood assured the doctor there was no other family.

The patient was propped up on the bed and stared at the blank TV with dull and glazed eyes. A little drool dripped slowly down from the corner of his mouth. Drood came in quietly and tiptoed over to the bed. McGrath didn't appear to notice. Drood looked back over his shoulder and saw the doctor watching him through the door. He'd have to play it a little cool. He just stood looking for a minute and then moved so his back was toward the door.

"McGrath. Are you awake?"

A dull, heavy head turned slowly to look at Drood. The eyes blinked carefully and tried to focus but couldn't. McGrath frowned but otherwise remained silent and motionless. "Good", thought Drood, "no commotion, no chance of me getting thrown out." He pulled the guest chair to the bedside and sat down. McGrath's eyes went slowly to the door and the window and he appeared to be considering an appeal for help.

"Don't worry McGrath, I'm not going to hurt you. Not really. If I wanted to do that, or if I wanted to kill you, you'd never see me, never know what hit you."

Silence.

"Memory come back to you yet? I think the last time I saw you, we were in a restaurant downtown, and you were getting ready to turn me over to the police, right?" Let him think that yesterday's bum was an apparition. McGrath's frown increased, but the drool was unchecked and the body was motionless. They must really have him doped up, Drood surmised.

"Well, just so you know, you're not crazy. I'm alive, and I'm here, and I'm never going to leave your side again, not until you let the world know what kind of person you really are. Not until you have suffered as much as I have. I lost my family, but all you care about is money and power, so I'll be around until every shred of any of that is gone from you. What do you think about that?"

McGrath's eyes got really big, but slowly, in an almost comic effect. His breathing was slow, but he began to labor at it and his chest heaved. He tried to speak, but his tongue wouldn't work and he only spluttered a guttural noise.

220

"Don't you worry." Drood patted his hand and stood. "The doctors here tell me you have a tumor in your head." Drood figured it would take them at least a month to get McGrath off that falsely planted idea after he came down from the drugs. "It will take some time for you to die. And you'll probably go insane first. But I'll be here all the time to make sure you appreciate the situation."

Drood stood and went to the door. He opened it and poked his head out, nobody around. He came back in and went to McGrath's bedside.

"And now, old friend, time for your medicine." More strangled sounds from McGrath and a feeble attempt to lift his hand as Drood removed the second vial of madness potion and a syringe from his pocket.

"Into the I.V. we go." And Drood sent the wicked droplets into the tube. He waved and smiled at McGrath, and tried not to enjoy the suffering too much. Gloating should be done at the campfire, not over the fallen victim, he remembered. He'd never again be seen in the hospital.

Now for phase 3 of the project. Hotel room. Tomorrow, time to go back to the lockers, get the suit out, and pay a visit to McGrath's business partner, Drood told himself as he walked the corridors of the hospital on his way out.

The appointment had been set up by phone the day before, at the same time McGrath was heading downtown with tampered coffee to begin his day. In the meeting Drood didn't even have to try hard to get some interest and a commitment from the business partner to work together. Drood dropped a few names; showed off a few expensive accessories, floated some jargon and buzzwords, and he had the guy hooked.

"Now, don't you have to consult with your partner, a Mr. McGrath, I believe?" said Drood.

"Well, he's a bit ill, right now, so I'm taking over the operations end of things for a while."

"I hope it's nothing serious?"

"No, he should be okay in a few weeks, thanks."

"Well, I'd be happier keeping him out of it anyway, if you don't mind. His reputation, you know, he's been associated with some difficult people in the past. I almost took this business to your competitor's at Jennings and Dougal because of him. You can handle it though. Just work closely with me and we should be all right."

He read the partner's face and saw that the partner was aware of and probably a part of McGrath's shadier dealings. The partner offered no resistance or challenge to Drood's machinations, even offering to keep their new project a complete secret from McGrath. Drood assured him that it wouldn't be necessary, that the partner needn't be completely forthcoming with details for McGrath. The client wondered how big a project Drood thought it would be and Drood almost stopped the man's heart by mentioning a ridiculous figure.

"Of course, you'll have to put up the usual bond to win the business."

The client frowned, but didn't disagree and Drood knew it was all going to be downhill from there. He'd be able to crush the whole business in three months by setting the right wheels in motion. He'd studied the partnership while pretending to be a bum and he knew they were overextended. Drood knew how to scare off the rest of their paying clients, knew how to force Chapter 7. Just a matter of timing and coordination and Drood had planned well and was ready for it.

The plan went well and McGrath was confused, seeing a therapist, and unable to work. His company was falling. Drood believed it was time to pay one more visit to McGrath just to say goodbye and to make sure his work couldn't be undone. It was a Friday and he had on a business suit as he stepped out of the cab in front of McGrath's apartment building. He nodded to the doorman and went to the elevator, looking for all the world as if he were a contemporary well-to-do broker in the capitol of capital on his way to visit a sick friend. Drood thought about the art of disguise. He realized that he had neglected to train young Tag in the art. You focused people on certain aspects of your appearance, keeping in mind to produce re-cognition. A person's short-term memory had to be combined with focus and attention. It was a remote possibility. People liked to categorize, so you helped them by making sure to use the right categories of focus with the right types of people. You couldn't control what was in the short-term memory, so you worked with focus and attention, same principle as magic, sleight of hand. Get 'em to look at the wrong things. The other idea was appropriateness for the setting. You had to also blend correctly into the surroundings. In his recent Manhattan campaign, he'd been a bum, a yuppie jogger, a stockbroker, a family friend, and just an ordinary citizen and he was confident he'd not be caught. No one ever gave him a second look.

* * *

A couple of weeks later, Drood was at the door to McGrath's apartment and rang the bell and then put his hand over the eyehole. He looked around the foyer for cameras and didn't see any, but figured that even if they had them, in the condition McGrath was in he wouldn't be able to tell Drood apart from any other businessman. Drood rang the bell again and heard some motion behind the door. It swung open and groggy McGrath stood there in a bathrobe, unshaven. He looked dubiously at Drood and then his eyes widened. His mouth fell open and he froze.

"You! What do you want?!!" McGrath sputtered.

"I just want to talk to you for a few minutes. Can I come in?" Drood breezed past McGrath, who staggered. McGrath might be considering calling the police, but he also might reconsider when he realized that they'd had enough of his wild fantasy about this dead man coming back to life to haunt him. Or, McGrath might wonder if Drood wasn't a ghost come back to haunt him for his misdeeds.

Drood plunked himself down on the sofa and looked out the high windows at the city. The sun turned the gray buildings white and frosty clouds hovered as a backdrop for the skyline.

"Nice view, McGrath. Too bad you'll be losing this place. I hope you can find someplace warm. If you like, I can give you some tips on living on the street and on the run, how would that be?"

McGrath said nothing but took a seat in a chair opposite Drood. He just stared.

"Yeah, a couple of words to the co-op board about your mental state, the state of the finances of your company, things like that, and you'll be gone. It doesn't take much for things to turn in the other direction, and when they do, momentum builds, and it's awfully hard to turn back the tide. Especially for a man in your condition. How are you feeling by the way?"

McGrath, helpless and weak, merely shrugged.

Drood continued. "Well, just thought I'd let you know, that I'm not really the vindictive sort. I'm going to be leaving you alone

223

now. I think you've been paid back enough for what you did to me so many years ago. You're in a tight spot and you may have to begin living life like a real person now. I doubt you will, but I've given you a great opportunity. I hope you can learn from it and take it."

Drood got up and went into McGrath's kitchen. He opened the refrigerator and flipped off the top of the milk. McGrath was still sitting in the living room with his back to Drood and a wild look on his face. Drood removed the third and final vial of "medicine" from his pocket and dumped it into the milk.

"Mind if I have some water?" He took a bottle of spring water. Drood returned to the living room and sat down again. McGrath's face twitched, his mouth opened as if to speak and then closed again quickly. Something Drood said about what McGrath had done to him so long ago seemed to set him to trying to remember something important.

"The satisfaction of revenge does not necessarily mean destruction and permanent damage of the enemy, especially if, in this case, the enemy has the opportunity to learn to do things right." Drood lectured, barely even paying attention to McGrath. He didn't notice McGrath begin to smile.

Drood was talking about playing God, but McGrath had stopped listening. McGrath stood up and turned to face Drood. They stared at each other for a moment. McGrath's face slowly broke into a broad grin. McGrath began to chuckle and then pointed a bony finger at Drood and began to laugh out loud. Drood was arrested in mid-speech.

"I know something you don't." McGrath said between guffaws. Drood edged closer and McGrath backed up to the couch.

"The whereabouts of your wife and your daughter."

They stared at each other, McGrath no longer laughing, and Drood no longer certain. Drood realized the game and the fun were over. It was time to finish what he had set out to do. He advanced on McGrath and McGrath retreated with his eyes on Drood. He backed toward the bedroom and curled around the door, closing it and locking it behind him.

Drood was chagrined that he had been so stupid, so cocky, so satisfied. The fact that he hadn't seen his wife and daughter in so long, hadn't been able to find them had put something on hold inside him. He forgot that McGrath had never left this world and probably still knew where they were. There was no sound from the madman's bedroom.

Drood floated like a ghost back to the hotel in Times Square, moving through the city, disconnected. What should he do now? His plan for McGrath was finished. He had planned to leave for L.A. right away. He couldn't let McGrath hurt Claire. He had to find her. His dreams told him the boy and the girl were together in L.A. The connections between all the events of his life were almost clear to him now. It was all pointing somewhere. The great plan of the gods was like the veins of a translucent fish, just below the surface, sometimes visible, sometimes not, depending on the light. If he could just make the final connection right, he could settle the hash for Mannanan, the god of this Otherworld. Then he could be done with life once and for all. He realized now that his suicide attempt years earlier had been premature. The story had barely even begun to be written at that point. Although losing his world, betraying his best friend, losing his wife and daughter certainly seemed like a final punctuation, the wheel had now spun again and now it was coming to another of those bizarre, fantastic and beautiful intersections in life that indicated some kind of pattern. "Every day life is just a thin disguise," he reminded himself. "The awesome tricks of the Gods." Now he could see the end coming and he wanted to make no mistakes now, at this crucial time, when all accounts would be settled. He had to find Claire and realized with a start as he stared out the window of his hotel room, he could get the boy to get the girl to give him the address.

Chapter 24

When Tag and Digger left Digger's apartment building there was a man leaning against the wall right next to the doorway. They glanced at him and walked by, looking down the street to the parking lot where Digger kept his car. Digger was going to drop Tag at Deirdre's and head to the beach and they came back out into the street in the car and the man who had been leaning on the building was sitting across the street in a car. Tag and Digger noticed him at the same time and looked at each other. The car pulled out behind them as they headed for the freeway.

"I think that guy is following us," Tag said.

"Dude, I didn't want to say anything, but I think I saw that guy yesterday outside my house."

"You think he's watching you for some reason?" Tag asked him.

"Must be. Emilio?" Digger said.

"Humph," said Tag. They drove the rest of the way in silence, both frowning.

* * *

Deirdre thought she would die if she had to interview one more law enforcement official, one more sociologist, or one more historian. They were all so righteous about weapons and it was always a moral cause with them and a political cause, and they could never admit that they were just fascinated by weapons. She was having trouble with the other angle, the user, the citizen, or the criminal, who sees the weapon as a tool, something for protection or entertainment or aggression. They were reluctant to talk about weapons because they feared the law. Her being a reporter was not very reassuring to them. Her doorbell rang and it was Tag.

They kissed and Tag sat down at the table where she had spread all her photos, transcripts, photocopies and books on the subject. Tag idly picked through the things while Deirdre tried to finish a thought on the laptop. He knew he must wait. He saw a photograph on the kitchen counter he had never seen before. He retrieved it and sat down again. The people in the picture were at a party, and it looked like an old photo, the styles of dress being late eighties or early nineties.

"What's this?" he asked.

She looked up from her laptop. "Picture of my parents, before my father died."

"Which one is he?"

"The one in the black jacket, with his face partially turned away."

Tag held the photo closer to his eyes. Then he held it real close. He stared at it for several seconds and then turned it in a couple of different directions.

"What?"

"Your father looks like my teacher, Drood."

"Well, it's not Drood. It's Sean Melvewin, my father."

"Drood's name is Sean, too. It's weird, man. This looks exactly like what Drood must have looked like when he was younger."

"Well, my father is supposedly dead."

She wanted to drop the matter, but there was a seed of discomfort in Tag's head, something about "the father of my love." Where did it come from? He drummed his fingers on the table and Deirdre shuffled more papers around.

He snapped his fingers. "Wait a minute. What was it that guy on the beach said, 'your teacher is the father of your love?' Well if you're my love, and you are, then he was saying that Drood was your father. And he looks exactly like the guy in this picture, only older."

Deirdre got up from the table quickly and went into the kitchen. "Let's just drop it Tag, OK? It's every kid's fantasy that their dead parent is alive somewhere and can't get to them. I don't want to go through all that. My father hasn't been heard from in years. Don't you think if he were alive he would have surfaced somehow? Besides, from what I've read about him, the FBI and the police and everybody else were looking for him and they all believe he's dead. So he's dead, O.K.?"

"O.K. Sorry. Just a coincidence I guess." Tag didn't want to discomfort her any further, but Drood had taught him about coincidences, and how there were no such things. Everything in the universe was connected to every other thing, you just didn't always know it or see the connection, or even if you did see it, you didn't understand it. He looked one more time at the picture and knew he was looking at a younger Drood. How on earth did it come to pass that he'd fallen in love with Drood's daughter? Did Drood even know he had a daughter? He'd never revealed much information about his past life except to say cryptic things about having lived in different eras, in different cultures. He had a vast repository of information about human beings and about life, but he'd never shared the specific details with Tag on how he had accumulated such a storehouse of knowledge. Drood always talked about the "training" and the "teachings" as if they were part of some school or tradition of philosophy, but Tag had always assumed it was just a quirky fantasy (bordering on a neurotic compulsion) of Drood's, that Drood felt he had to invent a validation for the things he was teaching Tag. Tag began to suspect Drood might be more than just his slightly cracked teacher, that there might be a gigantic and awesome story behind the man he knew as Drood. Where did Drood come from and who was he?

He went into the kitchen behind Deirdre and put his arms around her. She struggled for a second and then backed into him and pressed her shoulders against Tag's chest. They swayed for a few minutes, thinking their own separate dreamy thoughts. Tag was trying to figure out exactly what message he could send that would bring Drood out to L.A. to meet his daughter. How could he reveal it to Drood? He had to plan the reunion and the revelation carefully. "Finally," he thought, "I've found a way to repay Drood." This wonderful woman he was holding was Drood's daughter and he was going to give her back to Drood, so to speak. Drood was right, he considered, the universe was an amazing, miraculous place. Tag smiled and felt that he was being given the opportunity to commit one of the most significant acts of all time. He silently thanked whatever Gods and forces there were that had moved all the pieces in exactly the right way to make this happen. Tag anticipated the reunion and felt a swelling in his chest and a quivering pain deep in his abdomen. Tremendous currents of fate were swirling around him.

At the same time, Deirdre was feeling a little lost, grateful for the strong, warm arms holding her. She felt she could fly apart at any moment and her knees were weak. She didn't like the discussion they had just had and she didn't want to think about it, but she poured herself into Tag through her skin and her muscles. It was a wonderful thing to be with a kind, warm man like Tag. He was there, she could trust him, and he would hold her and protect her if he had to. He respected her wishes and he held her just right. Deirdre got anxious whenever she started to think of the photograph again, but then she just focused on feeling Tag around her and it went away.

She also resented Tag a little. His dropping the subject so quickly was a little like walking up the stairs and thinking there is another step when there isn't, and stumbling and coming down hard on your heel. Tag should have pushed the issue and they could have laid it to rest. He should have made her cry. "That's what we needed right then," she thought. Her mind was still trying to fight that fight and kept returning to the photograph. If that was her father and Drood at the same time, it was just too much, just an impossibility. Things just didn't happen like that. "Enough," she broke out of his embrace and started shuffling pots and pans around and getting ready to make dinner.

"Anyway," Tag said, "Emilio has got someone stalking Digger, I think. I don't know if I should go to the police or what. Eventually they'll find me from Digger and then they'll rob me, maybe worse. I wonder what Drood would tell me to do." At the name of Drood, Deirdre winced.

"It's probably time for me to take that big trip to Vegas. Stay there a week or two and practice and learn, maybe win a little, come back when the whole thing died down. Digger can go up to San Francisco, where his folks live. He doesn't have to be here for any particular reason right now. What do you think? Want to come?"

"Nah. I'll stay here; I've got a lot of work to do. I'm going to try to write all the pieces of the serial as one big story and then break it up and move things around when I'm done. I've got about all the information I need. It's time to hole up and put it all onto paper. And if I'm all wrapped up in that, I won't miss you so much."

Tag smiled at her. "When I come back, we can have a big reunion. Maybe then it will be time to...you know...get to know each other better." And he looked up from under his eyebrows at her with one corner of his mouth turned up in a devilish smile. They had not had sex yet though they had been dating for some time. It would be the first time for both of them.

She smiled back at him. "If my writing goes well, and your gambling goes well, who knows, we might be on top of the world by the time you come back. I suppose it would be a good time to ..." she paused and noticed him on the edge of his chair, and she finished by yelling. "...DO IT!" They laughed and laughed. They said no more as she went about the kitchen and he wandered around the living room picking things up and reading them. They had no moral reservations about having sex, but they were both young and on their own and it seemed sex was the first thing most kids in love would do in that situation, so they resisted for that very reason. They hung back and teased themselves and let the tension build and they purposely delayed it longer and longer, though of course, they knew they couldn't hold out forever. They believed the next big step into adulthood was coming at just the right time in their lives. Their lenses were clicking into focus.

* * *

Tag had time at the airport before his plane left for Vegas. He called Tom, laconic Tom in Syracuse New York.

"Tom? It's Tag. I need to talk to Drood; he's got to come out here to visit. I'm going to Vegas for a little while, but I really need Drood to come here. Can you tell him it's urgent?"

"Yup. Let me just write it down. He left a message for you too. Let me see if I can find it."

Tag heard Tom rummaging around and the sound of papers flapping and an occasional soft oath from Tom. Finally the receiver picked up again.

"O.K., let me give you Drood's message and then you can run that message by me again. Here it is, Drood said to make sure that you get your girlfriend to give you her mother's address. Drood needs it right away. And I should tell him that he has to go out to L.A. right away? Is that all?"

Tag was stunned and didn't respond for a moment. Drood knew about Deirdre. How?

"Yeah, but make sure you tell him it's urgent." He gave Tom his address and phone number again. "Why won't he call here directly or let me call him directly?" Tag asked.

"I don't know, Tag. All he said was he was on a mission that nobody could know about and that he didn't want anyone to know where he was. I don't know what he was up to. He also said it would be good for you to be cut off from him for a while. Time for you to do things on your own a little bit. Anyway, I'll give him the message. How's it going out there? You winning?"

"Yeah, I'm doing good Tom, I'm winning. And tell Shiny that he's never seen women like they have in Southern California. That ought to drive him crazy."

Tom chuckled. "O.K. You take care."

"Thanks Tom." His plane was boarding and he hustled onto the runway. He thought about what Tom had said as he stood in line at the doorway to the plane. He was better off doing things on his own for a while. Probably true, he thought, although he resented being out of contact with Drood. Drood wasn't just his teacher. Drood was his best friend and he could use the support. Well, he had learned an awful lot out here struggling on his own, but he'd feel better if Drood would come out to visit. But, now it was on to Vegas. Money, cards, lights, women, money.

Deirdre had all the food and drink she needed to stay in and work. Tag was gone and she had all the facts and photos she needed and she had all the writing materials she needed. She had to come up with five stories on weapons and she had to make each one connected and yet separate. They had to be fascinating but not too controversial. She had to sprinkle facts and figures throughout all the pieces and put the photographs in all the right places. She needed live quotes and she needed to arrange it all carefully. Each separate story had to make a point and in the end, she had to say something. As she started work on the writing, she realized that she didn't really know what she had to say. It was such a conglomeration of information and it could go in so many different directions. As usually happened when she went to work on a project, as soon as she writing, infinity began poking its way in, demanding that she run down all its millions of little alleyways, of potential tangents.

232

She reminded herself to start in any direction, but not to make any decisions until she finished with a first draft. Once she had a story she could read, then she could figure out what she wanted to say, what was right and wrong with it, where the weaknesses were and what the tangents were. "Writing and editing are two completely different skills," she reminded herself. She spent all of the first day and most of the second day putting all her thoughts in order on the computer. She got down her observations, her quotes, her facts, and she threw in everything she could think of. She went back over her material and put in everything else she had missed. By the third day she was ready to write the conclusion and she got it off in a hurry, ending up with "weapons are tools that can be used or misused." She didn't like it. It sounded obvious and trite and a little too close to the stance of the NRA for her politics. Well, she could re-work that later.

Those first three days she had worked in a hurry, writing feverishly, racing the clock, setting up her own little imaginary deadlines and then killing herself to make them. She wrote all day, taking short breaks to let her fingers, wrists, and shoulders relax and unwind. She ate little, but drank gallons of water and coffee. The phone was off - she had warned Tag it would be- and she went to bed early. She got up early and went right back at it. Her mind was turned off to life and was focused on the linguistic and metaphorical world of writing. By the end of the third day, she was satisfied with her progress, though of course she knew she had a long way to go and the condition of the story was raw. To leave it alone now would be akin to walking out in the middle of a birth when you were the only doctor available.

The fourth day came and she meditated to start her day and then took a quick walk around the neighborhood. It was time to change gears and use a different part of the brain. Now she had to be an editor, cutting, pruning, redirecting, rewriting. She had to be ruthless, cynical, harsh, and unconvinced about every aspect of the story. She had to go slow and think hard, taking every word, every sentence, every idea, every theme to task. At the same time, the mechanics of the writing had to be corrected automatically, accurately and swiftly. Grammar, syntax, and punctuation had to magically heal as if she weren't involved at all.

On days four through seven it was a struggle and she had to fight the temptation to be distracted, to go for a walk, to go to the beach, to call people. She took more frequent and longer breaks and had to recollect mental energy more often. The stories began to take shape and by the eighth day, she thought she finally had enough to take a couple of days off. She had enough done that if the deadline came up on her suddenly she could cram enough work time in to get at least the first piece ready for publication. From here on it was just dotting the I's and crossing the T's, checking everything again, tweaking, making it just right. She hoped this would be the easy part where she felt good about what she had done. It was before the doubt set in again and before it was time to move on to another piece of writing. Deirdre was putting her things away for the day on the eighth day when the phone rang.

"You Deirdre?"

"Yes. Who is this?"

"You know where Tag is?"

"Who is this?"

Click. Deirdre stared at the phone. Someone acting very suspicious, calling her looking for Tag. She dialed * 69 and heard the phone ringing on the other end. No answer and finally an answering machine kicked on. It was Digger's answering machine, but the voice she had spoken to on the other end was definitely not Digger. She hung up without leaving a message and wracked her brain trying to remember if Tag had said Digger was definitely leaving for San Francisco or not. She hugged herself and looked around the room. She checked the chain and the deadbolt and went to the windows. She had never liked the idea of a fire escape outside her window. She checked the locks on all the windows and wished she had grates. What if it was Emilio and his people looking for Tag? They had broken into Digger's apartment and she hoped to God that Digger was in San Francisco. Tag would be home soon? She had to warn him.

She left messages for Tag every day for the rest of the week and she made quick trips to the grocery store, checking all around her each time. She felt sure she was being followed but she could never quite see anyone. She called Digger's a couple of times but got no answer until the end of the week. Digger had just returned from San Francisco, but swore his apartment looked normal and there were no signs of a break-in. He thought Deirdre was "just being a woman" and she hung up from him, angry that she had even worried about him. Why didn't Tag return her calls and when was he coming back?

Deirdre was certain now that someone was following her and she began to feel frightened. The phone calls increased, and they began to come at two or three in the morning. She thought a thousand times about going to the police, but she didn't believe they could help unless some act of violence was actually committed. She was also certain that Tag would be back any day, but where was he? It was almost two weeks now and she didn't think he really had planned to be gone all this long. She kept calling his apartment and hanging up when she got his answering machine. Digger was no longer being followed and he still didn't believe his apartment had been broken into. He kept telling Deirdre she needed some mental help and he kept offering to stay over at her place to help. She began to suspect that Digger was not such a good friend of Tag's after all and his urgent offers of help didn't sound genuine to her. It was a lonely place to be. She kept working on the story. She thought that when she got paid, maybe she'd quit working at the tutoring center and concentrate full time on writing and generating assignments. She was drinking a lot of coffee, not sleeping much, looking over her shoulder. It was a lot of pressure for a woman as young as she and one day she found herself weeping with the frustration of it all.

She was beginning to shut down and she didn't realize it. She began to talk to herself out loud in the middle of the day; she lay on the couch without moving or sleeping for hours. She began to imagine killing intruders and wondered if some of the contacts she had made from writing the story could supply her with weapons. She'd learned enough to be able to shoot somebody, she thought. She triple checked the door and the windows whenever she was at home.

Chapter 25

Drood watched the building all day and finally, when he was about to give up and go back to his hotel, he saw her. His heart stopped and he began to sweat. The love of his life, the mother of his daughter, and the woman who had hated him and turned him away forever, was coming out of the building and crossing directly to the corner where he stood. He was at a pay phone outside a delicatessen, and he had been up and down the block several times, finally settling each time at this corner where he could at least be a part of the street scene, rather than the lone stalker that he was. People came in and out of the deli, used the pay phone, sometimes stood and talked to one another, or hailed cabs. Drood watched the building and now here came Claire. He felt exactly the same way he had felt the first time he saw her: helpless, stricken, and relieved, all at once.

She obviously had no idea he was there, didn't even look in his direction as she watched the traffic and the doorways of the street. She appeared to be heading for the deli itself. Her hair had streaks of gray, but her eyes were still bright blue and she seemed as put together as he remembered her. She had on a blue t-shirt, shorts, and sandals and she looked more casual, more lived-in than he remembered her. He surmised that her soul had weathered and grown. How would she feel about him?

She stepped onto the sidewalk about thirty yards from him but he stayed facing the street. He tried to watch her from the corner of his eye, but she moved too fast. There were a few seconds when she was still coming toward him but out of his sight behind him. Surely she'd recognize him if she looked at him at all, and it would be obvious he was there to see her. He made a decision at last and turned to face her as she came closer behind him. When he turned, she flinched and she seemed to be trying to hurry to get into the deli. Just another strange man in New York turning to check her out, she thought. He was tempted to forget the whole thing and just leave it and go away and die and not say anything, but something desperate and confident was in command of his heart.

"Claire," he said so she just heard him.

Her head whipped around at him and she paused in mid stride. She looked at him and her eyes opened wide and her jaw dropped open. Her shoulders went slack.

"You!!!"

"It's me. I'm real."

"What are you...?"

"I'm not a ghost ..." he trailed off and they stared at each other. Drood tried again. "I just wanted to see you...

Claire staggered and put her hand to her forehead.

"Here," Drood tried to steady her with a hand on her elbow but she pushed his hand away. They stood staring at each other: he leaning forward with an anxious look, she stared, open-mouthed.

Drood tried again, "I can't change what I wrote in that letter or how I lied to you." He paused. His speech came haltingly. "That's the way it had to be and I'm sorry we lost each other. I don't know what else to say. I'm going away for good this time...." and his voice trailed off again. He was saying the wrong things.

"Where have you been?" she said.

At this, Drood hung his head. He didn't know what to say.

"I mean where the hell have you been?!" Claire's voice was rising.

"Listen, can we sit somewhere and talk?" Drood was desperate.

Claire took a deep breath and glanced wildly around. She waved her hand at the coffee shop on the corner. It offered a neutral atmosphere.

They sat in the coffee shop trying to talk. They fingered porcelain cups and looked at and then away from each other and sighed. Pain. Drood knew this would be the last time they saw each other. They spoke about jobs and Syracuse and the passing of time. Occasionally they would just stare at each other in shock and language would not come. Drood tried to remember and to feel and Claire tried not to feel or to think. She tried to focus on what to do next. The other diners in the coffee shop clanked their silverware and chattered and laughed.

238

"Sean, are you crazy? I mean, are you really crazy? Where did you come from and how did you get here? Why were you gone so long, why are you back now?" Claire started to cry.

Drood sighed and reached his hand across to cover hers. This time she didn't shrug him off. "I seem to be helpless. I don't really know about crazy and I'm no longer sure about where I've been and came from and all that. I can't really explain anything. I just know I had to see you." Drood couldn't imagine what else he could say.

Claire tried to smile through her tears, but she looked very far away to Drood. Then she stunned him, "You know I married McGrath when you left, and I'm married to someone else now."

Drood could again see McGrath's leering face. He could just get out the name, "McGrath..."

Claire nodded. "It was a mistake. He hit me."

Drood patted her hand. He debated telling her about McGrath's demise, but she'd find out soon enough. Keeping it secret and refusing to get credit for it with Claire would make up for the past when she had discovered his other secrets: his betrayal of Kilty, his crime. The time ticked on. He leaned back in his chair. "But, are you happy now?" he asked.

She nodded and smiled thinly. She shrugged. Drood thought she looked like she wanted to say more but decided, as he had, what was the point? They both looked out the window for a few seconds.

The thought of their daughter hung between them in the air. Drood had been restraining himself as they negotiated their complicated and painful past. Finally, he could bear it no longer. He had to force his dream to happen and bring Mannanan's cycle to a conclusion. He knew it was time and he could feel the gods whispering in his ears and poking him. And he said, "Where is she? Is she O.K.?"

Claire knew what Drood meant. "She's out in L.A. becoming a writer. I'm dreadfully worried about her, but says she's doing fine. She's a lot like you."

Drood sat back in his chair. He hadn't expected her to give him that. He'd expected her to try to protect the girl from his "madness" and to be less forthcoming. He certainly hadn't expected Claire to admit to him that the girl was a lot like him.

"How so?" he responded after a long pause.

"She's very serious and very mysterious. Very independent and righteous."

"Hmm," he said. And then, "I think those qualities will make her a good writer and a decent person. But I can't imagine she doesn't also share your warmth and your sense of humor and your attraction to beauty."

Claire smiled but Drood could see her begin to pull back in her mind. Her eyes got serious and her mouth set briefly. She seemed to come into focus finally. "Don't go and bother her. She thinks you're dead. We all thought you were dead. Those notes they found in Montauk."

Drood vaguely remembered writing and ranting about death at a beach motel. It was the end of his last life.

"Right." Another long pause. "What name does she use? I tried to find her."

"My mother's maiden name, Dewar." Claire frowned and groaned. She began to cry. She took a deep breath. "I don't know what to do."

Drood tried to move his chair over and put his arm around her, but again she wouldn't let him. He saw how absurd and painful it all was for her, and he realized too that though she still loved him, she didn't want him to stay in her life. The pain in his chest was severe and breathtaking. Deirdre, though. He could find Deirdre. He would go to Los Angeles immediately. With a dawning horror, he realized that he would again be abandoning the woman he loved. He stared at the street through the coffee shop window. Everything moved in slow motion. He struggled for something to say to the distraught woman – his long-lost wife.

"Well. I'm sorry. I should have left you alone, but I couldn't help it, any more than I could help what happened so long ago. I still love you. I won't bother you again. Please try to forgive me."

Her head hung and she fussed with tissues. "Damn," she said in an exhausted, resigned voice. Drood rose to leave and she looked at him with suddenly dull eyes. She shook her head and dismissed him with her hand.

He walked to the door and went outside and he thought he was going to faint. His heart was pounding in his chest and he couldn't breathe. Was he really never going to see Claire again? He tried to shut his mind down. The will of the gods was that he not be with her, ever, it had all been a mistake. He was staggering away from the coffee shop when she caught up to him from behind.

She threw her arms around him and her mouth smashed into his. They held and kissed for a long time and the street melted away and finally they separated.

"I love you too," she said. "I forgive you. Come back if you can. Good bye." And she walked away, kicking herself for asking him to come back. It was the wrong thing, but it was also the thing that she had to do. They both wept silently as they went in opposite directions down the street, unseeing, unknowing, exhausted. Their dance was finally over.

Chapter 26

Tag arrived in Las Vegas and took a cab to the Grandee Palazzo hotel casino. He had been playing and studying cards for several years now and finally, here he was at the capitol of cards and gambling, with a decent bankroll and a couple of weeks to use it. The airport seemed like any other airport, the city like any other city, with highways and convenience stores, but the lights and the gambling were different. Tag arrived in Las with a lot of hope. He believed in himself and he believed in fate and he believed in gambling and he believed in Drood. No way he could ever imagine himself changing or aging or seeing some of the shine come off of life. No way he could see the shine fade and not worry about it, not consider it a tragedy and a betrayal. If things weren't the way he thought they'd be, he'd be betrayed and that would have to be pinned on someone. His eagerness and his willingness, and his desperate craving for buzz and tingle were glowing all over him as he walked from the cab to the carpeted steps of the hotel where a man in a gold uniform wanted to take his one tiny bag from him.

This was it. It was time for glory to hit him and he knew he had an advantage that a lot of people who came here didn't have. Drood had taught him clear thinking, his monitoring of his behavior and his bets, his careful choosing of his games made it certain to him that he was on the verge of something big. Every nerve cell in him was alive and he wished Deirdre could be here with him. Then he thought again and thought maybe she would just distract him, when he really wanted this life all to himself. He could feel the money in the air, he could feel the juice in the city and he thought the lights and the extravagant "family" atmosphere and the glitz everywhere were completely unnecessary. All you needed was the gambling and the money. The rest did not exist.

Even though he had done a fair amount of gambling, Tag had never had the fever before. He had always been calculating, and practicing because he had a knack for it and it was a good mental exercise, a good way to tackle the world, but he had never until this time actually been caught by the fever. Drood had taught him to focus on his vision and remain true to it and Tag entered his hotel room and reminded himself of it. But for the first time his young spirit which had till now always been defending and preparing; that young spirit was soaring and he was by himself and had no idea this could happen and no idea what to do about it. His vision of the house in California paled in comparison to the juice in the air and the fever in his blood.

Tag began to embellish on the dream that he had and after his first several hours in Las Vegas the vision changed. Now he thought that he would spend only part of the year in Los Angeles and the rest of the time he would have a luxury suite here in Las Vegas. People here would get to know him as a big-timer and he would have honor and respect. He began to add women besides Deirdre to his fantasy and soon he had a whole harem in several suites of a hotel. He thought about managing and even owning a casino. He'd fly friends and family to Las Vegas and he'd give them a thousand dollars each to gamble with. He'd have a diamond ring - why not? - And he'd drive a beautiful huge, restored, old-time Cadillac. Cigars. Power, money, sex, wealth. The fever was on him hard and he didn't even know he was sweating. Night, day and the rest of the world fell away and Tag was caught.

He started that first day playing black jack, best odds and easiest choices to make. He didn't want to go crazy and at least he believed he was exercising restraint and self-control. He didn't admit to himself that he was teasing himself, that he was really just delaying the anticipation, making himself wait until the pain of it was so sore that the pleasure of it would be increased tenfold. He won $550 the first day, not much, but he had played for ten hours. He rewarded himself with a steak dinner in his room and then he took a long sleep. He was exhausted and he didn't think of anything, nor did he have trouble sleeping. Life was good. He was a professional gambler and he was starting to win his money and he'd be home soon a rich man.

The second day he did craps and keno and he lost $2000. No problem he told himself. Those weren't really his games anyway, and he had plenty more and he could afford to lose it. The third day he got into poker and won $4000. This got him into a bigger game on the fourth day and that is where Tag got lost and discovered the lie that so many before him had discovered.

Each day in the big game they took his money from him in the same way and each day he didn't understand and couldn't struggle up to the surface. The fever deluded him and stripped him of everything he had learned about gambling and stole his memory and didn't let him remember any of Drood's teachings. He occasionally thought about how Drood would be disappointed in him and he occasionally thought about how Deirdre would feel about him, but mostly that just made him more determined to succeed and made him dive back into the game he couldn't win. He thought about calling Deirdre to let her know where he was and that he was okay. He had long since stopped thinking about her as anything but an obligation in some vague other place, but he didn't call because he had to wait until he was back on top.

He would get on top, he was sure of it, and all of life had to wait until then. He'd eat and sleep right, he'd call the people he needed to call, he'd take care of bills, and it would all be done okay after he got back on top. He began to bargain with the cards in his head. "Just get me back to even and I swear I'll quit." "I'm a professional," he'd tell himself, "and professionals lose sometimes. I just need to get back to within reason," as the thousands slipped away and he came to the point where he was going to have to quit or find more money because he wouldn't have the stakes.

He thought about calling Deirdre but she didn't have any money, neither did Digger, and Drood was incommunicado. Tag began the fantasy of self-pity. He wondered why he had to be born to people and a life without money. Some others who were no more deserving than he were born with money to burn. And his reasoning began to slip towards robbing people and taking what was owed him and Tag was going down the dark road that lay beneath the pavements of gold paint in the city of cheap lights.

He was exhausted by the dawn of his ninth day in Vegas and he hadn't slept at all for three days and he was almost out of money and his mind just wouldn't work. He was numb, staggering through a neon fog toward a pile of green and he just couldn't find it anywhere but he knew it had to be somewhere close. He was angry at Drood for teaching him a bunch of crap that could never help him and had only deceived him and he was angry at Deirdre for not coming with

245

him to give him emotional support and balance when he really needed it. He was angry at his mother. He began to mutter and swear while he was playing. He began to get into arguments with dealers and with other players. There was an incident in which he accused a dealer of cheating.

Finally, the manager of the casino took him aside and told him he couldn't play any more until he rested. He was upsetting the other players. Tag swore at him, but knew he was right and he went off to his room and lay down. His mind was turning over cards for three hours before he finally collapsed into sleep.

He slept the entire ninth day and woke up at midnight feeling sick and weak. He ordered a meal and ate slowly and stared about the room until his senses returned. He began to recognize his condition and realized he had to pull himself together. He rested and dozed the rest of the night and watched T.V. to try to bring some kind of normalcy back into his head and he went down to the floor the morning of the tenth day in a little better frame of mind. He walked around looking at all the people in the casino and he thought about Drood's teachings and the way of life Drood suggested he should live. He couldn't believe Drood would let him take this path, make this choice in life. He speculated that he probably would never have let Drood talk him out of gambling, but still it seemed strange to him that Drood didn't even try to dissuade him from this lifestyle. Did Drood know this was coming or didn't he? Then he remembered that Drood had always exhorted him to learn from every situation no matter how negative or positive.

Tag looked at the people around him again and wondered suddenly if this wasn't meant to be a lesson. He was having an awakening. Is that what Drood expected? What was the realization he was supposed to have? Tag looked around him again. In contrast to what he had seen when he arrived, he saw people all around him with no shine. They were throwing all their money and their lives away and they were sick and they were deluded. Las Vegas was a big center of disease, not fun and excitement. The veil was ripped away and Tag was watching a different world than the one he had arrived in. He noticed that many of the people were not even aware of their surroundings, that they were glassy eyed, out of control, lost. Hopeless zombies shuffling and spending their lives away. Some of them talked about leaving, but they never did. Their

246

skin looked gray and their eyes were red and they had terrible posture and they looked as though they couldn't breathe right.

And Tag knew he had to get out of there and he knew suddenly that he could never be a professional gambler and he knew there was no such thing. Tag realized that Drood had seen all this coming and had let it happen and that he was right to and that Tag had now learned a gigantic lesson and it freed him. The fever left him and though he was tired, he knew what he had to do. He had to gamble, one last time, the way Drood had taught him. With his head and with strategy. And so he set about it with dedication and intelligence and he attacked gambling as a man who was doing it for the last time and with the only intention of saving his soul and his self-respect. He realized at the same time that these were the worst reasons to gamble, but he went ahead anyway. It was subtle, this gambling addiction, but Tag wanted to drink it to the last drop and he wasn't far from the last drop.

And as he came to this point, he began to win. A little at first and then a lot. He struggled to feel no joy and forced himself to focus only on the shame and the debasement of having to gamble, of having no choice and of knowing that he was only riding it to the end and that this involved no choice or moral decision, he was just a passenger.

He would get his bankroll back and $10,000 more and go back to L.A. On the plane back he would not wish away the experience, but he would live his life completely differently from that point forward. He didn't know what he was going to do, but he knew the value of visions and he knew the value of disillusionment, and he knew humility. He was lucky to be alive and he was lucky to have what he had and it was time for him to grow up and get on with life. Thanks to Drood, he would be ready, willing and able to do that.

As he sat down for his last game, Tag realized he had never even called Deirdre. He had promised to, he had meant to, and he had started to or thought of it a hundred times each day, but always put it off, as he had put off all of life during his spree. It was suddenly incredulous to him that he had been gone two weeks and hadn't called her once. She was all he cared about. She was his life. What had happened to him? Was she okay and was she angry? Tag sighed as he watched the dealer shuffle and replace the shoe. He craved Deirdre and couldn't bear it. He realized then that he would return to L.A. late at night, but he wanted to hold her and to smell her and to just feel the warmth of her body against his. He wanted to beg her forgiveness and place his love in her hands and thank God for having her. He decided to skip calling her and to just go straight over to her apartment to be with her. He'd arrive in the middle of the night and wake her up with his blooming, newly awakened love. The first card in his last hand was an ace.

Chapter 27

Sleep. Sleep was a most precious skill, one that was underrated and taken for granted by those to whom it came naturally. Deirdre had always had trouble sleeping, since childhood. She was a nervous person with a lot of mental energy and when she laid her head on a pillow, she never knew what surge of electricity her brain was going to experience or why it always had to come right at the end of the day like that. On the night before she believed Tag absolutely had to come home, she got ready for bed with a determination and a seriousness that would have made her father proud if he had known about it. She was ready to tackle her disability and over the years of her young life had learned many ways to trick herself into relaxation. Then too, she had the pills, prescription and strong, that were guaranteed to drive her deep into the recesses of the underworld in the mind. She held the vial in her hand and struggled with herself. As a young person, she believed strongly in her own will and strength and never wanted to give in to pills. She felt that she should be able to sleep on her own, dammit, and she didn't want to have to rely on the pills that would screw up the rest of her system for things like eating and drinking and thinking and having energy during the day. To her mind, it was a toss-up between no sleep and drugged sleep.

She lay down and closed her eyes and here it came, the thoughts going around like crazy and she piled it all on: her articles, Tag, the people stalking her, her mother, her father, Digger. She kept going around and around the same circle, over and tediously over again, with no rest. Occasionally she would stop the cycle and demand of herself that she stop and try to think about something else, something pleasant and innocuous like lying on the beach with the waves and the gulls and ...no good, she was off on Tag again, then came with Digger, the mother, the father etc. She stopped to pray to God for relief and closed her eyes. The cycle started again. She got up to practice yoga and stretching and got into the most restful exhausted state she could imagine. She slumped back into bed, confident that she'd now drop off, but no, the damned cycle began again. She opened her eyes and just stared at the ceiling in the dark and she was oh, so desperately weary of herself and of her own mind. She thought about suicide, but then reminded herself that this was not cause for panic. She could sleep late if she had to. Tomorrow would just be a tired and crappy day, that's all, not a crisis or a tragedy. She'd been through this so many times before. It would just take a while for the cycle to exhaust itself and there was nothing she could do to break it. Besides, she thought, looking at the clock, it was 3 a.m. now and too late for a pill and she had made the choice to fight this battle. It was too late to go back. She had decided against the pill tonight. "So toughen up," she told herself, "so you're tired tomorrow, so you lose a little sleep. So what? Follow the cycle around and maybe you'll learn something. Maybe your mind is obsessing for a reason and you need to work on this particular cycle of worries and resolve something. Maybe by the time you get up in the morning you'll be farther along toward something than you were before."

Click. A loud click on the living room window by the fire escape.

She sat bolt upright in bed. With athletic youth she was on the floor in an instant. As quietly and quickly as she could she slid open her closet to look for the bat she kept there.

Deirdre's nerves were wired. A surge of adrenaline pumped through her. She wasn't thinking now. The cycle was gone and her mind and body were taut. She could feel every muscle in her as she finally handled the bat and drew it carefully out of the closet. She straightened, very afraid, but calm and full of purpose.

She heard another click. It sounded like the window being pulled open. She looked quickly around the bedroom. There was no place to hide. The closet would be the first place to look and would be directly in the line of fire if the intruder had a gun. She breathed as deeply and as quietly as she could to counteract the panic that started to seep into her chest and lungs. Whoever it was would now be completely inside and heading for her bedroom. She had nothing to steal. With a sudden click in her brain, she knew that it was rape and violence that was tiptoeing toward her in the dark. Reality slapped her. All pretense of safety, of personal inviolability, of

250

being a citizen in good standing and of being right with God dropped away in an instant, and she stood in panties and t-shirt with a bat and knew that she was about to battle for her life. She stepped behind the door - stepped back far enough to give herself room to swing the bat.

She had to time it just right. Her eyes had adjusted now to the dim light, but tears were running down her cheeks now. She heard a step outside the door and then a slight sound of friction as the doorknob turned. One quick prayer went through her head. "God don't let him have a gun or a knife" and the door came open and a shadowy head came into the room, aiming itself toward her bed. Deirdre swung as hard as she could and hit the head directly in the side. The figure fell forward and landed half on the bed and bounced onto the floor. It groped itself to a half standing position. She swung again as a hand came up with a knife, but the hand was directionless. The intruder appeared still groggy from the first blow. Her second swing hit the arm with the knife and it fluttered away into the darkness. The shadow man grabbed his arm with his other hand and yelled and then moaned. He leaned against the bed, half-kneeling.

Deirdre screamed, "Rape!" as loud as she could and jumped for the door. The man stuck his leg out and tripped her as she went by. The bat went flying. She got up and dashed to the front door and pawed at the chain and deadbolt. He stumbled after her. She got the door open and lurched into the hallway as the man got a fistful of her hair and yanked her head back. Instead of open hallway in front of her, there was a man standing there too. She screamed in desperation and then stopped short as she recognized the man in front of her. Tag's teacher.

Drood grabbed her wrist as the man behind got his arm around her waist. She twisted to the side. Drood's hand shot over her shoulder and his fingers jabbed at the man's eyes. The evil grip on Deirdre loosened as the stranger screamed. Drood yanked Deirdre completely into the hallway free of the hands. Drood kicked the man in the groin as hard as he could. The man went down, groaning. Drood turned to Deirdre, "Call the police. Go to a neighbor's." He calmly reached into his pocket and tossed her a cell phone. "Don't come out unless you hear my voice. My name is Drood."

Deirdre simply nodded and scampered down the hall to Mrs. Greeley's. Drood turned his attention to the writhing man on the floor. He kicked him hard to move him out of the doorway and stepped inside and closed the door behind him. He found a light switch and turned it on.

"Now, my friend," he said, and sighed. "You have made a series of errors in your life that have brought you to this pass. You will now be punished, all at once, for all those errors. If you have gods, speak to them now and beg for mercy. Because you will not get it from me." And Drood rolled up his sleeves and went to work.

Deirdre and Mrs. Greeley listened inside the bolted and chained door, not moving and barely breathing. They heard nothing from the hallway. Mrs. Greeley asked once what it was all about, but Deirdre was panting and crying and listening and she could only say, "Someone broke in and a friend of Tag's knocked him out." They heard the squawk of a police radio in the hall and then there was a knock on the door. Mrs. Greeley looked through the eyehole and then opened the door to the police. Deirdre quickly explained what happened and told them Drood's name. She asked them to be careful because Drood was a friend and might be the only one conscious in her apartment. They wanted to know why and Deirdre explained about the bat.

The police told them to stay in the apartment and wait. Mrs. Greeley made some tea and sat on the couch with Deirdre and put her arm around her. The T.V. was on and it was a late-night special. It seemed longer than ten minutes when the police knocked again on the door and Mrs. Greeley let them in. Drood trailed in behind them. Deirdre stood up and stared at him as the police explained how they'd have to do an investigation, but that it looked like Deirdre's story would be the one that would matter. As the police wrote their reports, Deirdre and Drood and Mrs. Greeley all sat in silence, occasionally looking at each other or at the TV. They waited for the police to leave. EMT's went by in the hallway with a stretcher and emerged a short time later with the unconscious, bloody attacker strapped down. As the police prepared to leave, one of them said to Deirdre, "Just to be on the safe side," with a nod toward Drood, " what is his relationship to you?"

Deirdre looked at Drood. She opened her mouth, but before she spoke, Tag's head appeared in the doorway and then the rest of him coiled into the room. Tag answered wearily before anyone could say anything, "He's her father."

Chapter 28

Father and daughter and young prince sat on a wall overlooking the great Western Capitol of the world. They were at the great Observatory, where so many millions of people had stood, where so many ideas and romances were bred.

After the police had left them, they had not known what to do. Drood and Deirdre belonged to each other but they didn't know how to talk to each other. Tag took charge and drove them in Drood's rental car. Soon the sun would be rising. He led them to the wall looking over the valley and they watched the winking lights of the city below. Occasionally they'd hear a shout or a siren, but mostly they just sat in the soft breeze. They breathed the rhododendron. Tag's heart was full to bursting. The things he had learned, the things he had to tell them both, and the love he felt for Drood and for Deirdre. From early childhood he had no one to love and to love him. He couldn't believe he'd been fortunate enough to find them both now. He was exhausted and weak with relief and love, but he knew he had to get his teacher and his love through until morning. He had to help them find each other. Tag looked at each of them and he saw the great fear in their eyes. The pain from not knowing each other was now at its strongest as the safety of fantasy was ripped away. It would be daylight in two hours and Tag knew they had to talk now, as tired and rattled as they were, or they'd never again have this openness, this vulnerability, this desperate need for each other.

Tag said, "Drood, can you tell us how you came to be at Deirdre's apartment at that exact moment?" He knew Deirdre was too stunned and traumatized to speak. She sat quietly leaning on Tag's shoulder with tears streaming down her face.

Deirdre wondered if she could explain any of this to her mother or if she would ever be the same. She was sure she'd have to redo her entire life. The terror of the attack was beginning to subside and she felt empty and weak. She could barely keep her head up and it seemed to her that the air she was breathing was dangerously thin. She shivered.

Drood started, "If I tell you anything, I've got to tell you the whole story. For once, I have to do this right. You may not believe me or you may think I'm crazy, but to you, my children, it's time to tell the whole story. Yours is the judgment I have been seeking."

Tag stared at Drood and felt something evaporate that had always been invisibly between them. His mouth hung open. Deirdre smiled weakly. She knew what was coming, and as she looked at Drood's deep blue eyes and the lines in his face, the high forehead, and the white hair, she knew that his story was true. Whether it was real or not, it was true. As Drood looked off into the night and began again to intone his story, Deirdre began to love her father.

"Well, I was born in Ireland, in 550 a.d." He looked at both Tag and Deirdre. Tag frowned but said nothing. Deirdre looked at him with wide-open eyes. Drood spoke of his magical arrival to New York from the mists and the sea. He told them of the adventures with Kilty and the mafia, the suicide attempt and rescue, the years of institutions and drug-induced stupor, the return to life and the calm years of boredom and safety in Syracuse. He left out the final chapter, the revenge on McGrath and the meeting with Claire, because he wasn't ready to tell it yet and Deirdre wasn't ready to hear it. He finished by telling how he had come to find her apartment that night, just to see where it was. It was the only place he wanted to go in L.A. When he realized that the shadowy figure on the fire escape was on Deirdre's floor, he hurried to investigate. That was how he came to be standing outside her door when he heard her scream. When he had finished talking he looked at Tag and tried to gauge the boy's reaction. Tag was staring at him, silently concentrating. Drood saw the boy make up his mind, either to believe or to excuse Drood's crazed story of time travel, and then the boy turned to look at Deirdre. "Such beautiful presence and perspective in the boy," Drood thought.

"Now Deirdre," Tag said, "Tell Drood how you came to L.A."

She sniffled and wiped her face on Tag's sweatshirt sleeve. Drood stared at her and tried to absorb her entire being through his eyes. His daughter in front of him. And Tag to introduce him and bring the two together with love. It was unbelievable, a moment that made the ridiculous story of his life sensible. For the first time, Drood silently thanked Mannanan. Nobody would believe this story.

"I have always been alone, or not really, … just missing something. When I was a kid I spent a lot of time by myself imagining things and describing things in my journal. My mother is an unhappy woman," and here she paused to check Drood's reaction, but he didn't move. Her mind was jumbled and she couldn't make any sense of her own life, so she continued. "…. And I needed to get away from New York and from her, and I have always been noticing, observing, recording. Writing and reading gave me a life when I was so alone…". She stopped. It was too much. Drood reached out and held her hand.

"I'm sorry," was all he could get out, before he began to sob. Tag put his arms around the suddenly old man and hugged him. Drood's heart broke open and a lifetime of loss poured out from him. Deirdre was still stunned and didn't know what to do, but she put her hand on Drood's shoulder and Drood immediately clasped it in his own and squeezed, still sobbing. The sun broke over the mountains and the pale light bathed the ocean across the valley. They were all crying now. The joyous agony was in all three hearts at once and would never be lost again.

Chapter 29

The months of preparation and getting to know each other were finally over. The three of them stood on the cliff not talking. Drood represented parents and priest. He thought suddenly, incongruously, of Mickey as they watched the sun begin to shine over the ocean and they could see the gleam far out at sea. He wondered if the spectacularly crazy Mickey would be able to understand that his own ranting prophecies had been directed by an ancient sea-god who captured souls and dragged them to and from the Otherworld. He wondered if Mickey would be happy that his prophecies had come true and Drood had found his daughter through Tag and that he would finally be released. A lone wisp of purple cloud turned bright white as Drood turned from the cliff to prepare the herbs.

Deirdre went inside and came back with the food and drinks and set them on a plastic table. There were apples and plums, hare and venison, potatoes and yams, cheeses and several kinds of wine. They had carefully followed Drood's instructions. Tag had dressed himself as instructed, with amulets he had made from Deirdre's possessions and robes he borrowed from Drood, his teacher and spiritual father. When he had looked in the mirror after dressing, he looked half hippy and half Native American, but what he couldn't know was that he looked almost authentically Celtic, minus the tartan plaids. It was improvised, but Drood approved. Drood had painted swirly lines on his face with blue ink. Tag was made vivid and bold.

Deirdre was in normal street clothes, her preparations would be done alone and last while Drood and Tag performed the final preparations outside. It was dawn of a Sunday. Nobody else in the condo complex was awake yet and the only sign of human habitation outside were two wine glasses left empty by the side of the community Jacuzzi on the cliff edge. It had taken Tag some doing to borrow this place for the week. Drood and Tag stared out to sea while Deirdre finished setting up the table. She didn't know what the bowls and glasses that Drood had given her were for, but she arranged them as he requested.

When Deirdre went back inside to prepare herself, Drood removed some packets of paper and some leather pouches from a burlap bag he carried by his side. He set them down on the other side of the table. Then he reached into the bag again and pulled out an immaculate white robe with a gigantic hood made from a heavy cloth. He slipped it on over his head and began filling its pockets with little items he lifted out of the bottom of the bag. Tag tried to see what he was doing, but Drood shielded his actions with his back. He appeared to be muttering to himself but Tag couldn't make out any words. Tag marveled at how old Drood had become in the months since he'd been in California. His hair was completely white now and he had grown a white beard in the weeks since his arrival on the West Coast. The wrinkles around his eyes and mouth had lengthened and somehow his eyes had gotten even bluer. Tag also noticed that Drood spoke even less now, had become quite taciturn. His eyes were very expressive but he was mostly silent. Tag realized as he left Drood's side to stand on the landing of the stairs that led down to the beach that he was witnessing some kind of transformation in his teacher. It seemed to Tag that the depth in the man was impossibly vast. Imperfections and impurities had melted away and looking at Drood was like gazing into a polished stone.

Drood had been staying at Tag's apartment and Tag sometimes came on him unaware and found Drood having animated conversations with unseen people. At first he thought Drood really was going mad, but his everyday behavior was not only sane and rational but also intelligent and focused. Drood helped Tag and Deirdre with practical things like writing, or money plans, or testifying to put away Emilio and his thug. He was solicitous of them and went out of his way to take care of them. He cooked for them, he walked with them, and he bought little things for them. He was silent, no teachings, but very present. Tag thought now as he stared out to sea that Drood was becoming Sphynxlike, inscrutable, implacable. It was as if Drood had somehow been perfected over the last several months, more so these past weeks, and Tag was now seeing the finished, final man. Tag was in awe of Drood, and as much respect as he had always had for his teacher, this was something completely different. This was a man who had become a presence, a power, someone connected to other worlds. Tag wanted to be near him as much as possible and his mind didn't take anything in, but his spirit soaked in the power and refreshed itself and filled up on the light emanating from Drood. Drood began to glow.

At the same time a great, dark sadness seemed to come over the old man. He sometimes looked at Tag or Deirdre from a depth of pain that moved them both to tears. They tried to reach out to him and to soothe him, but he was far away, a whole universe away. As the days leading up to the ceremony got shorter and summer turned to fall, Drood became more silent and he frowned and seemed to be concentrating carefully on every little action. The most trivial tasks of making a meal or shopping seemed charged with power and urgency. The opening of a door became a slow-motion act of ceremony when performed by Drood.

Finally, the day had come and they were there on the cliff, the sun had come up and it was all going to happen. Tag wondered what was going on in Deirdre's mind. He went back to the deck and set up the video camera. Deirdre was getting dressed and having a time with all the undergarments and accoutrements for this wedding of the twenty first century. She didn't understand why Tag would be wearing the weird costume from a different time while she had to follow the contemporary tradition. "Maybe it kind of makes sense," she thought, "if you looked at this wedding symbolically as a merging of past and present. Like a kind of reconciliation. A blueprint for the future drawn from the details of the past and the present." She thought about her father. It would be a wonderful thing to shock her mother by announcing to her that she and Tag were married and that her father had performed the ceremony. It didn't matter to them that the ceremony was not sanctioned by the state. It was a marriage ceremony and all the more important because Drood was the one performing it. It would be permanent and lasting. She sighed and finally thought she had the dress in the right place and fastened properly. The headdress and the veil next. She went to the door of the room and looked through the living room to the deck. Tag and Drood were all ready and were standing with their backs to her. They seemed to be watching the sea, the sky, and the wind. Deirdre took note of the glow of energy that seemed to emanate from the two figures in the foreground of the incredible swirling blue, white, and yellow scenery.

Deirdre marveled at the combination of the two of them, young and old, learned and learning, both filled with an unearthly energy and beauty. How could this all be happening to her, an ordinary girl from New York? And her father's belief that he was an ancient Druid, and Tag's tutelage and his odd choice of a gambling life-style. What would he do now? They both came from far away and she had not known of the existence of either one of them just a year ago, and yet here they were, her father and her husband. Deirdre made a mental note to herself that some day she would have to describe this wedding carefully, to write about it all. She would describe exactly this moment when her life became absorbed by, and in turn, absorbed these two unbelievable men.

There were no other witnesses or family or friends, and part of her regretted it. It was her day to shine and she should have an audience. But this was private, it was strange, and it was secret. She was accepting both of these men into her heart, and at the same time she was giving herself to both of them. She began to cry when she saw Drood reach out and pat Tag's shoulder just once before dropping his hand back to his side. They were motionless with the morning light on their shoulders as they stared out over the cliff.

She got the headdress and the veil on and looked herself over again. She crossed herself, and then felt silly and went into the living room and opened the sliding glass doors.

"I'm ready," she called.

Tag went to the video camera and turned it on while Drood stepped back to the railing of the deck next to the table. He motioned to Tag to stand beside him and to Deirdre to come to his other side. They took their places and they faced half into Drood and half out to the camera. Deirdre and Tag looked at each other and they quivered and felt raw and they both wanted to cry. Drood lowered his chin to his chest and the hood of the robe completely hid his face from the camera. He began to speak in a strange language, but he paused after each sentence to put it into English.

"The Gods have chosen to allow this union of Taggart, the son of James, the son of Edward with Deirdre, the daughter of Claire, child of Sean of Cathal, of Cairgus, of Dubhan, of Niall, of

Connaught. The rites shall now be performed and they cannot be undone, not even by the will of Lugh."

He paused and shook his fist at the sky and shouted, to the alarm of Tag and Deirdre, "You hear me Mannanan. They are not yours to play with, they belong to the sky and the sea now, they are not yours!" There was no reply – no sound but the soughing wind and the far-off screech of a gull.

Drood stared at the sky for a long time. He finally came back to them and composed himself. He turned to the table behind him and took two flasks. With his thumbs he opened them and asked them to join their hands in front of him. He poured liquid over their hands and they felt at first a cold stinging and then a very warm peaceful feeling in their hands. He set them down and took a drop from one and smeared it with his thumb first over Deirdre's heart and then over Tag's. They felt peace settle over them. He took a drop from the other flask and smeared their foreheads. They felt a clarity come over them as the liquid dried. Tag and Deirdre suddenly realized that something in the liquid had changed them, and they were sharing exactly the same thoughts. They were amazed and tickled and they began to giggle.

Drood turned to the bowls of herbs and food and raised them one at a time to the sky and then out to the sea. He spoke now entirely in Irish, but Tag and Deirdre seemed to be able to understand him. He was talking to the Gods, making offerings. He took a pinch from each bowl and sprinkled it over their heads. He lit a match and burned the rest of the herbs in each bowl. He repeated the procedure with the bowls of fruit, meat, and cheese, but instead of sprinkling it over them they took a bite of each. Drood threw the remainder over the cliff. The sun was high and hot now.

The wind picked up and Deirdre struggled to retain her veil.

Drood turned to them. "Down to the beach now. Be cleansed in the water at dawn and you will have a successful marriage," he advised them. "Make sure you are entirely wet, but don't swim. Come right back."

They held hands and silently went down the twisting wooden steps until they hit the sand. They were both barefoot and the wind kicked up and pulled at Deirdre's veil. She ripped it off her head and threw it to the sky and watched it soar away into the blue. She unpinned her hair and tossed her head and laughed. Tag pulled her

261

to him and kissed her warm neck. They ran to the water, they shouted and screeched and held hands and when they were stumbling into the surf, they threw each other forward and down. The joy spilling out of them was more than this planet had ever seen and light glowed from their eyes and their skin.

When they had climbed back to the deck they were shivering but smiling broadly. They came up the last step and Drood was waiting for them. He held out his arms to them and they stepped into the folds of his robe and he enclosed them and held them. They quickly dried and the three hugged each other and happily loved each other. Finally, Drood slowly shuffled them around to face the camera. He opened his arms and the wings unfolded, revealing rumpled, wet, and happy Tag and Deirdre to the camera. Drood bellowed very loudly,

"By the powers vested in me by the lunatic Gods of the sea and the earth and the sky and the wind, I now pronounce you husband and wife." And they all laughed heartily and turned to the food bowls and began to eat hungrily. Tag looked at the several objects still under cover on the table and asked Drood what they were.

"Wedding presents!" Drood shouted. And he pulled the covers off, revealing matching gold neck torques, bracelets, rings, and brooches. They shone in the morning sun and Tag and Deirdre put them on and became Gods. Drood had put the spells into the beautiful gold work, and the young husband and wife were immediately made flawless and beautiful. The wedding ceremony and celebration was successful and Drood smiled broadly and could not utter another word. His time was done and his training was over and his tasks had been completed. He stared at the two people before him, and marveled at what had occurred. "There is a purpose in living, no matter what happens, and it is good," he concluded, "and it is worth it, no matter the pain and loss you have to endure to get there." He closed his eyes, but he could still see them, their youth exploding into the air around them, their love gilding everything it touched, their truth and their beauty and their justice making the world a better place just by their existence. He had witnessed and taken part in the birth of two demi-gods and this was the privilege for which he had paid by the cost of his entire life. Drood was complete.

Epilogue
Chapter 30

The most beautiful love was sleeping, side-by-side, holding hands. If one could have looked down on them from above and photographed or painted it, one would have captured a work of art that would defy time and sum up the history of art. It would be a work that would culminate what had begun with the caves and the rock drawings, and would finish the need for art for the rest of human history. Woman was sleeping on her back with her head turned to her left side, black straight hair splayed out on the ice-blue sheets. Her mouth was slightly open; two swelled red lips just not quite covering two upper teeth. A slight tremor indicated breath. The skin was white as snow and the bones of her face were so smooth and symmetrical that she could not have been from earth, from nature. Her relaxed limbs were free and fully articulated and they moved slightly every now and then to show their potential vigor. A sheet covered her hips and her abdomen, but her breasts were pushing out and up, full of youth and sex and potential. She was beautiful by herself, but she was part of Man next to her as well. Her right hand was grasped in his and he was darker and made her whiteness shine brilliantly. Her skin was the color of the beginning of life.

Man was turned on his side toward her with his right hand across him grasping hers. He was breathing more heavily and the muscles in his back and his arms were still taut as slowly, slowly, he eased into deeper sleep. He was hard looking, all angles and abrupt contours, ending everywhere in refinement. It was easy to see how all was connected to the center of him and his muscles twitched with each movement. His light hair looked soft and healthy on the pillow and his cheekbones and chin jutted out, making his the face of a strong warrior. He appeared to almost surround her beauty, her softness, her whiteness, and his skin looked brown and sunful. He would have been too vivid to behold without her by his side to

263

complete him. They were a demonstration of the animal and the angel combined as human.

They had made love for long hours and it was the first time they had been this way together. They had had to teach each other about their bodies and so they had to go slowly and they did because they were not afraid. It was the first experience of sexual ecstasy for both of them and it had occurred the way it was supposed to. They were Woman and Man and it was destined to be this way for them. They had not thought too much and had become subsumed and burned up and overwhelmed in this night together and they would wake up tomorrow as new people, as nature's husband and wife. Their perfect union was legend, their love and their pleasures mythical, their ending and their beginning cosmic. Man and woman forever joined, no matter what the rest of time might bring to them, in them, on them, around them.

As Tag caught up to Deirdre in the slow sinking into the deepest brain wave-restoration-sleep, he moved closer in the bed and removed his hand and put his arm over her and one hand on her left breast. She smiled and pushed her back into his chest. They were still together in unconsciousness. They began to move in synch, and they appeared to be acting different parts of the same drama. A leg moved and the other's leg moved. They swayed together and frowned together. They breathed deep sighs together and their hands eventually sought each other and held on again.

They had come to a place in their dreams where they were together and they both looked at each other with surprise. They were in the same dream and they both knew it, and at the same time they could both feel their dreaming bodies way back in the west, in Los Angeles, in Deirdre's apartment, in the bed, on the ice-blue sheets. Their bodies' warmth comforted them as they moved about in the coldness of the dream world. They were walking hand in hand and it was nighttime somewhere. It was cold, bitter cold and they huddled together for warmth. As they walked further they could see that there was a tremendous amount of snow on the ground, the piles were very high, several feet high. They came into a parking lot and Tag recognized it at once as the parking lot to the old magic factory complex in Syracuse.

"This is the factory, where we played cards and where he taught me everything. But it's changed. It's older now. Another part of it has collapsed. I wonder if Tom still has his workshop here."

As he spoke the wind whipped up the snow and they could barely see anything. Deirdre scanned all around her, trying to take it all in. They huddled closer and back in their bodies in L.A. they shivered again.

"C'mon, I'll show you around." And he started to tug on her arm.

"Wait!" she said. "Look!" She pointed to a dark figure, huddled against the weather, trudging slowly down the sidewalk on the street. As they watched, it turned and came into the parking lot toward them. They stayed where they were as the figure seemed to be making straight for them. It moved very slowly and faltered several times, as if old, drunk, or sick. It was a black figure. They couldn't make out any details until it was almost right on them.

Tag spoke to the person, "Hey." But the figure moved right past them, completely unheeding. When it was a few feet beyond them it hesitated and then continued. They followed along behind the figure, which now appeared to be a male, as it headed toward the old door at the back of the factory complex. The person knew where he was going, Tag thought. He didn't bother to try any of the side doors or garage doors. They followed behind him. It was pitch black inside and the person stopped to remove his hood. Snow fell on his shoulders and on the floor. Tag and Deirdre moved closer.

"Is it him?" she asked, a tremor in her voice.

Tag simply nodded.

"He doesn't know we're with him, does he?"

"No. I don't think he can hear or see us."

They moved closer and sure enough, Drood moved as if he was in another dimension, aware only of himself and the place and the dismal cold. He shook himself and almost lost his balance. Tag and Deirdre gasped at his appearance. He was gray and he had purple circles under his eyes. The cheekbones and jawbones stood out so far it was clear he was nearly a skeleton. He looked as though he hadn't eaten in a long time and he was very frail. Drood paused to catch his breath and coughed loudly and painfully. He swore.

Finally, Drood moved into the factory with his hands extended in front of him as if he were having trouble seeing. He bumped into walls and banged into things as Deirdre and Tag walked behind him, watching carefully. They were both afraid for him and they wanted to help, but when they tried talking to him, they went unnoticed. They wondered if Drood was in a dream as well and if so, why couldn't he hear or see them? Drood appeared to be wandering around the inside of the ruined building, groping, looking for something. He was following all the walls with his hands. "He might actually be blind," Tag thought. Drood came to the collapsed heating duct and when his hands found it, his face relaxed and his movements became quicker, more positive.

Drood patted the duct as he made his way around it and found where it curved upward. Drood quickly scooted under the duct and went through the door behind it. Tag and Deirdre followed and almost ran into him. He was inside the door, stopped, trying to peer down into the darkness at all the boards and junk piled at the bottom of the stairwell. He had another coughing fit and they waited while he regained himself. He swayed a little and stood for a long time waiting for strength. Tag and Deirdre looked at each other with concern. They began to have an inkling of what Drood was doing and their emotions overcame them and they emanated love and tried to pat the old man and tried to send it into him. It seemed to help and he stepped with more surety into the stairwell going down.

They followed him as he climbed painfully over the boards, plucking and hauling, and moving things out of the way. He stepped on and over things as he balanced himself and made his way down to the first landing. He didn't hesitate this time, as if he knew he only had enough strength left to get him right to the bottom and no more. When Tag and Deirdre also got to the bottom, Drood was already kneeling by the opposite wall. It was dank and dark in the basement, but Tag and Deirdre could see Drood clearly. Drood began feverishly pulling a pile of plywood sheets away from the floor. When the pile was gone and Drood hunched over, hands on his knees, panting, Tag and Deirdre saw another set of stairs going down. Drood staggered down the stairs hanging onto the railing and they went right behind him into what must once have been a boiler room. There were giant gray pipes and tanks everywhere.

Drood found a corner of the room, directly behind an old boiler, and lay down on his side and was still. Tag and Deirdre moved closer, squeezed around the tank and yelled at him and tried poking him, but he couldn't hear them. They couldn't touch him. He didn't move. There was just enough room for them to kneel by his head and they put their faces down close to him.

They told him that they loved him. They told him they would always be with him. They begged him to come back, to wake up. Finally, they just stared, their ghost-dream hands resting on his shoulders. Drood's eyes emptied and his chest rattled and they watched as the life went slowly out of him. The man they called Drood left this world. He could have been a homeless bum, hidden in the basement of a burned-out factory, where no one would find his body for years. He wore nothing but rags and the homemade, recent tattooed list on one forearm that read "Claire, Tag, Deirdre." Tag and Deirdre wept and stood and held each other. They would wake up hours later knowing that Drood was gone.

Chapter 31

Drood woke to find himself in the magic glade where he had seen Tag and Deirdre. Somehow he knew they were not here now and he knew they were forever gone to him. There was a thickness in his head and he couldn't quite remember why he wouldn't see them anymore. They were fading in his memory, and it was like a vivid dream that was going away as he woke in this new clearing. The magic glade did not bring him any peace this time, as the old dream had, and as his senses returned to him. He saw that it was just a clearing in a wood, no place in particular, no symmetry, no magic. He looked at his arms and they were fleshy and he felt a bounce in his legs. Something had changed. He was younger, stronger, and the memories of the Otherworld were gray and thin.

He moved further into the clearing and saw a path on the other side. Drood stopped without thinking and knelt by the entrance to the path.

"Mannanan, guide me now on the path to my destiny. Send the wind to speed me, the sun to warm me, the rain to refresh me, and keep the path clear before me."

Drood stepped into the path and walked for many miles, through dark woods and quiet valleys. He crossed two streams and stayed on the path. He began to get tired, but he felt happy and free. Drood heard a strange humming sound and it came back to him, from long ago, from his youth several thousand years ago. It was the sound of the sea in the distance. He paused and put his hand on the trunk of an oak tree. He could hear the night and the animals all around him. He longed to get to the sea; he felt somehow that he belonged there. He began to cry happy tears as he waited to catch his breath. The night seemed to go on forever.

The leaves on the side of the path in front of him rustled. Drood started, but he felt no real fear. He knew that all was going as it was supposed to and that he was where he was supposed to be. The leaves parted. A large head peeked into the path and Drood saw the outline of a wild head of hair. Spying Drood, the giant shadow stepped into the path with his head craned in Drood's direction. The man held a huge sword and he smelled of a campfire and Drood strained to make out his features. As the man came forward, the moon slipped out from behind a cloud and Drood could suddenly see the man directly in front of him clearly.

Drood bellowed, "Hah!" and then leaned over and put his hands on his knees and began to laugh. The shadow-giant also began to laugh. They bellowed and snorted and guffawed, and Drood laughed until tears poured down his face. The man's hair was gleaming red and his eyes were crystal blue. The white skin of his face was covered with ugly scars. And Drood laughed and wept and knew he had been forgiven his most heinous crimes.

"Kilty," he said. "I'm sorry."

And the giant man laughed and threw an arm around Drood's shoulders.

"Failte abhaile. (welcome home). I've been sent to bring you to the campfire by the shore. We will eat, drink, and sing and at dawn you will speak with Mannanan." Drood started and stared at Kilty. Again, Kilty roared a hearty laugh and Drood trembled. In his great joy and relief, Drood hadn't noticed, but a mist had begun to rise from the ground and curled around the oaks and the yews. The moonlight was suddenly distorted and fuzzy and Drood's weary eyes began to lose focus. He hurried to follow the big man through the bushes to yet another path.

Contact us:

Green Boat Press
P.O. Box 135
Manlius, NY 13104

editor@greenboatpress.com

or

Join our reader's forum at

www.greenboatpress.com